THE LADY OF THE RAVENS

Joanna spent twenty-five years at the BBC writing and presenting for radio and television. Gripped by Shakespeare's historical plays, Joanna originally began researching King Henry V's 'fair Kate' as a schoolgirl and the story of Catherine de Valois and the birth of the Tudor dynasty went on to become her first Historical novel, *The Agincourt Bride*. Joanna is now an internationally bestselling novelist with a legion of fans around the globe. *The Lady of the Ravens* is her sixth novel. She is married with a large family and lives in Wiltshire, England.

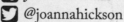 Joanna Hickson
@joannahickson

BY THE SAME AUTHOR

The Agincourt Bride
The Tudor Bride
Red Rose, White Rose
First of the Tudors
The Tudor Crown

THE LADY OF THE RAVENS

JOANNA HICKSON

HarperCollins*Publishers*

HarperCollins*Publishers*
The News Building,
1 London Bridge Street,
London SE1 9GF

www.harpercollins.co.uk

HarperCollins*Publishers*
1st Floor, Watermarque Building, Ringsend Road
Dublin 4, Ireland

Published by HarperCollins*Publishers* 2020

This paperback edition published 2021

2

A catalogue record for this book
is available from the British Library

ISBN: 978-0-00-830561-1

Set in Adobe Caslon by
Palimpsest Book Production Limited, Falkirk, Stirlingshire

Printed and bound in Great Britain by
CPI Group (UK) Ltd, Croydon CR0 4YY

MIX
Paper from
responsible sources
FSC
www.fsc.org   FSC® C007454

This book is produced from independently certified FSC™ paper
to ensure responsible forest management.

Find out more about HarperCollins and the environment at
www.harpercollins.co.uk/green

'For my ever-supportive husband Ian, who calms me down when I'm up, lifts me up when I'm down and always has a bottle of champagne in the fridge on publication day!'

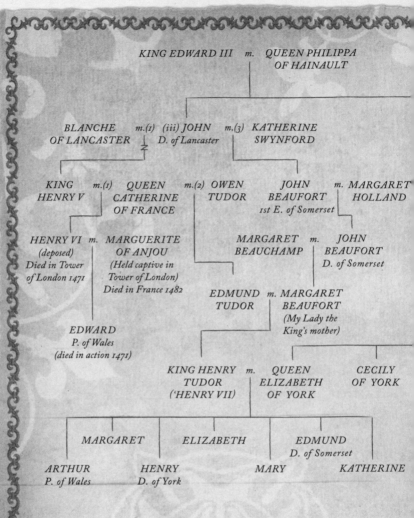

KING EDWARD III   m.   QUEEN PHILIPPA
OF HAINAULT

BLANCHE   m.(1)   (iii) JOHN   m.(3)   KATHERINE
OF LANCASTER   D. of Lancaster   SWYNFORD

KING   m.(1)   QUEEN   m.(2)   OWEN   JOHN   m.   MARGARET
HENRY V   CATHERINE   TUDOR   BEAUFORT   HOLLAND
      OF FRANCE   1st E. of Somerset

HENRY VI   m.   MARGUERITE   MARGARET   m.   JOHN
(deposed)   OF ANJOU   BEAUCHAMP   BEAUFORT
Died in Tower   (Held captive in   D. of Somerset
of London 1471   Tower of London)
        Died in France 1482   EDMUND   m.   MARGARET
                         TUDOR   BEAUFORT
         EDWARD   (My Lady the
         P. of Wales   King's mother)
        (died in action 1471)

KING HENRY   m.   QUEEN   CECILY
TUDOR   ELIZABETH   OF YORK
('HENRY VII)   OF YORK

MARGARET   ELIZABETH   EDMUND
                           D. of Somerset
ARTHUR   HENRY   MARY   KATHERINE
P. of Wales   D. of York

TUDOR
ANCESTRY

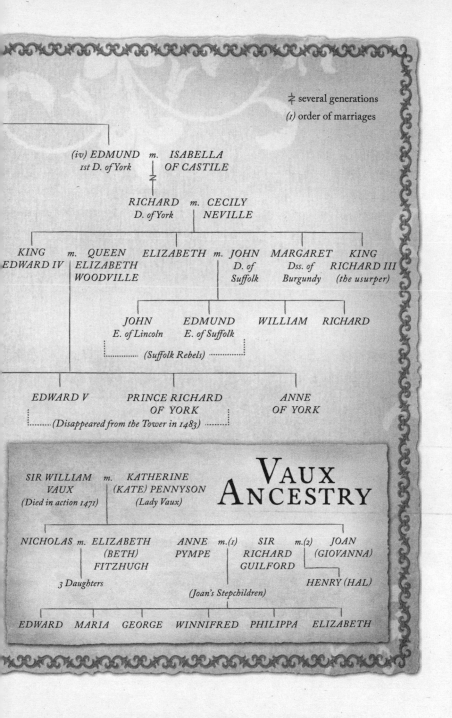

≠ several generations
(1) order of marriages

(iv) EDMUND m. ISABELLA
1st D. of York OF CASTILE

RICHARD m. CECILY
D. of York NEVILLE

KING m. QUEEN   ELIZABETH m. JOHN   MARGARET   KING
EDWARD IV ELIZABETH   D. of   Dss. of   RICHARD III
WOODVILLE   Suffolk   Burgundy   (the usurper)

JOHN   EDMUND   WILLIAM   RICHARD
E. of Lincoln   E. of Suffolk

········· (Suffolk Rebels) ·········

EDWARD V   PRINCE RICHARD   ANNE
OF YORK   OF YORK

········· (Disappeared from the Tower in 1483) ·········

VAUX
ANCESTRY

SIR WILLIAM m. KATHERINE
VAUX   (KATE) PENNYSON
(Died in action 1471)   (Lady Vaux)

NICHOLAS m. ELIZABETH   ANNE m.(1)   SIR   m.(2)   JOAN
(BETH)   PYMPE   RICHARD   (GIOVANNA)
FITZHUGH   GUILFORD

3 Daughters   HENRY (HAL)

(Joan's Stepchildren)

EDWARD   MARIA   GEORGE   WINNIFRED   PHILIPPA   ELIZABETH

DRAMATIS PERSONAE

Royal Family:

Henry Tudor – *King Henry VII*

Lady Margaret Beaufort – *'My Lady the King's Mother'*

Elizabeth of York – *Queen Elizabeth*

Princess Cecily of York – *the queen's sister & 1st Chief Lady-in-Waiting*

Princess Anne of York – *the queen's sister & 2nd Chief Lady-in-Waiting*

Dowager Queen Elizabeth (Woodville) – *the queen's mother*

Arthur, Prince of Wales – *born 20th September 1486, the Tudor heir*

Margaret Plantagenet/Pole – *the queen's disinherited York cousin*

Edward, Earl of Warwick – *Margaret Plantagenet's younger brother*

John, Earl of Lincoln – *son & heir of the queen's paternal aunt Elizabeth, Duchess of Suffolk*

Margaret, Dowager Duchess of Burgundy – *the queen's other paternal aunt & a focus of Yorkist conspiracy*

Jasper Tudor, Duke of Bedford – *King Henry's paternal uncle*

John, Viscount Welles – *the king's maternal half-uncle*

Princess Margaret Tudor – *born 28th November 1489, eldest daughter of the king*

Prince Henry, Duke of York (Harry) – *born 28th June 1491, the king's 2nd son*

Princess Elizabeth Tudor – *born 2nd July 1492, 2nd daughter of the king*

Princess Mary Tudor – *born 18th March 1496, 3rd daughter of the king*

Prince Edmund, Duke of Somerset – *born 21st February 1499, 3rd son of the king*

Lady Meg Poyntz – *queen's illegitimate cousin by Anthony Woodville, Earl Rivers (see English citizens & Deceased characters)*

xi

Royal Households:
King Henry:
PC=*Privy Councillor*
KG=*Knight of the Garter*

Sir Richard Guildford – *Master of Ordnance & Armaments & PC Later KG*

Nicholas Gainsford – *Usher of the King's Chamber*

Lord Thomas Stanley – *Earl of Derby, High Constable of England & PC Husband of the king's mother*

Sir William Stanley – *Earl of Derby's brother, 2nd Lord Chamberlain, PC & KG*

John Morton – *Archbishop of Canterbury, Lord Chancellor & later Cardinal*

John de Vere, Earl of Oxford – *1st Lord Chamberlain, PC, KG & Arthur's Godfather*

Sir Henry Wyatt – *Master of the King's Jewels & Comptroller of the Mint*

Giles, Lord Daubeney – *succeeded Sir William Stanley as Lord Chamberlain, PC & KG*

Queen Elizabeth:
Joan Vaux – *former ward of Lady Margaret, later Lady Guildford*

Katherine Pennyson/Lady Vaux – *Joan's mother, known as Mother Vaux*

Lady Mary Rivers – *widow of the queen's uncle Anthony, Earl Rivers & former ward of Lady Margaret Beaufort*

Eleanor Verney – *Lady-in-Waiting, married to Sir Ralph Verney, sister of Richard Pole*

Elizabeth Jerningham – *Keeper of the Queen's Robes*

Thomas Butler, Earl of Ormond – *Queen's Lord Chamberlain*

Lady Elizabeth Stafford – *3rd Chief Lady-in-Waiting & daughter of the Duke of Buckingham*

Guildford Family:
Sir Richard Guildford of Halden, Kent – *Master of Ordnance & Armaments*

Sir John Guildford – *Richard's father & Comptroller of Royal Household*

Richard's children in age order:
by Anne Pympe:
Edward (Ned)
Maria
George
Philippa (Pippa)
Friedswide (Winnie) – *Friedswide a popular saint in this period, also known as Winifred*
Elizabeth (Lizzie)
by Joan:
Henry (Hal)

Elizabeth (Bess) Mortimer – *Richard's ward*

English citizens:

Rosie – *a London silkwoman*

Nicholas Vaux – *Joan's brother, a landed esquire, later knighted*

Beth Fitzhugh/Vaux – *his Yorkist bride*

Lambert Simnel – *name given to the pretend Edward of Warwick*

Richard Pole – *Esquire (later Knight) of the King's Body, brother of Lady Eleanor Verney & husband of Margaret Plantagenet*

Martin Steward – *a senior Guildford servant*

Hugh – *a scullion training as a server*

Luce – *a Guildford maidservant*

Jake – *the Guildford cook*

Wynkyn de Worde – *printer at Caxton's Westminster press*

Mistress Wood – *governess to the Guildford children*

Sir John Digby – *Lieutenant Constable of the Tower of London*

Lettie Stock – *a London midwife*

Mistress Strood – *a Kent farmer's wife & breast nurse to baby Hal*

Hetty Smith – *a maidservant from the Kent village of Rolvenden*

Sir Robert Poyntz – *a landed knight, husband of Meg Woodville*

Anthony Poyntz – *their eldest son*

Jane Howell – *governess to Prince Henry & former nurse to King Henry*

Mistress Brook – *2nd governess to the Guildford children*

Deceased characters:

Queen Marguerite – *Marguerite of Anjou, wife of King Henry VI the last Lancastrian King of England*

Edward (Édouard), Prince of Wales – *their son*

Sir William Vaux – *Joan's father*

Edward IV – *Yorkist king who deposed Henry VI*

Prince Edward of York & Prince Richard of York – *The Princes in the Tower, deaths unknown*

Richard of Gloucester – *Richard III (the usurper), Edward IV's brother*

Anne Pympe – *Sir Richard Guildford's 1st wife*

Anthony Woodville, Earl Rivers – *executed on Richard III's orders (father of Meg Poyntz)*

PART ONE

I

THE CART RUMBLED PAST so close that it almost killed me. I was forced to flatten myself against the gatehouse wall or I would surely have been crushed before I had even entered the Tower of London. Limewash and mortar flaked off the masonry, smearing my gown with white dust. Then suddenly, above the diminishing sound of rolling wheels and clattering hooves, I heard the rasping 'kwaark' of a raven and a childhood memory rushed in to swamp my senses. I became my nine-year-old self, trembling under the gaze of a large black bird with a bill like the hook of a soldier's halberd and an eye that could pierce the soul. Then that fearsome beak had opened to emit a hoarse cry, bringing tears to my eyes, and I heard the gravelly voice of my escort, an elderly knight from the Tower's garrison.

'Think yourself honoured, young mistress. The ravens avoid us men because the archers use them for target practice. But there is a legend, which says that as long as they haunt the Tower, it and the kingdom will stand. Just lately they've been coming and going, so perhaps there's something in it.' At the time I didn't understand what he meant but so vividly had the raven's image imprinted itself in my mind, that the incident and his words had remained with me ever since.

Now thirteen years later another cart, heaped high and shedding fragments of its cargo as it juddered over the cobbles, made me press even harder against the wall and my heart thudded as a real raven was suddenly there at my feet, rushing in with a triumphant flap of feathers to peck up a speck of shiny discarded metal that glimmered in the gatehouse gloom. My daydream dissolved into reality. The carts were carrying gold and silver scrap to the Royal Mint and the raven scampered away with its booty, rising on beating wings as it cleared the archway. Hastening into the daylight, I watched it carry off its treasure, to secrete it somewhere high on the battlements.

I stood transfixed, admiring its fluid, swooping flight until an angry shout from behind alerted me. 'Hey! Clear the way! D'you want to get killed?' I jumped to the side again as another laden cart trundled past, the driver red-faced and yelling. 'God's blood, woman! There's no room for stupid skirts in here.'

Fearing more vehicles, I made a run for the gate at the other end of the moat bridge and took refuge through a door in an adjacent building, which I knew should contain the office of the man in charge. I felt in the purse on my belt and removed the letter within.

'Tell me, what business can a female possibly have in a military fortress?' The young Lieutenant Constable was hook-nosed and handsome, with all the hubris of noble privilege and not a hint of charm. He had given my letter barely a glance.

'I am on royal business, sir, as the letter says.' I held out my hand. 'May I have it back? I know where I am going.'

His eyes scanned the page and rested on the signature

at the bottom. 'Who is MR?' he asked, refolding the note and handing it to me.

I could have remarked that he should know but I desisted. 'Margaret, Countess of Richmond, is the king's mother – MR is her cypher.' Knowing the lady well, as I did, I reflected that it could equally be a monogram for 'Margaret Regina' but resisted the temptation to point this out.

He did not respond verbally but his curled lip and disapproving sniff were revealing. It was only weeks since Lady Margaret's son, Henry Tudor, had taken the throne 'by right and conquest', to become King Henry the Seventh of England and there were still plenty of dissenting Yorkists among minor royal officials. I didn't give this one many more days in his present post.

As I hurried along the narrow street between the twin curtain walls that defended the fortress from a river attack, I couldn't resist searching for more signs of ravens on the battlements of the main keep, which reared above me to my left. These enigmatic birds had haunted my dreams ever since I had made that first fearful childhood trip to the Tower to visit my mother. Whatever the men had said about it being no place for women, I could have begged to differ. My mother, Katherine Vaux, had lived within its intimidating walls for two years and the captive lady she had served there had once been Queen of England.

My grandfather, a doctor from Piedmont, had been physician to the Duke of Anjou's family and in her childhood my mother had been invited to join their schoolroom. When the duke's daughter Marguerite married King Henry the Sixth of England, she had travelled with her to his court and later married one of his household knights, Sir William

Vaux, becoming an English citizen. When civil war erupted and Edward of York snatched the throne, forcing King Henry and Queen Marguerite to flee their kingdom, my loyal Lancastrian parents escaped with my young brother Nicholas to my mother's birthplace in Piedmont. A few months later, I was born and baptised Giovanna, after my Italian grandmother.

My baptismal name may be Giovanna, but English is not a lyrical language like Italian is. Here in my mother's adopted country I have become plain Joan; and plain is what the English think me, as I am not pink-cheeked and golden-haired like the beauties they admire. I have olive skin and dark features – black brows over ebony eyes and hair the colour of a raven's wing. With my full lips and straight nose, many consider me odd, or probably, to put it bluntly, ugly. '*Jolie-laide*' is what the French used to call me, more kindly. Perhaps that is one reason why I habitually wear dark colours and am so drawn to the big black birds that haunt the cliff-like walls of the Tower and why, as I hastened to my meeting on that late September day, I was enraged at seeing one of the sentry archers on the battlements take aim at a raven as it flew close to his position on the roof of the Royal Palace. Luckily the arrow missed its target but I was still seething while I negotiated my way past another set of guards and into the fortress's intimidating limewashed keep, known as the White Tower.

'May I ask what a young lady like you is doing here?'

At least this time the inquiry was couched politely and came from a trimly bearded man of obvious status, wearing a furred gown, with a gold chain about his shoulders and a black hat pinned with a jewelled brooch. I had almost run into him in the gloom of the main troop-gathering hall, which was empty and echoing and lit only by the daylight filtering through a few high barred windows. Swallowing my first indignant riposte, I made him a brief curtsy.

'I've been sent by My Lady the King's Mother, sir.' Once again I offered my letter of charge.

'Have you indeed? Let me see.' In order to scan the script he had to squint and hold it up to what little light there was, then he made me a courteous bow. 'Welcome to the Tower of London, Mistress Vaux. I am Sir Richard Guildford, the king's Master of Ordnance, in charge of the guns and weapons that are held here. But I cannot believe they are relevant to your purpose. I see you are bidden to the Chapel of St John. For what reason, I wonder?'

I shook my head. 'We would both like to know the answer to that, Sir Richard, but it is a royal command, which one does not query.'

He inclined his head. 'Indeed.'

'I have a question for you though, sir.' I took a steadying breath before plunging on. 'If you are in charge of weapons, why are the archers wasting arrows, firing them at the ravens? What harm have they done?'

Even in the dim light I could see his cheeks flush and his next words were delivered with savage emphasis. 'Those ravens are the devil's demons – filthy scavengers and harbingers of death! All soldiers hate them and the archers are encouraged to use them for target practice. An arrow is retrievable, preferably with a dead bird attached.'

Or possibly a dead passer-by, I thought. I bit back any comment but he must have noticed my look of angry astonishment. I wondered how a man who lived and worked in

7

the Tower could be ignorant of the widespread belief among Londoners that the presence of ravens was essential to the fortress's security and that of the city and the kingdom they inhabited. This folk legend and its subjects had stayed with me ever since I had heard it as a child from the old garrison knight and over the ensuing years I had made it my business to read whatever I could find on both the birds and the belief.

During the resulting silence he recovered his composure and gave me a brief smile. 'Now, Mistress Vaux, may I call someone to show you to the Chapel of St John?'

Although I could not bring myself to return the smile, I made an acknowledging bob. 'Thank you, Sir Richard, but I know the way.'

I sensed his puzzled gaze following me to the foot of the long stair. Like all castle chapels, it was situated above the other chambers, giving prayers a clear path to heaven, and on other visits to my mother and the captive queen I had made the climb to the top of the White Tower to find them at Mass. On this occasion two Ushers of the King's Chamber were there still wearing the blue and murrey household livery issued under the Yorkist kings, along with an assortment of other men in civilian dress. I was acquainted with one of the ushers, a landed squire called Nicholas Gainsford, and as soon as I arrived he began lecturing us on how anything we saw or heard that morning was to be considered a state secret and revealed to no one; everything had to be committed to memory and nothing written down. Having calmed my alarm on behalf of the ravens, I felt my heart flutter anew at Usher Gainsford's stern admonishments.

Bizarrely, the frame of a large bedstead had been erected

in the chapel nave and it was to this that he proceeded to direct our attention, impatiently beckoning us to gather around it. I received curious glances from the strange men as we jostled for position, aware that the presence of a woman was perplexing to them. Not for the first time I wondered what I was doing there myself.

'You are all here to learn precisely how to make the king's bed,' the usher continued, as if reading my mind. 'At present his grace is living at his manor of Kennington, a small palace over the river, which is easily secured and presently inhabited only by people well known to him and sworn to his affinity. But after his coronation he will be living in many larger royal palaces including the one located here, within the Tower of London. Such buildings are a warren of chambers, passages and staircases, containing many entrances and large numbers of people – not easy to keep secure. So when King Henry inhabits these palaces, or visits the homes of his favoured subjects, he will always have his own secure royal quarters, an area known as the Privy Chamber. Only trusted subjects who have sworn an oath of allegiance will be admitted into this reserved area, which will contain all the rooms necessary for his ease and comfort, where he can consult with his advisers and councillors in certain knowledge that what is said and done within its walls will go no further. And of course the most important of these rooms is that in which the king takes his rest – his bedchamber.'

He let his gaze roam over the gathering. 'You men have been appointed Yeomen of the Guard of the Body of our Lord the King and, apart from protecting the king wherever he goes, an important part of your duties will be to make the monarch's bed daily. To ensure that it is clean and comfortable and, most importantly, free of any hazard from hidden blades, poisonous plants, or biting insects that might cause him ill, injury or irritation. And naturally, when his grace marries he will want his queen's rest to be as free from danger and discomfort as his own; therefore we have a lady here with us.' My eyes flicked nervously about as everyone turned in my direction. 'Mistress Vaux is charged with relaying all that she sees and hears to the sworn women of the bedchamber of his eventual bride. Before you leave today, all of you will be required to take an oath of loyalty before the Lord Chamberlain of the King's Household.'

Having long lived under Lady Margaret Beaufort's roof, I was probably already as familiar as any there with the best way to prepare a bedstead for the nobility but Usher Gainsford was taking no chances with royal security. He literally started from scratch, feeling with the tips of his fingers and scraping with his nails all the way around the wooden bedframe and headboard, looking for any crack or crevice where something sharp or noxious might be hidden. Then he ordered one of the men to strip to his chemise and hose and, to the obvious amusement of his fellow yeomen, roll around on the thick rush mat spread over the ropes, to test it for needles, thorns or twigs.

'A sharpened twig soaked in the juice of deadly nightshade berries can work its way through to the sleeper, who falls into a stupor from which he does not wake,' he warned, then lifted the straw mattress and dramatically sliced open the end with a sharp knife. 'You need to distinguish between the different plants used to stuff this layer. Ladies' bedstraw is best and this one,' he picked out a dried stem with leaves larger than the rest, 'is called woodruff and has a scent like freshly mown hay.' He picked up a handful of the stuffing and peered closely at it. 'This mattress should be opened and refilled and all feather beds shaken and checked regularly. Some of you yeomen will be appointed Keepers of the Wardrobe of the Beds, in charge of storing the royal bedclothes in locked and insect-proof chests every day and responsible for ensuring that a record is taken of when checks are made.'

One of the men spoke up. 'In view of these precautions, sir, how would anyone manage to corrupt the royal bed? If everything is so carefully locked away and checked and the Privy Chambers are restricted to sworn servants, it does not seem very likely.'

Usher Gainsford cleared his throat and a flush stained his cheeks. 'One of a yeoman's duties is to report any hint of a colleague failing in his loyalty. You have all been chosen because you are known to be staunch Lancastrians but King Henry is anxious to unite the country, bringing York and Lancaster together under his rule and the Tudor name, ending the recent years of strife. So it is to him and the family he intends to have that his household will swear allegiance and obedience. This will be a Tudor reign and in due course, God willing, a Tudor dynasty but to begin with this may not content everyone. Dissidents may contrive to be appointed to the royal household. Treachery can emerge anywhere. You, as individuals, will be responsible for reporting anyone criticising the Tudor reign, or showing the slightest preference for another house, to the Lord Chamberlain or his deputy.'

I had no great sympathy with dissidents, having lost my father to a Yorkist army fourteen years ago, but I found this last order bittersweet as I took my oath of loyalty and I hoped I would not be expected to observe and report on the new queen's commitment to the Tudor dynasty that she would be expected to provide. Officially, six weeks into his reign, we still did not know the identity of King Henry's eventual queen, although the fact that his mother had selected me to attend this meeting strongly suggested that it would be the young lady currently living under her roof at her palace of Coldharbour on the banks of the River Thames.

Elizabeth of York, to whom I had almost inadvertently become servant, companion and friend, was the eldest child of King Edward the Fourth and the princess Henry Tudor had vowed to marry in order to boost support for his ultimately successful expedition to establish his own claim to the throne of England. But this had only happened after Edward died unexpectedly and his two young sons were brought to the Tower's Royal Palace to await the elder boy's coronation as King Edward the Fifth. This was because their uncle Richard, Duke of Gloucester, apparently unprepared to act as mere Protector to a boy king, contrived to get parliament to declare them illegitimate and to have himself crowned instead. Within weeks the York boys had disappeared from public view and two years later the usurping king, who as their Protector must surely have known what happened to them, had died fighting Henry Tudor's invading army without revealing their fate.

From my staunch Lancastrian viewpoint, I considered the York history a chequered one; however it also greatly concerned me that Elizabeth and her mother and sisters might never discover when or how the two young princes died – if die indeed they both had. As I left the White Tower I paused to gaze up at the windows of the adjacent Royal Palace where the princes had been accommodated and in which soldiers and other Tower residents had reported catching occasional glimpses of their small, pale faces – until all sightings mysteriously ceased.

Although his victory in battle against the usurper Richard had brought King Henry to the throne, I was aware that it must also have left him with an urgent need to feel secure on it and a strong sense that he was not. Several leading Yorkist knights and nobles, captured after the battle, were now incarcerated in towers around the fortress and might expect to lose their heads as traitors to the new crown. However, peering through the open gate in the wall, which led onto the green beside the castle's Church of St Nicholas, I could see that no scaffold had yet been erected there. Instead, bowmen had set up butts and were using them to hone their archery skills.

Remembering Sir Richard Guildford's vehement comment that all soldiers detested ravens, I became anxious when one of them landed on the gateway arch. Within moments I heard the threatening zing of an arrow and intuitively ducked, as it seemed almost to skim my headdress. My heart skipped several beats but relief flooded my veins when I saw the raven fly off and the arrow drop harmlessly over the outer curtain wall, presumably into the moat.

'Devilish bird!' I heard an archer shout. 'I'll get you next time.'

2

THE PALACE OF COLDHARBOUR had acquired its royal status after King Henry repossessed it and granted it to his mother, knowing her fondness for the old mansion where she had lived during the happy days of her marriage to Sir Henry Stafford. After his death she had been obliged by King Edward to marry his Steward of the Household, Lord Thomas Stanley, and move to his London home at St Paul's Wharf, a house that held no fond memories for her.

Coldharbour was a stately but rambling residence, set high above the Thames with views of London Bridge and across the river to Southwark. Its long garden sloped down to a private dock, making travel between it and the other Thameside royal palaces swift and easy. On my return there from the Tower I found Elizabeth of York seated under the light of a casement window reading a letter, which she waved at me fretfully.

'The king's messenger has been, Joan. Henry has not visited me for a week and now he apologises that he cannot invite me to witness his coronation. What am I to think?' She was an undeniably beautiful girl, blue-eyed and alabaster-skinned, just coming into full bloom as she approached the end of her teenage years. But at that moment her face was flushed and her brow creased in frustration.

I made a brief curtsy and took the letter from her, perusing it quickly. In order to usurp the throne, Richard of Gloucester had managed to persuade members of parliament that his dead brother's marriage was invalid, rendering its offspring illegitimate and the eldest boy therefore ineligible to inherit the crown. The letter explained, quite apologetically I thought, that as long as this heinous Act of Royal Title remained on the statute book, according to law Elizabeth was still illegitimate. Therefore all the noble ladies due to witness the king's coronation at the end of October would outrank her, so King Henry felt it was not advisable for her to attend. Once he had been crowned and a new parliament assembled, the Act would immediately be repealed and she would be restored to her rightful position as premier princess of the realm.

'Henry will be crowned king but the letter makes no mention of me becoming queen,' Elizabeth complained. 'I begin seriously to wonder if he intends to marry me at all and if not, what does he plan to do with me? I feel insulted and abandoned – no longer even sure that I wish to marry him, but whatever would I do otherwise?'

The intensity of her resentment alarmed me. She was usually so calm and serene and I searched for words to soothe her anguish. 'He signs the letter as "your loving friend",' I pointed out. 'And has he not sent you bolts of velvet and damask cloth and scores of ermine skins for trimmings? These are hardly the presents of a man who does not intend marriage. They will make a gown fit only for a queen.'

Elizabeth's frown deepened. 'I suppose you're right, Joan,' she said with evident reluctance. 'On the surface he appears all kindness and generosity but he is miserly with his time. Not only do I have no date for my wedding but I hardly know the man who has supposedly vowed to marry me. I feel like a prize heifer in the sale ring, on offer to the highest bidder.' Her fingers strayed to her temples and she rubbed them distractedly. 'Where have you been anyway? I have another headache and I was looking for you to go to the apothecary and fetch more of that vervain potion.'

I folded the letter, written in King Henry's own looping hand; surely another sign of his wish to please his intended bride. 'I will go now if you like,' I suggested, handing it back. Conscious of Usher Gainsford's warnings, I refrained from making any mention of my morning activities.

'Yes, thank you, Joan. But I think I will lie down meanwhile. Will you draw the curtains around the bed and help me remove my gown before you go? Wake me when you return if I'm asleep, won't you?'

Elizabeth was encouraged not to venture out into London's streets, even in a concealing hood. Most Londoners had always heartily supported her charismatic father, King Edward, and probably would welcome a glimpse of his daughter but King Henry cited the violent street clashes of persistently opposing factions as a reason for her to keep out of sight. Clearly it was considered that a lowly commoner like me could run the risk. Before I left I set a maid outside her door, who might hear her if she called.

Coldharbour was situated not very far from the Tower but it was quite a walk to Blackfriars at the western end of the city wall, where Elizabeth's favoured apothecary had his shop.

However, despite the gutter stink of emptied piss-pots, I enjoyed negotiating the bustle of Thames Street and, in daylight at least, the greatest danger was only from the flyblown offal and dead vermin that littered the thoroughfare.

To my delight, in one of the alleyways leading down to the river, I spotted a busy flock of ravens squabbling around the carcass of a stray dog. London was full of such carrion, which attracted these large birds in considerable numbers. Goodwives might chase them away but they were surely of help to the unfortunate gongfermers, overwhelmed by the task of waste disposal in the city. Over the years I had learned that most of the citizens did not share the Tower garrison's intense dislike of ravens. Stopping briefly to watch, I admired the birds' glossy black feathers, which seemed to throw off blue and green reflections under the stray rays of sun that pierced the gloom under the overhanging timber-framed houses flanking the alley.

When I reached the apothecary's shop in the black monks' walled enclave, I took it upon myself to ask whether any harm could come of taking too much of the vervain potion but was reassured that its soothing qualities were potent but harmless, so I gave an order for several bottles. While this was being fulfilled, I stole an hour to pay a visit to my mother, who rented rooms in the Blackfriars' extensive demesne. Katherine, Lady Vaux, to give her official title, although her friends called her Kate, was a popular resident of the tenements there, which had been built to house the widows and families of knights killed on the battlefield. Whenever I called in, I usually found some other lady with her, seeking comfort or advice from one who was known to be wise and well acquainted with grief. On this occasion however, I found my mother in the process of teaching her maidservant, Jess, how to write but the instant I arrived she put aside the waxed tablet they had been using and shooed the girl away into the scullery.

'What a treat to see you, Gigi!' she exclaimed, embracing me warmly and delighting me, as she always did, with the use of my childhood nickname and the slight foreign lilt in her voice. I had always thought her a handsome woman, whose dark features I had inherited, although sadly not, in my view, her marvellous warmth and generosity. 'I expect you have been very occupied with your bride-in-waiting. And I gather Lady Margaret is now ruling the kingdom, while her son is closeted away learning the laws and liberties of England. How is my old friend? In her element I warrant.'

Her friendship with the king's mother went back more than thirty years, to when she had been a maid of the chamber to Queen Marguerite. They were much of an age and Lady Margaret had been a maid of honour at court before her brief but fruitful marriage to Edmund Tudor, King Henry VI's half-brother.

'Indeed. She is officially presiding over the Privy Council,' I said, taking a seat on the carved settle beside the well-stoked fire. 'I don't sit in the council obviously, but I can imagine her style of leadership rather resembles the red dragon on King Henry's battle banner, breathing flames of fire.'

My mother shrugged and gave a rueful smile. 'She may be fierce in public but she was always the kindest of friends. I would never have married your father if she had not promoted our match with the king. Even after Edward of

York took the throne and forced us to flee back to Piedmont she always wrote to me. And what would I have done with you and Nicholas when poor Queen Marguerite begged me to stay with her as she was taken prisoner to the Tower? Margaret took you in and refused any payment.'

Her memories of that time always made her a little sad. England had been in turmoil. Edward of York had been victorious at yet another bloody battle in which my father was killed, fighting alongside Queen Marguerite's treasured only son, who also died. In mourning and despair, the two bereaved friends were taken captive to the Tower of London and that is how my brother and I had gone to live with the present king's mother. Although neither royal nor noble, the life of the Vaux family had not been without incident.

I nodded in acknowledgement. 'It's true that she's always been generous and now she is also working hard on behalf of her son. While he is closeted away making plans for England, my lady leaves Coldharbour after Prime and rarely returns before Compline. But we talk together at supper and she tells me that she misses you greatly. However I can assure you that she doesn't miss a Mass, even though these days her chaplain has to follow her around like a lap dog.'

This picture made my mother laugh. She had poured two cups of ale from a jug and carried them over to sit down beside me. 'Margaret's always been punctilious in her piety; but I hope you're not implying that I was once her lap dog,' she added, passing me a cup.

My walk had made me thirsty and I sipped eagerly before responding, 'Far from it, Mamma. You will always be Lady Margaret's greatest friend. If you were ever anyone's lap dog it was Queen Marguerite's. There is no denying that you were a martyr to her.'

For the second time that day I found myself recalling my first childhood visit to the Tower when, after the encounter with the raven, I had found my mother still trying hopelessly to console the bereaved and captive former queen. Out of her mind with grief, Queen Marguerite had taken one look at me and dissolved into tears, wailing, 'I lost *my* one child, my beautiful Prince Édouard, slain in battle; only seventeen and dying unshriven!'

I had then endured a sobbing hug that lasted for what seemed like an age. Subsequently, during the scant hour's visit I had been permitted, it had been impossible for us to share our own grief over my father's battlefield death along-side the prince, without his mother's continuous keening as an accompaniment. Then, after the French king at last paid her ransom, Marguerite had somehow persuaded her faithful companion to go back with her to Anjou and leave my brother and me with Lady Margaret. During the next six years I saw my mother only once, when she managed to escape to England for a brief visit. As a result I always wondered whether such selfless loyalty should have taken precedence over motherly love.

Now my mother regarded me solemnly. 'You are right, I was. I admit it. But look what a superb education you received as Lady Margaret's ward. Few girls are granted such a chance and you have made the most of it.'

I nodded again and took another gulp of ale. After a pause I added, 'I see you are teaching Jess her letters.'

She rolled her eyes. 'Well, I'm trying, but she makes a better scullion than a scholar.'

It was my turn to laugh. Now in her early forties, my mother had never known the luxury of having her own household or even bringing up her own children and yet she displayed a sense of humour and a zest for life that never ceased to surprise me. Where I wore dark clothes out of choice, she preferred to dress in light colours, sewing her own kirtles in blues and pinks and somehow acquiring gowns in colours like mustard yellow and dove grey, trimmed with rabbit fur, and displaying her widowhood only in the rather old-fashioned white veils she chose to wear. Or perhaps she could not afford to replace them with the new headdress fashions, as a result of having served an impoverished ex-queen and being short of funds all through the York years.

I changed the subject. 'What news of Nicholas? Has he taken possession of the Vaux honours yet?'

After King Edward seized the throne, his first parliament had confiscated the properties of all those Lancastrian land-holders who had fought against him. Thus on reaching his majority, my brother had been denied his inheritance. Now that King Henry had taken the throne he expected to reclaim it.

My question kindled the light of battle in my mother's eyes. 'No, and he is very keen to do so. King Henry has called a parliament for November and promises it will revoke the attainders; then it will be a matter of reclaiming the manors, but I imagine in some cases that may not be easy.'

'I thought King Edward granted you your dower lands when you returned from France after Queen Marguerite died.'

'Yes, he did, but I have been subsidising Nicholas and the income barely covers our basic needs. I am hoping my well-connected daughter will acquire me some employment in the household of the new queen, when we have one.' She gave me an inquiring look. 'When is that likely to be, do you know?'

'No – and neither does Elizabeth. She fears King Henry may even call the marriage off.'

'Surely not! His mother would never let him do that. Margaret has promoted that marriage for years and there is no doubt it would do much to placate persistent Yorkists. Why should he back out now that he has the throne?'

'Perhaps because he wants to establish a *Tudor* dynasty.' I laid stress on the Tudor name, recalling the words of Usher Gainsford. 'A queen without ties to any English house might suit him better than one who has a claim to the throne that some consider stronger than his.' I dropped my voice as I said this, conscious that Jess might have Yorkist leanings and her ear to the door.

'You mean marry a foreign princess?' My mother gave a dismissive wave of her hand. 'I don't think so. None of Europe's present rulers would risk giving a daughter to a king who'd won his throne by a twist of fate. They'd want to see him keep it for a few years first and Henry Tudor needs to get his dynasty started as soon as possible. I'd say he's just waiting to be anointed with the holy chrism and then Elizabeth will be whisked to the altar!'

My mother made a good point, although an opposing view was aired at my next port of call. Having collected the apothecary's order, I took a roundabout route back to Coldharbour so that I could also drop in on my friend Rosie in Crown Seld, a square off the busy Cheapside market, where her mother ran a business devoted to the arcane craft of passementerie: the production of decorative trimmings in silk.

The workshop was a riot of gossip and colour. Spools of silks in a score of hues were stacked on shelves along the walls and on the tables at which the weavers were working, cones of costly gold and silver thread were in constant use by rows of females of all ages. Young apprentices worked under the eagle eyes of older workers, whose gnarled and calloused fingers revealed their experience in fashioning the delicate braids and laces used to embellish and fasten the gowns and robes of the wealthy and noble.

This form of employment was the exclusive domain of women, men lacking the dexterity needed to handle the delicate threads involved. The practitioners were called silkwomen and inevitably, when a group of females were gathered together employing busy fingers while their minds roamed free, there was always plenty of chatter. In days gone by, Lady Margaret had often sent me there to collect her passementerie purchases and during these errands I had discovered the stimulation of city scandal and become particularly friendly with Rosie, a bright, forthright woman a few years my senior, quick-witted, married to a mercer and a fount of information from the streets and guilds.

Knowing that she hated stopping in mid-weave, I pulled up a spare stool beside her and, like my mother, she immediately sought inside knowledge about the new royal regime. 'What a welcome guest you are, Joan! I hope you're going to tell us why we've heard nothing more about our new king's much-vaunted marriage to Elizabeth of York.' Blonde and buxom in a blue kirtle and brimmed linen cap, Rosie winked at me at the same time as she expertly tied off the end of a gold lace, clearly part of a batch destined to attach sleeves to a gown or doublet belonging to some exalted personage. 'Since her triumphant return to London she seems to have disappeared entirely. I could say much like her brothers. Where's she hiding and why?'

It was true that Elizabeth's arrival in the capital five weeks before had been greeted with great joy and celebration by its citizens, who had lined the streets waving banners, throwing flowers and shouting her name as she rode past – in marked contrast to the somewhat muted reception afforded the new, self-declared king, Henry Tudor, some days earlier. However, not wishing to feed the city rumour mill, I dodged the question. 'You're obviously working on an order for some rich customer, Rosie,' I remarked, fingering the lace she had just completed. 'This looks fit for a queen.'

My evasive reply drew a frown from my friend. 'Well, there's no secret about this,' she said, taking back the lace and adding it to the pile beside her. 'Tomorrow we've got to send two hundred gold cord-laces to the pointmakers, who'll fit the aiglets, and then they're going to George Lovekyn up in Threadneedle Street.' Wasting no time, she hitched a fresh length of gold thread to her thumb and finger and began another line of loops, her fingers flying up and down and to and fro like shuttles, so fast that I couldn't begin to follow the pattern they made, only witness the ever-growing length of the braided lace they produced.

'Wasn't Master Lovekyn recently appointed Royal Tailor of the Great Wardrobe?' I asked. 'You must have heard that news, if I have.'

Her expression cleared. 'Ah, so you think these laces are

meant for the Lady Elizabeth? For her wedding garb perhaps?'

'I'm saying no more, except that some fabulous fabrics and furs were delivered to a certain lady recently.'

'Then why wouldn't we send the laces to where the lady is staying?'

I affected wide-eyed innocence. 'Because I haven't mentioned who the lady is, or where she is living.'

Rosie cast an exasperated look at the other women working nearby, whose ears had all been tuned to our chat, and they exchanged dissatisfied shrugs. I knew that my hints would be embroidered and spread almost as fast as their fingers wove each lace but I considered that a few rumours refuting the prevailing gossip that the Lancaster–York wedding was in doubt could only be beneficial to both the ladies I served.

Her fingers still flying, Rosie took another tack. 'They say King Henry won't marry King Edward's daughter until he has proof that his sons are dead. But some of those new yeomen guards searched the Tower for days and found no sign of them.'

'Well, if they were alive after Richard was crowned, don't you think he would have shown them to the people of London? After all, parliament had declared them illegitimate so they were no threat to his reign.'

'That depends if you really believe they were bastards.' It was one of the older women who spoke, her voice sharp with sarcasm. While King Edward had been almost universally admired in London, the same was not true of his brother Richard, whose main support had been in the north of the kingdom. 'Henry Tudor's yeomen might have been sent to make sure the boys definitely *are* dead now, if they were not before.'

'That's possible,' Rosie agreed. 'What does their sister think, Joan?'

'I have no idea,' I replied truthfully. 'But I'm certain she would not marry Henry Tudor if she thought he was in any way involved in her brothers' deaths. She mourns them deeply.'

I didn't stay long with the silkwomen but even so dusk was beginning to fall as I made my way back down towards the river. To my alarm, as I descended Soper Street I ran into a rowdy gang of men who had apparently been quenching their thirst after a long day's work in the Tanners' Seld, a fetid centre of their odorous trade. My heart lurched with dread as they halted in front of me, barring my path, and I looked urgently around for help but found none.

'Here's a posh skirt out late, boys!' gloated one, leaning into me with alarming menace. I gave an involuntary gasp at the stench of urine rising from his stained clothing and backed away, but another of the gang had circled behind me, blocking my path. 'Are you trading, mistress?' The first man's laugh was harsh and ugly with lust. 'There's a dark alley just here and we can all take turns. This could be your lucky night. Come on, men, get her in there!'

My limbs turned to jelly out of sheer terror. I was only too aware how easy it would be for such a threat to be fulfilled in the lawless streets of a city where rape and murder went daily unpunished. I felt hands pushing under my cloak and my mind told me to scream but when I opened my mouth no sound came out. My feet were almost pulled from under me as two of the gang began shoving me towards

26

the alley. I tried to struggle against them but their strength and the smell of their clothing were overpowering and the sound of their crude comments and evil laughter were blood-chilling. Terrified and outnumbered, I thought my worst fears were about to be realised but still my voice failed to let me scream.

Then rescue came from an unexpected source. Out of the very alley into which the gang were forcing me strolled, all unsuspecting, a young man in a leather apron.

A voice from the midst of the tanners' pack yelled, 'There's that little shoe-shit Seb! Come on, let's get him!' and all at once their attention shifted from me to him.

The lad in the leather apron did an abrupt about-turn and disappeared back up the alley. Realising all at once that the groping hands had been withdrawn, I took my chance and made a dash for it, running as fast as I could downhill towards the river, panting with panic. Luckily even though my brain was scrambled with fear, the route to Coldharbour remained familiar and I just kept running until I saw the entrance. Never had the flaming torches, flickering and spitting in their gatehouse sconces, been so welcome. Unaware of my situation, the duty guard recognised me, raised his eyebrows at my obvious haste and admitted me with a jocular inquiry: 'Where's the fire, Mistress Vaux?'

Once safely inside I flopped back against the courtyard wall to catch my breath. My chest was heaving and I felt as if my lungs would burst. Still trembling with shock, I closed my eyes and relived the whole horrific incident in flashes of terror. However as my breathing eased, sanity returned and I sent up a heartfelt prayer of thanks to God for my escape. I worried whether the boy in the leather apron got away and if it would really ever be possible for the new king to clear the city streets of danger and provide the peace and prosperity he had promised his new subjects.

And also amidst all this I worried whether King Henry was having second thoughts about marrying Elizabeth of York. Tucked away across the river in his secluded Palace of Kennington, was he aware of the mood in the city? Did he realise there was every chance it would erupt in rebellion if he reneged on his marriage vow? The thought of thugs such as those I had recently encountered running amok in the streets made my stomach churn all over again. I decided not to tell Elizabeth of my brush with danger and felt in my skirt pocket for the small leather bottles of vervain tincture I had set out to fetch. They were all there, unaffected, as if nothing untoward had happened.

3

WHEN A BARGE WAS sighted on the river flying Lady Margaret Beaufort's portcullis emblem, the Coldharbour household went into high alert. With his coronation only a few days off, she had been staying with the king at Kennington Palace to assist in the arrangements and her return to her own home so close to that date was a surprise.

I watched with Elizabeth from a window in the great hall as the noble lady disembarked, along with a procession of porters bearing gifts, doubtless gleaned from among those presented to King Henry to celebrate his crowning: baskets of oranges probably from Spain, crocks of honey and casks of wine from France. As usual she was elegantly garbed in a deep red velvet gown trimmed with gold fringes and a close-fitting black chaperon hat against the sharp river breeze. Although she had accepted the somewhat ageing title of 'My Lady the King's Mother', at not much more than forty she was still fit and energetic and strode briskly up the garden path that led from the quay to the mansion, taking the slope without slowing her pace.

She did not come to the great hall however, but went to her solar and sent a page to summon me, rather than first paying her respects to Elizabeth, who was more than somewhat peeved. 'She will not acknowledge the servant before the mistress when I am married to her son,' she muttered, sinking back onto the cushions of the window seat and taking refuge in her embroidery, while I blushed furiously, murmured an unnecessary apology as if it were my fault, and fled from the hall to obey Lady Margaret's call. Not for the first time I felt the strain of being Elizabeth's attendant as well as, at present, her only friend.

The kind lady who had been my foster mother was now the first lady in the land; at least until King Henry took a wife as queen. I had been with her almost throughout the time of her son's exile, grown up under her strict but compassionate care and stayed with her as a companion and foster daughter until the usurper had discovered her part in a rebellious attempt on his throne and sentenced her to house arrest under the supervision of servants loyal to him. Her own household had been forced to leave and I had not returned until after her son Henry had fought for the throne and won it.

'How are things between you and Elizabeth, Joan?' she asked as soon as we had exchanged kisses of greeting.

'They are fine, my lady,' I replied, 'or they were until you summoned me ahead of greeting her.'

'Oh dear, have I offended her?'

'Just a little I think.' I smiled at the slight note of insincerity in her voice.

'Well, she is not queen yet and until she is I remain first lady in the land. It will do her no harm to accept this for the time being.'

'I'm sure she will do so graciously – for the time being.' I laid a certain stress on the last words and received my patron's smile in return. She was a tiny woman with a big heart and a sharp intellect; I admired her enormously.

Except when on her knees at prayer she was rarely still and at this moment she tucked her hand in the crook of my arm and walked me towards the window of her solar, which overlooked the Thames. 'It pleases me greatly that you have obviously become a good friend to the Lady Elizabeth, Joan, but you must realise that you do not have sufficient rank to hold a senior position among her ladies when she becomes queen. The king has asked me to supervise the appointment of her female household and I think it would look good if her sister Cecily were to be chief among them. But I am not sure how well the two get on. Do you happen to know whether such a partnership would work?'

I hesitated before answering. Having only observed the two princesses together as young girls, on the odd occasion they had been there when I had attended Lady Margaret at their parents' court, I had not gleaned any real idea of how they got on. 'I couldn't say, my lady,' I admitted. 'She talks about her sisters often and worries how they are, but I don't get the impression that she and Cecily were particularly close. I think Princess Mary was her favourite and closest to her in age but of course she died.'

I felt Lady Margaret give my arm a gentle squeeze. 'Yes, how sad that was. Do you think you could sound Elizabeth out about Cecily for me, Joan? I don't want to suggest she appoint her as chief lady-in-waiting, only to have her immediately veto the idea. It might jeopardise our future relationship.'

I took a deep breath. Negotiating royal relationships was

not something I had ever imagined doing. 'I can try, of course, but would this not be something their mother might advise you about?'

Lady Margaret glanced around, as if there might be a spy lurking in her solar. 'Their mother is presently living at Sheen Palace and has yet to demonstrate reliable support for the Tudor crown. My son does not believe her to have entirely abandoned the Yorkist cause but by bringing Cecily into her household, Elizabeth would be indicating that her whole family supports King Henry's reign. And after suffering the humiliating marriage foisted on her by the usurper, as the queen's chief lady-in-waiting Cecily would acquire high status once more and a good income, which should inspire her gratitude, if nothing else. By the way, I will be telling Elizabeth that her sister's regrettable misalliance is to be officially annulled by the consistory court in York in December.'

This would be welcome news to Elizabeth, who had fretted much over the fact that in order to provide for the nieces he had rendered illegitimate, the usurper Richard had arranged a marriage for Cecily with one Ralph Scrope, the younger brother of a Yorkshire baron, and I assumed that at only fourteen, it was not a union she had entered willingly.

'How well do you get on with your sister Cecily, Lady Elizabeth?' I tried to slip this question in casually as I helped her to dress on the day of King Henry's coronation, hoping that her mind would be occupied and she might not question the query.

But she did. 'Why do you ask, Joan?'

'It's been suggested that you might appoint her as your chief lady-in-waiting – after your marriage, of course.'

'When I am queen you mean.' Her chin lifted. 'Who made the suggestion? Was it the king's mother?'

Blood rose to my cheeks. 'Well, yes, it was Lady Margaret. Does that matter?'

Elizabeth gave a considered sniff. 'No, not really, but now I know why she snubbed me and commanded your presence the other day without greeting me first. That will not happen when I am queen. I will be first lady and she will walk behind me, whether the king likes it or not. I was reared to be a queen, Joan. She was not.' She turned to gaze out of the window, which faced west, the direction in which lay Westminster. 'I do not need anyone to tell me how to perform my duties, or what respect I should be owed.'

I bit my lip before responding. 'I do not believe there was any disrespect behind the suggestion that you might appoint your sister as your chief attendant. Lady Margaret thought you might feel more comfortable with a member of your family at your side.'

'I will have the king at my side. He will be my family and when we have children, so will they.'

I dared to pursue the point. 'Does that mean you would prefer not to appoint Lady Cecily?'

The expression of offended nobility left her face and was replaced by one of mischievous intent. 'No. It means I will do my own appointing and when I require her help I will ask for it. You can tell Lady Margaret that if you like, Joan.'

Two days after the coronation the king's mother came to Coldharbour again, this time to give Elizabeth a description of the event and the celebrations that had followed. I could tell from her expression that Elizabeth was in two minds as to whether she wanted to hear this, probably preferring to have had King Henry's impressions from his own lips. However, having already been waiting impatiently for longer than she liked, she was not about to refuse Lady Margaret's account.

It was a highly charged one. 'It was an extremely moving occasion, dear Elizabeth!' she began. 'A ceremony of such immense significance! I do not know how the king remained dry-eyed. Of course I should not have succumbed to tears but when the archbishop placed the crown on my son's head I admit I was overwhelmed. Nor was I alone in this. Even his uncle, the great Jasper Tudor, had tears sliding down his cheeks as he knelt to be the first to make his oath of allegiance.

'God's presence and approval was divinely evident throughout the ceremony. Henry's anointing was truly awe-inspiring, even though it was performed under a canopy and hidden from view; as the holy chrisom was applied the choir's anthem rose in a glorious crescendo and I felt as if my heart would burst. Everywhere was brilliant spectacle; the new green and white uniforms of the yeoman guards, the red robes and jewelled coronets of the barons and the splendidly embroidered copes of the clergy, led by the bishops with their gilded mitres and gem-studded croziers. It was enough to bring pride and joy to every heart and a prayer to every lip.'

She reached out to take Elizabeth's hand and held it between her own, her face charged with sympathy. 'I am so sorry you were not there. Had it not been for the question of rank, of course you would have been and I'm sure you'd have been more thrilled and proud than anyone. The king has asked me to assure you that when parliament meets next week, after the Act of Royal Title has been repealed and every copy consigned to the bonfire, there will be parliamentary endorsement of his long-avowed intention to marry you and to unite the warring factions of Lancaster and York under a new Tudor dynasty.'

Gently and politely Elizabeth removed her hand, clasping both of hers tightly together in her lap once more. 'I will look forward to hearing that from the king's own lips, my lady,' she said. Her back grew straighter and her head seemed to rise above Lady Margaret's.

My glance swung from one to the other and I noticed a marked similarity in their expressions. Both women were direct descendants of King Edward the Third and pride was etched into each face; steely resolve glinted in the blue eyes and the grey. For a time I had fretted that Elizabeth might have met her match in My Lady the King's Mother but at that moment I recalled her recent forceful declaration that she would be first lady and walk beside the king. 'I was reared to be a queen, Joan. She was not.'

I felt a surge of relief. The wedding was on and Elizabeth was exerting her authority. The fear of rebellion receded and with it the prospect of violence in the streets of London and a resurgence of civil war. I wished I could be at the Tower, to see if ravens were flocking in on a new sense of national security.

4

AS HER WEDDING DREW nearer, Elizabeth had taken the initiative and invited Cecily to lead her ladies-in-waiting. When the two sisters put their heads together to select the ladies and gentlewomen who would be invited to attend the new queen, it made me smile to see how they joined forces, gently but firmly, to inform Lady Margaret of their choices.

Just as she had claimed a seat at the right hand of the king at the meetings of his Privy Council, My Lady the King's Mother had automatically assumed that she would supervise the selection of his queen's ladies, but although she was consulted, the growing list of possible attendants gradually began to show more bias towards York than she liked. 'This one does not ring any bells with me,' she commented, pointing to a name on the list, 'unless she was the Lady Katherine Grey who served your mother with me and was then widowed. I don't know who she married afterwards.'

'Yes, it is the same woman,' Elizabeth said with a smile. 'I always liked her when she served my mother. Sadly, she has no children and has made it known that she would be available to serve me, should I wish to welcome her into my household.'

'But her husband is an esquire, so she would have to

accept that she could not be a lady-in-waiting but only a gentlewoman of the bedchamber.' I sensed rather than saw Lady Margaret cast a glance at me, where I sat in my usual discreet corner, book in hand. 'Joan Vaux is an equally experienced attendant, is she not? Would she not be a better appointment in that capacity? You might also consider appointing Joan's mother, Lady Vaux, as your chief lady of the bedchamber. That is if serving under her mother would not discomfort her daughter. Would it, Joan?'

With the attention of all the royal ladies on me I closed my book and rose to reply, grateful for Lady Margaret's promotion of my mother because I had been dreading having to make the suggestion myself. 'I had not dared to assume that I would be on the list, my lady,' I said. 'But if I am to be so honoured, of course I would have no objection to serving under my mother. In fact both she and I would be privileged to serve the queen in any way she commands.'

But then Lady Margaret caused my heart to miss a beat when she mentioned something I would have much preferred she had not. 'Joan may not have told you, Elizabeth, but when the king asked me to nominate a female to attend security instruction from his Ushers of the Chamber I asked her to go, knowing she could be relied on to remember all the details without writing them down.'

Elizabeth gave me a quizzical look and I felt my cheeks begin to burn. 'I was ordered to tell no one,' I admitted. 'Usher Gainsford told us that it was information only for the ears of those who had taken an oath of loyalty to the king.'

Elizabeth's expression turned from curiosity to anger. 'And I had not, is that it? Indeed will not, until I make my marriage vows. But how did they know that you would be among my attendants when – if – I became queen, Joan?'

I could hear the hurt in her voice and hung my head. 'I cannot say, my lady.'

The king's mother replied for me. 'Because I vouched for her, believing that you had found Joan as clever, kind and obliging as I always have. If I have made the wrong assumption I can only apologise.'

I held my breath, fearing that in doing Lady Margaret's bidding and keeping faith with my secrecy vow, I had destroyed Elizabeth's trust and lost places in her household for both my mother and me. When I risked a glance, her face was a picture of indecision. I could see by the way her mouth was working that she was considering whether or not I had betrayed our friendship by appearing to favour Lady Margaret over her. She was anxious and bewildered, a bride at the steps of the altar, wracked with nerves about what the future held for her.

To my surprise Cecily spoke up on my behalf. 'Surely there can be no one more trustworthy and helpful than Joan, Elizabeth. Look how she has served you and consoled you through all these months of waiting, wondering whether you were going to be forced into a misalliance like I was, or enclosed in a convent, or raised to the consort's throne, as is your right and due as our father's heir.'

I looked at Lady Margaret, who appeared delighted with Cecily's robust defence of both me and her sister's rightful place in the kingdom. Then I hung my head once more and waited, hoping I had not condemned the Vaux name to ignominy, not daring to look at Elizabeth, for fear of seeing her friendship fading away and with it my own future as a member of her court.

At length she spoke. 'I have to acknowledge the truth in that, Cecily,' she said. 'I must have tried her patience horribly.' She rose from her seat and came towards me. 'I am sorry I doubted your loyalty, Joan. I admit that you have been my rock in a sea of uncertainty. Of course I can trust you above all people.' She placed her hands on my shoulders and kissed my cheek. 'I cannot imagine my royal bedchamber without your presence. Whatever top-security secrets you hold in that book-filled head of yours, I'm sure they will protect me from all manner of harm.'

Retiring once more to my corner, I reflected what a momentous and hazardous life Elizabeth had ahead of her. For all her claim to have been reared to the role she had to play, she was still only a girl of nineteen; she would need all the help and support of her mother, her sisters, her ladies and her gentlewomen, if she were to achieve all that was expected of her as England's first Tudor queen and the fertile heart of the Tudor rose.

In early December, once parliament had confirmed the marriage contract between Henry and Elizabeth and set the wedding for mid-January, I had been surprised at the speed of subsequent arrangements. Even my friends at the silk workshop commented on it.

'There is little more than a month to make preparations,' Rosie remarked when I went to the passementerie workshop to collect supplies of trimming braid. 'We're already working flat out on orders for our products. Yet as well as gowns to be made and feasts to plan, there are tournaments and processions and entertainments to organise and they'll never get papal dispensation through in a month! Anyone would think there was a reason for speed.' She grinned slyly around at her fellow workers and I grasped her implication. It was common knowledge that at least a third of brides marrying in London were already pregnant when they took their vows, although few would have admitted the fact.

I had sudden recall of an incident shortly after the wedding date had been announced. With Elizabeth then officially queen-in-waiting, King Henry had granted her the use of Baynard's Castle in which to gather her household and wardrobe ready for her new life, and she and her sister had immediately taken up residence there. After the Tower, Baynard's was London's most imposing fortress, located on the Thames and guarding the western corner of the city wall, and my mother and I had moved there together, awaiting the rest of the new royal household.

Shortly after we had settled in, King Henry had made a surprise visit, delighting Elizabeth, who had been frowning with Cecily over a list of possible candidates for her staff. Mother and I immediately withdrew to an antechamber and within minutes Lady Cecily had joined us. 'The king says he wants to take Elizabeth into the garden,' she said with a knowing smile. 'He has some private business to discuss with her.'

My mother was sympathetic. 'And why should he not? Heaven knows they have a great deal to discover about each other. But it will be cold in the garden. Joan, you should fetch a cloak for her grace.' As a practised servant of queens, Lady Vaux was already using the royal form of address and indeed the king had specified that Elizabeth should now be regarded as if she were already his queen.

I had run to the Wardrobe, housed in a tower overlooking

the garden, and selected a fur-lined mantle, but when I tried to deliver it, after searching every bush and bower, I could find no sign of the royal couple. Wherever they had gone, it was not into the garden. Surprised and even a little alarmed, I looked for them in the long gallery overlooking the river, thinking that in view of the December cold they might have decided to hold their private conversation there, but the only sign of the royal presence was at the entrance to Elizabeth's bedchamber where two yeomen guards stood barring my way, holding their crossed halberds against my entry.

'The king has asked for privacy, mistress,' one announced. 'And we are here to make sure he has it.'

With my thoughts whirling, I made my way back to the Wardrobe Tower, replaced the mantle and returned to the river chamber. I did not confide what I had seen to the others. An hour later we heard the sound of King Henry's departure but Elizabeth did not reappear until supper, when she drew me aside. She looked unusually flushed and I wondered if she might be starting an ague.

'After the king left I felt a little unwell, Joan,' she said, 'and I lay in the bed to rest. When I woke I found that there was blood on my shift and on the sheet, so my month-lies must have started early. Please be so kind as to deal with the laundry and do not mention this to anyone else. I know I can rely on you to be discreet.'

And of course she could, no matter what.

At her wedding Elizabeth looked every inch the royal bride, in a gown fashioned from the rolls of red satin and crimson damask and trimmed with the almost priceless ermine tails that had been her first gifts from King Henry. I had suggested then that these could only be the presents of a king to his bride and she had used them triumphantly to present herself as his true consort.

For many years Mary, Countess Rivers, had been one of my fellow 'nestlings', as Lady Margaret had called her clutch of young wards, and she had also been appointed a lady-in-waiting, so my mother and I had enlisted her help to present the queen-to-be as bridal perfection. We had dressed Elizabeth in the spectacular crimson gown, brushed her long red-gold Plantagenet hair down her back as a sign of her virginity and threaded it with jewels to glint in the myriad candle flames of Westminster Abbey. A diamond-studded coronet proclaimed her lineage and a collar of gold, pearls and rubies encircled her neck and breast. Her train was fashioned from cloth of gold and lavishly embroidered with heraldic badges – the falcon and fetterlock of York, the swan of Lancaster and the new Tudor rose – Lancastrian red outer petals and the York white rose at the centre.

In the abbey I watched the bridal procession make its slow, rhythmic progress through the choir screen and towards the chancel. I was immensely proud that my mother was among the trainbearers, especially as the others were, to a greater or lesser degree, all relatives of the bride or groom. Two York princesses, sixteen-year-old Cecily and nine-year-old Anne, led the chosen eight, who all wore red velvet gowns, complementing the bride but without the costly and spectacular ermine and jewels. Significantly, however, on their heads were coronets of red and white silk roses, celebrating the crucial union of the royal houses taking place before our eyes.

Ahead of them Elizabeth walked unaccompanied, gliding like a swan, head high and proud. Even from my lowly place at the back of the choir I could see that King Henry was awestruck by her beauty as he watched her approach him at the chancel steps. She, as much as the kingdom he had conquered, was the prize he had won five months before on that bloody battlefield in Leicestershire.

5

IT WAS A PEAK time for nuptials. King Henry had been busy matching up his trusted and unmarried Lancastrian followers with women of Yorkist family, in order to build Tudor support. I thought it rather an unpleasant way of coercing loyalties. It reminded me of the heinous '*droit de seigneur*' tactics of the Normans I had read about, after they first conquered England, whereby the new foreign lords of the manor claimed the first night of every village wedding, with the aim of impregnating the bride and spreading Norman blood across the formerly Saxon kingdom.

In the midst of the ten days of royal marriage celebrations in London and Westminster, my mother and I had to request leave from the queen's service in order to attend my brother's wedding to Beth Fitzhugh, the young widow of Sir William Parr, who had been Edward the Fourth's Comptroller of the Household. Somewhat to my surprise, despite her Yorkist background, Nicholas seemed rather taken with his pretty, cheerful bride and quite undaunted by the prospect of playing stepfather to the children of her first marriage. And Beth confided to me that she was looking forward to life with a young husband, instead of one nearly thirty years her senior.

'When you marry, as I'm sure you very soon will, Joan, I urge you to try and acquire a husband nearer your own age, rather than one old enough to be your father, as my first was. It can make for a difficult relationship.'

I bit back the temptation to confess my secret hope of avoiding the state of matrimony and motherhood altogether and assured her that my brother, as well as being much her own age, was also relatively easy-going. 'And Nicholas is particularly happy now that he's recovered our father's estates,' I added, delighted at last to visit Harrowden Hall, my brother's birthplace and the seat of the Vaux family, which had been granted away to a supporter of York in the newly crowned King Edward's first parliament. 'He's been almost penniless all his life until King Henry took the throne – not a very good catch for anyone. But you'll be able to live a comfortable life here now.'

'While you and your mother work your shoe-leather to shreds in the service of our new queen!' Beth cast her eyes skywards. 'I know what it can be like. I served Queen Anne for the last years of her life, poor sickly lady.'

I decided to avoid the subject of the new queen's predecessor. 'And my brother?' I inquired. 'Will he take royal service with King Henry?'

'I believe so but not yet.' Beth laughed. 'I think we have been granted a few weeks to "get to know each other", as they say. No doubt he hopes to sire an heir for his restored estates.'

I decided there and then that I liked my candid sister-in-law and waved in the direction of her two young sons, playing a game together in a corner of the hall. 'He has reason to believe you will have no problem in providing that.'

She smiled fondly at her boys. 'There are two little girls as well but they are too young to be present. The poor man is already a stepfather of four.'

I was tempted to ask her how she was so confident of supplying more children for my brother without mishap to herself but resisted, not wishing to saddle her with my own pessimistic attitude towards childbirth or to be told that there was nothing to it. My fear of giving birth sprang from the time I had acquired enough Latin to read the Bible, which had coincided with the start of my menstruation. Reading of Eve's punishment for giving Adam the apple and beginning to suffer its consequences at the same time had been enough to set me against the whole idea of becoming the vessel of man's procreation. And rather than arguing with her about it, I preferred to part friends with my new sister-in-law.

A more politically important match was that of Queen Elizabeth's thirteen-year-old cousin, Margaret Plantagenet, who was living and serving among her maids of honour. King Henry had sent Margaret's younger brother, eleven-year-old Edward, Earl of Warwick, to live at the Tower of London.

'Not as a prisoner,' I had heard him assure Elizabeth when she protested. 'He is lodged there as my guest, in comfort and security, in order to avoid Yorkist sympathisers being tempted to use him as a focus for rebellion.'

Margaret and Edward were the orphaned offspring of the late King Edward's younger brother George, who had been Duke of Clarence. They were legally excluded from the royal succession due to his attainder for committing treason against his brother; otherwise young Edward would have been next in line to the throne of his grandfather, outranking all other contenders including Henry himself, a position I assumed must be of serious concern to the newly-crowned king. Their father's mysterious death in the Tower of London during the York years was widely believed to have been a clandestine execution.

Two weeks after their wedding, when the official celebrations had died down, King Henry came unexpectedly to Elizabeth's robing chamber. It was the first time he had ventured into her private quarters other than to her bedchamber, which was always after her ladies had been dismissed, and I was fascinated to see him close up and dressed as plainly as a king could ever be, in a grey wool doublet and short black fur-trimmed gown. Apart from his splendid ruby coronation ring, his only jewellery was a gold chain about his shoulders and a pearl pin in his black beaver hat. He looked relaxed and cheerful, albeit perhaps a few years older than the twenty-nine I knew he had recently celebrated, with signs of grey mingling with the smooth brown hair at his temples. And I was happy to see him bend to kiss his new wife and return her warm smile before taking the cushioned stool I set beside her.

Eleanor Verney, a lady-in-waiting of much the same height and shape as the queen, emerged from the next-door room, making a surprised curtsy on seeing the king.

'We are deciding which gowns and kirtles to take to Greenwich next week, my lord,' Elizabeth explained to her husband. 'I have so many new ones and Lady Verney is kindly modelling them for me so that I can see how they look.' She nodded at Eleanor to carry on and the king watched attentively as the model demonstrated an elegant green brocade gown, showing how the skirt flowed behind her as she walked, and the full marten-trimmed pink sleeves, tied with silver laces, were draped from the elbow to show the tight cream-embroidered linen sleeves of the kirtle beneath. His obvious interest led me to surmise that the world of female fashion was something of a mystery to him.

When Lady Verney left to change Elizabeth turned to the woman standing behind her chair and made a brief comment. This was Mistress Jerningham, her Keeper of the Wardrobe, who would be responsible for making sure that the selected apparel was packed ready to be transported to the queen's next destination.

King Henry cleared his throat to attract her attention. 'Fascinating though this process is to an ignorant male, dear Elizabeth, I came to tell you what I have arranged for your cousin Margaret's future.' The queen immediately turned from her wardrobe mistress with an apologetic gesture and adopted an attentive attitude, joining her hands in her lap. The king continued. 'I intend betrothing Margaret to one of my prominent household squires, a man called Richard Pole. He is my mother's half-nephew and coincidentally the elder brother of Lady Verney here, who we have just been watching. He is of good family obviously and without doubt will progress well in my service, so I believe they will make a good pair.'

Elizabeth looked a little doubtful and cast an inquiring glance at her sister, Lady Cecily, who sat behind them both and, no doubt remembering her own recently annulled misalliance, immediately commented, 'Surely she deserves a marriage of higher status, your grace? After all she is the daughter of a royal duke.'

The king swung round with a swift and negative reaction. 'Yes, Lady Cecily, but a duke who forfeited all his honours when he betrayed his monarch, not once but three times! Besides who knows what rewards young Pole could reap while serving the Tudor crown? By the time they marry he might be a knight or even a peer.'

'Or she might find herself a country squire's wife living in a dilapidated rural hall, far from her friends and family,' Elizabeth observed flatly, no doubt recalling her sister's recently departed circumstances. 'I believe she is better and safer remaining here under our care, my lord.'

There was a tense pause and Eleanor Verney appeared once more in a fresh gown. King Henry dropped his voice to respond to Elizabeth's remarks. 'Since she is only thirteen she will remain here for the time being anyway and in the presence of Pole's sister it is perhaps invidious to discuss the subject further.' More loudly he added, 'I chiefly came to tell you, my queen, that plans are now completed for us to depart after Easter on a royal progress to East Anglia and the north of the kingdom. It is vital that we show ourselves to as many of our subjects as possible and besides I need to acquaint myself with the far reaches of my kingdom.'

I drew a sharp breath and clenched my teeth, my gaze flicking from the king to the queen. As Elizabeth's most intimate attendant and knowing what I did, I wondered how she would react to this announcement.

Her cheeks flushed bright pink and her voice trembled a little as she almost whispered, 'I fear it may not be possible for me to accompany you, sire.' During a brief but fraught hiatus before she spoke again, deep creases appeared between

49

King Henry's dark eyebrows. 'I cannot yet be completely certain but I believe I may be with child.'

The king's brow cleared and his pale blue eyes grew round with wonder; his chin dropped and he gave a loud gasp of surprise, then he flung himself from his chair to his knees and took his queen's hands in both of his. 'This is wonderful news, Elizabeth! I cannot believe it has happened so quickly.' He drew her fingers up to his lips and kissed them passionately, one hand after the other, several times. 'Let us pray to God there is no mistake.'

'Pray by all means, my lord,' she said with a smile, 'but not in words that may be heard outside this room. It is very early days and I am told that the initial months of pregnancy are fickle.' She gestured at the rest of us, all privy to this momentous news and sworn to absolute secrecy. 'These ladies can be trusted not to tell a soul and I'm advised that it would be best to wait until the child quickens before we make a public announcement.'

The light of pleasure in the king's eyes receded and he stood up, returning her hands to her lap. 'I'm sure you are right, my dearest lady,' he acknowledged. 'But I will find it very hard to keep such tidings a secret.'

Elizabeth laughed. 'I am sure you have kept plenty of secrets in your eventful life! Think of this as just another.'

'When do you think he will be born?' he asked.

She raised both hands to express uncertainty. 'In the autumn – September – October – I am no expert. But do not pin your hopes entirely on a boy, my lord. It is just as likely to be a girl.'

He shook his head so violently that he had to throw up his hand to secure his hat. 'I suppose I should declare that a healthy child is all that matters – but forgive me if I pray secretly for God to grant us a son. A Tudor heir, with the blood of both York and Lancaster flowing in his veins, to take the throne after I am gone.'

This elicited an immediate protest from the queen. 'Do not even hint at your demise when we have only just begun our reign, my lord! Is it not treason to speak of the king's death, even if the words are spoken by the king himself?' Elizabeth placed her hands over her belly as if to protect her unborn child from its father's words.

King Henry made her a low bow and lifted one of her hands again, to kiss it in farewell. 'I will take my leave and vow to keep my silence in every way that my queen commands. Only God will know my true desires.'

He departed with a smile on his lips – a happy king. But Elizabeth was not a happy queen. As soon as the door closed behind him she gave me an anguished look and I rushed to fetch the bowl that I had hastily hidden away when his arrival was announced. I needed no bidding because she had been hunched over such a receptacle every morning for the past week and had sent me on yet another errand to the apothecary's shop at Blackfriars. The suffering already evident in this royal pregnancy had done a great deal to nurture my conviction that motherhood was to be avoided at all costs.

6

WHEN THE TIME CAME for the court to move down-river to Greenwich, Elizabeth sank gratefully into the royal barge that was to take us to the Palace of Placentia, where we hoped fresher air and more restful circumstances would ease her condition. She was happy to have the company and advice of her mother, the Dowager Queen Elizabeth, who joined the royal party along with My Lady the King's Mother. Personally I thought the presence of both matriarchs might blight the newlyweds' chance to grow closer as a couple but they seemed delighted to welcome them. As it was proving a mild winter, the ground remained unfrozen and it was not long before King Henry decided to take the six-mile ride to inspect Eltham Palace, returning at dusk full of eager plans to make improvements there.

'Even in winter I think Eltham has a most pleasing climate, being set on a hill away from the odours of the Thames. Instead it has distant views of the river through stands of magnificent trees. I think that with some renovations it would make the perfect place for our children to grow up. But you know Eltham well, don't you, Elizabeth?'

We'd all stood up at the king's entrance and he took a seat beside her, displacing his mother, who beckoned rather petulantly to one of the duty pages to set another; but the Dowager Elizabeth had commandeered the only other spot near the fire, obliging Lady Margaret to settle for one within draughty reach of the constantly opening door, as servants came and went. I hid a smile. First gain to the queen's mother, I thought.

Unlike many of his sex, King Henry seemed quite comfortable being a lone man in the company of women, although he sometimes brought members of his court to share the ladies' society. On this occasion however he had come alone and straight from the saddle to the queen's commodious solar, where we spent the short winter afternoons reading and embroidering. When it grew too dark for these pastimes, candles were lit and musicians came to play and sing for us. On the king's arrival they had just begun setting up their instruments.

Being Lady Vaux, my mother qualified for a place near the queen but I usually took my book and embroidery to a discreet corner, chilly and suitably distant from the nobility but not too far from the queen's frequent summonses. However, I freely admit that when the Dowager Queen and Lady Margaret were both in attendance neither book nor embroidery held my attention, for I found the interplay between these two senior royal ladies fascinating, especially when they began to vie for the queen's attention, as they invariably did when in the presence of the king.

The Dowager exploited her memories of family life. 'You used to love staying at Eltham as a girl, didn't you, Elizabeth? You and your father enjoyed wonderful rides there together.'

The queen nodded and smiled, reminiscing. 'Oh yes, and

it is a marvellous place for hawking. You gave me a merlin for my twelfth birthday, do you remember? I wonder what happened to it after . . .' She let her voice trail away, presumably not wishing to revive sad events. Instead she turned her attention to the present. 'Isn't it too soon to start planning a nursery, Henry? I feel it might be tempting fate.'

It was the first time I had heard her address her husband by his name and hoped it was a sign of their growing fondness for each other. Certainly the king's elation had not diminished since learning of the coming child. 'Not at all,' he responded, lifting his chin. 'I am God's anointed. He has brought me to the throne and I believe that He would not have done so if He did not intend to grant me the gift of children to perpetuate the Tudor dynasty. We must have faith in the Almighty's purposes, Elizabeth.'

'I do not lack faith, I assure you.' She gave an audible sigh. 'I only wish the task of producing your children was less taxing, then I could have ridden with you to Eltham and shared your thoughts and plans on the spot.'

The Dowager Queen intervened again. 'But you soon will, my daughter,' she said encouragingly. 'By spring you should feel quite different. It will bring warmth and fresh vegetables and you will stop feeling sick and be filled with energy and vigour. I have carried twelve children, Elizabeth, and I know this. I continued to ride until quite near my time – not for long journeys obviously, but for short trips and exercise.'

Lady Margaret could not remain silent. 'But not all mothers are the same, are they, my lady? Carrying her first child is an anxious time for every woman. I think the queen should follow her instincts.'

I saw Elizabeth glance from mother to mother-in-law, probably sensing an argument brewing, which she hastily set out to dispel. 'Well, my instinct at present is just to curl up beside the fire and let nature take its course, but my sense of duty urges me to support my husband. At present I can do neither to my own satisfaction.'

King Henry smiled sympathetically and supplied a practical distraction. 'At this moment, my dearest queen, you can support me by ordering wine and spices. I did not stop for dinner and I don't think I can last until supper without some sustenance.'

Looking at the king's slim figure I was amazed that he could go from dawn to dusk and ride for most of it without some form of nourishment, but he seemed to have a will of iron. I had heard from members of his household that he sometimes rode fifty miles a day if necessary, as well as keeping up his knightly training. There were obviously muscles of iron within his wiry frame.

'Forgive me, Henry, I should have thought.' Elizabeth looked contrite and beckoned me to her side. 'Please organise refreshments for his grace, Joan, some wine and wafers and perhaps some sweetmeats. The king is hungry.'

'And find some cards, Joan,' added Henry as I curtsied compliance. 'Lent is looming, when we must not gamble, but today we can still allow ourselves a small flutter.'

I heard a distinct 'tut' coming from Lady Margaret but the Dowager Queen clapped her hands enthusiastically. 'Oh yes, good idea, your grace! A game of chance will cheer us all up. You'll play, won't you, Lady Margaret?'

I hurried away to follow my orders so I did not hear the response of the king's mother but from what I had observed of the newlyweds' card play, their 'game of chance' would entail more than just a 'small flutter'. Elizabeth had already been obliged to borrow money from her ladies to pay her gambling debts, including a significant sum from my mother, who did not indulge. I estimated that if the king continued to encourage her reckless wagers there would surely come a time when he would have to increase her income in order for her to pay them back, to himself included!

As I hurried away to fulfil my duty, I heard the king's mother's flat refusal. 'No, gambling is a sin, in or out of Lent. I do not choose to play cards.'

So here was another thing over which the two ladies could argue. I had observed the Dowager Queen's face closely and gleefully tucked away the image of her lips curling with irritation when Lady Margaret appeared to challenge her advice. Obviously a young woman like Elizabeth, only days off turning twenty, would appreciate having her very experienced mother close at hand during her first pregnancy, but equally the king was making up for lost time with his mother, from whom he had been separated for fourteen formative years of exile before coming to the throne. If the rivalry continued between the Dowager Queen and My Lady the King's Mother it would be very interesting to see who won.

Personally I was discovering that serving a queen was a very different proposition compared to the role of friend, servant and counsellor I had been playing before the royal marriage. Being on robing and disrobing duty early in the morning and late at night, and being expected to accompany Elizabeth to Mass and court gatherings during the day, was tiring, to say nothing of almost constantly running errands and fetching and carrying on her behalf. In addition, despite my terrifying encounter with the drunken tanners, I missed my sorties into the London streets and my informative gossip sessions at the silk workshop.

But the thing I found most inconvenient was the dress code. King Henry was determined that his court should be favourably compared with others in Europe, particularly France and the Burgundian duchy, which were renowned for their glamour and culture. So both the men and women of the English royal households were expected to wear fashionable apparel at all times. We were paid a dress allowance but I was always in trouble with Princess Cecily for failing to wear bright enough colours. Stubbornly however, I persisted in sticking to deep blue, brown and black, which I thought suited my dark colouring. Nor did I like being obliged to change at least twice a day in order to be clad in the right apparel for the various court activities. Not only were we expected to dress to impress but also to entertain guests with our dancing and singing and cultured conversation. I could readily discuss art, philosophy and literature in four different languages but when it came to dancing, singing and playing a musical instrument my skills were grievously inadequate.

My mother decided that I should take some lessons. 'I'm afraid Lady Margaret let you down in those departments, Gigi,' she admonished me one day. 'Which surprises me because she herself is a beautiful dancer and has a lovely voice.'

I had to make a confession. 'Do not blame her, Mamma. She organised teachers for us in all those skills but I'm afraid I skipped their classes, preferring to study in her library. Besides I have two left feet when it comes to dancing.'

She gave a dismissive wave. 'I do not believe that. Everyone can dance. It's just a matter of learning the steps and keeping time with the music. Some of the other ladies are also rather inadequate in that department so I am going to suggest to Lady Cecily that she ask the vice-chamberlain to organise some classes. It will come in useful for when you marry and become a lady-in-waiting rather than a minion of the bedchamber.'

I stared at her, eyes wide. 'Assuming I will get married,' I said.

She gave me an exasperated look. 'Of course you will, Gigi! All women get married, unless they enter a convent and I do not detect any inclination in you to take the veil. However learned you have made yourself and whatever you say to the contrary, I cannot believe that you don't want children.'

'I love children,' I said defensively. 'I just don't want babies, especially now that I see how sickness is plaguing Elizabeth. Nor do I feel the need of a man in my bed, or whatever the euphemism is for copulation in polite circles.'

Now I had shocked my mother. 'You should confess that remark the next time you face the priest, Gigi! The Church declares marriage to be "the mystical union between Christ and His Church, ordained for the procreation of children", not "a man in my bed" as you so coarsely put it. And whatever you say, I think you will find that sooner or later, if you remain in royal service, you will be required to enter its honourable estate. Single members of the royal court are generally regarded as loose horses, which need to be tethered.'

I flared up. This was not the kind of conversation I had come to my mother's private chamber to have. 'I refuse to be considered a "loose horse", Mamma, or forced into being "tethered" by royal decree!' Then, seeing her disappointed expression, I relented. 'But I will attempt to learn to dance and sing, if that will please the queen. Now tell me how you think she and the king are getting on in *their* marriage? Does the early conception of a child necessarily indicate a successful relationship?' I drew a joint-stool up to the hearth where my mother was seated and settled myself beside her.

She paused before answering but her sombre mood did not lift. 'In a royal marriage it certainly helps matters along. If Queen Marguerite had not taken seven years to conceive her prince, the nobility might not have become so restless and many lives might not have been lost on the battlefield.' And of course she meant that of my father most of all.

This conversation sparked a dream during the night that followed. I was back at the Tower of London, as if on another visit to my mother and the captive queen, but this time it was night and I seemed to be considerably older than the nine-year-old girl who had made her first visit. The fortress precincts were in deep gloom but when the moon appeared through the clouds I could see that the green in front of the Church of St Peter was packed with guns and siege weapons – huge and cumbersome cannons that could be hauled out onto battlefields to roar death and defiance at the enemy, or turned on castles to shatter the walls and the will of defending garrisons. Ranged there too were rows of smaller, old-fashioned bombards with squat, fat barrels that could be loaded with small shot to wreak havoc among foot soldiers.

Wandering among these deadly weapons, some dream connection led me to expect an encounter with the king's Master of Ordnance, Sir Richard Guildford, but instead I was confronted by a weird woman dressed all in grey, with a grey veil and a grey face. On her arms and shoulders were perched several ravens: mysterious black companions with shiny hooked beaks and small piercing eyes, which seemed to absorb the light of a gibbous moon. Their fierce claws should have drawn blood from the lady's pale skin but none was evident. Strangely I was not afraid and even asked her name.

She shook her head but the raven perched on her left shoulder spoke in a rasping croak. 'She is our lady – the lady of the ravens. Men say we are the harbingers of death but they are wrong. On a battlefield, it is the guns and arrows and blades that do their work, and if they have not completed it, human scavengers come stealthily at night to cut the throats of the wounded, then to steal their clothes and armour, leaving them naked. When we venture there we take only the eyes of the already dead, so that their souls may enter heaven obedient to God's will, that man shall never look upon His face.'

Then I asked the question burning in my head. 'Was my father helped to heaven at Tewkesbury? Did you take his eyes?'

Now the lady spoke, in a voice weird and echoing, as if it came from deep inside a cave. 'Your father was a hero who stood over his wounded prince and defended him to his own death. When he fell, his body covered the prince's, but when the victors came they threw him off and desecrated the prince's corpse. My birds took your father's eyes so he would not see what they did to him. He is in heaven now and in the arms of God, where all heroes go.'

I opened my mouth to pose another question but the dream and the lady of the ravens faded. I woke with a sense of abandonment.

AS PLANNED, IN MID-MARCH King Henry departed on his progress to the north and Lady Margaret returned to London, leaving the queen, her mother and her three younger sisters who joined them for Easter at Placentia. All seemed peaceful and pleasant in the kingdom and the queen's court. But at the start of April, before the festivities could begin, a messenger arrived with emergency orders. Agents had brought information that a force of Yorkist adherents had assembled in the northeast, planning a rebellion. The queen and her household were advised to return to the shelter of London's walls and take refuge with Lady Margaret at Coldharbour. The Dowager Queen and her younger daughters were to go back to Sheen. Guards soon arrived to escort the separate parties and farewells were said but I noticed no kisses were exchanged between the two senior ladies.

'Is it not significant, Joan, that the Dowager has been removed from the queen's company?' It was Rosie who voiced this question, setting my teeth on edge. I had come to the passementerie workshop soon after arriving back in London to fetch fresh supplies of laces and silk coifs and, of course, to glean the rumour and wisdom of the streets.

'In what way significant?' I prompted. Rosie's opinions were often couched in ambiguous terms.

'By all accounts King Henry is facing a Yorkist rebellion and so he straight away separates his wife and her mother, the two leading members of the House of York. Does he perhaps fear that either, or both, are involved in some way?'

Indignation surged through my body. 'Well, if the queen were involved I am sure I would know and I certainly don't. She has been almost prostrate with pregnancy sickness, hardly in a state to plot armed rebellion. As for her mother, I cannot say, except that she has been living cheek-by-jowl with the king and queen since February. Not the easiest of circumstances in which to conspire with the Yorkist under-world, I think you'll agree. Anyway, if the Dowager Queen were to be plotting any kind of revolt my inkling is that it would be against the king's mother. Relations between those two are not exactly cordial. Surprisingly though, the queen doesn't seem to have noticed.'

Rosie grinned. 'Or else she's feeling too weak to care. I remember how I felt in the early weeks of carrying my little girl. I just wanted to curl up and sleep until she was born.'

'That is more or less what the queen felt. She's much recovered now though and had talked of joining the king on his progress, not that he'll allow that while rebels are mustering. You may have noticed that Lady Margaret has doubled the guard on London's gates and ordered men in from loyal Lancastrian territory to reinforce the city's defences.'

'We certainly have noticed!' One of Rosie's young apprentices stopped weaving to receive nods of agreement from the others. 'They're country hicks, all of them, who reckon us city girls are easy game. We soon put them right about that though, don't we, ladies?'

Rosie stamped her foot loudly. 'Carry on working please, Mary! It's not time for a break yet.' The guilty weaver hunched back over her half-completed lace, muttering under her breath. Rosie shrugged at me, adding, 'Laces don't make themselves, Joan.'

As I gathered up my order of two hundred of these essential royal items, I speculated how many fingers had fluttered for how many hours to make them and was grateful that mine were not among them. It occurred to me that had I not been so fortunate as to be fostered by Lady Margaret, I might have been apprenticed to such a craft.

'Has there been any trouble in the locality, Rosie?' I asked. 'All seemed quiet as I made my way here.'

'Scores are still being settled, especially after sunset,' Rosie replied, calloused fingers still flying. 'There was a body lying at the entrance to the Seld this morning, so I don't let my girls go out at night at all. Take care to get back well before dark, Joan.'

When I left the workshop her parting words had me looking over my shoulder, my mind suddenly alive with memories of that ugly encounter with the drunken tanners. Instead of being noisy with banter and bonhomie, the Cheapside market felt ominous and threatening, its stall-holders grim-faced. It was as if London was closing in on itself and I saw a hawker spit and make a sign against the devil as he passed a soldier in northern livery. At first we had not taken the rebellion very seriously at Coldharbour, as we had witnessed no outward signs of unrest, but when I returned with the silk necessities, I found the courtyard noisy with the sound of horses' hooves and voices shouting in unfamiliar accents. Extra men at arms had been sent to protect the queen and I had trouble getting through the gatehouse, until one of the household guards recognised me and ordered my admittance. When I finally reached the queen's apartment I found her pale and shaking, while Lady Margaret sought to comfort her.

'One of the king's knights came,' my mother revealed, keeping her voice low. 'He brought a posse of men at arms to boost the watch and told us that in York there has been an attempt on the king's life. The Earl of Northumberland tackled a lone assailant as he drew out his dagger not a yard from his grace's back. Somehow the wretch had infiltrated the mayor's welcome party at the city gate. When he was searched, a purse of gold was found and he confessed that he had been paid to kill the king by Lord Lovell.'

'Lord Lovell?' I murmured, cogitating. 'Wasn't he one of the usurper's cronies?'

My mother nodded. 'Yes. Many of his close followers were wounded and captured in King Henry's victory battle, but Lovell escaped and has apparently emerged again. The queen is now convinced that the whole country will erupt.'

'And what does Lady Margaret think? She's the one charged with protecting Elizabeth in the king's absence.'

'Oh, she's as calm as a millpond. Look at her. You would think there were alarms like this every day. But then she survived two years of house arrest under the usurper, while still managing to conspire on behalf of her son. It takes a lot to rattle Margaret Beaufort's cage.'

Lady Margaret had not entirely allayed Elizabeth's fears however, for while we were disrobing her that night she suddenly said in a choked voice: 'Henry could be dead. He might have fallen foul of a rebel army and my baby will be born posthumously, like he was. Whatever would happen then?'

Seeing her tears welling once more we hastily pulled the heavy gown and sleeves from her arms and shoulders. Then she suddenly pressed her hands against her belly. 'Oh! I can feel something. There! I think it is the baby. Could it be the baby, Mother Vaux?'

My mother moved swiftly forward, made a brief curtsy and held out her hands. 'May I feel, your grace?' Their palms changed places and a smile spread across my mother's face. 'The babe is quickening. Shall we take off the kirtle? Then we'll be able to feel it better.'

But by the time the under-dress had been unlaced and removed the movement had ceased. Nevertheless Elizabeth's pessimistic mood had undergone a sea change and the anxiety brimming in her eyes had become tears of joy. 'Oh, the baby is definitely there! It is not a fantasy after all. I shall write to Henry tonight.'

In her sudden euphoria she seemed to have abandoned her fear for the king's life but I didn't share her sudden change of mood. King Henry had won his throne on a battlefield – he could easily lose it on another. The ogre of bloody civil war would be sure to rear its horrible head again and more fathers and brothers, husbands and uncles, nobles and commoners would die on the battlefield, leaving wives and mothers and lovers to grieve and suffer the consequences. I studied my mother's face and saw a similar fear in her eyes.

A few days later, in the garden at Coldharbour, I was

gathering fragrant herbs for the queen's bed when I noticed an authoritative figure in a fur-trimmed gown and jewel-pinned hat approaching from the house. He called out as he drew close and I recognised him as Sir Richard Guildford, prominent courtier and Privy Councillor; the man I had once confronted about the ravens at the Tower.

'A word with you privately, if you please, Mistress Vaux,' he said in a tone that instantly told me this was not a social encounter.

I straightened up. 'Could it not wait until I have fulfilled my duties to the queen, Sir Richard? I will not be long now.'

He stood firm, shaking his head. 'No, mistress, this will not take long and the garden is a suitable location. I would rather there were no eavesdroppers. I merely wish to establish whether you spoke alone with your brother's new wife when you attended their wedding in January.'

His question astonished me, setting off alarm bells in my mind, not so much because of its content but the tone of his voice; it held an accusatory note. 'Of course I spoke with her, sir. She had just become my sister-in-law. Why do you ask?'

He had the grace to look somewhat embarrassed. 'I ask on behalf of those appointed to investigate the recent attempt on King Henry's life. Perhaps you do not realise that your new sister-in-law's sister is married to the rebel who paid the man who drew a knife on the king in York.'

I took a few moments to comprehend exactly what he'd said. 'Do you mean Beth Vaux's sister is married to Lord Lovell?'

He nodded. 'Yes. Her sister Anne was married to Lovell when they were children. After their father fell in battle, both girls were made wards of King Edward's sister, the Duchess of Suffolk. They were brought up in her family and all of them were – indeed most still are, it would seem – committed Yorkists.'

At this point he became almost apologetic, as if he was not even convincing himself of the heinous nature of Beth's relationship to the king's enemy. 'As you know, Lovell is on the run and is suspected to have fled to Flanders with the help of his wife and these Suffolk allies of his. At the king's request, your brother Nicholas agreed to marry Elizabeth Fitzhugh in order to bind her and her children to the Tudor cause but these are early days in their marriage and your brother became concerned when he remembered that you had some private conversation with his new wife. He suggested that, perhaps without realising its significance, you might have supplied her with some useful information. Perhaps details of the king's progress?'

At this my anger flared uncontrollably. This man who on first meeting, apart from his regrettable soldier's attitude towards ravens, I had considered civil and personable, was proving to be anything but. 'Are you saying that my brother implied that I might have been conspiring with his new wife? That is ridiculous, Sir Richard! Nicholas and I are the children of a Lancastrian war hero and former wards of My Lady the King's Mother. Now I am a gentlewoman of the queen's chamber. You can hardly get less Yorkist than that! Nicholas's wife and I spoke only of marriage and children and my brother's prospects as a husband – the sort of thing women talk about all the time, which does not include details of royal activities. So I cannot help you with your inquiries. I can only wonder why you or anyone else ever doubted my total loyalty to the king and queen.'

I turned to pluck more leaves haphazardly from the herb bed, throwing them into my basket. 'I have nothing more to tell you but I would be grateful if you would kindly inform my brother that I do not appreciate being placed under suspicion by my own flesh and blood!'

'You are not under suspicion, Mistress Vaux, merely assisting our inquiries,' Sir Richard tried to reassure me but I had snatched up my basket and was striding away.

It was only later, when I had cooled down, that I pondered why the Master of Ordnance should be acting like some kind of spy-catcher. Should he not have been ensuring that the king's men were supplied with all the guns and weapons they needed to defeat the rebels? Not sniffing around the queen's household looking for closet Yorkists. Or did King Henry have all his Privy Councillors nosing out closet Yorkists and making staunch Lancastrians utterly furious? So far I had escaped a royal invitation to bring some former York loyalist safely into the Tudor fold by marrying him but, still fuming, I told myself that if I ever did marry, Sir Richard Guildford was one courtier who would not be invited to the wedding.

8

THE COURT MOVED TO Windsor Castle for the summer
and in late August, Elizabeth took me aside in the
privy garden. It was just after Terce and I thought the sun
not yet high enough to have raised the colour that stained
her cheeks, as speaking softly so that her voice did not carry
to any of the other ladies taking their outdoor exercise she
said, 'You are the only one of my household who may realise
that this baby could be born earlier than expected, Joan.'

Her words instantly carried me back to the previous
December, when she had asked me discreetly to arrange the
laundering of her bloodstained shift and sheets after the
king's pre-nuptial visit to Baynard's Castle, suggesting that
her monthlies had come early; but there had been no more
stained linen that week and no monthly bleeds since. I had
often speculated secretly over what I had come to assume
had been an anticipation of the royal wedding night. Had
an uncontrollable passion suddenly overwhelmed them?
Could it possibly have been a cynical desire on King Henry's
part to ensure that his beautiful bride was a virgin? Or had
there been a romantic and mutual decision that they had
waited long enough to satisfy what had been an instant
physical attraction? After all, their wedding date was less

than a month away. Of the three choices I would have preferred it to be the first or the last and greatly hoped it was not the second, which did not seem to chime with what I had since observed of King Henry's character. Whatever it was, I had already drawn my own conclusions that this baby might be born sooner rather than later.

The queen quickly came to the point. 'King Henry is presently staying with Bishop Morton in Kent, planning among other things the bishop's installation as Archbishop of Canterbury, and sees no reason to hasten back. But Henry passionately wants the child born in Winchester, to indicate his hope that the Tudor dynasty will unite England, just as King Alfred set out to do from his Saxon capital. And so I feel that it is time I was travelling there. What do you think, Joan?'

What was she trying to tell me? That as a first-time mother, unfamiliar with the signs of impending birth, she was merely anxious that the king's wishes should be granted? Or was she suggesting, without actually admitting, that her child just might have been conceived a few weeks before the wedding night?

'I think that if you write to him of your worries, he will immediately take horse for Windsor, your grace,' I said. 'It is obvious to the dullest observer that the king would grant your every wish at this time.'

A coy smile lit her face. 'You are right; he would, because he believes I carry the Tudor future, and pray God that I do. But I would rather not worry him myself. Would you write to him for me, Joan? The king knows that of all my attendants you are the most perceptive of my moods and needs. You can convey your belief that I am fretting for my confinement and need reassurance that the birth will be where he wishes it to be – in Winchester. The letter can be sent under my personal seal so that none but he sees it.'

I dropped her a curtsy. 'Of course, your grace, as soon as I have returned you to the safekeeping of your other ladies.'

She clutched my hand tightly. 'Thank you, Joan. Make sure you couch the letter in terms that inspire immediate action.'

After much chewing of my quill I completed my letter that same afternoon.

> *To His Grace Lord Henry, King of England and Wales and Lord of Ireland, humble greetings.*
>
> *I beg forgiveness for writing privily to you but I do so out of concern for my royal mistress. I know her grace would be hesitant to write of this herself because of the important business you are conducting with the archbishop elect, but I have noticed her growing anxiety over the imminent birth of her child, particularly over when and where it will be born. She is acutely conscious that you wish the birth to take place in Winchester and therefore I dare to inform you that in my opinion she would be much quieter in mind and body if she were to travel there as soon as possible.*
>
> *I send this under her personal seal and for your perusal only and hope you will forgive my presumption in expressing my own unease about her condition. I am her grace's loyal servant and intimate companion and assure you of her otherwise good health.*

*I also pray for yours and beg once more for your
tolerance in receiving this letter.*
    Your grace's humble subject,
    Joan Vaux
    *Written at Windsor Castle on the twenty-fifth
day of August 1486.*

Very soon orders came for the queen's baggage and chariot
to be prepared and then King Henry arrived himself, damp
and dishevelled from riding through a summer thunder-
storm. Dried off and with a change of clothes, he came to
find the queen, who was watching her maids of honour on
the tennis court from the shade of the netted viewing lodge.
After he had conversed urgently with her for some time he
kissed her hand and cheek in farewell and then caught sight
of me, sitting in the gloom at the rear of the lodge.

'Never far away, are you, Mistress Vaux,' he said as I rose
at his approach and made a curtsy. 'The queen is very lucky
to have such a sedulous attendant. I thank you for drawing
her anxiety to my attention.'

I found myself blushing and hoping Lady Cecily, sitting
beside her sister, had not heard this last comment. Elizabeth
had stressed the need for discretion regarding my letter and
so I murmured my response. 'I thought it no more than my
duty, your grace.'

'Well, I hope you will stay close by her during the journey
to Winchester,' he added. 'It may seem hasty to some, but
there is no point in taking risks with such a precious cargo.
I, too, shall ride alongside the queen's chariot and pray for
fine weather.'

I nodded agreement. 'And perhaps ask for light cloud

rather than hot sun, sire. Too much heat makes her grace very uncomfortable.'

He smiled without showing his teeth, as was his habit. 'Let us hope the Almighty looks favourably on us. It will be a nail-biting journey, Joan.'

It began the following morning, with Elizabeth sitting under a canopy although there were kind and fluffy white clouds in the sky to shelter her from much of the sun's heat. With hurriedly arranged overnight accommodations providing ample rest stops, her chariot carefully slung between four steady horses and the pace kept to a gentle walk, it would take all of four days to reach Winchester. In view of what I knew about the need for haste and aware that any untoward jolting could result in a roadside birth, I gave thanks that the dry summer had left the highways relatively free of ruts and potholes. There would be much explaining to do if the potential heir to the throne were to be born under a tree, rather than beneath a tester bearing the royal coat of arms.

9

WHILE THE QUEEN WAS making her slow and hazardous journey, servants were hurriedly preparing her lying-in chamber in the recently renovated Priory of St Swithun, the patron saint of the ancient city of Winchester. The prior had vacated his luxurious house in her favour and his great hall had been hung with tapestries and swathes of scarlet cloth embellished with gold fringes. All doors and windows were covered by velvet curtains with the exception of one, which was left free to let in light and air, and the great bed was built in the centre, adorned with satin hangings and a counterpane of cloth of gold. Plush carpets were laid over the stone-paved floor to dull the intrusive sound of footsteps.

Caught short by the sudden summons from Sheen, the Dowager Queen and her daughters hurried to be present in time and, not to be outdone, so did Lady Margaret. We all attended a special service in the cathedral to pray for Elizabeth's safe delivery, before the king escorted her to the door of her confinement and then went hunting with his friends and courtiers to take his mind off his great hopes for a son.

After only two weeks' lying-in, considered barely respectable for a queen, Elizabeth's babe was born a few minutes after the cathedral clock struck midnight on the twentieth day of September. In the early hours and probably much to the discomfort of its sleeping citizens, every church bell in the city was carolling the arrival of a Tudor heir. I took the tiny prince, inspected, bathed and wrapped in his swaddling, to his carefully prepared stateroom and placed him under a crimson coverlet in his gilded cradle of estate, the tiny reality of the Tudor rose. King Henry and Lady Margaret stood together beside the cradle, gazing down on the realisation of their dreams with tears coursing down their cheeks.

'God has answered our prayers, my lady mother,' said Henry, when he managed to find the power of speech. 'He has truly favoured our cause.'

In the confinement chamber the queen had been carried from the delivery pallet to a warm, herb-scented bathtub and once she was washed and gently dried, I helped to dress her in a clean linen shift and lay her in her scarlet and gold bed. All signs of the sweat and effusions of childbirth were removed and fresh rose petals were strewn on the carpets and bedding before her chaplain was admitted to say prayers of thanksgiving. The Dowager Queen, who had been beside her daughter throughout her long labour, retired to her chamber looking exhausted and when the new prince was brought through from his stateroom to be placed in the arms of his breast nurse, the king and his mother followed. Those of us who had attended the birth were gathered around like a guard of honour and I was one of several whose eyes swam with tears, which for the others might have been due to an overflow of joy, but in my case was evidence of shock and distress.

Elizabeth was already drowsy with sleep. 'You will have

to imagine my curtsy, my lord,' she murmured to the king when he leaned over to kiss her cheek. 'I am very tired.'

'May God bless your rest, Elizabeth,' he said. 'There can be no woman in England who deserves it more than you. You have brought joy and hope to a divided kingdom and granted me my dearest wish. May the jubilant ringing of the bells be a lullaby to your slumbers.'

Her eyelids drooped as a frown creased her brow. 'They are very loud, my lord,' she complained and immediately fell into a deep sleep, oblivious even to a loud clap of thunder outside, accompanied by the sound of sudden torrents of rain. I rushed to close the single open casement and the noise of the storm faded behind the thick tapestry hangings and velvet-draped rafters.

King Henry welcomed the downpour. 'Even the heavens show their approval of this night's events,' he said, making the sign of the cross.

Lady Margaret took a more pessimistic view. 'Let us hope the rain does not turn the roads to quagmires,' she said. 'The child's early birth will have taken important guests by surprise, who will now have to hurry here for the christening. The babe should not be baptised without his godfather and Lord Oxford has to come all the way from Suffolk.'

Henry was undeterred. 'The midwife said the boy is strong and healthy, so we can wait a few days if need be.'

'We cannot ignore his premature arrival though,' repeated his mother firmly. 'He must be carefully watched.'

These would have been wise words indeed, had it been a premature birth, but I had seen the child delivered, pink and robust; far from frail or underdeveloped. In fact he looked much stronger than I felt after witnessing the pain and effort his mother had endured to bring him into the world. Elizabeth's labour had lasted more than twenty-four hours of mounting agony, culminating in alarming bloody effluence, and I had found the final heart-rending groans and humiliating loss of dignity as the lusty boy was finally hauled from her body such a traumatic ordeal to witness, that any scrap of ambition I might have still harboured to have a family myself vanished without trace.

If my mother's warning was true and there could come a time when preserving my position at court might oblige me to marry, I decided my only option would be to seek a way of preventing any possibility of my bearing a child as a result. Tucked into my baggage was a copy of a compendium of women's medicine written in Latin by doctors at the university of Salerno in Italy. I had found it in Lady Margaret's library and asked if I could borrow it, which she was happy to permit. Because she had only church Latin, I knew she could not have read it herself. If she had she would never have lent it to me, for it contained among its venerable pages several suggestions 'For Those Who Do Not Wish to Conceive'.

When the king and his mother left I sat on watch beside the sleeping queen's bed as the babe was suckled and rocked by his various nurses to the sound of hammering and sawing from the nearby cathedral, where joiners were preparing for the baptism. I sympathised when, on waking, the queen complained of acute discomfort in her breasts, but hearing the carpenters at work she was nevertheless eager to know how arrangements for the christening were going.

'You are good at describing things, Joan,' she said while I helped a team of chamberwomen adjust her bedclothes, tie tight strips of linen to stop her flow of milk and feed her nourishing beef broth. 'Please go and see how the preparations are proceeding for the christening.' As yet no one, not even the child's mother, had called the baby by name, which would not be spoken until it had been delivered to him at the font by the bishop.

Weary from lack of sleep and grateful to leave the stuffy atmosphere of the confinement chamber, I took deep breaths of the fresh air outside. The rain had stopped and there was an invigorating smell of damp earth and wet leaves. When I entered the cathedral I found it transformed; the great pillars of the nave were hung with red satin, while costly bright-coloured Persian rugs laid a path from the font to the altar. In the chancel the half-moon lids of two great cope chests had been lifted to air the glittering embroidered and jewelled vestments that would be worn by the attendant bishops and high-ranking clergy and the magnificent vaulted ceiling echoed to the sound of choristers practising their psalms and Te Deums.

Elizabeth's eyes shone as I described the scene and tried to give her an idea of the ceremony she would not witness, partly because of exhaustion but mainly due to the Church's demand that new mothers be cleansed several weeks after childbirth by the solemn ceremony of 'churching', before they were once more permitted to attend services.

'As the bishop immerses the child in the water of Jordan,' I explained, 'he will call out his name, while making the sign of the cross on his forehead and breast, and when the Holy Spirit descends to claim him, a hundred torches will be lit. So a brilliant burst of light will welcome your royal son into Christ's Holy Church.'

'Oh Joan, you make it all so vivid I can almost see it now!' she cried. 'But my mother tells me that Lord Oxford has not yet arrived, so the service must be delayed another day.'

I understood the note of anxiety in her voice. Without the protection of baptism even the most carefully tended newborn might suddenly be snatched from life while denied God's Holy Spirit to carry him to heaven. I looked down into the cradle set beside the queen's bed, where a crumpled little face was all that was visible of the baby, tightly wrapped in swaddling. At that moment he looked quiet and peaceful in his sleep, pale lashes lying against his cheeks, his nose faintly twitching as he breathed.

By the next morning the Earl of Oxford still had not arrived but King Henry ordered preparations to be made for the service. Although she was slightly feverish we made the queen ready in her bed, propped up on the pillows wearing her crown, with her ermine-trimmed mantle of state carefully arranged around her shoulders. Then the babe was placed in her arms and the principal participants were admitted.

At the last minute it was revealed that Lady Margaret would not be attending. It was my mother who made the announcement. 'My Lady the King's Mother is unwell and begs to be excused. She has developed an ague overnight and fears she may cough during the service and make a disturbance.'

While Princess Cecily took the child from the queen's arms and arranged the long train of his mantle ready to carry him to the cathedral, I managed to slip across to my mother's side and murmur, 'Is she really ill, Mamma? This baby is the emblem of her son's hopes for his kingdom and

Lady Margaret has written almost the entire order of service herself.'

My mother replied from the corner of her mouth. 'But the king determined the sponsors and she doesn't wish to walk behind the Dowager Queen and her two daughters. Too many vivid memories of having to kneel at the feet of York.'

For the first time my foster mother, the woman who had nurtured me and claimed my admiration, now earned my disapproval. If she could not quash her antipathy for the York affinity, how could she expect the rest of the king's subjects to adopt a sense of national pride and abandon their adherence to one side or the other? Suddenly I felt deep pity for the little boy with the mixed blood of York and Lancaster, who was expected to become the symbol of unification in the divided kingdom his father had so unexpectedly acquired. Where was the legendary Merlin, to teach this child how to achieve this incredible task, if even a woman with the intelligence and wisdom of his grandmother could not shelve her own deeply held loyalties in the interests of her son's ambition?

The baptism went smoothly and the baby cried loudly when the devil was banished as he was submerged in the holy water. I was seated with the rest of the queen's gentlewomen at some distance from my mother but I saw her astonishment when the bishop made the sign of the cross on his forehead and pronounced his name as 'Arthur'. Judging by the whispers in the nave, it came as a surprise to the whole congregation, which had doubtless been expecting the boy to be called Henry after his father. I supposed that King Henry had thought as I did, that the name might serve his son well, referencing the legendary king, believed to have united the ancient realms of Britain under one crown.

Another surprise awaited us and caused quite a commotion when the soldierly Earl of Oxford appeared in half-armour, damp and mud-spattered straight from the saddle, and strode up to the altar, just in time to play his vital role as godfather at the confirmation service that followed the baptism. Perhaps he was the wise councillor who might guide the young Arthur in his quest to complete his father's reunification of England.

During the days of celebration that followed, meetings were held between King Henry, his mother, the godparents and the Bishop of Winchester, at which serious consideration was given to the baby prince's immediate future. Still weak and feverish and in confinement, the queen was not included but my mother and I were present when the king and Lady Margaret came to tell her of the outcome of these talks.

'It has been decided that in view of his early birth, Prince Arthur should not come with us to London but remain out in the countryside where the air is fresher,' King Henry began. 'The bishop has kindly offered to accommodate him and his household in his palace at Farnham, a small, peaceful town, protected by a well-garrisoned royal castle, where he will be safe until he is strong enough to withstand the rigours of palace life.'

Accustomed as I was to reading Elizabeth's mind, I realised that this information distressed her considerably, although she fought to conceal her feelings. 'I thought you had decided that Eltham was the place to bring up our children, my lord,' she said.

King Henry gave her one of his charming smiles. 'Indeed I did, my dearest Elizabeth, and to that end I have already instructed masons to carry out extensive alterations, which means that at present it is something of a building site and hardly suitable to house the newborn heir of England. My lady mother has shown me the list of appointments you have made for the prince's household and I am sure your choice of Lady Darcy as his governess will be perfect.'

Elizabeth's brow knitted and she shot a fierce glance at her mother-in-law. I could have sworn this was the first she had heard of this appointment. 'Lady Darcy was certainly very capable as my brother Edward's first governess,' she observed weakly, 'but I wonder now if she might not be a little too old for the task.'

'Oh dear no, your mother did not think so,' Lady Margaret remarked.

Lady Cecily echoed the persuasion of the Tudor pair. 'It is true that our mother held great store by Lady Darcy, sister. I'm sure you remember.'

Having completed her duties as godmother, the Dowager Queen had returned to Sheen with her daughter Anne, and Lady Margaret had made a suspiciously swift recovery from her ague. However Elizabeth was far from fully fit. Having witnessed the severe handling her body had received during the delivery I was not surprised that there were still postnatal complications and although I could see that she had no wish for her son to stay at Farnham, in her present state of health she could not summon the strength to argue.

King Henry quickly continued conveying the arrangements. 'On her way back to Woking, my lady mother will make sure all is well at the bishop's palace and when you are quite ready, Elizabeth, we will arrange your churching in the cathedral. I have ordered your tailor to make you a splendid gown for the ceremony and he will deliver it here in a week or so.' The king stood up. 'But now I can see that we tire you and so we will take our leave.' He bent to kiss her cheek, pausing to stroke her forehead in a gesture of tender sympathy.

When he and Lady Margaret had left, Elizabeth turned to my mother. Tears began to run down her cheeks and she gestured weakly at the cradle in which her son lay sleeping. 'Arthur is Henry's longed-for heir, Mother Vaux, yet he did not even glance at him and wants to leave him with strangers in a strange town. Perhaps it is because he spent so many years of his childhood separated from his own mother that he does not find that odd but I find it very hard to forgive.'

10

DURING THE CHRISTMAS FOLLOWING Prince Arthur's birth, the first moves were made towards planning Queen Elizabeth's coronation and all seemed amicable between her and King Henry. She had apparently recovered her health and with it her good spirits. The two exchanged magnificent New Year's gifts and wore their crowns and state mantles, as the whole court at Placentia made a splendid procession to the palace chapel to hear Mass, before sharing a sumptuous banquet when gifts were distributed and I was touched and thrilled to receive a beautiful pearl pendant from the queen. On Twelfth Night there was another feast with entertainments in the great hall and choristers harmonised while the wassail cups were passed from hand to hand for a collective health to be drunk to the coming year. Many a couple went to bed in merry mood and the king and queen were no exception.

However, in mid-January a rumour flared in London that the Earl of Warwick had appeared in Ireland, publicly mocking King Henry as a 'Welsh pretender', who had laid claim to the throne that should be his. Except that King Henry and his Privy Council knew very well that the real Earl of Warwick, a little boy of twelve, was still safely living in his comfortable quarters in the Tower of London.

At the time I was in the queen's entourage staying at Farnham Castle while she visited her baby son, something she had been pining to do throughout the Christmas festivities. We were all enchanted with four-month-old Prince Arthur, who had put on weight, grown a fuzz of reddish-brown hair and greeted his mother with smiles and gurgles. 'I believe he knows me,' she said with glee, happy to hold him on her lap for hours at a stretch, sleeping and waking. The threat from some imposter Earl of Warwick in Ireland seemed distant and minimal.

In the middle of February Elizabeth's mood changed radically however, when she read one of King Henry's regular letters, delivered after one of our afternoon visits to Prince Arthur's nursery. Her complexion paled as she perused his familiar hand and she kept glancing up at my mother, as if trying to decide whether to confide its contents. 'The king wants me to return to court,' she said eventually. 'There have been developments in Ireland regarding the young man pretending to be my cousin, Edward of Warwick.' Suddenly her face crumpled and she waved the letter like a distress signal. 'And oh, Mother Vaux! They have sent my lady mother to Bermondsey Abbey.'

'But why, your grace? And who are "they"?' My mother's hand went to the cross she wore around her neck, a frequent gesture when she was anxious.

Elizabeth's hand reached out, the missive drooping from it like a dead animal. My mother took it from her but immediately passed it to me. 'You read it, Gigi,' she said. 'My eyes are not good enough in this winter light.'

I scanned it quickly. 'His grace does not say that the Dowager Queen has been sent to the abbey; rather that she has chosen to go there herself. Perhaps she is in need of a retreat. She has been through so much in these last few years and she is not young any more.'

Lady Margaret had once told me the history of Bermondsey Abbey. It was a royal foundation on the south bank of the Thames, diagonally opposite the Tower of London. As well as being a Benedictine monastery, and not officially a place of detention, it had sometimes been used as a 'refuge' for out-of-favour royals and nobles.

'But he does not say what has happened to my sisters. Bridget is only six and such a shy little thing.' It was typical of Elizabeth to think of the children. She had always been like a second mother to her younger siblings. 'And Katherine is just eight. Has she left them alone at Sheen? They will wonder why.' She crossed herself and rose from her chair. 'I must go to them. Anne is not old enough to know how to comfort them. Oh, but I do not wish to leave little Arthur. Dear God! Why has she done this? Why has Henry done this to her?'

When she finally tore herself away from Farnham and confronted him, King Henry must have managed to explain the situation to Elizabeth, but it was done in private and she did not reveal what he said. The following week twelve-year-old Edward of Warwick was brought from the Tower, walking with an escort through the City of London, to hear Mass at St Paul's. Afterwards he was taken to meet the city burgesses, assembled at the Bishop of London's palace, in order to demonstrate to them that the real Edward of Warwick could not be in Ireland because he was alive and well in London. He was then brought upriver by barge to Sheen, where the court was staying, when the queen was able to confirm to members of the Privy Council, who had never met him, that this was indeed her cousin, the genuine Edward, Earl of Warwick.

Edward's thirteen-year-old sister Margaret also spent some time with her brother and afterwards, while she helped us prepare the queen for an evening entertainment, the two cousins compared notes.

'At first I could hardly get a word out of him, Margaret,' Elizabeth admitted, permitting the girl to roll up one of her hosen and tie the garter. 'But then there were several other people in the room who were strangers to him. Perhaps he opened up more freely to you?'

The girl glanced up from her kneeling position. 'No, your grace, in answer to most of my questions he merely grunted something inaudible. He was never the brightest candle in the room but he seemed unwilling to acknowledge me.'

Elizabeth looked shocked. 'He didn't know you – his own sister?'

Margaret finished adjusting the garter and stood up. 'Well yes, he certainly knew me – but he almost seemed frightened of me, as if he didn't want to say anything in case it got him into trouble.'

Elizabeth nodded in agreement. 'I had exactly the same impression but I thought he might be wary because he knew he was on show. He never actually held my gaze during the whole of our encounter, so it was hard to tell what he was thinking.'

'I mentioned the hiding games we all played at Sheriff Hutton, do you remember, your grace? Before our uncle . . .' Margaret suddenly stopped and went red in the face, wringing her hands, '. . . well, before we were brought to

London. Edward used to love those games but he just shrugged. I'm sure he did remember but just wouldn't admit it.' The usurper had sent his young nieces and nephew to his stronghold of Sheriff Hutton in Yorkshire for safety, before raising his army to confront Henry Tudor.

Elizabeth altered her approach. 'He is quite small and thin. Did he seem healthy to you?'

Margaret took a few steps back, allowing me to approach with the queen's girdle. 'He is pale but I don't think he's ill, my lady. I got the impression that he doesn't get much exercise, especially in the winter. I asked him if he rode out at all but he just said "No". Is that right for a boy of noble blood?'

While tying the girdle I glanced back at her and thought she looked guarded, casting her eyes down as she said this, perhaps fearful of being accused of criticising the king.

'I've made sure he has books and lessons and regular visits from a priest and doctor,' Elizabeth responded sharply. 'The reports from his tutors indicate slow progress in all subjects and activities. The king thinks he is not cut out for knightly training.'

Margaret caught my eye and rolled hers briefly as I crossed the room to fetch a frontlet for the queen's headdress. She had clearly understood that the king was loth to allow a boy so close to the succession to receive any training that might assist his capacity to rule.

Elizabeth made minor adjustments to her girdle before raising her head. 'You are growing into a clever and capable damsel, Margaret. I think you are taller than me now. You'll be fourteen this summer, won't you? We must consider arranging a date for your marriage. Your betrothed is one

of the king's most promising Squires of the Body –
a candidate for knighthood, I should think. You must be
very proud.'

'Yes, your grace,' said Margaret dutifully, recognising this
change of subject as a hint for dismissal and making a curtsy.
Her expression as we passed each other again did not imply
that she looked forward to marriage to Richard Pole Esquire,
a man twice her age. I would not have called her pretty but
she was handsome and, whatever the intellect of her brother,
Margaret Plantagenet was, as Elizabeth had deduced, a
shrewd and intelligent young lady.

Edward of Warwick went back to his tutors in the Tower
and the subject of the young pretender, now identified as
an Oxford lad with the curious name of Lambert Simnel,
slipped temporarily from palace gossip. However, to
Elizabeth's further distress her Suffolk cousin, the Earl of
Lincoln, suddenly left court and a week later was reported
to have arrived in Flanders at the court of their mutual
Aunt Margaret, the Dowager Duchess of Burgundy, an
infamous focus for Yorkist conspiracy. Furious that the
duchess should be giving shelter to such a prominent rebel,
the king called a halt to all English trade with the Low
Countries, igniting the fury of London merchants, who
relied on it for their wealth.

The queen's alarm at all these developments was alleviated
by reason to hope she was pregnant and once again she asked
King Henry to excuse her from a progress to East Anglia.
But as soon as he had left London on his travels, she ordered
her barge for a visit to Bermondsey Abbey, taking with her
Princess Cecily, my mother and me. 'The three people I trust
the most,' she said. 'This trip is confidential.'

The abbey occupied a walled enclosure on the high ground above the flood-pastures that lined the south bank of the Thames below London Bridge. Our approach had been observed and we passed easily through the sentries at the gatehouse, where a cowled monk bowed and led us to a long stone building adjoining it, with windows overlooking the river. Once inside we climbed a wide, palatial staircase to a series of ample chambers reserved for royalty and nobility.

Tears filled the eyes of the Dowager Queen as she embraced her two daughters. 'God is good,' she said in a voice hoarse with emotion. 'I have prayed that you would come. I do not know what King Henry has said to you but let me give you my own version of events.'

The former queen had not adopted any official form of religious dress but compared to the glamorous style that she had affected at her grandson's baptism she looked plain and nun-like, her gown dark blue and her headdress a simple veil and coif of unbleached linen. She appeared drawn and tired and kept using the kerchief she held ready to wipe her eyes. As she waved her daughters to seats close to her and to the blazing fire in the hearth, at a sign from the queen my mother and I took up a removed position on cushioned stone benches either side of a deep window embrasure.

Seeing the Dowager Queen's disapproving frown, Elizabeth's eyes flashed. 'I wish them to stay. They can both be trusted as you know and I need their witness.' She did not explain further and her mother sighed and nodded, outranked. 'I had to come, my lady mother, because I cannot believe you are here voluntarily. You have lived too much of your life in sanctuary to willingly submit yourself to further religious confinement.'

'That may be true,' the Dowager agreed, 'but nonetheless I did ask the king for protection. Coming here was his suggestion and it certainly does serve that purpose. I am safe here from Yorkist intimidation.'

'Intimidation?' Cecily's voice was raised with indignation. 'Who would dare?'

Her mother's reply came terse and swift. 'Your cousin the Earl of Lincoln dared. When the king was absent for meetings in Westminster and you were at Farnham, Lincoln came at night to Sheen Palace with a proposal that I give my support to the rebels in Ireland. Of course I laughed in his face. Why on earth would I support the cause of a boy pretending to be the son of the traitor who rebelled not once but thrice against his brother the king – my husband? The idea is too absurd.'

'But you agreed to let your husband's other brother marry me to a penniless nobody!' Cecily almost spat her accusation.

Elizabeth hushed her with a curt wave. I was impressed by her determined grasp of this rather fraught meeting. 'Our lady mother was not herself then, sister. She had lost her father, brother and several other members of her close family, been forced to take sanctuary for the second time, informed that her marriage was invalid and her children illegitimate and feared that her two royal sons were also dead. It would be no surprise if she were out of her mind with grief when she agreed to that marriage. But as yet, we have no idea why she has now decided to commit herself to this new religious confinement. We've come to hear her story, Cecily, without interruption.'

The Dowager Queen smiled wearily at her elder daughter. 'Thank you, Elizabeth, I appreciate your spirited defence.

When I asked Lincoln why he was supporting a churl who was no more the Earl of Warwick than my Aunt Alice, he admitted that his plan was to lure Henry into battle in order to procure his death. At which point he, John de la Pole, Earl of Lincoln, who the usurper had named as his successor, would step forward to claim the throne. I informed him that in my opinion you, Elizabeth, are the rightful York heir and as you are already queen I was hardly likely to support his cause. I ordered him to leave but he pleaded with me, saying that under Henry's rule he was down to his last half-crown, having sparse income and no prospects, even though he had made a show of swearing loyalty. It was then that he threatened to turn the whole York affinity against me personally, if I did not get behind his scheme.'

She drew a deep breath to steady her emotions. 'I believed him. I know a desperate man when I see one and your cousin John of Lincoln is dangerous. I fear for myself and for my little girls, who do not have the shield of royal guards as you and Cecily do. So I asked King Henry for his protection, for them and for myself. He agreed to look after them if I would come here to Bermondsey Abbey, where royalty has previously taken refuge. He also pointed out that as it was a royal foundation I would be able to live board- and rent-free and he would use my widow's dower to boost your income sufficiently to attend to your sisters' welfare and eventual marriages. He kindly added that I could spend feast times with you and your sisters and with my godson Arthur. We do not have to be strangers.'

She spread her hands. 'He was very persuasive. How could I refuse?'

'But what immediate provision was made for my sisters?'

Elizabeth persisted. 'I will take Anne and Katherine into my household but Bridget is too young, and I cannot imagine her being happy placed in ward with a noble family. She will feel abandoned.'

Her mother shook her head. 'Do not worry about Bridget. As you know she has always been destined for the veil and before I came here I took her to the nuns at Barking Abbey, where she has spent time already. They know her delicacy and her precocious love of the church. She was quite content to stay there with the other young novices. I have no qualms about Bridget but I know she would love a visit from her big sister, if you have the time and the inclination.'

Elizabeth was only too eager to oblige. 'Of course I will visit her. I want to be certain that she is well treated and content. And you must not be a stranger to any of your children, or your grandchildren, dearest mother.' She rose and moved across the hearth to kneel and embrace the Dowager warmly. 'You do not have to remove yourself from the world. If you prefer, I could rent you somewhere where you can live your own life – be independent. If I am to have the income from your dower, which I admit I can very well use, I would willingly do that.'

Her mother smiled. 'No, Elizabeth. That would incur all the expense of a household and guards to deter Lincoln's cronies. Besides, I am quite content here. I have my personal maids, comfortable accommodation, plentiful food and, best of all, I feel very safe under God's protection. Not even the most fanatical rebel is going to storm His sanctuary. But thank you for the offer.'

The queen nodded and rose to return to her seat then, just when I hoped there might be complete rapport between mother and daughter, beneath her wimple the Dowager's face resumed its earlier austere expression. 'More importantly though Elizabeth, when is Henry going to authorise your coronation? Is it not time that you were in your rightful place alongside him, as joint sovereigns of England? Was that not the purpose of your marriage – to unite the two royal houses? When a York queen is consecrated and enthroned alongside Lancaster, it will surely put a stop to all this rebellious conspiracy. You must insist upon it, Elizabeth. It is your duty to your father's house and your brothers' memories.'

The queen visibly cringed and I felt a surge of sympathy for her. She was suddenly a little girl, shying away from a mother's reprimand. I willed her to face off the Dowager's fierce gaze but, as I could be with my own mother some-times, she was overawed. The blood crept into her cheeks. 'Plans were discussed at Christmas but put on hold when Lincoln's defection altered the security position. Now that Henry has gone on a progress I cannot reinstate them without his endorsement.'

The Dowager sniffed loudly, clearly unimpressed by these excuses. 'Henry undermines you. He wants to reign alone, denying your better claim to the succession. He will suffer the consequences, of that you can be sure. This farcical Lambert Simnel pretender is just an overture. Others will follow with more convincing claims.' Her eyes misted over but her voice lost none of its fervour. 'To prove to the people for absolute certainty that my two lovely boys are dead, you must be God's consecrated and crowned queen, not just a womb to carry Henry's heirs. Stand up to him, Elizabeth – and his bossy mother! You are his equal, in right and lineage.'

II

ON RETURNING TO WESTMINSTER we realised that Elizabeth was not pregnant after all. I felt her loss profoundly as I dealt with the bloody evidence of her disappointment. There was no knowing whether the meeting with her mother had sparked a miscarriage or if it was merely a matter of her monthlies still being irregular after the birth of Prince Arthur. However, when she had dried her eyes and talked it through with us, she decided to instruct her Master of Horse that she intended to join the king at the Shrine of our Lady at Walsingham, in the midst of his East Anglian progress. At this famous Norfolk place of pilgrimage, where so many women had sought help with matters of childbirth, she wished to entreat the Virgin to look kindly upon her and grant her another child. And, since conception was unlikely to occur for a couple at odds with one another and despite the Dowager Queen's outburst, for the time being Elizabeth deliberately avoided any mention to the king of her coronation.

In the event this turned out to be a wise move, because the Earl of Lincoln had not postponed his desperate plan to wrest the throne from King Henry by forcing him onto the battlefield. He left Flanders for Ireland and somehow convinced a number of Irish lords that his poor young scapegoat actually was Edward of Warwick. He even managed to have the lad paraded through the streets of Dublin and crowned as King Edward the Sixth in the cathedral, which persuaded two thousand gallowglass mercenaries to join his cause and take ship for England.

The true King of England moved his entire court to Kenilworth in the Midlands: a castle completely surrounded by a lake, which represented a safe base from which to confront any incursion, whatever direction it came from. And so it was that in the middle of June I knelt with Queen Elizabeth, Lady Margaret, their officials and attendants, in the Kenilworth chapel, echoing their fervent Ave Marias, as King Henry led an army into the field for only the second time in his life.

The Battle of East Stoke, as it came to be called, was fought on the River Trent near Newark, in the heart of England, and our all prayers were answered as Henry sent his army into a pitched battle that developed into a bloody rout, resulting in the death of many of the ill-equipped Irish mercenaries and a number of the rebel Yorkist leaders, including the Dowager's nemesis, the Earl of Lincoln. The boy who had masqueraded as Edward of Warwick was captured, cowering in the enemy camp with the priests and the whores. Although many councillors called for his execution, the king merely had him stripped of his silks and gold coronet, pardoned him and handed out a sentence he regarded as punishment enough for a sadly exploited twelve-year-old. Showing unusual clemency for an aggrieved monarch, he sent him to work in the Westminster Palace kitchen.

At the other end of the scale King Henry also knighted many outstanding members of his army for their part in what had been an even more ferocious battle than the one that had brought him to the throne; including, to my mother's delight, my brother Nicholas, appointing him to a court position as a Knight of the King's Body.

I recognised when the time came for Elizabeth finally to confront her husband over the matter of her coronation, because she insisted that she be dressed in her most alluring gown and headdress and armed with a formidable array of jewellery, like a knight donning his attire. Obviously I was not party to what took place in the king's private chamber, nor did any inkling emerge from within those walls, but when I saw her face after their meeting, I knew she had conquered him as thoroughly as he had triumphed on the banks of the River Trent. Within two days a decree had been issued announcing that the queen's coronation would be celebrated at Westminster Abbey on the Feast of St Katherine, November the twenty-fifth. I hoped the Dowager Queen was smiling in her safe Bermondsey retreat.

For the first time in my life I wished I had married some random knight, so that I was a 'lady' and could take an active part in Elizabeth's coronation ceremony, but instead I stood in the nave of Westminster Abbey alongside the queen's other common women of her chamber, just one of the crowd of citizens watching the procession move slowly down the long aisle. I so wanted to celebrate Elizabeth's consecration at her side, like my mother, helping to remove her outer clothing and smelling the fragrant oil as it was applied to her head and breast. I felt a fierce sense of outrage at the rigidity of court protocol that kept me away from her. I was her friend as well as her servant and I hoped she was missing my attendance as much as I regretted my absence.

Outside the sky was a dull grey and occasional showers of rain and sleet battered the clerestory windows. It should have been cold inside the abbey but it was so crowded that although a fortune had been spent on fragrant beeswax, in the nave there was more body heat than candlelight and a pervading smell of sweat. Even clouds of incense rising from the priests' censers failed to dispel it. I wondered how the choristers managed to sing in their high, clear voices when they were breathing such clotted air but sing they did, magnificently, as Elizabeth made her stately progress towards them preceded, as protocol demanded and despite his son Lincoln's recent treachery, by her rather doddery uncle the Duke of Suffolk carrying her sceptre, the Earl of Arundel with her rod and the king's silver-haired uncle, Jasper Tudor, Duke of Bedford, bearing her crown. When she had passed into the choir and out of my line of vision, I closed my eyes. Since I would not be able to witness her consecration, nor watch the crown lowered onto her head, I would relive all the memorable moments I had shared with Elizabeth, leading up to this glorious event.

I had been thrilled to travel from Greenwich aboard her royal barge to the Tower of London, gasping at my first view of it dressed *en fête*, fluttering with banners and bustling with gorgeously uniformed men. The queen was greeted by a deafening salute from a row of guns deployed on Tower Wharf, which had her ladies jumping with fright and then collapsing into relieved laughter on realising that the bangs were all gunpowder and no cannonballs. Personally I was

98

more enthralled by the small flock of big black birds, which rose in panic from the battlements of the White Tower, signifying that, despite persecution by the garrison soldiers, some ravens still haunted the fortress's ancient walls, keeping the legend of their protective role alive. That night, on the eve of her coronation, tradition dictated that the queen would reside in the Tower's Royal Palace and I promised myself that even if it were at midnight, I would go and visit their autumn roost in the trees on the green.

Surging under London Bridge on the ingoing tide, we were treated to another glorious shock. A huge and ingenious red dragon came racing towards us, looming out over the prow of a winged wherry and breathing flames of fire, which flew sizzling into the river; a nod to the legend that both Henry and Elizabeth were descended from the Welsh hero King Cadwallader and the ancient rulers of Britain. Much enthusiastic waving of the York colours of murrey red and blue indicated that Londoners saw this coronation as a sign that King Edward's daughter was taking her rightful place as his successor on the throne of England and made me wonder how favourably King Henry would greet such abundant evidence of enduring allegiance to the House of York?

Any negative thoughts he might have had were well hidden, however, when he greeted his queen back at Tower Wharf. He embraced and kissed her warmly on the lips before bending to take the train of her gown from the young bearer, draping it over his own arm and tucking his other hand into the crook of Elizabeth's to personally escort her into the Royal Palace. Afterwards, courtiers who attended the reception in the great hall feasted on roasted swan, gulls' eggs and other rare delicacies, enjoyed some nimble tumbling and juggling and remarked on the close affection so evident between the king and queen. From a raised dais they watched proceedings seated on gilded chairs of estate, eating from the same gold plate and drinking from the same jewelled cup, and King Henry gave every sign of being delighted not only at the prospect of sharing his throne but also his hearth and his bed with the beautiful woman at his side.

At this reception I sighted Sir Richard Guildford, last met when we'd exchanged harsh words in the garden at Coldharbour and he had more or less accused me of having Yorkist leanings. I thought he looked drawn and less robust than at that time; his gown hung loosely, as if he'd shrunk a little. However, his beard was neatly trimmed as usual, his dark hair curled thickly over the neck of his fine silk doublet and his smile showed a complete and very straight set of teeth when I greeted him cautiously. 'You have been absent from court of late, I think, Sir Richard,' I said. 'Yet I've heard that you are in charge of the jousting to celebrate the coronation.'

He nodded affably. 'You are well informed, Mistress Vaux. I hope you will attend. I assure you the entertainment promises to be spectacular.'

'If the queen commands my attendance, of course I will be there. It depends on precedence, as you know, and frequently on these very grand occasions the gentlewomen come well down the pecking order.'

His sympathetic expression surprised me. 'Is that so? If you wish me to arrange seating for you in the household stand please let me know; I will be happy to do so.'

I gave a bow of acknowledgement, surprised that he had made the offer to someone he had cross-examined only months ago. 'I thank you, Sir Richard, that is kind of you. I haven't noticed your wife here at such an exciting event in the Tower. Is she perhaps ill?'

A shadow crossed his face. 'Anne gave birth last month and unfortunately has been ailing since. Sadly she is unable to attend.'

'I'm very sorry to hear that. I will include her in my prayers for the sick and hope there is some improvement soon. How does the baby fare?'

'She is well, I am glad to say. We have called her Elizabeth.'

'I expect that name will be given to many a newborn girl this year,' I said, with a gesture towards the dais.

'I'm sure you are right, Mistress Vaux. Certainly my wife wished to mark the occasion.' With a wistful smile Sir Richard bowed and left me – clearly a man with a weight on his mind.

Later the queen attended another formal gathering in the White Tower, and this was followed by a torchlit procession of boats on the Thames, the evening being calm and clear with a beautiful sickle moon hanging in a star-filled sky. While the attention of the crowd was focused on the river, I had turned to watch at least a dozen ravens settle to roost in the alder trees on the green and quietly exulted in their presence.

The climax of the river display came as a complete surprise. Among the participants on the wharf I spotted Sir Richard Guildford again, now in an elegant fur-trimmed gown, prowling restlessly in a roped-off section of the wharf. A number of men were standing at posts erected on the waterside and several boats began to row out over the glistening water as music swelled from trumpets, sackbuts and drums, reinforcing the softer sound of viols and lutes. As a band of choristers began to sing the first verse of a popular ballad, the wharf and the river suddenly burst into life with a series of loud bangs and sprays of coloured sparks.

Standing beside me, my mother cried, 'Holy Maria preserve us!' and crossed herself several times. 'What is happening, Gigi?'

I had kept my eye on Sir Richard Guildford and noticed him nodding in turn at the men, who were holding smouldering ropes, which they applied to the top of the posts. This appeared to be the initial source of the bangs and sparks but pretty soon they also began to zing up from the boats, making impressive arcs of light as they burned, finally fizzling out as they disappeared into the river.

'Fireworks, Mamma,' I shouted over the noise. 'I've read about them but never seen them before. Don't they make a thrilling show?'

My mother's hands flew to her ears and she shook her head violently. 'No! They are terrifying. So loud!'

Then I heard an even louder noise rising behind us and turned to see the flock of ravens, screeching and croaking in alarm as they abandoned their roost and flapped up into the sky, turning their backs to the river and fleeing over the battlements of the White Tower to seek quieter territory outside the city. Sir Richard Guildford and his explosives had achieved what the archers and their arrows had failed to do, drive the ravens away from the Tower. I only prayed that they would return, unable to forget the superstition that when the ravens left, the kingdom would fall.

12

As soon as the excitement of the coronation died down some of us among the queen's gentlewomen were detailed to assist in wedding preparations for young Margaret Plantagenet. Her bridegroom, the king's cousin and Lady Margaret's half-nephew Richard Pole, had earned the nickname Rich, although he was far from wealthy. However, even at the tender age of fourteen Margaret was intelligent enough to realise that although she'd been born a princess, her father's erratic swerves of loyalty during his brother Edward's reign and his consequent conviction and execution for treason had destroyed any chance of her making a noble marriage. A role as the wife of one of the king's preferred knights was as high up the court rankings as she was likely to go. At least Rich had been among the squires knighted after the Battle of Stoke and had also inherited his father's Buckinghamshire holdings, so she would not exactly be a pauper.

That might be so, I thought as I watched them take their vows in the Chapel of St Mary Undercroft at Westminster, but it was noticeable that neither king nor queen attended their wedding, unlike the next one, which took the court by surprise. King Henry had decreed that once more

Christmas would be celebrated at the Palace of Placentia and the seasonal entertainments and feasts had been particularly boisterous, including a rowdy banquet on Holy Innocents Day when courtiers wore exotic costumes and drank copiously, encouraged by a very daring Lord of Misrule. One of his 'dares' lured Princess Cecily from her table of ladies-in-waiting into the centre of the great hall and challenged her to choose her favourite from among the king's courtiers present. Blushing prettily, apparently having partaken freely of the festive mead, to the amusement of the large gathering she pranced up to a table close to the royal board, where the king's uncle, Jasper Tudor, headed a well-lubricated party of senior knights and noblemen.

'The man I love is here,' she declared loudly, making a sweeping gesture to indicate the dozen male courtiers seated there. Then she turned to face the high table where King Henry and Queen Elizabeth were hosting the Lord of Misrule, who had climbed up to stand on the seat of his wooden 'throne' set between them, wearing his paper crown and wielding his wooden sceptre.

Lady Cecily continued coyly, slightly slurring her words, 'But I cannot reveal his name unless the king allows it.' She made a deep curtsy to her brother-in-law and the hall held its breath as she wobbled alarmingly, almost unbalanced, before righting herself and rising. 'Do you allow it, your grace?'

King Henry appeared to greatly enjoy taking part in this episode, standing up with a merry grin and making a flourishing bow to the Lord of Misrule. 'I defer to the lord of the feast,' he cried. 'Does Misrule insist that the lady reveal her true love? I only warn her that if she does, she must save his reputation and her own by agreeing to marry him before the Feast of Epiphany.'

A buzz of excitement fluttered around the hall like a swarm of bees. Epiphany was only a week away. I turned to Elizabeth Jerningham, the queen's Keeper of the Wardrobe and my neighbour on the gentlewomen's table set at the far end near the service screen. 'I smell a conspiracy,' I said in her ear. 'Have you noticed the knowing little smile on the face of the king's mother? I predict that she's in on this charade.'

'What sort of conspiracy?' Mistress Jerningham was sceptical. 'Do you think Lady Cecily will really be obliged to marry the man she names?'

'Look at the candidates,' I persisted. 'There's only one man on the table who isn't already married.'

My neighbour studied the dozen noblemen. 'Oh yes,' she said with a smirk. 'The king's mother's brother. Ha! She's at it again!'

Even as she spoke, Lady Cecily approached the man sitting at the end of the trestle: Viscount Welles, Lady Margaret's younger half-brother John, a man who had been prominent among King Henry's companions in exile and on the battlefield that won him the throne. He was obviously in on this Christmas comedy because he was ready to jump to his feet when Cecily took his hand and led him towards the high table. 'Here is the man I love, my lord,' she said proudly and without the trace of a slur.

The following week, on the eve of Epiphany, all the queen's ladies and many of the king's men were invited to the palace chapel to witness the marriage of Princess Cecily to Viscount

Welles. My mother took great glee in telling me that, due to her friendship with Lady Margaret, she had known for some time that a romance had blossomed between these two but had been sworn to secrecy. 'And as luck would have it both the king and his mother thoroughly approve the match, so let us hope Lady Cecily finds some real happiness at last.'

'And another knot is tied between Lancaster and York,' I remarked cynically. 'Does anyone marry without political advantage, I wonder?'

My mother frowned and laid a finger on her lips. 'You can try and avoid it, daughter, but I wish you good luck. At least Lancaster is in the ascendant under King Henry.'

I gave her a sideways look and murmured, 'I think you mean Tudor, Mamma. Be careful.'

At the Epiphany feast that closed the Christmas festivities Lady Cecily was announced as 'the Princess Cecily, Sister to the Queen and Viscountess Welles'. She was fêted and favoured and songs were sung in her praise and no one remarked on the twenty-year age gap between the bride and groom. Margaret Plantagenet the new Lady Pole, was nowhere to be seen but a few days later I was delighted to greet her as she quietly returned to the queen's service to take up her role as a lady-in-waiting.

After the feasting and entertainments were over, a sad announcement was made at morning Mass. Sir Richard Guildford's wife Anne had died at their home in Kent. I sent up a prayer to the Virgin Mary to ease her passage through purgatory. Surely a lady who had borne six children and expulsion from her husband's lands during the reign of the usurper, only to lose her life when the tables had turned for the better, deserved to find a place in paradise? The perils of marriage and childbirth loomed ever larger in my quest to avoid both.

Easter was spent at Windsor and immediately followed by a splendid service and ceremony in which Lady Margaret was created a Lady of the Garter and her half-brother Viscount Welles, now a member of the royal family, was made a knight of the same order. These processions and ceremonies always demanded robes and jewels of particular splendour and the queen had brought costly pieces from London, including the gem-studded coronet she had worn in her coronation procession. Usually Lady Cecily supervised the collection and return of these royal items to the Jewel House at the Tower but this year, before we left Windsor, she announced that she was pregnant with her first child and would be retiring to the country. Her office as chief lady-in-waiting had been officially assigned to her twelve-year-old sister Anne, but she was not considered experienced enough to perform this task, so the queen's Lord Chamberlain, the Earl of Ormond, had appointed me to accompany the yeomen guards who were to deliver the jewellery.

'It will be your responsibility to ensure that each item is correctly itemised and listed as having been returned, Mistress Vaux. These objects are very valuable, as you know, and most of her grace's attendants are not sufficiently literate or numerate. The queen trusts you to read the ledger accurately.'

I was delighted at the prospect of visiting the Tower once more, as it would give me a chance to see if the ravens had returned after being frightened away by the coronation fireworks, but I was not foolish enough to mention this particular preoccupation to the Lord Chamberlain.

'I think most of the ladies outstrip me when it comes to

needlework, my lord,' I responded, giving him a rueful smile. 'If her grace had to rely on me to sew her smocks she would be badly served, I fear.'

At this point he gave me an enigmatic smile and I understood why the suave but ageing Lord Ormond had once had a reputation as a ladies' man. 'Some horses gallop in the lists and some pull in the traces, mistress. We need both types, do we not?'

Without royalty in residence the Tower had reverted to its everyday role as a busy military base and coin mint. By May the ground was hard enough to roll out the big cannons for servicing and allow heavy carts to deliver their loads of precious metals for melting down and striking. However, the cart carrying the strongbox with the queen's jewels was given precedence and there was little opportunity for me to check whether there were any ravens about as our mounted posse made swift progress through the barbican, across the moat and through a series of guarded gatehouses to the Tower's Inner Court, the secure eye of the fortress. The Jewel House was part of the Royal Wardrobe, attached to the Queen's Lodgings adjacent to the White Tower.

Sitting behind the large receiving table was a disconcertingly handsome man of no more than thirty, wearing apparel that looked dangerously close to contravening the sumptuary laws – a pale grey Kersey wool doublet trimmed with what I took to be marten but which might just as well have been summer ermine, and a cap trimmed with a white feather, exotic enough to be from the tail of an ostrich. He stood up when he saw the yeomen in their royal livery but sat straight down again when he realised they were not accompanied as usual by Princess Cecily.

'Well, who have we here?' he demanded, eyeing me curiously with one sandy eyebrow raised. 'A blackbird, I declare.'

My hackles rose instantly. I was particularly sensitive about reference to my dark hair and features and made the sketchiest curtsy I could manage. 'Joan Vaux, sir, gentlewoman to the queen; I am here to check the inventory.'

His second eyebrow rose to join the other in surprise. 'Whatever is old Ormond doing sending a commoner to replace a princess? What has happened to Lady Cecily?'

The straining yeomen lowered the jewel chest onto the table with a thud and turned away, one of them giving me a wink of sympathy when his back was to the receiver. 'She is on leave, sir,' I replied succinctly.

'On leave, eh? I heard she was married so now I assume she is breeding. That was quick work.'

I took offence at this and told a white lie. 'I do not know the reason, nor would I tell you if I did. May I ask to whom I am speaking?'

He frowned and puffed out his chest. 'Sir Henry Wyatt, Master of the Jewel House and Comptroller of the Royal Mint.' He thrust out his hand and added peremptorily, 'Key?'

My gowns always had a hidden slit, through which I could reach the concealed purse beneath. Ignoring his hand I removed the key to the chest and bent to unlock it myself. As I did so he stretched his arm further and rubbed the cloth of my sleeve between his thumb and his finger. 'Hmm. Dull in colour but very fine cloth. Some might say too fine for a commoner, even one in royal employ.'

I jerked back and snapped, 'Pot calling the cauldron black, Sir Henry?'

He gave a nasty laugh. 'Blackbird pecking at a wolf,

Mistress Vaux?' He flipped open the lid of the chest, which almost hit me in the face.

One of the guards stepped forward hastily. 'Have a care, sir!'

Wyatt gave him a long, hard look, trying to stare him out, but the yeoman held his gaze, one hand on the hilt of his poniard. After this the inventory was checked in heavy silence, precious item after precious item being lifted onto the table, examined, ticked off and set aside. Finally the Master of the Jewel House turned his leather-bound ledger around and pushed it across the polished wood. 'Check it and sign, mistress,' he said.

I ran my eyes down the columns; halfway down the second I placed my forefinger on an entry. 'This gold chain is marked as worth six marks. It should read six pounds.'

With a muttered expletive Wyatt swung the ledger back to face him and studied the entry; he picked up the chain in question and placed it on the scales at his side, adding weights until the scales tipped. 'Saints be praised! You found the deliberate error and win my respect, Mistress Vaux. You may come again.'

I made no comment and swung the book round once more. There were no further errors and I handed the key to the yeoman sergeant who shut the chest and locked it, handing back the key. He and his partner then lifted it and carried it out of the room. 'I hope you have a deputy, Sir Henry,' I said, pocketing the key before I turned for the door. 'Because if I do come again, I would prefer to see him.'

I left the Jewel House with a bad taste in my mouth, which must have shown in my expression. 'He's an awkward customer, that Sir Henry Wyatt,' remarked the sergeant.

I nodded agreement. 'A little too fond of himself, I'd say. Would you be able to take my horse back to the palace, sergeant? I have a desire to walk.'

'Yes, we can do that but don't leave it too late, Mistress Vaux. It's not safe for a woman in the city streets after dark.'

I gave another nod. 'I know. I have a few errands to do but they'll not take long.'

Leaving the Inner Court, I made my way to Tower Green and was delighted to find one lone raven perched on the side of a horse trough, intently watching a row of soldiers with rags, each polishing a cannon. The bird was so interested in this activity it did not notice me approaching from behind, treading softly on the grass. Bright sunlight flashed off its raised band of neck feathers, turning them a greenish blue, and I was entranced. How did something so intrinsically black suddenly become radiant with colour? Then I heard swift footsteps approaching from behind and a grey-clad figure rushed past me muttering, 'Filthy bird! It'll be fouling the water.' With one swipe of his arm he would have shoved the raven into the full trough, perhaps intending to drown it, but it was too quick and managed to get airborne in time, making a loud alarm call – 'kaark, kaark!' I had not seen the assailant's face but the curly white feather in his cap made identification easy. Sir Henry Wyatt was obviously another man who despised ravens.

When I entered the passementerie workshop I noticed some changes. Instead of all the women finger-weaving laces, several of them, including Rosie, were using small hand-looms to make wider, ribbon-like strips of patterned silk fabric in a variety of colours.

'What cunning little machines,' I remarked, approaching the table on which a row of them were lined up while the weavers wielded shuttles at lightning speed.

'You'll be wearing one of these frontlets soon, Joan,' Rosie said, managing to talk as well as fling her shuttle to and fro and change the heddle as she wove. The ribbon of fabric seemed to grow amazingly fast on the warp, despite the fineness of the silk thread loaded on the bobbin. I never ceased to admire the skill and stamina of these hard-working silkwomen.

'The queen's Wardrobe Keeper has ordered scores of them for you ladies to wear under the new lappet hoods,' my friend continued. 'They will replace your coifs and veils. It's the latest fashion in the French court.'

I picked up a sample from the growing pile on the central table. The frontlet was black with a subtle pattern in the weave and the warp ends had been finger-woven into thinner ribbons, waiting to be finished with aiglets. 'Why are these so long?' I asked her.

'They can be crossed behind your head and tied prettily at the throat to secure the frontlet. You can hang a gem or a locket from it to adorn your neck.'

I replaced the item on the pile. 'I'm not sure I like the idea of having a ribbon tied around my neck. It has connotations of the hangman's rope,' I added with a shiver.

Rosie shrugged. 'Nevertheless they're the fashion and the queen's ladies are expected to be elegantly clad and right up to date, are they not?'

'But not strangled with a string,' I complained.

She shot me a fierce look. 'Huh! You can tie it at the back if you prefer. And our beautifully woven ribbons are hardly strings.'

I sat myself down on an empty stool. 'That's true; I take it back. Your work is extraordinary. Now tell me the latest from the Cheap.'

Rosie paused briefly in her weaving to dig into her apron pocket, pulling out a crumpled pamphlet. 'This,' she said, passing it to me and returning her attention to her heddle and shuttle. 'They're all over London. The rumour's rife that Lambert Simnel is actually a farmer's boy called John Brown. That's why King Henry was loth to have him hanged with the other rebels after the battle of Stoke and sent him to work in the palace kitchens instead.'

I scanned the print on the pamphlet and read it out.

'Lambert at the kitchen fire
Boasts he had a royal sire
But when truth is said and done
John be just a farmer's son.

'It's doggerel, Rosie. By an untaught poet.'

'Doesn't mean it might not be true.' Rosie gave a mischievous grin and expanded her theory. 'Lovell escaped the Stoke battlefield and took the real pretender back to Flanders with him. And for those who want to believe it, the boy they crowned in Dublin was not Edward of Warwick at all but Richard of Shrewsbury, Queen Elizabeth's youngest brother.'

'He certainly wasn't Edward of Warwick,' I said. 'I was there at Sheen when they brought the real Warwick from the Tower to meet the queen. She knew him instantly and was obviously not surprised when he avoided her gaze and only made a few grunts in response to her questions. He was always like that, she said. And now she's met Lambert

Simnel as well and says he's much the same. Not much brain between them.'

'There you are then,' said Rosie, still grinning. 'Neither of them was the boy who was crowned in Ireland. That boy easily convinced the Irish lords and clerics that he was a real prince but Lovell didn't want to risk his skin and so replaced him on the battlefield by a local yokel. The real pretender will be back, you'll see, and this time he'll be Prince Richard. King Henry will never sit easy on his throne.'

'Well, there may be gullible Yorkists who like to think that, Rosie, but take it from me, King Henry and Queen Elizabeth are here to stay.'

13

OVER THE FOLLOWING WEEKS things were not all honey and wax in the queen's hive. After Whitsun the royal household moved to Woodstock for the summer months and although the hunting there was excellent, it proved unfortunate for Queen Elizabeth, who suffered another miscarriage soon after our arrival. She plunged into depression, blaming herself because, having been without any warning signs of early pregnancy, she had enjoyed some strenuous hunting, remaining in the saddle for many hours a day.

Whereas Lady Cecily might have known how to comfort and distract her sister by organising card games and musical entertainment, the new chief lady-in-waiting, Princess Anne, was a young girl with an inflated sense of her own importance and incapable of running a children's party, never mind the Queen's Chamber. Her instinct was to leave its organisation to the rest of us and to keep out of Elizabeth's way, avoiding her weeping and complaints. As a result my mother and I were constantly on call, as were Mary Rivers and the matronly Anne Hubbard, who had been sent from Woking by Lady Margaret as soon as she heard of the queen's disappointment. Mary and I were delighted to see her, for

Mother Hubbard had been our governess as Lady Margaret's wards and although she was now getting on in years, there was no one better at nursing the sick and cheering the miserable.

Her first recommendation was one which none of us had considered. 'Why is Prince Arthur not brought here for his summer holiday?' she asked. 'Nothing will cheer the queen up faster than the feel of her own babe in her arms. Also you can tell the king that close contact with another infant after a miscarriage often inspires a fresh conception. I've heard it said that it acts better than a pilgrimage to the Shrine of Our Lady at Walsingham.'

'Well, that didn't work for the queen,' I told her sadly.

That evening the king joined the queen for supper and after hearing Mother Hubbard's suggestion was content to send a contingent of the yeomen guard to Farnham to fetch the prince and his nurses. This meant that the accommodation for gentlewomen became overcrowded and I was grateful to accept my mother's invitation to move into her lady's bedchamber. It also meant that I could act as her clerk, as the task of organising the roster of duties in the Queen's Chamber seemed to have devolved onto her, while Lady Anne enjoyed playing cards and bowls with the king's young squires and the queen chased her nearly two-year-old son around the privy garden. When the king wasn't hunting he held meetings with Spanish ambassadors, who had come to begin negotiating a marriage treaty for the little prince with a Spanish princess. I wondered if perhaps the reason he had agreed so readily to bring Prince Arthur to Woodstock was to show them how fit and healthy the royal toddler was.

Meanwhile a few weeks later a cannonball landed to disturb the even course of my life. It came in the shape of Sir Richard Guildford and in view of his position as Royal Master of Ordnance the analogy with a cannonball was particularly appropriate. I should have known when he asked me to take a walk with him after morning Mass that he had more than simple conversation in mind.

'I hear you had something of an altercation with Sir Henry Wyatt in the Tower Jewel House recently, Mistress Vaux,' he began. 'I hope he did not upset you.'

'Not at all,' I said, hoping my nonchalant wave of the hand convinced him. 'At least not in the Jewel House. I was angered on behalf of a raven when he tried to drown it in the horse trough on Tower Green. Fortunately it got away. But you know my penchant for the big black birds, Sir Richard. I hope they did not leave for good as a result of your amazing but noisy firework display at the queen's coronation.'

'You'll be glad to hear that they did not.' I was surprised when he smiled rather than frowned as he told me this happy news. 'And I hope you enjoyed the display nevertheless.'

I gave him a sideways glance. 'As a matter of fact I did, Sir Richard. It was truly extraordinary. But please let me offer you my condolences on the death of your wife. You must have been desolated.'

To my consternation tears sprang to his eyes. 'Yes, I was. Anne seemed to have recovered her strength after our daughter's birth. Yuletide is always a delightful holiday in the Kent countryside and she was out in the woods collecting holly with the children when she was suddenly unable to breathe and fell to the ground. Luckily my eldest son Edward is fourteen and a sensible boy. He told his sister Maria to take the younger ones home and send out the steward, while he tended his mother. But there was nothing to be done. The physician who came said she'd had some kind of paroxysm of the lungs. He'd seen it before in older mothers who had recently given birth.'

A cold shiver ran through me – yet another reason to avoid childbirth!

'God rest her soul. I have remembered her in my prayers,' I said truthfully, hastening to change the subject. 'But what brings you here in midsummer, Sir Richard? Would you not normally be back on your estates for the harvest?'

I couldn't think why such a question would cause him to blush but his cheeks had definitely coloured. 'I have been to see the king,' he said. 'I wish to remarry and as you have a court position it is protocol to ask for his permission to approach you, especially as you have no father.'

Now it was my turn to blush. 'To approach *me*,' I echoed. 'Are you asking me to marry you?'

He stopped walking and turned to face me, so suddenly that I almost collided with him. 'Yes I am and the king has given his permission.'

I took a deep breath and a step backwards. 'Does that mean I have no choice?'

His colour deepened. 'No, but I hope you will agree. I know I am a few years older than you but you would not be a child bride, Mistress Vaux. I would be honoured if you would consent to be my wife. Will you marry me?'

In retrospect my response was gauche and stupid but his proposal had come out of the blue. 'I don't know much about you, Sir Richard, and to be frank it seems too soon. You have only been a widower for six months and besides you have six children, I believe. I know nothing of motherhood. Why should I marry you?'

He began wringing his hands. Maybe he had been led to expect a more positive reaction. 'I cannot answer that. Perhaps you should ask someone else that question; someone who knows us both and whose answer you trust. I will leave you to think about it and wait for your reply.' He coughed to clear his throat. 'But I will not wait long, Mistress Vaux, and it is a good offer. Anyone will tell you that.'

He was angry – and understandably. I had not handled his proposal very well but he had taken me completely by surprise. Of course I should have believed what my mother had told me, that the king liked his courtiers to be married because it gave an impression of permanence and stability around the throne. The queen knew of my preference to remain single but had probably not communicated it to the king, so when Sir Richard asked his permission to approach me King Henry would not have hesitated to agree. He would probably have considered me lucky to attract the attention of a knight and Privy Councillor: one who rode high in his opinion.

By that evening he had also told the queen, and while we were preparing her for bed she mentioned it. My mother was present and Lady Anne, Mary Rivers and Anne Hubbard, plus a couple of maids of honour.

'I believe congratulations may be due, Joan,' Elizabeth said with a smile, as I removed the pins from her wired gauze veil and lifted it away. It was high summer and she liked her headdresses to be as light as possible while court life was not so formal out in the country. 'My lord tells me Sir Richard Guildford has made you a proposal of marriage.'

I caught my mother's startled look and gave a slight shake of my head. 'Yes – and no, your grace,' I replied, feeling my cheeks burn. 'That is, he has made a proposal but I have not yet given him my reply.' I carried the veil over to the young maid of honour waiting to fold it ready for storage. Among the queen's attendants there were those who actually touched her person and those who remained at a distance.

The queen had noticed my mother's astonishment. 'Had Joan not told you of this, Mother Vaux?' she asked.

'No, my lady, she had not.'

Hearing the hurt in my mother's voice I felt a stab of guilt. 'He only asked me this morning and our paths have not crossed today until now. Besides, as I said, I haven't given him my reply yet.'

'Why do you hesitate?' asked the queen. 'It is a good offer, is it not?'

'I could not tell you, your grace, I hardly know Sir Richard.'

'But the king knows him very well. They were fellow exiles and he has entrusted him with several important offices. I should have thought that was enough to recommend him.'

Trying to bring the conversation to a halt, I resumed my share of removing the queen's clothes by beginning to unlace one of the sleeves from her gown. 'I am honoured that the king should consider me worthy to be the wife of one of his friends, my lady, but I need time to consider.'

Lady Anne spoke up from the cushioned seat where she usually sat to watch the rest of us perform our familiar tasks.

'You're quite old, Joan. I would have thought you might be pleased to be taken off the shelf.'

As I was so close to her, Elizabeth could not help noticing my angry frown. 'I think Joan is only twenty-four, sister,' she chided. 'Many women do not marry before that age.'

Lady Anne's eyes rounded in surprise. 'But you mean common women, don't you, sister? Women who have to work and have little dower.'

For once the queen took issue with her sister. 'All my ladies work, Anne, Joan more than most. And it wouldn't harm you to make a little more effort yourself to earn the money I pay you.'

I winced at that; not because I disagreed with Elizabeth but because I knew her last remark would backfire on me, for I was not Lady Anne's favourite among the queen's attendants. But she was only a child and her eyes filled with tears at the rebuke. Elizabeth was like a mother to her younger sisters and immediately crossed the room to console her. 'Please do not cry, Anne. I know you are finding it hard to take Cecily's place but you will learn quickly, I know you will.'

The subject of my proposal was dropped and eventually we left the queen with her night lamp and Mary Rivers, who slept in a truckle bed in her chamber. The two were great friends, closely related by marriage and much of an age. Elizabeth did not like to sleep alone and Mary was content to depart for her own bed whenever a Yeoman of the Chamber brought news of the king's approach.

My mother did not let the subject of Sir Richard's proposal slip however. She turned on me as soon as the door closed on the queen's bedchamber and we were alone in the passage that led to hers. 'You want to turn him down, don't you, Gigi?' She did not need to say whom she meant. 'But you must not!'

'This is why I did not tell you, Mamma. I knew you would say that and I haven't decided.'

'Why not? He may be some years older than you but it cannot be more than ten and you can hardly expect love's young dream at your age.'

I tried to contain my anger but it flared nonetheless. 'I do not want to marry at all, never mind love's young dream. You know that.'

She stopped short and took a look behind us to make sure no one was there. 'Gigi – the king wants you to marry his friend! You cannot turn him down. You will lose your place at court and then how will you live? Your brother will not house you. He already has four stepchildren and I am not getting any younger. Do you want to rot away in some almshouse like I was doing before King Henry took the throne? You have a life to live and you need to grab it. Sir Richard may be no heartthrob but he is a nice man and very high in the king's favour. He already has estates and will inherit more when his father dies. It is the best offer you will ever get.'

I stamped my foot in frustration. 'I know it is, Mamma, but that is what irks me. Why should I have to marry at all? It's not fair!'

'Huh!' My mother made an exasperated noise. '*Life* is not fair, Gigi! We are in this world to accept our place and do God's will and then, perhaps, we'll get to paradise. You are one of the lucky ones. Girls a lot younger and more beautiful than you fall over each other to obtain places at court in order to find themselves a good marriage. Sir Richard is a king's knight and you will be a lady. You can keep your place at court and be paid more for it.' She clapped her hands to her temples in despair. 'I do not understand you.'

I walked off down the passage with a huge lump in my throat. In the part of our lives we had spent together, I had almost never defied my mother, and when she hurried to catch me up all I could do was give her a silent hug. What could I say? I knew she was right but with marriage went the prospect of motherhood and she did not fully comprehend the very real fear I had of childbirth. Nor did she realise that having lost my father when a child, as I grew older I had found living free of male authority a boon. Now I had clashed with the king – the highest of them all and I resented his dominance and his demand that I submit to being shackled. But could I – should I – defy him?

14

AFTER ATTENDING MASS NEXT morning I was astonished to receive a summons to the King's Chamber.
This was unexpected, because King Henry usually communicated through the queen's ushers and pages and we only
saw him when he visited her Great Chamber or we attended
her at his official court functions. At Woodstock his apartments were in another wing of the palace and I grew more
and more nervous, the closer I got to the entrance. When
I gave my name to the yeoman guards one of them immediately opened the door. I was clearly expected because a
page was waiting to guide me to the right room.

The king was alone in what I took to be his private office,
for it was lined with shelves of leather-bound ledgers, one
of which was open on the table before him. I had heard
that he liked to check his accounts daily and frequently
added items in his own hand. He was a king who saw a
healthy bottom line as the sign of a successful realm.

When I entered he put down his pen and rose from his
chair. 'God's greeting, Mistress Vaux,' he said as I bent my
knee.

'God give you good day, my lord king,' I replied, embarrassed by the nervous tremor in my voice.

He took his seat again. 'Please rise, mistress. I have summoned you to discover your reply to Sir Richard Guildford's proposal of marriage.'

I was almost dumbstruck. Was Sir Richard so nervous of a face-to-face refusal that he had delegated the task to the king? 'I – I told him I would consider it well, your grace.'

'And have you decided?'

I thought his tone slightly irritable and I swallowed hard before answering. 'My mother told me I would be foolish to refuse, sire, but in truth I have still not decided. Sir Richard has six children and I have no experience of motherhood.'

His thin lips spread in a patient smile but did not part. 'Well then, I have a suggestion, which you might prefer, Mistress Vaux.' He picked up an open letter from his desk. 'Here is a written request from another widowed member of my court who seeks permission to offer you marriage. He had no children with his first wife. Are you acquainted with Sir Henry Wyatt? He is Master of the Royal Jewels and Comptroller of the Mint. Another of my worthy court officials.'

I could hardly believe my ears. After I had discovered a discrepancy in his receipts, Sir Henry Wyatt and I had not exactly parted amicably. Nor had I liked his manner of address. What could have led him to imagine I would welcome an offer of marriage?

'Yes, we have met, sire.' I hoped I had managed to conceal my dislike.

There was a brief silence. King Henry laid the letter back on his desk and studied my face for what seemed like a long time before he spoke. 'You are not a young girl, mistress, and I have heard that you are highly intelligent.' I could feel the infuriating blood creeping up my neck to flush my cheeks. 'The queen and I agree that it is time you entered the married state. She cannot promote you further, as she would wish, unless you acquire a higher status. I hazard a guess that you cannot before have had two knights offer you marriage within two days and I would like you to decide which of these two you intend to accept.'

I took a deep breath and played for time. 'They both have their very different points, my lord. I need to seek advice. May I have your permission to deliver my decision tomorrow?'

He shook his head. 'No. At first light tomorrow I leave for an urgent meeting of the Privy Council at Westminster and I would like this matter settled today. You have until the Vespers bell to give your answer. Good morning, Mistress Vaux.'

As I was backing away I saw him pick up a small green leather-covered volume from the corner of his desk and wondered if it was the notebook, which court gossip said he kept close at hand in order to write impressions of the people he met and his conversations with them. I wondered if I would now feature in that book and if so, what impression of me would be inscribed. The thought made me shiver. On his visits to the queen's Great Chamber King Henry invariably showed a pleasant, social manner. Today I had experienced at first hand the resolute, businesslike King Henry, the man who had won his throne by sword and cannon but was determined to rule a well-ordered and peaceful kingdom of high repute. I was just a very small cog in his master plan.

Returning to familiar faces and surroundings in the queen's apartments was reassuring and I sought out my mother immediately. She was among a gathering of ladies and gentlewomen doing intricate repair work on the elaborate embroidery of a velvet coverlet. They were seated in a close circle and the cloth was spread out between them, each one with needle and coloured silk threads to concentrate on her section of the border of exotic flowers and fruits. I caused a gap in their teamwork when I took Lady Vaux away.

As we paced down the passage towards the ladies' chambers I said ruefully, 'I'm sorry, Mamma. I know repairs are important but I must talk to you again about marriage.' She must have understood how stressed I was because after we entered her chamber she immediately secured the bolt on the door.

'Come, Gigi, let us sit down. We have plenty of time to talk because the queen has had some bad news and has gone to the chapel with her chaplain and the Lady Anne.'

'Not about her mother?' I asked with concern. The Dowager Queen had joined us for Easter at Windsor and seemed in good health.

'No, no; but she will also be affected because the message concerned her youngest brother, Sir Edward Woodville. Apparently he had taken a force of English archers across the Channel to support the Duke of Brittany's stand against a French threat to his border but before they could make the rendezvous he was killed in an ambush along with most of his troop. The queen was very fond of her uncle, as was King Henry. They were brothers-in-arms before the change of thrones.' She took a seat in the window embrasure and gestured to me to take the opposite one. In the orchard outside the trees were beginning to droop with fruit. 'There always seems to be war somewhere,' she sighed.

'Including inside my head,' I said. I had not known Sir Edward Woodville personally but as he was Admiral of England I realised this must be the reason for the urgent meeting of the Privy Council. However, my own quandary was uppermost in my mind. 'You'll never guess what's happened, Mamma – the king summoned me after Mass and told me that Sir Henry Wyatt has also sought permission to make me a proposal of marriage. I might call it an embarrassment of riches if I actually cared for him any more than I do for Sir Richard Guildford or if had any desire to marry at all.'

'Sir Henry Wyatt? Isn't he the one who was so rude to you when you returned the queen's jewels to the Tower?'

'Yes, him. King Henry seemed to think I would jump at his offer because he's nearer my age and has no children by his first wife. I did not tell him I would rather face the hangman.'

My mother looked horrified. 'Don't say that, Gigi! It's tempting fate. I told you to accept Sir Richard. He really is a nice man.'

I pressed my palm to my forehead in despair. 'I'm sure he is, Mamma, but I do not want to marry anyone, particularly someone with six children under fifteen!'

'I see that must be a consideration for you but you're a resourceful woman and you might be surprised. Look how well Lady Margaret cared for you and your brother and her other nestlings, when she wasn't much older than you are now.'

I hung my head because this had already occurred to me

and was one of the reasons I had not sought advice from My Lady the King's Mother. My own mother might think me resourceful but I was definitely not saintly like her friend.

My gloomy silence inspired a maternal revelation. 'I will let you in on a secret now, Gigi. When I married your father it was a court scandal. He was heir to considerable estates and I was not even an English citizen, just a young foreign maid in the queen's household. I brought him nothing, except a connection to the royal family. William Vaux had been expected to marry infinitely better but he wanted me and Queen Marguerite agreed the match. What was I supposed to do? I had no choice but to cross my fingers and take my vows. Only afterwards did I discover what manner of man he was – a kind young man and a fearsome knight, who fought like a demon for my queen. In a twist of fortune his father died before he could fulfil his threat to disinherit his son for marrying me and by the time your brother was born, William was knighted and I was in love; happy to give him an heir for his substantial estates. But within two years he – we – had lost everything – attainted for supporting the wrong side. We had to flee across Europe to my family. It was ten years before we returned and then William was killed. You see, we can never really know what God has in store for us.'

She leaned over and took my hand. There were tears in her eyes. 'Why not go to the palace chapel and lay your problem before St Margaret? She is the patron saint of women and I'm sure she will help you to make your choice better than I can.'

I knew why she suggested I consult a saint who was primarily the patron of women in childbirth; because

Mamma was the only one who had any inkling of my morbid fear of giving birth. However, lacking any other suggestion and hoping for some form of guidance, I did what she suggested. Queen Elizabeth and Princess Anne were leaving the chapel as I arrived but I ducked behind one of the entrance pillars to avoid them. I had my own problems and didn't want to be obliged to comfort them in their grief.

Once the coast was clear I slipped inside. At the top of the north aisle there was a small shrine to St Margaret. The dramatic icon image showed her bursting out alive from the belly of a dragon, to which she had been fed as punishment for refusing an emperor's suit, one of his many attempts to achieve her death in vengeance. Her escape from the dragon's belly was the reason why pregnant women called on her in their labour but marriage and childbirth were the very situations I was praying to avoid. Surely I would find no guidance from that source?

Wandering disconsolately back down the nave, my gaze was drawn to a colourful mural in the plasterwork on the south wall. It depicted St Francis, surrounded by birds and animals, which he had loved and protected from harm. Approaching nearer, I let my eyes wander over the image and felt a sudden jolt of recognition. Perched on a branch behind the saint were two large black birds with beaks like shears. Memories of my various encounters with the ravens in the Tower of London flashed into my mind and at the same time I knew exactly where my future lay. St Margaret may not have had any message for me but St Francis did. Sir Richard lived at the Tower of London, alongside the ravens, and although he had expressed his aversion to them,

I had never actually seen him harm one. Sir Henry had deliberately tried to drown a raven in my sight. I felt I had received a divine clue as to what course I should take. I slipped a coin into St Francis's offering box and asked him to send me luck and fortitude.

PART TWO

15

BOTH THE KING AND queen attended my wedding, a huge honour I had not expected and which I assumed showed the respect King Henry had for the man I was marrying. The result was that the undercroft Chapel of St Mary at Westminster Palace was crowded with members of the royal household, whose regular place of worship it was, leaving St Stephen's Chapel above for the exclusive use of the royal family. But the fact that St Mary's was a crypt beneath a superior church did not mean it was of secondary beauty. The chancel gleamed with gilding and the extensive nave contained gloriously painted pillars, supporting four wide bays lit by luminous stained glass windows. As a place to begin a marriage it should have been uplifting.

Sadly I did not hold out much hope of the mutual satisfaction, which had been specified in the marriage contract drawn up by the lawyers for my union with Sir Richard Guildford. I could not say he was bad looking, especially when a fashionable cap with a folded-back brim and a jewelled pin disguised his receding hairline. At thirty-three he could be said to be in his prime, fit and muscular due to the regular arms practice demanded of a Knight of the Household and the Master of Ordnance and Armouries,

135

but he was strong and silent, a man who could wield a pen to design a new gun but found writing anything other than his name a chore and reading equally tedious. He was a man of action, not words. In our attitudes to life we were curds and whey and if I was the whey, I very much feared that I was about to disappear down the marriage drain.

My friend Rosie had scoffed at my misgivings. 'You should thank your lucky stars, Joan Vaux!' she cried, when I told her gloomily that I dreaded my wedding day. 'You will move from commoner to lady in one wave of the priest's hand. The queen will have to promote you up the court hierarchy and you will have all the privileges of a lady-in-waiting. Now if I had married a Master Mercer I would be a happy woman. I could have set up my own business and employed apprentices myself but instead I'm still tied to my mother's workshop until my husband makes Master grade, which I encourage him to do with all means at my disposal. There is much that can be achieved in the marital bed, Joanie, you'll see. And I don't just mean by pillow talk, if you get my point?' She winked at me. 'Bear that in mind and don't lose heart.'

Rosie's words echoed in my head as Sir Richard and I were declared man and wife and the priest gave the blessing. Her reference to pillow talk had, if anything, lowered my expectations of marriage even further. In the few meetings we'd had between his proposal and the wedding, our talks had been stilted and practical. I held out little hope that the marital bed would provide any sudden bursts of intimate conversation, let alone irresistible action.

When we rode through the City together to visit the house on Tower Wharf, which would be our London home,

I had tried to discover his reason for asking me to marry him but somehow the crowded streets, hawkers' cries and loud noises from open workshops allowed him to evade giving me a satisfactory answer. 'It seemed a good match and the king approved,' was all he said. I began to wish I could have consulted his first wife about how to break the ice with her taciturn husband. I'd been nervous at the prospect of meeting his children for the first time but when I asked where they were he told me they were in Kent, preparing to celebrate Christmas. Sir Richard would be going to join them the following day. I don't believe we exchanged more than five or six sentences during the whole excursion. Nor did I manage to spot any ravens at the Tower, an equal disappointment.

We married two days after Epiphany and just before the opening of King Henry's second parliament, another reason why so many courtiers attended, because they were in London anyway. After the wedding the queen kindly provided a reception in her Great Chamber, during which her Lord Chamberlain, Lord Ormond, spoke on her behalf of her happiness at another union of the two royal households and her wish that, on my return from my marriage leave, I should no longer serve her as a gentlewoman but join the exclusive company of ladies-in-waiting, with all the privileges that entailed. Obviously I showed immense gratitude but it was the mention of 'marriage leave' that stuck in my mind.

Although kind-hearted and open-handed in every other way, Queen Elizabeth was notoriously ungenerous when it came to granting leave of absence, preferring to keep her favourite attendants with her as much as possible, especially those that served in the most intimate capacities. I could understand her feelings about constantly swapping dressers and bathers, to say nothing of those who attended her at the stool, but procreation being of as much importance to landholders as to the monarch, there was an inevitable maypole-dance of ladies and gentlewomen coming and going for reasons of fruitfulness. With my secret fear of childbearing and my new husband's ready-made family, I hoped fervently to be among those who proved infertile. When I spoke with my new husband's father however, I realised that would not go down well with the head of the Guildford family.

I knew little about Sir John Guildford except that all his life he had been a staunch supporter of Lancaster and now effectively controlled the loyalty of the county of Kent for King Henry, being one of his most senior Knights of the Body. Sir John was an old man now though, probably over seventy, but nevertheless a force to be reckoned with and one who knew his own mind. Although Sir Richard had never said so, I surmised that he and his father were not the best of friends, because I only met Sir John for the first time at my wedding and saw little of him after it.

'Welcome to the Guildford family, my lady,' he said when Sir Richard introduced me in what I thought a rather abrupt manner. 'I'm pleased to see that you're young enough to breed. My son has plenty of children already but far too many girls. What you need to do is give him a son.'

My brother Nicholas, who happened to be standing beside me, gave a harsh laugh. 'Ha! Good advice, Sir John! Perhaps you'd have a stern word with my wife as well. She's over there.' He pointed out Beth, conversing with my mother a little distance away but possibly within earshot, if she was listening. 'She gave her first husband two sons but so far she has produced only girls for me, the latest only a few months ago. It is very frustrating.'

I suppressed a desire to protest that he should be grateful that his girls were healthy and Beth had survived their births and instead I gave my new father-in-law a dutiful bridal smile and said, 'I will do my best, Sir John, but of course it is in God's gift.'

Because King Henry had called the parliament so early in the year, Sir Richard was unable to leave London again so soon after Christmas to introduce me to his children or his Kent tenants. Our wedding night was to be spent at the house on Tower Wharf, for which I was extremely thankful, because it meant there would be no ceremonial bedding of the bride and groom at the palace, with all the court banter and ribaldry this inevitably entailed. Instead we were able to ride away through the City, reaching the top of Ludgate Hill just as the sun was beginning to set. Beside St Paul's churchyard we paused to drink in the view over the rooftops of London. The River Thames, which usually flowed a muddy brown, was in disguise, as the flat beams of the sinking sun bathed it in a golden glow and, where it churned under London Bridge, caused it to throw up diamond-studded spray. We could see our eventual destination, the White Tower, gradually turning pink in the reflection from a strip of fluffy clouds banked in the western sky.

To my surprise Richard was inspired into speech. 'Surely there must be a God,' he said.

I turned to gaze at him, eyes wide. 'You mean you need convincing?'

He gave me a rueful smile. 'I'm afraid so, yes – sometimes.'

The thought of this shocked me. 'But why?'

'Because in my life I have seen terrible destruction.' He turned away and gathered up his reins. 'It will be dark soon. Come, we must go on.'

He was right, we needed to complete our journey before the thieves and footpads came out to prey, even on mounted passers-by. But I was disappointed. I had really thought he might open up a little, even though his chosen subject had alarmed me. Having been brought up in Lady Margaret's household and spent my subsequent years in royal service, I had never questioned the fact that there was a God, loving or avenging.

Our first meal together as man and wife was embarrassing and uncommunicative, but no more so than I expected. The steward of the house and a young helper served supper, introduced to me as Martin and Hugh respectively. Martin struck me as just the sort of person Richard would employ to keep his house and servants in good order; punctilious and polite, his conversation restricted to the shortest possible reply to any inquiry. Hugh on the other hand was a bright youth, willing but not always careful. More than once I feared for the fine damask of my best gown as stews and sauces slopped over the rims of dishes when he placed them on the table, staining the brilliant white of the cloth.

Sir Richard's Tower House was situated on the wharf, outside the castle walls and at one end of a tenement of houses that were rented out to other permanent members of the fortress staff: the families of sergeants, cooks, guards, masons and moneyers from the Mint. The rents were part of his grant from the crown to add to the income of the

Master of Ordnance. It was the largest of the houses in the row, comfortably furnished but prone to draughts due to the chill winds that blew in off the river. We dined in a panelled hall on the first floor where a good fire blazed in the hearth; much needed, for it had grown very cold as the January night fell.

'How long has Hugh been working here?' I asked when he had disappeared through the service screen.

Richard frowned. 'Not long,' he said, using some bread to wipe sauce from the edge of one dish and popping it in his mouth. 'He'll learn.'

I grimaced. 'Yes, he'll need to.' I took it that the previous Lady Guildford had been too ill to instruct him and made a mental note to speak to him myself.

The food was tasty; some shellfish in spiced sauce and a mutton stew. 'You have a good cook,' I remarked when we had both eaten our fill.

'Tell Martin. He will pass it on.' Richard sat back and wiped his beard carefully with his napkin.

He drank freely of the red wine the steward had poured into silver cups. I sipped sparingly of mine, pondering the night ahead with growing apprehension. To distract myself I persisted with another question. 'Has Martin been with you for some time?'

'Quite a good while.' He swirled the wine in his goblet and took another gulp, gazing into the cup longingly as if he wished to find it full again, before putting it down.

After an awkward pause the steward brought sweetmeats and a bowl of shelled nuts and filled small glasses with sweet wine. There was no lack of fine tableware.

I racked my mind for further topics of conversation.

'I would like to visit the domestic quarters. I did not see them on our last visit.'

He reached for a sugared plum. 'Plenty of time for that.'

'Will your children be coming back to London soon?' I plunged in with the question that plagued me most. 'I look forward to meeting them.'

'Not while parliament is sitting.' He caught my inquiring look and misinterpreted it. 'I have to attend daily but will return before dark.'

Had he thought I was asking what I would do all day, or reassuring me about what we would do at night? How little he knew me. My days would be full in this amazing fortress but the prospect of the nights filled me with foreboding.

I watched him rise, my stomach churning. 'Come,' he said calmly. 'Our chamber is prepared; a fire will be burning and lamps lit.'

The house was lath-and-timber built under two dormer-roofs with a stone spiral stair linking them. The main bedchamber and solar were above the hall and he climbed ahead of me. Behind us Martin must have entered through the screen door. I heard his discreet cough and call after us, 'God give you goodnight, sir, my lady.'

I ducked back down to wish him goodnight. 'And please tell the cook it was a delicious meal.'

I saw sympathy in his responding smile. 'I will, my lady. God bless your rest.'

I got little rest. Oh, not because I had married an insatiable and demanding lover but because, after he had politely and considerately introduced me to my marital duty and satisfactorily come to his own release, he had fallen asleep and I had lain awake until the small hours, wondering what all the fuss was about regarding the preservation of virginity and the life-changing significance of its loss. To me it had been an anti-climax, a messy and unfulfilling rite of passage from maidenhood to matronhood. I had found more meaning and excitement in any of Odysseus's adventures while reading Homer and anything less likely to result in the conception of a child I could not imagine.

I must have eventually fallen asleep because I was woken by a girl in a brown dress, white coif and apron, and wearing an 'anything-to-please-you' smile. There was no sign of my husband. She held out a mug containing a liquid that gave off a fragrant, herbal aroma. 'I made you a bridal posset, my lady. The apothecary said it would fortify you after your wedding night.'

I reached out to take the drink but it burned my fingers and I thrust it back at the girl. 'Put it down somewhere,' I suggested. 'It is too hot to drink now.'

With a contrite look she scuttled off to put the mug on a trivet by the hearth. The fire had died in the night. 'Shall I relight the fire, my lady?' she asked.

'I don't know. What is the hour?' Even under the covers I could tell the room was cold but I was used to being up and dressed before dawn to attend the queen's awakening and fires were never lit in the gentlewomen's quarters.

'The bells rang for Terce a little while ago, madam. Shall I bring water for washing?'

I sat up in surprise. I had never before slept through Prime and Terce. What would the household think of me? 'Yes, bring water please, but first tell me your name.'

'I am called Luce, my lady.'

'Luce? Just Luce – not Lucy?'

She looked puzzled, as if I had made an odd suggestion. Perhaps she'd never heard of St Lucy. 'Yes, just Luce.' She turned to select some kindling from a log box beside the hearth and swiftly had the fire going again, as it caught in the residual heat from last night's ash. I did not think she was very old but she obviously knew what she was doing. I stretched luxuriously under the warm covers. The bed was very comfortable; being a bride had some advantages.

'When did Sir Richard rise?' I asked. 'Is he breaking his fast?'

'The master left the house at first light, my lady.'

'Do you know where he was going, Luce?'

'No, madam. You would need to ask Martin. Shall I pass you the posset now?'

'Yes please. And is that my chamber robe on the clothes pole beside you?'

She was still standing by the fireplace, where the fresh logs were beginning to catch. My baggage had been brought to the Tower House the previous day and the clothes chest unpacked for me. I felt my cheeks flush as I recalled undressing the previous night. Richard had attended to unlacing my gown and kirtle with the practised skill of someone who had performed the task many times before. Still in my smock, I had removed my hosen and headed for the bed, but he had stopped me.

'We will not need this,' he said casually, lifting the smock over my head. Standing in his own chemise, he had run his gaze briefly over my body as if I were a brood mare at a horse sale; then he'd smiled and said, 'Lovely. Quick – get under the covers. It is freezing!' On his way round to the

144

other side of the bed he had hauled his own chemise over his head and discarded it before extinguishing the night candle and climbing in to join me. Ten minutes later I was no longer a virgin. There was no more to it than that really, except a series of grunts, a stab of pain and a few drops of blood, which I did not discover until I emerged to don the chamber robe handed to me by Luce.

She saw me look back at it and helped me tie the belt of the robe. 'I will see to that, my lady, don't worry,' she said, turning to fetch the posset.

'Are there any books in the house, Luce?' I asked on an impulse.

'I do most of the cleaning, my lady,' the maid said as she approached with the mug, 'and I have not noticed any books anywhere except school primers when the children are here. The master has papers strewn all over the desk in his work-room but they are mostly drawings of some sort. He orders me not to touch them so I do not.'

I took the posset and drank it. There were things that would clearly have to change, if I was to live at all happily in the Tower House.

16

My first day of married life was spent familiarising myself with the house and its surroundings. As I'd discovered already, the building was divided into two wings around the spiral stair I had climbed the night before. The main bedchamber, spacious and well furnished, was above the hall on the second floor of one wing, and beneath an attic in the dormered roof, which held pallet beds for domestic staff. I was to discover that a team of male retainers slept over the stables, acting as grooms, porters and messengers and drove the family cart for journeys to and from the estates in Kent.

In the attic under the second roof there was a partitioned room for a tutor and box beds for the girls' nurses, all presently unoccupied. Below this second attic were two chambers on each upper floor. Judging by the presence of a cot in one of the second-floor rooms the baby slept there, presumably with a nurse in the box bed beside it, and the governess occupied the other. The back room on the first floor was fitted with a large tester bed for the girls, while the boys shared another in the chamber overlooking the wharf. As far as London accommodation went it was luxurious living but I did not find any sign of a bookshelf, except in the governess's room where, as well as a box bed, there was a trestle table and benches and a cupboard containing primers and slates for teaching.

On the ground floor, at the foot of the stair, was an entrance porch with doors on either side, one of which was firmly locked. I assumed this must be Richard's office, which Luce had mentioned; on the other side a room contained benches along two walls, trestles balanced against a third and little else. Perhaps it was a waiting room or a guardroom or a servants' hall, or perhaps all three. At the back of it was another door, which led me into a walled rear courtyard. Here were all the usual domestic buildings, timber lean-to stalls for a number of horses, an empty kennel, a dairy, a large stone-built kitchen with quarters for the cook and, in the far corner, a latrine with drainage into the castle moat. The fact that the moat was tidal, like the river that fed it, meant that the inevitable smell was less pungent than it might have been. In fact, due to its location at the moat's confluence with the Thames, where the tide rushed in and out with cleansing power, it was possibly the least offensive privy in London. Having found it unoccupied I made timely use of its facility before venturing out onto the busy Tower Wharf.

I was glad I had added a fur-lined cloak over my kirtle and gown because a sharp winter wind blew off the river, rattling the rigging of the row of ships docked against the wharf. Cargoes of guns and ammunition were being unloaded for the Armoury and I watched nets full of stone cannonballs being lowered into carts, pitying the teams of oxen waiting in the traces to pull their heavy loads over the wharf draw-bridge and into the inner ward of the castle. The shouts of porters and mariners exchanging orders carried over the noise of the wind rattling the rigging and were then drowned every time a net was deposited with a deafening clatter. I didn't linger at this dock but made my way down to the far end of the wharf, attracted by the glinting of the cargoes emerging from one particular barge. This was a load of precious scrap metal for the Mint, arriving from some coastal port to boost the stores waiting to be melted down and struck into coin.

I soon regretted my curiosity in approaching the upper wharf, for a richly dressed man watching proceedings spotted me immediately. Because his head was down against the wind I couldn't see his face clearly but I knew instinctively that it was Sir Henry Wyatt.

As he drew near he swept into an unnecessarily elaborate bow. 'Lady Guildford, I declare! Welcome to your new fief.' Whereas a smile would have countered the mockingly effusive greeting, his expression remained stony. 'How was your wedding night?'

The last remark was shouted over the wind so that any of the nearby porters might hear and it stung me into anger. 'I am extremely happy to say that is no business of yours, Sir Henry!' With a stiff bow I pulled my hood down over my forehead and added, 'God give you the day you deserve.' And with that I turned away and headed for the drawbridge that would take me into the castle precincts.

Unfortunately I had to wait to cross, standing back to allow an empty oxcart to pass onto the wharf. The wind threatened to whip my hood back and I had to hold it in place, so I did not detect the knight's approach from behind. I jumped when I heard his voice very close to my ear. 'You slighted me, Blackbird, and it will not be forgotten.'

I swung round to confront him but he was already two strides away with his back turned, leaning into the wind. I knew he would not hear me. Besides, what could I say? He was right; in effect I had slighted him, preferring Richard's suit over his. Now the two men would have to work together because the Armoury and the Mint shared dominion over activities in the Tower. But while Wyatt knew that I'd chosen Richard, my new husband did not know that Sir Henry Wyatt had also sought my hand – unless the king had told him, which I very much doubted. As I walked up Water Lane between the twin curtain walls I pondered whether it would be wise to tell Richard of my encounter on the wharf and the reason for Wyatt's vindictive attitude but decided the most sensible strategy was to ignore it and hope for the best. There was no reason to think Wyatt would hold my husband responsible for my marital choice. It was entirely possible that the two men were rubbing along together perfectly well in their working environment.

My musings on this matter vanished as soon as I reached the Wakefield Tower and turned through the archway beside it into Tower Green, intending to visit St Peter's Church. I was also half-hoping to spot a raven, as I knew from my previous visits that this green area with its grove of alder trees, was a favourite haunt of theirs. For once its grassy open space was devoid of archers or gunners, I presumed because the strong wind made target practice and firing training impossible.

As I walked through the gate arch I came to an abrupt halt, backing swiftly under its shadow again. A pigeon was pecking at a muddy patch in a corner of the green, while a raven approached it from behind, stepping cautiously into the wind rather like a drunken man, while the pigeon remained blissfully unaware of its presence. Suddenly the raven darted forward and snatched at the pigeon's tail, pulling a feather free and retreating before its owner could retaliate. However, neither I nor the unfortunate pigeon had realised that another raven was lurking behind the nearby horse trough and while the pigeon flounced after the first raven, the second pounced, pinning it down with its mighty claws. I became rooted to the spot, watching in fascinated horror, aware that the pigeon was about to become the ravens' dinner, half appalled at the destruction and half pleased that the big black birds, which were so hounded and despised, were going to get a decent meal. Although it was two against one, as the first raven rushed forward to share in the banquet, I could only admire the way they had worked together to achieve their feast.

Things were not so simple though. A guard on duty at the entrance to the Lieutenant Constable's house had also been observing the incident and, abandoning his post, he rushed forward, yelling abuse at the ravens, which were forced to take flight, leaving the stunned pigeon flapping helplessly on the ground. The guard did not see me but I saw him grab the pigeon, hastily wring its neck and stuff it into the front of his brigandine. I waited for him to return to his post before I stepped out to continue my way to the church, seething on behalf of the ravens, for it would be a beefy well-fed soldier who would feast on pigeon for dinner, not a cunning pair of ravenous black raptors.

Before Richard returned from attending the opening of parliament, I had ventured into the Tower House kitchen to speak to the cook, a surprisingly thin man called Jake. His slight build was a wonder to me because Brice, the queen's cook, who travelled faithfully with her wherever she went, was red-faced and rotund, as if he had done more than his fair share of tasting the rich dishes he set before her. He was also of fiery temperament, whereas Jake seemed to be a genial fellow, eager to please and willing to adjust mealtimes to suit his employers. He readily agreed to hold dinner until his master's return. The presence of cheery Hugh darting about the kitchen in his scullion role prompted me to ask Jake whether the lad had been given any training in serving at table, a task I thought probably the steward's responsibility. On hearing to the contrary I decided to raise the subject with Martin.

The steward ruled over a pantry and wine cellar off the kitchen, where he also had an office-bedroom next to the stair that led up to the serving screen at the end of the hall. As well as a box bed, it contained a desk and cupboard to keep his accounts, a duty he clearly pursued with characteristic efficiency, for I found him there, wielding his quill in a ledger. My arrival took him by surprise and colour flooded his pale cheeks as he leapt to his feet, but not before he had meticulously placed his pen in the inkpot.

'My lady! Give you good day. Are you seeking to break your fast?'

'No, Martin, thank you. I never eat before dinner, which I have asked Jake to delay until Sir Richard returns from parliament.' His look of mingled alarm and irritation prompted me to add, 'I hope that does not interfere too much with your routine.'

He adjusted his expression into one of polite acquiescence. 'You are the mistress here, my lady. Everything shall be as you wish.'

I smiled. 'In that case, Martin, I wish young Hugh to be given some instruction in how to serve at table. He is very willing but a little careless in his delivery and at supper last night I feared some of the sauces might have splashed their way onto my gown. I take it he has not been doing it for long.'

He cleared his throat. 'Ahem. No, my lady. In fact last night was his first attempt. I am sorry if he displeased you but with the mistress no longer with us, and the children away, Sir Richard has been dining at court or in the White Tower. I had been supervising Master Edward in the rudiments of table service, but he has now joined the royal household as a page. Hugh is only a temporary replacement until young Master George returns from Kent. However, he is only eleven, early days in his noble training, and may be even less dexterous than Hugh – until he learns, that is.'

Martin was proving to be more loquacious and informative than I had estimated and I began to realise that he might be of a great deal more help than Richard in giving me an introduction to my new family. 'I see. I didn't know Edward is now serving in the king's household. That is a great honour. Please tell me the order and ages of the other children if you have the time. Who comes between Edward and George, for instance?'

Martin puffed up with pride at the prospect of describing the family he served. I was beginning to warm to him. 'Maria is twelve and although perhaps I should not say so, rather her father's favourite. I believe he intends to name one of his ships after her this year.'

'One of his ships? I'm ashamed to say I had no idea that Sir Richard owned ships. I thought he designed big guns.'

Martin looked astonished. 'Yes, my lady, but Sir Richard is an engineer. He designs guns, ships, bridges, castles, sea walls – anything that requires accuracy and ingenuity. His family have a shipyard in Kent and the king has commissioned two vessels for his new navy.'

'Goodness, I had no idea.' I paused, letting this unexpected information sink in. 'But tell me more about the children, Martin. Who comes after George?'

Rather to my annoyance the steward sighed. 'Nothing but girls after that, I'm afraid, madam. Philippa is eight and Winifred six, then there is the baby Elizabeth.' His face clouded then, as if a painful memory rushed in. 'Sir Richard joined the first rebellion against Richard of York – the usurper, I should say – and was obliged to flee and join the king in exile. He was away for two years and the master and mistress – late mistress, begging your pardon, my lady – they were so glad when she expected another child a year after his return.' He stopped abruptly, pressed his hand to his mouth and turned away, embarrassed to show the emotion he clearly felt at the loss of his previous mistress.

'Oh dear, Martin, it seems I have special shoes to fill,' I said gently. 'I will trouble you no longer but thank you for letting me know. I will do my very best.'

The steward shook himself fully erect again and coughed. 'I think I hear the master's horse, my lady. I will inform the cook to prepare to serve the meal.'

I watched him disappear hastily into the kitchen and made my way through the screen door into the hall, shedding my cloak on a hook in the hall as I moved towards the main staircase. If my new husband was home I supposed it behoved me to tidy my windblown appearance a little. As I climbed I pondered how remarkably my brief talk with Martin had shifted my hitherto uninformed opinion of both Richard and his steward. I had so much to learn about my new family.

17

PARLIAMENT WAS PROROGUED AFTER only ten days and Richard decided his children should return from their Christmas holiday in Kent. At the same time I received a message from the queen's vice-chamberlain informing me officially that my marriage leave was coming to an end and I should prepare to rejoin her service as soon as possible at Sheen, especially as her cousin Lady Margaret Pole was with child and due to retire to her family home quite soon.

When I informed Richard of this he looked displeased. 'This is unfortunate,' he said. 'I think you must warn them that you have not yet been able to establish a relationship with your stepchildren and require a few more weeks to do so.'

I gave a decisive shake of my head. 'I can't do that. You must know that part of the reason the king and queen promoted our marriage was to allow me to become a lady-in-waiting. I cannot now renege on my obligation to take up my new responsibilities.'

His expression darkened further. 'If I require you to do something, as my wife you are obliged to obey me, Joan.'

We were at supper together following his return from a lengthy final parliamentary session at Westminster. I lowered my head and wrung my hands under cover of the cloth.

Although our union could hardly be called a romantic triumph, this would be our first confrontation since our wedding, but I knew it had to come.

'Legally that is true, sir, but may I suggest that using the need for me to establish a relationship with your children as an excuse will not go down well with the queen; a woman who was obliged to leave her firstborn son with a nurse and governess at Farnham only weeks after giving birth to him. We have to face the fact that our marriage was made by royal command for the queen's convenience, not for ours or your children's.'

Richard banged his hand down on the table, his colour rising. 'I thought we married at the king's command because he dislikes his courtiers remaining single, not for the queen's convenience. I admit that I needed a wife but my children also need a mother!'

I sighed. 'Then perhaps you married the wrong woman, sir. I pledged my allegiance to the queen when we were both unmarried and unless she releases me from my duty, or I become incapable, I owe her my obedient service.'

His brow creased further but his colour faded as he fell silent for a brief spell. 'You said you were especially needed back because Lady Pole was retiring with child. Supposing you were to be pregnant, Joan? You would have to retire then too, would you not?'

I had to suppress a smile at the sly look that accompanied this sally. 'Temporarily yes, I would. But I am not pregnant now and even if I were it would be at least three or four months before I was permitted leave.'

His face fell at that but quickly brightened again. 'Let us come to a compromise then. The children will be here in two days' time. You can write to the queen's chamberlain and say you will return at the beginning of February – weather permitting, of course, and it may be snow and ice by then. But you will have at least a few days to get to know the children before you leave. Meanwhile we can do our best to ensure that you become pregnant so that you will return to us in spring. How does that sound?'

His suggestion wasn't funny really but I had to laugh. 'That is the longest speech I have heard you make since our wedding, Sir Richard!' I saw his frown return but I couldn't resist pursuing the teasing note. 'Very well, husband, as you tell me I am obliged to obey you, I will write the letter and submit to your other suggestion. However, do not blame me if the second part of your ruse is not successful.'

He pushed back his chair and stood up. 'If it is not it will be through no fault of mine. Come, we will start now.'

I rolled my eyes in surprise. The meal was not over. There were dishes left untasted. 'Will you go hungry, sir?' I asked, rising slowly.

'There is more than one type of hunger, my lady, as you have learned. You bring the candle.' He headed remorselessly for the stair.

As I took a candlestick from the table Hugh arrived through the screen door carrying sweetmeats on a platter. 'Will you not partake of the void, my lady?' he asked, puzzled. The 'void' was a court term used to describe the honeyed wine, spiced cakes and sweetmeats served at the end of a meal. Martin must have been coaching him as I had requested.

Richard turned back from the hall doorway, holding out

his hand. 'Give those to me, Hugh,' he ordered. 'We may need them later. Goodnight, boy.'

Hugh's face assumed a knowing look as he passed the platter over and made a rather impressive bow. I suppressed another smile.

For the first time our congress that night might have been described as lovemaking. Even though 'babe making' was Richard's driving force, nevertheless it spurred him into treating the event less as a means of personal release and more like a joint venture for our mutual benefit. Afterwards, as we munched on the contents of the platter, I reflected that I could almost have said I enjoyed it but Richard had reverted to his usual strong and silent self and of course we did not discuss it.

The following day he had duties to perform as the Master of Ordnance and he set out later than usual as he had only a short stroll across the moat rather than a horse or ferry ride to Westminster, which gave him enough time for a repeat performance of last night's pursuit of pregnancy. After Luce had brought my warm water for washing and helped me with the ties and laces of my kirtle and gown it had been my habit to walk through the Tower's Outer Court to the little church of St Peter ad Vincula, either to attend one of the Masses or just to say my own prayers in the quiet nave.

However, on this occasion, perhaps because I had found myself enjoying our repeated marital activities more than I anticipated, I decided instead to make my way to an apothecary's shop I had noticed on Cheapside, during my visits to Rosie's silk workshop. I could not go to the queen's favoured apothecary at Blackfriars, partly because it was too far away and Richard might question my absence at dinnertime but mainly because I was known there and the purpose of my visit might get back to Elizabeth. I hardly liked to admit to myself the reason for my excursion so I pretended that I was intending to visit Rosie, then swerved into my destination at the very last minute, almost as if I was fooling myself into believing it was a sudden decision.

To my intense relief the shop was attended by a woman, and a woman of some age and experience who I hoped might be sympathetic to my request, as indeed proved to be the case. I left the premises after no more than a few minutes with a small linen bag containing an object she had assured me was the most popular and effective remedy against the condition for which I required it. It also happened to coincide with one of the recommendations I had read in the book on women's medicine from Salerno University. Well before the bells rang for Sext I was back within the Tower precinct and reckoning I had time to visit the chapel on the green to pray to St Margaret for understanding and forgiveness.

On this fine and dry day the green was busy with gunners practising firing routines and, as usual, muttering and grumbling about the presence of a female. Unhappily their presence also deterred the ravens, of which there was no sight. However, as I walked back over the moat through St Thomas's Tower I caught a glimpse through a narrow window-slit of a big black bird swooping down onto a cart that was parked on the wharf and surrounded by gulls pecking away at spilled grains of corn on the ground nearby.

I decided to see if I could creep up on it while it was distracted and darted down the spiral stair onto the wharf.

The raven was perched with its back to me on one of the cart's rails, edging its way nearer and nearer to where the gulls were gathered. There wasn't much wind but the slight breeze was in my face so I hoped I could get to the cart without being detected. My heart began to beat so hard in my chest I thought the bird would hear it but very slowly I managed to reach the shelter of the cart's high end, so that I was not much more than arm's length from the raven, peering through the two top rails over piled sacks of corn. Up close I was struck by the size of it: as large as a chicken but more finely built, with smooth gleaming blue-black feathers spreading back to its spade-shaped tail from a thick ruff of upstanding neck pins. I thought it so beautiful I could scarcely breathe.

The raven suddenly sensed my presence and turned its head; otherwise it did not move. One peat-dark eye fixed me with a fierce glare but my own eyes were drawn to its magnificent raptor's beak, the sharp, curved tip of the upper bill hooked over the lower. There was no mistaking the flesh-ripping potential of this mandible and I gulped, imagining it tearing at mine. Nevertheless, despite the thudding of my heart, my hand seemed to reach out almost of its own accord and the tip of my forefinger lightly stroked its polished black surface – once, twice, three times. The beak opened and I thought the hook was going to strike me but instead a hoarse growl emerged from the raven's throat. That bill looked hard as nails but plainly it was acutely sensitive and my soft caress was welcome and enjoyed. I had long admired these enigmatic black birds but in that moment I fell in love.

My euphoria lasted for all of five breaths, then suddenly the grateful growl turned into an aggressive 'arrrk' and the raven dug its hook into my thumb before lifting off with an energetic thrust of its wings, followed by a cloud of surprised gulls. With a cry of pain I thrust my thumb into my mouth and tasted blood. I had received my first lesson in raven handling; don't, unless you're prepared to take the consequences. Pulling out my kerchief, I wrapped it around the injury and set off for the Tower House, more than somewhat chastened and surprised to find that the sudden attack seemed to have had an unexpected effect on me. Not only did my thumb begin to throb but I also felt queasy, as if I was about to be sick. I wondered whether it was delayed shock or if eating sweatmeats late on in bed the previous night could have upset my stomach. In any event I decided it would be better if I were inside.

Luce was sweeping the hall when I returned and became quite concerned when she saw my bandaged thumb. Propping her broom against the wall she sat me down and removed the stained kerchief. The sight of blood aggravated my queasiness and I pressed my good hand over my mouth.

'You've gone very pale, my lady. Shall I fetch a bowl?'

I nodded and mumbled, 'I think you had better, Luce.'

She wrapped the kerchief back and hurried through the screen door, as I took some deep breaths. Luckily she was back within a minute, having grabbed the wooden bowl Martin used to wash his precious sweet wine glasses after the void. While I hugged the bowl with my other arm and retched, with little except bile to show for it, she fetched water and linen waste and attended to my thumb.

'How did you come by this hurt, my lady?' she asked. 'It is not a big wound but quite deep.'

'I was trying to make friends with a raven, Luce.' There was a pause as she stared at me, open-mouthed. 'I know, you think me crazed and perhaps I am – a little – but they fascinate me.'

Luce raised the wad of linen waste she was using to stop the blood flow and I risked a quick look at the slit in the ball of my right thumb. I could see that it was going to be a nuisance for a few days. She placed the wad back and said, 'If you can keep this pressed over the wound, my lady, I will go and fetch some wine and honey to wash it with before I bind it.'

I did as I was told and blessed her for not scolding me. The washing and dressing was soothing but I had not escaped castigation. When Richard came back for dinner he spied the bandaged thumb immediately. 'What have you been doing, Joan? Not playing with sharp weapons, I hope.'

I laughed sheepishly. 'No, just getting to know a raven.'

'What! Jesu, please tell me you jest.' His incredulity gave way to anger. 'You know I dislike the way you champion those filthy creatures. Exactly what happened?'

I told him, which I quickly realised was foolish.

'You literally asked it to peck you? Joan, ravens are scavengers. They feast on dead creatures. Pray God the thumb will not fester. I forbid you to go anywhere near those devilish birds again!'

Perhaps I should have been grateful that he was concerned for my wellbeing but I bristled at this high-handed demand. 'They are wandering birds, just as likely to visit our back court as the wharf or the castle,' I pointed out.

He drew a sharp breath and puffed out his chest like a fighting cock. 'There is no reason for my lady wife to be visiting the back court. That is why we have close-stools. As for the wharf – Sir Henry Wyatt told me he met you out there while they were unloading cannonballs and scrap metal. That is a dangerous activity and no place for a lady to be. Why did you go there?'

'I was on my way to the church. At the time I did not know I could cross at the Watergate. I am still finding my way about.' I tried not to sound churlish but that is how I felt. Also my thumb was throbbing again and I confess to being close to tears.

Richard did not appear to notice. 'I would prefer you only to use St Thomas's Tower to make a crossing and you should restrict your visits to St Peter's. It is not necessary to go every day.'

For fear of dissolving completely into sobs I stood up. 'I cannot be confined to this house all day. I need air. And right now I need peace.' I headed for the hall door.

He followed me and caught my arm; at least it was the uninjured one. 'Joan, stop! You do not eat breakfast and now you intend to miss dinner. Are you ill?'

I halted but avoided his gaze, keeping my eyes pointedly on the stairway. 'No, sir. I am in some pain. Get Luce to bring me some bread and pottage if you wish but please let me rest.' I shook off his grip but at the foot of the stair I turned. 'I will write to the queen's chamberlain as you requested and were there any books in this house I would sit quietly and read; but there are none. If you intend to keep me housebound, sir, I will have to do something about that.'

18

Iate the bread and gruel Luce brought but could not keep it down and lay in a cold sweat, fearful that, as Richard had predicted, my encounter with the raven had started something sinister. However, within two days the wound began to heal and the sickness abated so I decided to make good my vow to import some books into the Tower House. When I mentioned this intention, perhaps out of guilt Richard offered to escort me to Westminster, where Master Caxton had located his celebrated printing presses in a workshop behind the abbey, aiming to find customers among the monks and the lawyers of the bench as well as the royal court.

'Lady Margaret buys books there,' I told him as we were rowed upriver in a hired ferryboat. 'I realise now how lucky I was to be brought up in her household, for even if my father had not been killed and my mother obliged to serve Queen Marguerite, our family would never have been able to afford the books I found in my lady's library.'

Sir Richard's expression was more of a grimace than a smile. 'Book learning was never for me but I would like my girls to read and write. Their mother was more interested in teaching them to dance and sing. She hoped to get them positions like yours, in the queen's service.'

This came as a surprise to me, almost as much as his unexpected urge to converse. 'Did she serve the Dowager Queen then?'

'No, she didn't.' He shrugged and I thought he might go silent but his loquacious mood continued. 'The Pympes are a well-known family in Kent but not in court circles. Anne's father was a landholding squire – more of a farmer than a courtier. They made their money in sheep wool. Besides, like us they were Lancastrians and we all kept our heads down during the York years, until our fathers chose to support the Duke of Buckingham in his rebellion against King Richard – not a good idea, as it turned out.'

'That was when you joined King Henry in exile. And then, when you returned from exile, she had another child and died,' I mused. 'That is sad indeed.'

His response was brief and gruff. 'Yes.' And silence prevailed once more. But in a way I was pleased to have stirred painful memories in Richard as well as Martin, because it showed me that Anne Guildford had touched a tender spot in the men who had been close to her.

The creak and splash of the oars filled the rest of the journey. However, although he blanched slightly at the cost, Richard readily pulled out his purse to pay for the books I chose from William Caxton's shelves. The entrepreneur who had brought the magic of printing to England was not there himself but his aptly named printer, Master Wynkyn de Worde, was more than willing to break away from his imposing presses for one of the king's Privy Councillors. Remembering how much I had appreciated the work of a female French writer called Christine de Pizan when I had the run of Lady Margaret's library, I was delighted to find another book by her on the Caxton shelves. It was in the original French, with the title *Le Trésor de la Cité des Dames*, and I presumed it to be a follow-up to the one I had previously read called *Le Livre de la Cité des Dames*. Then, although I had already read it in Latin as a girl, I picked an English translation of Varagine's *Golden Legend*, thinking that the stories of the saints would surely interest Richard's older daughters. It wasn't until I was sitting in the ferryboat, being rowed back downstream, that I realised I had been thinking like a mother.

Richard's children arrived from Kent the following afternoon and the house erupted into a fever of activity as chests of belongings were hauled up the stairs and the walls reverberated with the sound of young treble voices. Richard went out to greet them but I decided to wait in the hall until the governess managed to restore some sort of order and usher them in to meet me. The eldest boy, Edward, was absent, having already joined the royal household, and so the first to be introduced was twelve-year-old Maria and as he drew her proudly forward it was clear to me that, as Martin had indicated, this girl was the apple of Richard's eye. She was certainly pretty in her sky-blue kirtle, its yellow sleeves tied on with dark blue laces, showing little puffs of her white linen smock and a white kerchief tucked tidily into the neck. Her blonde hair was plaited up on her head under a short white linen veil and her polite smile would have lit her rosy-cheeked face, if only it had reached her bright blue eyes. I had a brief glimpse of the challenge contained in her glance, before she dropped her gaze and made a correct little bob as she greeted me with a murmured 'My lady'.

I hoped the smile I gave her in return emitted more warmth. 'I am so happy to meet you at last, Maria. Perhaps since you are the eldest here you would introduce me to your brother and sisters?'

There was a pause while Maria decided whether she intended to comply, then she gave an impatient sigh and turned to the girl behind her. 'This is Bess,' she said abruptly. 'She's not my sister but she lives with us and is betrothed to my brother George, who is supposed to be next in line but is lurking at the back.'

Bess was a sturdy little girl who stepped forward shyly and made a neat curtsy as Richard intervened. 'My ward, Elizabeth Mortimer,' he explained. 'She was already motherless when her father died in battle. Sadly she is an orphan of war but the king granted me her custody and I think she is happy living with us. She is eleven and George is just twelve and it is intended that they should marry in due course.' He beckoned his son forward with a stern finger. 'George, come and meet your stepmother.'

I exchanged smiles and nods with Bess, as a sulky-looking boy in a brown jacket and grubby buff-coloured hose emerged from behind the rather stout woman at the back who was carrying a plump infant. His bow was sketchy and clumsy and his black felt cap remained firmly on his head.

'Doff your hat, George,' ordered his father sternly. 'You know very well how to greet a lady.'

The cap was pulled reluctantly from his thick tawny thatch of hair. 'Greetings, lady,' he muttered, eyes glued to the floor.

'Oh, go away, George!' said his exasperated father. 'I will speak to you later.' As his son slouched off Richard turned to the giggling little girl who was next in line and brought her forward with a fond arm around her shoulder. 'This little minx is Philippa, who we call Pippa. She can do a fine curtsy, can't you, Pip?'

The skirt of her fawn woollen kirtle folded around her feet as she proved him right. Straight-backed, brown hair braided neatly off her face under a narrow-brimmed coif and huge blue eyes fixed sincerely on mine, she declared in a clear voice with a slight impediment, 'Good day, my lady. I hope you are well.'

I rewarded her with a slight bob of my own and a grave nod of the head. 'I am very well, thank you, Pippa,' I said. 'And how old are you?'

'I am eight,' she replied, adding proudly, 'nearly nine.'

Not to be outdone, the next girl in line trotted forward and made a slightly wobbly curtsy, spreading her green skirt and piping up loudly and clearly, 'My name is Winifred after the saint but you can call me Winnie.'

I bent down to her. 'Thank you, Winnie, I will.'

The sturdy nurse moved up with her wriggling burden and put the child down on unsteady feet. Richard took the toddler's hand. 'This is Elizabeth, born two months before the queen's coronation. For the short time she knew her, her mother called her Lizzie.'

I squatted down to the infant's level. 'Then so shall I, of course. Good day, pretty little Lizzie.' She stared at me briefly, before turning back to her nurse for reassurance and being swept up once more.

'She doesn't say much yet,' said Richard. 'Mistress Fisher here has kindly stayed on to nurse her but I believe she will soon be weaned, is that not so, mistress?'

The nurse gave a brief nod. 'Very soon now, sir,' she said. 'My own children are expecting me home in Kent.'

I made a mental calculation. 'Lizzie must be about sixteen months old now. Many children are weaned by then, are they not?'

To my alarm Mistress Fisher lost no time in stating her case. 'Yes, my lady, and I am already giving her ewe's milk from a feeding cup. I would like to join the next party of Canterbury pilgrims if it is possible, then my husband can meet me at Rochester before Candlemas. Lizzie is a placid little girl. She will be no trouble to you.'

I looked at Richard in some panic. Having no experience with babies or children, weaning a toddler was not something I felt at all confident about, but he ignored my anxious gaze. 'That will be perfectly possible, Mistress Fisher. Your husband will be busy with the plough after Candlemas, no doubt.' He turned to me. 'Tom Fisher is one of our tenant farmers. He will need his wife home for the start of the farming year.'

I gulped. Just when I thought meeting the children had not been quite the nightmare I had feared – it was. Richard then added to my dismay by announcing that he must go and check on the night security at the White Tower and took himself off with a merry wave at his children. 'Do what your stepmother tells you,' he said airily.

For a minute or two after his departure we all stood looking from one to the other and my mind became a whirlwind of doubts. What should I tell them? What did children do as dusk began to fall? They couldn't go out anywhere and there was no sign of supper being served. Should I suggest a game or tell them a story? I felt helpless and useless. Then George took some knucklebones out of his jacket pocket and took himself off to a corner of the hall, rattling them from one hand to the other.

'Anyone want to play Jacks?' he asked vaguely, tossing the bones up and catching them on the back of his hand. 'I'll lay a ha'penny a game.'

None of the three older girls seemed interested and I didn't blame them at those odds. They took themselves off to play some hand-game on one of the window seats and Mistress Fisher sat Lizzie down on the floor with some bricks, so after a minute or two I wandered across to George and said, 'I'll play Jacks with you but I won't gamble, except to bet I'll beat you – best of three.'

That stopped his idle tossing for long enough to allow him to look up at me in surprise. 'Really? I don't think so.'

'You don't think you'll play me or you don't think I'll win?' I asked.

Ignoring my question he sprawled on the floor and scattered five bones, managing to collect up two of them while a sixth was in the air. 'I'm very good, you know.'

I picked up a cushion from another window seat and sat down on it, opposite him on the floor. Leaning over, I took one knuckle from his hand, threw it up and swept up the other bones before catching it. 'I used to play with my brother,' I said. 'Best of three?'

When Martin arrived to announce that the children's supper was ready I had not succeeded in making a friend out of George. Although he had won at Jacks, he suspected that I had let him win and he gathered up his knucklebones without saying a word, shoved them in his pocket and stomped off to help Hugh put up the trestle table. I was pleased to see him lending a hand and unconcerned about his huff. I guessed he might want to play again, to see if he could really beat me.

At this point the governess arrived and introduced herself as Mistress Wood. She told me she was the widow of a bowyer who had worked in the Tower for many years. She struck me as rather too old to be in charge of quite young children but of course I did not say so, being only too grateful for her presence.

'Sir Richard hired me when my husband died and his first wife became pregnant with little Lizzie,' she explained. 'I brought up six children of my own, taught them all to read and housewifery to the girls.' Her voice dropped when she added, 'But it has been difficult here since their mother died. The boy is rude and disobedient and the older girls have ceased to pay attention in lessons. I hope they take to you, my lady.'

I rolled my eyes. 'So do I, Mistress Wood, so do I,' I said quietly, watching the youngsters squabble over who would sit where at the table. 'But I will not be here for long. I have to return to the queen's service so I do hope you will persevere a while longer. Their mother is not long dead. Surely the children's behaviour will improve with time.'

While they ate their supper of bread and cheese and preserved fruit, I fetched my new copy of *The Golden Legend* and asked if any of them would like me to read to them afterwards. George was scathing. 'Stories about saints! That sounds boring.' The two older girls agreed with him, although I suspected Bess only did so because she was apt to copy Maria. So I settled down with Pippa and Winnie on a bench near the fire and read them the story of St Francis, because I thought the fact that he made friends with birds and animals might particularly please them.

George kept playing Jacks with himself, rattling his knucklebones in the background and scoffing at the thought of a man talking to the animals. 'Men hunt animals or farm them, they don't talk to them,' he muttered. But when he heard about the stigmata that appeared on the saint's body he stopped playing and although he did not move nearer, I had the feeling he was listening. Later, when I changed to the story of St Margaret being swallowed by the devil in the shape of a dragon, he crept up behind us and listened in with his back leaning against the bench. For the little girls' sake I missed out the final beheading but I was sure that would have gone down well with George.

Later that evening, before Richard and I partook of our own supper, I went up with him to say goodnight to the children. Maria and Bess were in the large curtained bed while Pippa and Winnie occupied a box bed set up beside it and George, who hitherto had shared a room with his big brother Edward, decided he did not want to sleep alone, so he pulled a truckle bed out from underneath it. 'I'll sleep here,' he announced defiantly.

Richard glanced at me and shrugged. 'Well, there's no harm in it. Mind you, George, you start your service training with Martin tomorrow and if I hear of you giving him any trouble you'll be sleeping in your own room alone – in the dark.'

'That's not fair!' George dived under the covers he had thrown onto the wheeled truckle and it rolled a few feet across the rush matting.

'You forgot to put the brakes on!' his father laughed and bent down to push a couple of wooden wedges against two wheels. 'And don't keep the girls awake with your snoring.'

The boy poked his head out, declaring indignantly, 'I don't snore!'

'Edward says you do,' retorted Maria from her cosy position in the big bed with Bess. 'But you'd better not!'

19

M<small>Y SUMMONS BACK TO</small> the queen's service had arrived by the last Sunday of January, specifying Candlemas, five days later, as the date I should report at Sheen. Sunday mornings at the Tower of London were quiet, as gun drills and archery practice were suspended, so I decided to take all the children, except the infant Lizzie, to Mass at the Church of St Peter. I also hoped to come across some of the regular visiting ravens on the green, knowing that it might be my last chance to encounter them for some time. Richard had ridden off to Kent the previous day, in response to an urgent message from his father, who kept an eye on the shipbuilding business for him during his absences, so there could be no paternal protests about taking the family through Tower Green.

It might have been that the ravens heard the bells ringing people to their Sunday worship, or else they recognised the lack of bustle within the castle walls, for when we emerged from the little church, together with other Tower residents, there was a noticeable gathering of black silhouettes in the bare branches of the alder trees at the far end of the green.

'Oh, I hate those birds! I don't want to go back that way,' protested Bess in alarm. 'Can we go via the Wardrobe Gate instead?'

I was disappointed. Richard had turned the children against the big black birds. 'If you like,' I said. 'Perhaps Mistress Wood might take you that way and I will take whoever would like to visit the ravens. I have never seen so many together before.'

The governess was well informed. 'They're all the young birds who haven't found mates. It's called a conspiracy, because they're up to no good,' she said with a shiver. 'I will gladly take those who want to avoid them by the other route.'

Bess, Pippa and Winnie went with her and although I was not surprised that George chose to come via the ravens, I was astonished that Maria also volunteered. 'Are you sure?' I asked her. 'Most people seem to be afraid of them.'

She was scornful. 'I'm not. Ravens are like us. They can tell if we're afraid of them but if we're not they favour us; especially if we give them presents, and I have something they will love.' She held out a polished black stone that glinted in the flat sun.

'Let me see that!' George pounced, grabbing at the stone, which fell to the ground. 'It's black. What does a black bird want with a black stone?'

Like lightning I snatched it up. 'How did you come by this, Maria?' I asked, although I knew very well, for it was mine.

I had bought it from the apothecary on Cheapside. She had told me that jet prevented conception if held under the tongue during congress. I know, I know, I should not have been deceiving my husband in this way but any woman with an abiding terror of childbirth, such as I have, would understand. One of the reasons I had agreed to marry

Richard was because he already had two boys and four girls and could surely not be too disappointed if there were no more children. Now here was my medicine stone exposed, glinting in the sunshine and claimed by an acquisitive little girl. It was an awkward situation.

While George protested about my determined grip on the stone, I repeated my demand. 'This stone is quite valuable. Tell me please, Maria, where did you get it?'

She bridled. 'I found it on the floor in the house. Someone must have dropped it.'

I put the stone carefully in my skirt purse, pondering her answer. My habit was to keep it in the purse, which I hung on my clothes pole every night. I had used it only two nights before, so she must have found it yesterday. Perhaps I had missed the purse when I returned it there the following day and it fell to the floor unnoticed. I would not have put it past Maria to have wandered into my bedchamber and gone nosing about while I was busy in the domestic quarters, inspecting the storerooms and checking the spice-cupboard as I did every day. But if she knew it was mine would she bring it out now, under my very eyes? Perhaps it had dropped somewhere else when I pulled my kerchief out of my purse. My thoughts raced to no conclusion.

'I will ask around the servants,' I said firmly. 'It may belong to one of them.' I just hoped that Maria had no idea what it might be used for.

'If no one claims it, can I have it back?' she asked slyly.

I shook my head. 'No, Maria, it doesn't belong to you. Nor will it go to the ravens. Come, I have some stale wafers. We'll tempt them with those. Let's see if we can get close enough before they fly off.'

I counted about twenty of them, spread among the small seed cones hanging from the bare branches of the alder trees. If they were juvenile birds, they might be feeling vulnerable, having recently been ejected from the nest site, like young apprentices thrown out into the street on a Saturday night and seeking the safety of a crowd. I hoped a quiet approach and an offer of food might encourage them.

We walked slowly, hugging the inner wall of the green until we reached the horse troughs where I had witnessed the raven pair ambushing a pigeon. Crouching behind one I whispered to George, 'We need to be very calm and quiet now. Try tossing out a few crumbs and see if any of them are brave enough to approach us.' I took a handful of the broken biscuits from the linen bag I had stowed in my purse and gave them to the boy but he was incapable of doing anything calmly. He chucked the wafers over the horse troughs with a shout and some wild arm movements and half a dozen birds rose into the air in alarm.

'That didn't work very well, did it, George,' I said, quickly pulling him down. 'What is calm and quiet about flinging your arms about and yelling? Let's see if Maria can do better.'

I could feel the excitement in the girl's body as I pressed a few wafer crumbs into her hand but she managed to throw them quite far, without disturbing any more ravens, and those spooked by George had settled down again. So we waited, peering cautiously over the trough, hoping for a daring approach.

'Ooh, look! There's one coming!' It was George again, leaping up and forgetting my blandishments about silence and composure. I hauled the boy back down as the brave young raven retreated on the wing. 'I want to catch one!' he complained fiercely in what he thought was a whisper.

'Why, George? What do you want to do with it?' I tried to keep my voice low.

'I want some black feathers to put in my cap.'

'Forget that, George. We're here to watch the ravens, not to catch them. I'm not bringing you again if you're not kind to them.'

'Why should I be kind? My father says they're filthy devils.'

'Why ever would you want feathers from a filthy devil in your cap?'

He looked scathingly at me. 'To scare off Satan, of course.'

I sighed. The task of saving the Tower ravens from destruction suddenly seemed beyond me. If every man and boy in England hated them so thoroughly, they were surely doomed to be hunted out of existence, despite the persistent folklore that their presence in the Tower of London ensured the endurance of both Tower and realm. Here in this fortress, legend and reality clashed, and I feared that any feeble attempt on my part to change attitudes would prove fruitless. Nevertheless I felt a strange affinity with these charismatic birds. I was beginning to believe we were fellow misfits in the world.

'Well, we're not pulling out any feathers today, George, or any other day if I have my way. Now you wait here with Maria. Despite your best efforts to see them off, I want to see if I can get near to these ebony beauties.'

George's outburst had scared all the birds higher and I no longer held out much hope of attracting them down, but I had some wafer crumbs left so I crept nearer and laid a trail backwards from the base of the tallest tree; then I sat down on the sparse winter grass and waited. I didn't even look round to see if the two children were still waiting behind the troughs, thinking that if they weren't, they both at least knew the way home. After what seemed like an hour but must only have been the length of a Mass, I saw movement in the high branches and a bird dropped to the ground not a stone's throw from where I sat. It pecked at the first scrap of wafer and then began to follow the trail, gobbling them up as fast as it could. I soon understood its haste, when another bird followed it and flew down to sample the larger pieces George had hurled at random. The wafers, sweetened with honey, were clearly to the ravens' taste and while there were still some tit-bits left, several more decided to follow the first two. I held my breath and wondered if any would dare to pick up those closest to me. I remained still as a statue, feeling instinctively that at least one might actually make eye contact with me.

Suddenly a loud report resounded around the green, echoing off the surrounding walls and buildings. The ravens all rose in fright, except for the one nearest to me, which struggled and squirmed on the ground, unable to get airborne and flapping only one wing, while the other hung uselessly. I scrambled to my feet and whirled round to check on the children. Sensibly both had crouched down behind the lead water-trough. Glancing the other way I saw a man standing in the arch of the gate, which led onto Water Lane. He held a handgonne in one hand and a smouldering touch-cord in the other. It was Sir Henry Wyatt, unmistakeable in his sumptuously furred gown and prominent curled-feather hat.

As he walked towards me the handgonne was still emitting wreaths of smoke. 'You should not be here, Lady Guildford, and certainly not with children,' he said as if nothing untoward had happened.

My voice shook with anger. 'It is Sunday, sir, and we have been to Mass. It is you who should not be here, at least not with a primed firearm. If you shot this bird, you might have shot me. You could have killed any one of us.'

'This is where we come for practice. The ravens make excellent targets and, as you see, I am a good shot.' He pointed his weapon at the bird, which was still struggling on the ground. A useless gesture because even I knew that a handgonne had to be reloaded after each shot and the process took at least a couple of minutes.

I shrank from the idea of putting the wretched bird out of its misery but nor could I bear watching its pain. 'I hope you will finish the foul job you started, Sir Henry,' I said, turning my back to go to the children, but George was already on his feet and intercepted the knight as he approached the dying bird.

'Will you wring its neck, sir?' he asked excitedly.

'Yes, boy, unless you want to have a try,' Wyatt responded, ruffling the boy's hair.

George almost nodded his head off his shoulders in his excitement. 'Yes please!' he cried, pouncing on the flapping bird.

I was on him immediately, preventing him from grabbing the raven. 'No, George, I forbid it.' I was furious with Wyatt for even suggesting it and clung on to George, who was doing his best to twist out of my grip. 'Finish it off yourself, Sir Henry; but for pity's sake do it out of the sight of the children.'

I began to march George away, dragging him firmly by the collar of his jacket. As he went he yelled, 'Keep me some wing feathers, sir! Please!'

Wyatt gave a grim chuckle as he walked away through the trees with the dying raven, making me suspect that he was wrenching out the big wing feathers while it was still alive. My skin crawled at the thought but George was making too much fuss to allow me to do anything about it. 'My father would have let me do it. I'm going to tell him you stopped me. I hate you!'

Not words I wished to hear. However, there was no doubt that Richard would ask questions, because there was to be evidence of our encounter with the ravens. That afternoon a messenger brought a package to the Tower House addressed to Master George Guildford. Inside was the body of the dead raven and a bloodstained note:

From Sir Henry Wyatt, Comptroller of the Mint and Master of the Jewel House.

I have taken one feather for a quill. Make your selection and pull them out yourself, young man. They will look good in your hat.

And tell your stepmother she should not meddle with the devil's imps.

20

I FELT PROUD WHEN the queen's personal barge came to the Tower Wharf to collect me, with one of her household squires in his royal livery there to supervise the loading of my baggage. The children had all come out to wave me off and the hustle and bustle had attracted a good deal of attention among the porters and mariners on the quayside, especially when the queen's crack team of oarsmen made nothing of tackling one of the narrow tunnel arches under London Bridge just as the tide turned.

It was the first time I had made the journey upstream alone and although it was February and the wind was cold, it was a bright winter's day and I wrapped myself in my fur-lined cloak and sat outside the cabin. Without company to distract me I was able to observe the passing scene change from the tightly packed houses and busy wharves of the City, dominated by the looming presence of St Paul's Cathedral on Ludgate Hill, onwards to the high crenellated towers of Baynard's Castle where the town wall ended, then outside it the parade of bishops' inns and gardens along the Strand, which gave way to the vast complex of Westminster Abbey and the sprawl of buildings that formed Westminster Palace.

I noticed that the royal standard was flying over the palace, indicating that King Henry was in residence, which made me wonder whether the Privy Council was in session without Richard, who was still in Kent, dealing with the problem at his shipyard. I had written to tell him of my departure for Sheen and he had replied that he would be delayed for another week and would then attend on the king, wherever his grace was staying at the time. If he was with the queen at Sheen, Richard would see me there; if not he would come to me as soon as he could. There had been no mention made about the incident with Wyatt and the raven, so I assumed no word of it had reached him.

When the barge docked in the rural tranquillity of Sheen Palace, I left my baggage to the porters and followed my escorting squire through the wintery orchards and gardens. How exciting it was to be shown to my new lady-in-waiting's quarters, the luxury of a chamber to myself containing a curtained bed and a hearth with a fire already lit. When I had warmed my icy hands, I spent my first few minutes examining every detail with proprietorial delight. A wash-stand stood in one corner and a close-stool in a wall-cupboard beside it. A casement window overlooked the orchards through which I had just walked, with a cushioned seat set in the recess beneath the sill. Several clothes poles marched like soldiers along the inner wall beside a space for my travelling chest, when the servants brought it in. I had hardly removed my cloak and rearranged my windblown headdress before the queen's page arrived with a royal summons. My arrival had been reported and no time had been wasted in calling me back to duty.

A guarded entrance connected her ladies' quarters to the

queen's Privy Chamber – her bedchamber, her dressing chamber, her solar and, most importantly, her Great Chamber with its elegant oriel window, which gave a view across a formal garden with hedged flowerbeds and heraldic statues and over a shrubbery leading down to a wide, lazily flowing stretch of the river. I was admitted to it by one of her grace's yeomen guards, resplendent in his tawny working livery. He recognised me and even acknowledged my new status as he saluted with his halberd and threw the door open.

'Welcome back, my Lady Guildford,' he said with the smallest hint of a smile.

A large number of ladies and gentlewomen were gathered in the long room, around the queen seated on her raised and canopied throne. As I rose from my curtsy, Elizabeth drew me close and kissed my cheek. 'I am so very glad to see you back, Joan. You have come at a time of sadness and celebration. My cousin Margaret is leaving us, which is sad, but it is for the happiest of reasons. She expects her first child in late spring.' She stood up and waited while one of her maids of honour gathered up her train. 'Her friends and yours are celebrating her joyful event, so let us go and join them.'

The former Margaret Plantagenet, now Lady Pole, would never be considered beautiful but she had grown taller and the lines of her face had softened, although she showed little outward sign that she was within four months of giving birth. I pitied her the ordeal of carrying a child and bringing it into the world while so young. To my mind it was a dangerous and daunting prospect at any age but to face it at fifteen seemed cruel. The queen left us together and went to converse with other guests.

'I am so glad you have come back, Lady Guildford,' Margaret said when I had wished her well. 'The queen has missed you sorely. She says no one reads to her like you do.'

As I prided myself on my ability to bring the written word alive, I was absurdly pleased to hear this but brushed it off with a return compliment. 'Ah, but she will miss her games of tennis with you,' I said. 'You were always the sporty one among us. I wonder who will challenge her with racket and ball now?'

She made a face. 'I fear my sporting days are over. I grow large and clumsy.'

'Far from it!' I protested. 'Are you sure you are with child? I can see little sign of it yet.'

'Ah, you flatter me, my lady. These court gowns hide a great deal, do they not? But you are just arrived and have no refreshment. Come, let me help you to some meats and cakes.'

As I followed her to a cloth-covered trestle spread with treats, I reflected that this very young woman bore her ill luck in life with laudable grace. Sir Richard Pole was a lucky man indeed.

Having done my duty by queen and hostess, drunk some wine and eaten a little, I made my way through the crowd to seek out my mother and found her talking with Lady Mary Rivers. After we had all embraced, they naturally wanted news of my wedding leave and my impressions of married life but I think they did not greatly like what I had to say.

'Having met Sir Richard's offspring, I find myself envying you both your single status,' I informed them with a wry smile. 'How you put up with my brother and I for the years that you reared us, Mamma, I will never know. I now believe that a governess is a wonderful creature and much to be desired.'

'As long as you have enough funds and lack of heart to employ one,' retorted my mother. 'Wait until you have a child of your own, Gigi. You will change your opinion then.'

Mary Rivers did not condemn me quite so roundly. 'If I could have had a child with my Lord Rivers I'm sure I would have adored it, but alas it was not to be. Instead I have only his young grandchildren to visit in Gloucestershire; the offspring of his daughter Meg. Children you know well, Joan, and, despite what you just said, I seem to remember you taking a particular shine to one of them.'

It was true. After Lady Margaret had been put under house arrest for her conspiracy in the failed Buckingham rebellion, the usurper's agents had ejected all her household companions and servants and I had taken refuge with Meg and Sir Robert Poyntz at their Gloucestershire manor. They had three young children then and I had taken particular interest in the eldest boy, a bright and entertaining lad of four called Anthony after his grandfather, Mary's cruelly executed husband and brother of the Dowager Queen, who at that time had been languishing in sanctuary with her daughters, for fear of the usurper's further retribution. This young Anthony had been a precocious learner and in the twenty months I had spent with them I had taught him to read and write English to a remarkably high standard. He was nearly six when I left and had already grasped the rudiments of Latin.

'You mean Anthony Poyntz, don't you, Mary? You are right, he was a clever child – still is, I imagine. Have you seen him lately?'

'I spent Christmas with them. He is nearly ten now and attends a grammar school in Bristol. His father wants him to follow his own path to the law schools in London and I have said I will help find him a court post to assist with the fees but he is a bit young yet. Perhaps when the time comes you might have a word with Sir Richard? I'm sure Anthony would benefit from the patronage of a Privy Councillor.'

'I certainly will. How many children do the Poyntzes have now?'

Mary laughed ruefully. 'Five; three boys and two girls. Their latest babe is a girl named after both queens. There must be thousands of Elizabeths baptised in England now!'

My mother commented at this point. 'It would be good if the queen could produce another child herself, whether it be boy or girl. She pines to breed again but it does not happen. And while we're on the subject, although I love your brother's two little girls, Gigi, Nicholas's wife shows no sign yet of giving him a boy. I would hate to see your father's Harrowden estates fall back to the crown again for lack of an heir.'

Knowing my shiny piece of jet was safely tucked away in my purse, I scratched my nose to hide a nervous smile behind my hand. 'I'm sure Nicholas is doing his best, Mamma,' I said.

'Well, if he isn't, it will be up to you. The Vaux estates can come down through the female line, you know. It only needs one male in the immediate family to inherit.'

Hurriedly changing the subject I turned back to Mary. 'I have a beautiful chamber now, overlooking the orchard. Are we accommodated close together, I wonder?'

'I think not. The married ladies and the widows are housed on different floors. The Lord Chamberlain doesn't want any husbands creeping into the wrong rooms by mistake.' She giggled. 'Although at Holy Innocents it has been known for the Lord of the Revels to swap door-labels as a prank.'

At this point Princess Anne approached our group. 'Welcome back to court, Lady Guildford,' she said. 'I have not yet had an opportunity to congratulate you on your marriage. I hope it will be a happy one.'

I made her a curtsy. 'Thank you, my lady.' I had not forgotten her remark about my advanced years at the time of my marriage dilemma. Now that she had attained the ripe age of thirteen, I hoped she had developed a little more tact. She had not.

'I have responsibility for the attendance lists now and since you fortunately obeyed the queen by accepting the king's recommendation for your husband, you are on the list of disrobing ladies. She will be pleased to see you this evening when she retires.'

I doubted if Elizabeth would have dismissed me from her intimate attendance just because I had not married the man of the king's choice but of course I did not say so. Anyway we were called to attention by the duty vice-chamberlain, who rapped on the trestle with his white staff of office. I was quite surprised that the princess had not acquired one of these sought-after wands herself but perhaps she considered it too servile an accessory.

'Ladies, the royal barge bearing his grace King Henry and My Lady the King's Mother has just docked, and word has been sent that they will sup with the queen and her household this evening. Please attend their graces here in the queen's Great Chamber after Vespers. And now her minstrels will play for dancing.'

Since I had yet to impress the queen's dancing master with my talent, I decided I could save myself for supper and leave the dancing to the maids of honour, most of whom were of a similar age to Princess Anne and made a prettier sight skipping down a set. Lady Mary and my mother also decided to bow out, choosing instead to come and inspect my new quarters in the 'married ladies' passage.

My mother was shocked that I had returned alone. 'Have you brought no maid with you, Gigi? How are you going to keep your smocks and coifs laundered, your gowns brushed, your room cleaned and tidied, your close-stool emptied and your bedding changed? We have to pack for the queen every time we move from one place to the next, supervise the making of her bed and the emptying of her close-stool, accompany her to Mass, fetch her drinks and comfits, read to her, sew with her, eat with her, attend court functions with her, dress her, undress her, ride out with her and hunt with her. The duties of a lady-in-waiting leave very little time for tending to your own needs. I have Jess with me, as you know, and you must arrange for a personal servant of your own as soon as possible. The Lord Chamberlain's office will arrange for her accommodation with the other retainers.'

I was startled. 'I confess it never occurred to me, Mamma. I was not permitted a servant as a gentlewoman. I should have consulted you before.'

'And you are entitled to stabling for your horses and an allowance for clothes,' added Lady Mary. 'Do you have enough gowns? Have you a gown for tonight's supper with the king, for instance? And who will help you to dress?'

Despite my mother being a lady-in-waiting and having served the queen for three years as a gentlewoman myself, I had failed to consider any of this. 'Perhaps I had better not attend the queen's supper,' I said.

My mother was appalled. 'Oh, but you must, Gigi. You are expected. The queen will notice if you aren't there. We can surely find what you need between us. Show us your gowns and jewel box and we will sort something out.'

My mother was generous enough to lend me her second-best gown that evening but not without provisos. 'Just remember that it's only to be worn when the king is present and I need it back as soon as you've acquired some suitable gowns of your own,' she warned me. 'It cost me nearly two pounds.'

'I thank you for this, Mamma. It is truly beautiful and it will go perfectly with the pearl pendant the queen gave me.'

It was fashioned from wine-red Italian brocade, which complemented a pair of embroidered pink satin sleeves I had brought with me and laced on myself before I donned the gown. I dressed my own hair into plaits and wound them into a coronet to support the fashionable black lappet-hood headdress my friend Rosie and her silkwomen had made for my wedding.

I walked with Mary Rivers as we lined up to follow the royal couple from Vespers in the palace chapel to the queen's supper.

'I believe I recognise one of Lady Vaux's gowns, Lady Guildford.' Princess Anne's appraisal of my attire was less than subtle as she approached her place behind her sister, making the implication that I could not afford such luxurious apparel myself.

Skilfully side-stepping the sin of mendacity, Mary Rivers was quick to my defence. 'And I believe it is not unusual for a mother and daughter to use the services of the same tailor, my lady. Such beautiful fabric certainly bears repetition, I'm sure you agree.'

'It is the only gown that comes out of a travelling chest looking the way its maker intended,' I added. 'That is what a costly fabric can do for you, is it not, my lady?'

The queen's sister passed on by with a loud sniff but no further comment. Mary watched her hurry to catch up with the king and queen and dropped her voice. 'If you ask me, the sooner that young lady becomes a Howard the better; then we might be rid of her sour tongue.'

'Is that marriage still on the cards?' I asked. 'I thought it was another of those cancelled by King Henry as being too Yorkist.'

'Had you not heard? Thomas Howard won a knighthood at the Battle of Stoke and his father has been reinstated as Earl of Surrey. But marriage to a mere knight is not nearly good enough for a princess. She doesn't want to lose precedence, so until the queen can convince the king to restore the Howard family to the dukedom of Norfolk, she remains chief lady-in-waiting. Meanwhile Surrey's heir is holding her to their betrothal; but it could be some time before he gets her to the altar, if ever.'

I grimaced. 'In that case I'd better start ingratiating myself with the Lady Anne by obtaining the right class of gown. Not too dull and not too splendid – one mustn't outshine the queen's sister!'

Mary gave me a lopsided smile. 'I think you're getting the idea, Joan.'

21

As spring moved towards summer, those of us who gave intimate service to Elizabeth had not failed to notice that her monthly effusions had ceased and drew our own conclusions but, as she had suffered two miscarriages since the birth of Prince Arthur, everyone remained tight-lipped on the subject. She knew she was being difficult to please, particularly over food and drink, but the king had headed north to preside over the trials of those involved in another failed uprising and she blamed her bad moods on worry for his life in that hotbed of Yorkist activity. We could do nothing but sympathise and bite our tongues.

Nor was she alone in hiding her condition. As the weeks went by I had to accept the appalling fact that I, too, was pregnant. The black and treacherous piece of jet, in which I had placed such faith, had utterly failed me and the time came when there was no longer any point in pretending to myself that I was suffering the effects of eating rancid cheese or drinking sour ale. I decided that my early bout of sickness at the Tower must have heralded the disaster but luckily there was no more nausea and so with careful loosening of my kirtle lacing I had no difficulty in hiding my plight, except for a sudden and violent distaste for fish, which luckily did not develop until after the Lent fast ended. However, my morbid fear of childbirth escalated and loomed over my future like an evil genie. I genuinely believed that I was living my final months and yet I confided in no one, definitely not in my husband and not even in my mother.

Being a mother though, of course she guessed. The queen had at last made her condition public and the court was making its way in procession from a celebration Mass in St George's Chapel, up through the Middle Ward of Windsor Castle and past the Round Tower, back to the Royal Quarter in the Upper Ward. There was to be a feast in the magnificent Great Hall and I was feeling sick already at the thought of the inevitable fishy smells, wondering if I could make my excuses and retreat to my chamber.

My mother read my thoughts. 'Don't tell me you are going to cry off again, Gigi,' she said. 'People are beginning to think you are seriously ill. Can't you follow the queen's example and announce your pregnancy? Then you can refuse the dishes that give you nausea.'

I glanced around to see if anyone was within earshot. 'How do you know?' I whispered. 'I'm sure it doesn't show yet.' I calculated that I must have conceived almost immediately after my wedding and was therefore more than halfway through my ordeal; or, in my worst nightmares, about four months from death.

Lady Vaux gave what was, for her, an unseemly snort. 'Goodness, Gigi, do you think I would not know when my daughter was carrying my grandchild! It is written all over your face. I grant you that it is not showing on your body yet but that is because you have not been eating properly.

If you don't begin to look after yourself your child will be the one to suffer. Which is why you should make your condition known. Then you can ignore fast days and make whatever demands you like of the cooks.'

I cast another glance around but everyone was busy chatting as they walked and taking no notice of the two of us. 'All I really want is manchet bread and fresh meat but all we seem to get is smoked fish, rye bread and hard cheese. It's the end of May, for heaven's sake. Is there no lamb or spring vegetables to be had yet?'

'Poor Gigi.' My mother's amused smile roused my ire.

'Pray do not laugh, Mamma!' I hissed my disapproval. 'And don't you dare to tell anyone yet.'

She had the grace to look contrite. 'Well, perhaps you will be lucky today. After all, this is a special banquet for the queen's celebration and she is also *enceinte*. Who will be first to give birth, do you think, you or her?'

'How can I be sure? We all knew she was pregnant before she announced it but how long had she been keeping it secret?'

'Well, by my reckoning yours must be a wedding night baby.'

I nodded glumly. 'Yes, it probably is.' I did not tell her about my use of the piece of jet and it was quite possible that I had already become pregnant before I started to use it. 'But we return to London next week and you're not to tell Sir Richard when we get there. He will insist I go back to the Tower House and I do not want to leave court before I have to.'

My mother frowned. 'I won't tell him but I think you should, Gigi. He has a right to know before the court does.'

We had to end our conversation there because the column of courtiers bunched up at the Norman Gate, which led into the Upper Ward. Royal guards checked us all as we filed through. At the entrance to the impressive Great Hall a troop of yeomen in their splendid Tudor green-and-white ceremonial doublets formed a guard of honour for the king and queen and their guests. It was too late for me to make a surreptitious exit.

During the banquet King Henry lavished love and gifts on his queen, thrilled almost beyond words that she was with child again, nearly three years after giving birth to their son and heir, Prince Arthur. Between courses grooms paraded between the garlanded trestles, bearing gifts from the king to his wife, bolts of velvet cloth, tapestries, furs, a carpet, feather beds and sheets of Rennes linen, all to make the remainder of her pregnancy and her eventual confinement as comfortable and luxurious as possible. I began to feel twinges of jealousy. I was married to a man who already had six children. I doubted Sir Richard would give me more than a napkin for what would be his seventh child, but then I reflected gloomily that I wasn't likely to live to appreciate gifts anyway.

The queen rarely managed an entirely private conversation with any of her ladies, except perhaps Mary Rivers when she shared her chamber at night, so I was surprised when Elizabeth made a point of singling me out during her daily walk in the privy garden. That morning the household had been ordered to prepare for departure to Eltham Palace the following day, before returning to Westminster later that month. Queen Elizabeth wished to visit Prince Arthur before travelling became too difficult for her.

'Heaven knows I am grateful to be with child again, Joan,'

she confided as we walked in bright sunshine, 'but it is easy to forget how it restricts one's movements.'

I sighed. 'I would like to be able to say I agree with you, my lady,' I murmured.

She gave me a sharp look. 'Which part of what I said do you disagree with, Joan? Are you perhaps also pregnant?'

I felt the blood rush to my cheeks and I certainly hung my head, so she cannot have doubted what my reply would be. 'I greatly regret to say I am, yes; but not grateful.'

Her face creased into an expression of incredulity. 'Not grateful – why is that? Is childbearing not part of a married woman's lot, ordained by God?'

My eyes remained fixed on the ground, where our skirts stirred the pebbles of the path. 'That is a part of the marriage contract I had hoped to avoid, your grace. Unfortunately it has caught me out.'

She took several more steps before responding. 'Well, it has caught me out too, Joan, because I had been hoping you would take charge of my confinement. You were such a support the last time but now I suppose I will have to rely on someone else.' She did not sound best pleased. 'When do you expect to be delivered? Have you quickened? You show no visible sign yet of being with child.'

'As your cousin Lady Pole remarked to me on her departure, these court gowns disguise a great deal. I think I must be at least a month ahead of you, my lady, perhaps two.'

'Then it is hardly worth you coming to Eltham, is it? I am travelling by barge, of course. Shall we drop you off at the Tower of London on the way?'

My reply probably came a little too hastily. 'I too would like to visit Prince Arthur. Would it inconvenience you to drop me at the Tower on your way back to Westminster? I am sure I will be able to serve you perfectly well for another fortnight.'

Elizabeth stopped and turned to confront me, studying my face. 'Are you not happy in your marriage, Joan?' she asked at length.

I sighed again. 'It is not my marriage that troubles me so much as what goes with it. His first wife is only recently dead and I find it hard being stepmother to his children. But Sir Richard is a kind and considerate man and his demands on me are perfectly reasonable. It is actually the prospect of giving birth that haunts me.' I could not wait for her to resume walking but plunged on up the path at some speed, obliging her to break into a trot to keep up. 'I never wanted children but not because I don't like them, your grace – I do. I love their inquiring minds and their quickness to learn. But I have the most dreadful fear of giving birth. I genuinely believe God does not intend me to survive the process.'

'Slow down, Joan!' Elizabeth panted. 'The others will wonder what on earth is going on and I don't want them to interfere. Let us walk on calmly.'

She was right. The sight of the queen running would bring my mother and Mary Rivers and probably some of the maids of honour who were also taking the air in the garden. I slowed my pace and Elizabeth suggested we take a seat under a trellised arbour where trailing roses were beginning to bud.

I suddenly felt contrite. 'I'm sorry, your grace. I should have given more thought to your condition.'

We sat down together. The warmth of the sun drew out

the nascent perfume of the roses and succeeded in steadying my nerves. 'It is not my condition that concerns me,' said Elizabeth. 'It is yours. I think your time is nearer than it might appear. If you do not wish to take your leave yet, I want you to get more rest. You have been serving me on rising and when I retire at night. I will tell my sister to reduce your duties and order Brice to prepare you some beef broth. My mother had some every day when she was pregnant and she successfully birthed twelve children – several of them in very trying circumstances. It need not be a death warrant, you know.'

Her words did not go far to console me but they did inspire a suggestion. 'You are right,' I said, 'and I will bear your words in mind. But as far as your own confinement is concerned, why don't you ask your mother to take charge of it again? You pointed out that she has more experience than anyone else and it would be good for you to spend some time together.' It was probably not necessary but I took the precaution of checking there was no one within earshot before continuing. 'I know she claims to be happy at Bermondsey Abbey and visits court at Christmas and Easter but I'm sure she would be delighted to spend more private time with you. Lady Margaret rather took over arrangements last time, especially after Prince Arthur's birth, but you have every excuse to hand responsibility to your own mother this time, do you not?'

I realised afterwards that I had probably spoken well out of turn but fortunately Elizabeth seemed to welcome the suggestion. 'That is a good idea, Joan, and she might be able to steer Anne a little in her role as chief lady-in-waiting. I think she has not grasped the social niceties of it. But first of all I want to see you smile again and I will join you. We have both been too melancholy of late.'

This conversation had consequences I had not foreseen, although I probably should have. When the queen and her ladies gathered for their afternoon recreation Princess Anne, with knitted brow and metaphorically breathing fire, immediately confronted me.

'How dare you announce your pregnancy directly to the queen, Lady Guildford?' she demanded. 'The protocol is to inform the chief lady-in-waiting, who will tell the Lord Chamberlain or his deputy, who will convey the news to her grace. She has the affairs of the kingdom to worry about. She should not have to listen to the minor worries of a servant, particularly not those of one barely qualified to be called lady!'

I closed my eyes and rubbed at the beads of the rosary I had only minutes ago been using to direct my prayers to the Almighty. If the Dowager Queen should attempt to steer her younger daughter in the best way to perform her royal office I wished her luck. She had a mighty task ahead of her.

But I knew how to calm the princess's easily raised hackles. 'I humbly beg your pardon, Lady Anne. I merely answered with the truth when her grace asked me a direct question. I hope you would not expect me to lie to the queen.'

'You mean my sister actually asked you if you were pregnant? Why would she do that? You do not look pregnant.' My grovelling did not appear to be working this time. If anything Lady Anne's indignation level had risen several notches.

I lifted my shoulders. 'I don't know. Perhaps it takes one mother-to-be to recognise another. But I did not mean to undermine your authority in any way, and nor did she.' I hoped my ingratiating smile would smooth the creases from her brow but I was to be disappointed. She left me with a pronounced flounce of her skirts.

I didn't know if she upbraided the queen as well but I would not have been surprised. There was a great deal of her mother in Lady Anne and I was glad I would not be sharing the queen's confinement with them this time. It was a slither of comfort in the purgatory of my own pregnancy.

22

I SAW VERY LITTLE of Richard after I returned to the Tower House towards the end of June. He was overseeing the supply of guns and ammunition to three of the king's ships and was due to captain one of them himself on a sortie to patrol the Channel in support of Brittany against renewed French aggression. I was rapidly discovering that there was no end to the versatility of my multi-talented husband – gunner, architect, shipbuilder, ship's captain, knight and courtier. When I did at last manage to tell him that he was going to be a father again he gave me a smugly satisfied look and at least promised to return from his mission in time for the birth, which I told him would probably be towards the end of September. 'Although that is a guess, rather than a certainty,' I added.

Having a well-practised facility with numbers it took him less than half a minute to work out when the baby had been conceived. 'You'd better make sure it's no earlier or people will gossip that we anticipated the wedding,' he remarked solemnly, but he was obviously pleased; I only wished I could feel the same way myself.

By time that I undeniably looked pregnant but was not yet too cumbersome to renew my acquaintance with the ravens. As soon as Richard left I began to seek their company again, visiting any of the towers and battlements to which I was admitted, and several where I was not. To my surprise, when Maria discovered that I was making daily trips to the alder trees on Tower Green she asked if she could come with me. Pleased to be able to share my obsession, I adjusted my visits to avoid her sessions with Mistress Wood and we made regular afternoon trips to the green together, taking a variety of bribes with which to tempt the birds into our company. After a couple of weeks we discovered that ravens will eat almost anything but their favourite treats were morsels of raw meat and any dead mice removed from the traps set around the house. Failing these we resorted to stale wafers and dried fruit. These wild birds had as much of a taste for sweet things as we did.

At first Maria was hesitant about getting too close to the ravens and balked at handling dead rodents but after watching me tempt the birds into several snatch-and-grab events, when brave juveniles made sudden raids on the treats that I placed within my reach, fluttering away joyfully with their treasures, she set about following my lead. Annoyingly she seemed to attract them closer and more quickly than I did. Perhaps they liked her triumphant giggles when they pecked up her offerings and one of them actually appeared to stop and thank her with a nod and a 'chirrck', before flying back to the shelter of the trees to consume its prize.

Sitting close to the trees meant we kept out of the way of the soldiers attending their regular practices on the guns and at the butts. However word of our presence soon reached Sir Richard on his return from his Channel patrol and it wasn't long before he confronted me with my misdemeanour.

'How dare you expose my daughter to those evil birds, madam!' he exploded over our family dinner one day. 'I have received reports that you and Maria have been feeding the ravens on a regular basis, encouraging them to haunt the Tower and spread their dirt and devilish influence on my men. I forbid you to continue this practice!'

I wanted to protest loudly that the ravens meant no harm to his daughter or his men but Maria leaped to their defence before I could speak. 'They are not dirty or devilish, Father! They are beautiful and intelligent and deserve our respect. And they bring good luck, not bad.'

Richard rounded on her. 'Who has filled your head with such idiocies, Maria? Surely not your governess?'

I felt bound to intervene. 'It has nothing to do with Mistress Wood,' I said. 'Maria asked me if she could come with me to feed the ravens and of course I agreed. Her opinions of them are her own.'

'Or are they yours, wife? You have been filling her head with ugly thoughts!'

I had never seen this side of Richard before: eyes narrowed, words delivered with angry ferocity. Once again Maria spoke up defiantly. 'I am not voicing anyone else's opinions, Father. I make my own decisions and I find the ravens creatures to be admired, not vilified.'

I don't believe Richard had ever heard his daughter stand up to him in this way before and it obviously stunned him. For several moments he was lost for words and then he switched his attention to me again, his voice now full of reproach. 'You have turned Maria against me, madam. How could you do such a thing?'

I was horrified. 'No, sir! I have merely watched her come

to realise that all God's creatures are His creation and we should treat them with respect. Ravens are part of His plan; they help to keep our city and castle free of pests and carrion and we should encourage them, not oppress them. If you look kindly into their eyes you will see intelligence and empathy but if you mistrust them and call them ugly names they will show you fear and anger. The Tower should protect them, not persecute them, and in return they will rid us of rats and mice and biting insects. That is what God intended. They are our friends.'

There was a tense silence as Maria swung her gaze from Richard to me, then back again. 'Mother Joan is right, Father. And plenty of people believe that when the ravens leave the Tower, the kingdom will fall.' I dared not show it at that juncture but I was astonished and elated to hear her call me 'Mother Joan'.

At this point George chose to weigh in with his view in his forthright way. 'Well, I think Father is right. They are the devil's disciples; that's what the soldiers say, because ravens haunt the battlefield and peck out the eyes of the injured as well as the dead.'

Further down the board Richard noticed his younger daughters' eyes widen in alarm and quickly picked up his knife to slice into his manchet loaf. 'We will not continue this conversation now; we will eat our dinner. But I would be obliged if you did not invite Maria to join you when you feed the ravens, Joan.'

I gave a sigh. 'Very well.'

Maria grabbed the last word and flummoxed us both. 'I do not need to be invited. I will feed them anyway,' she declared.

Maria was as good as her word and when I grew larger and slower to rise from my bed, I often found her already under the alders with her tempting tit-bits. I worried about her safety when so many soldiers and archers frequented the other end of the green but there was always a yeoman guard at the Lieutenant's lodging and I asked them to watch out for any untoward approaches. The haughty Lieutenant I had encountered on my visit to learn the bed-making system had been replaced and the new one was Sir John Digby, a young retainer of the Tower's Constable, the Earl of Oxford, who had been knighted in the field like Richard, during King Henry's victorious expedition to win the crown. I had made a point of becoming acquainted with him and discovered that he was also an admirer of the ravens. We were beginning to make some progress in bringing the inhabitants of the Tower around to our way of thinking.

At the start of September I began to make arrangements for my lying-in. I had no intention of going into confinement like the queen did, mainly because I wanted to enjoy every moment of what I genuinely feared might be my last days. Aware that Richard had lost his first wife to complications of childbirth, I kept silent about my own dread, telling myself it was entirely in God's hands and I should simply place myself at His mercy. I had gratefully accepted Rosie's recommendation of the experienced midwife she had employed for her own labour and arranged for her to be on standby towards the end of the month. Her name was Lettie Stock and she had asked me questions and felt my belly for signs, before nodding agreement about the probable week of delivery. Luce, as always, helped me with making sure there was plenty of fresh linen and I sent Hugh to the Blackfriars apothecary with a list of requirements.

Having stayed by Elizabeth throughout the birth of Prince Arthur, I thought I was fully aware of what to expect, only too aware indeed, but in fact everything about my delivery turned out completely different. Whereas she had been cocooned in peace and quiet for several weeks, with nothing to do but embroider and be read to, I was still making my rounds of the household stores, agreeing lists of necessities with the cook, attending the church regularly for Mass and visiting the ravens on the green. I dismissed the first signs of my labour as mere twinges of the sort I had been having on and off for days and carried on until bedtime without telling anyone. It must have been my way of denying the inevitable. I slept well because Richard had been in attendance on the king at Westminster Palace and decided to stay the night there, so I had the bed to myself. Waking early I felt the first real pangs of childbirth, so strongly that the first one took my breath away. I stumbled to the chamber door, calling out for Luce but she couldn't have heard me, for after two or three more calls it was Maria who appeared from the other wing of the house, rubbing sleep from her eyes.

'What is it, Mother Joan? Is it the baby?'

I nodded speechlessly as another spasm took my breath away and it was some time before I could summon words. 'Yes, Maria. Can you go and ask Hugh to fetch the midwife? He knows where she lives. But put on your chamber robe first.' She was wearing only her smock. 'And wake Luce too. I may need help getting back into bed.'

I stumbled back into my room but instantly understood

why we had prepared a special pallet bed for the delivery because I could not contemplate the effort of clambering back into the high tester bed I had left only minutes before. As another cramping pain tore through me I collapsed onto the large chest where my clothes were stored and concentrated on breathing, gasping air into my lungs. It felt as if this living creature inside me was wildly battering its way out with no consideration for the body that had carried it so safely for so many months. I suffered two or three more assaults before Luce put in an appearance, having obviously dressed in haste. By this time I was shivering, partly in fear and partly from cold, because at the end of September the mornings were chilly and a sharp breeze was swirling in the empty hearth. I had felt my way to the door without lighting a candle and the first thing the maid did was open the shutters on the window behind me so that she could see what was going on. Grey morning light revealed me to her as a gasping, shuddering figure slouched on the chest with her arms wrapped around her huge belly and her eyes wide with fright.

The first thing she did was to pull a cover from the bed and wrap it around me. 'Oh my lady, you are freezing! How long have the pains been coming?'

I shook my head and stuttered. 'I don't know. I was sleeping and they woke me up.' I paused to breathe through the next onslaught as Maria reappeared, wrapped in her chamber robe and remarkably calm.

'Where do you want us to put the delivery pallet, Mother Joan? If you tell us Luce and I will arrange it.'

But my brain seemed to have turned to pottage. I could hardly even remember what the arrangements were, let alone put them into words. 'So cold . . .' I whispered. 'Can't think.'

'The boys' chamber is free now that George insists on sleeping with us,' said Maria. 'I've been begging to move into it myself but Father won't let me sleep alone. We can set up the pallet bed in there but I don't like to leave Mother Joan on her own. Can you get the steward to help you, Luce? He should be breaking his fast by now in the kitchen.'

The part of my brain that still functioned recognised that Maria was proving to be a remarkably sensible young lady, even though she had only recently celebrated her thirteenth birthday. But as soon as a rational thought entered my head it was abruptly dismissed by another searing contraction in my belly and the real world vanished into a vortex of pain. I lost all sense of time and place and hardly noticed how I was transported from the bedchamber to the hastily arranged pallet bed, onto which I was lowered and into which I gratefully sank. Soon afterwards I became aware that Mistress Stock had arrived and begun to examine me in ways I would never have tolerated had I been in full possession of my faculties, which was far from the case.

My hearing was not affected however and although she lowered her voice I clearly heard her say to whoever was there in the room with her, 'The babe is breeched. I will need to try and turn it but it may be too late. It's a pity I was not called yesterday. My lady has been in labour for a long time already.'

'She showed no sign of it yesterday.' It was Luce who spoke, the trembling tone revealing her anxiety.

'This is her first child. Many inexperienced mothers think the pains are just the babe kicking harder than before. In my lady's case that may be true. This one is trying to kick its way out and getting nowhere. We need to get her on her hands and knees. I'll need your help.' The midwife threw off the quilt. 'First we must turn her on her side.'

I freely admit that I protested loudly at this treatment but my shouts were ignored as the two women managed to draw my knees up and tip me over onto them, then Luce supported my arms by the shoulders because they tended to buckle when the pain was at its peak. I had to use all my strength and hers not to topple down onto my belly, bolstered by an instinctive fear that by doing so I might seriously damage my unborn child. With my eyes tight shut I tried desperately to dismiss from my mind the fact that Mistress Stock was invading my woman's parts in an unimaginable way. I could not close my ears however and groaned at what I heard her say next.

'Her waters have not run. I will have to break the sac before I try to turn the child and then we will have to get the babe born quickly, otherwise it will not survive.'

At this point a crazy notion grew in me during the short pauses between contractions. It had been a mistake to employ such an experienced midwife. One with less knowledge would just have let me succumb to the pain and the wracking cramps and slip into oblivion, not insisted on trying to save both my baby and me. I had always known that childbirth would kill me and now I prayed that death would come like a benevolent angel. While this thought was occurring I felt a terrible tugging inside and my whole body seemed to lurch as something began to move slowly within, guided by strong fingers on the stretched skin of my stomach.

'I think the head is down!' There was a thrill of victory in the midwife's voice and somehow she lifted me bodily onto my haunches. My arms felt as if they would spring from their sockets until Luce took one and pulled it over her shoulder, allowing Mistress Stock to do the same with the other. I hung between them like pegged washing, my soaked smock clinging to my belly. 'Well done, Luce! Hold her tight. We'll let Mother Earth pull the baby out.'

By now I was completely heedless of what was happening to me or to my poor child. I felt like a rag doll being mauled by an animal and all I could do was hang my head and groan louder and louder as the pains went wild. There were no pauses now, just one long continuous bolt of lightning tearing me in half, and two panting, shouting women urging me to push down. It was all I could do to breathe, let alone follow their instructions, but suddenly and absurdly I had an irresistible urge to sneeze, and as she heard my jerky intakes of air I felt the midwife's hand, still sticky with the fluids of her earlier activity, suddenly clamp over my mouth and nose. The result was that the force of my sneeze was directed inward, pounding down on my womb and more or less expelling the child within like a cork popping from a fermenting cask. My eyes flew open with surprise to see a bloody, mucus-covered object fall at my feet, into the soft, wet safety of the ruined feather bed on which I had been laid a lifetime before.

Luce took my entire weight as the midwife pounced on the little body and whipped it away before I collapsed back onto the pallet, careless of whether I was alive or dead. In fact I was neither, as I had fainted. Luce kindly covered me, temporarily hiding the devastation that was now my lower half. They had saved both my baby and me but only time would tell whether either of us would survive the delivery.

23

'MOTHER JOAN! MOTHER JOAN! Oh do look, you have a little boy.' The voice reached me through a fog of dreams, which I had thought were visions or saintly visitations until my mind adjusted slowly to reality. It was not the Virgin Mary who was leaning over me but her namesake Maria, her pale blonde hair hanging in loose curls over her shoulders. As I blinked awake her bright blue eyes drilled earnestly into mine, bringing me gradually to full consciousness.

'A boy?' I echoed faintly. 'Does he live?'

Maria smiled. No one smiles at death, so that blessed parting of her lips told me that I must be alive myself. 'Yes, of course. He is perfect. Here, let me show you.'

I tried to pull myself up but pain shot through me like an arrow and I collapsed back on the pillows. I seemed to be in my own bed and beside me was the cradle I remembered buying from a city carpenter, what seemed like months ago. Maria was bending over it and gently lifting a linen-wrapped parcel from its shelter. 'Here he is,' she said, her voice soft with wonder. 'We all went to the church for the baptism and my father said his name is Henry. Sir John Digby, the Lieutenant of the Tower, is his godfather and I am his godmother. I hope you approve.'

She announced this so proudly that I tried to smile, although it was a weak effort. I managed to lift one hand from the sheets to touch the child's pink cheek.

'Do you want to hold him?' Maria sounded doubtful. 'Are you strong enough?'

I moved my head in weak refusal. 'No, not yet, Maria but I can see he is in safe hands. He has the perfect godmother.' She gave me another smile. If I did not recover my strength at least my son had a stout supporter in his half-sister. 'Does he have a nurse? Has she arrived?' I had appointed a breast nurse to feed my child and vetted her personally to make sure she was clean and healthy. She was the wife of one of the garrison's archers and had been intending to wean her own year-old daughter.

'Yes, she's already fed him twice. You have been asleep for a long time.' Maria turned to place the baby back in his cradle. 'Luce and the midwife bathed you and put you to bed and you never blinked an eye apparently.'

'It was not an easy birth,' I said, thinking what an understatement that was. 'Is the midwife still here?'

'No, she had to go to another birth. She carried the baby to the church though, as is her prerogative. He cried when he felt the holy water so the devil was dismissed. Are you happy with the name Henry?'

I grimaced. 'Don't tell your father, Maria, but I think there are too many Henrys and Elizabeths being baptised at present. I shall call him Hal and I hope you and your brothers and sisters will too.'

She gave it some thought before agreeing. 'Hal is a good name. I like it.'

'Good. I'll tell your father what we've decided and assure

him that if Hal ever gets a knighthood, then he can be called Sir Henry.'

'Luce said you'd probably be hungry when you woke. I'll go and get you something.'

'You might have to help me eat it. I doubt if I can lift a spoon.'

It pleased me so much that Maria had shed her initial hostility towards me. In the next few days and weeks she took it upon herself to be my personal nurse and I certainly needed one. Delighted though I was that Mistress Stock had succeeded in saving my beautiful baby boy, the process had undoubtedly used up every ounce of my strength and I still feared that my ordeal might not be over. I would like to have asked the midwife exactly what she had needed to do in order to deliver little Hal successfully and what advice she might have to stave off any post-natal problems, knowing as I did from my medical reading that fevers and other physical after-effects might not reveal themselves until some time after the birth. But it was not a subject I felt able to discuss with Maria or Luce because I thought neither would have the experience or the knowledge to help me. So when Richard finally visited my bedside, having returned from the works at Westminster Abbey, I asked him if he would summon Mistress Stock again.

He agreed to do so the following day. 'But you will recover, Joan, won't you?' he asked me nervously. 'I know it was a traumatic birth but Henry is fine and Mistress Stock said she was confident that you would be too, in time.'

'I think "traumatic" might be an understatement,' I responded. 'I would appreciate a visit from the priest as I think I will need the Almighty's help. By the way, I take it that Maria has not told you that I intend to call my son Hal.'

His brows almost met in a frown. 'Why? What objection can you have to calling him after the king?'

'Only that everyone has done the same lately and there will be far too many Henrys at court by the time little Hal is of an age to serve the king. I'm sure you can see that. What do they call your Edward at court? Not by his full name, I'm sure.'

He gave a rueful smile. 'They call him Ned.'

I gave an exhausted sigh and felt my eyelids droop. 'Exactly. So we might as well start straight away with Hal.'

This conversation turned out to be the last coherent words I spoke for some days. Unfortunately, although Mistress Stock came again she was only able to give Luce a detailed list of cures to get from the apothecary and advised against sending for the barber to bleed me, suggesting that I had already lost enough blood during the birthing. Later I was told that I burned with fever and might have died if it had not been for Maria and Luce's tireless sponging with cold cloths and spooning of a yarrow tincture down my parched throat. All I could remember afterwards was a series of vivid dreams of following Dante through the gates of hell and finding his chosen sinners languishing under their various forms of torture. When I finally struggled back to consciousness I felt so weak that any further loss of blood might have put a final end to me. I became nauseous at the putrid stench of the napkin when poor Luce had to change me every few hours like a baby. I do not know how she did it without vomiting and I promised myself to reward her lavishly when – if – I recovered my strength.

Young Hal proved to be a good deal more resilient than I was and Maria showed herself a perfect mother substitute, rocking her godson tirelessly and carrying him about when he was fractious. The nurse who suckled him slept beside his cot but if she failed to wake when he cried, it was often Maria who went to comfort him and rouse her to feed him in the night. I was tempted to try and suckle him myself but the fever and evil discharges had put paid to any chance I had of doing that.

It was not until the end of November that I was well enough to be churched and take the holy sacrament, which I had at one time feared I might only receive in the last rites. Walking very slowly through the green afterwards on Richard's arm, I was pleased to see a pair of ravens perched in the branches of the alders and if he was tempted to reprimand her, he desisted while we watched Maria pause to spread some tasty morsels on the ground below. To my surprise both birds quickly came to feast and even allowed Maria to approach and talk to them. She admitted to me afterwards that she had been visiting the roost regularly but only those two particular ravens had responded favourably to her presence.

'I think they are a bonded pair, Mother Joan. I know how to recognise them now; they are always together and act like a married couple, preening each other and roosting closely at nightfall. It has been lovely to watch their friend-ship grow. I was wondering if we should consider erecting a roost box for them. It would be warmer in the winter and it might protect them from hostile soldiers.'

'Have you seen any sign of soldiers persecuting them?' I asked. 'Sir John Digby assured me that under his lieutenancy the garrison archers would not use the birds for target practice any more.'

Maria looked dubious. 'I'm not sure if they all obey that order. When they haven't known I'm nearby, I've certainly heard some archers making bets about who will make the first raven kill. How sad it would be if one of this pair were to be killed and the other left alone.'

The following day Sir Richard returned unexpectedly early from a trip to Westminster Palace with worrying news. 'I could not gain admittance,' he said. 'Apparently the queen gave birth to a daughter yesterday and at the same time an outbreak of spotted fever was reported in the City. The palace is in lockdown, for fear of it spreading into the royal lodgings and particularly the new princess's nursery. She has already been baptised Margaret after the king's mother, just in case. Young children are particularly susceptible to the disease apparently, so I have ordered our baggage to be packed ready to depart for Kent tomorrow. We cannot risk the health of the children.'

'There are many types of spotted fever,' I observed. 'Did your informant know which kind it is?'

'He said it was the measles – the type that affects the eyes and ears as well as spreading a rash all over the skin. We need to avoid it at all costs as it is quite often fatal but can also cause deafness and speech defects. I've hired two baggage wagons and if you are not up to riding a horse, Joan, you can travel on one of them.'

I gave it some thought and decided that the cart would be more uncomfortable than a horse. 'I will ride side-saddle but I fear the breast nurse will not be able to come with us. She will not wish to leave her family and so we will have to acquire some ewe's or goat's milk during the journey to keep Hal going, until we can hire another nurse in Kent.'

Richard grunted. Such domestic details were not his field of concern. 'This move into country air could be good for you, Joan. You must stay at Halden Hall until you are completely well.'

Luce began packing the travel chests while I took time to pen a letter to the queen, congratulating her on the birth of Princess Margaret and apologising that I would not be able to return to her service as soon as had been expected. I also said I would pray that God would protect them all from the spotted fever. After the messenger had departed I realised that I should probably have directed my communication through the chief lady-in-waiting but if the Lady Anne objected I would not be there to receive her reprimand.

I had not been on horseback for some months and had no idea how much my muscles had softened. I was at the stage of recovery when I could haul myself up the stairs in the Tower House but just sitting on a horse sideways at walking pace for hours on end meant that when I dismounted my legs threatened to throw me to the ground and my back shrieked with pain. At our overnight stay in a Maidstone inn I was barely able to climb the stair to our chamber and had to leave Hal to the care of Luce and Maria.

'I have fed him all the milk the breast nurse gave us,' the girl confessed when she brought Hal to me later. 'We'll have to find a fresh supply tomorrow. I've also fed and watered the ravens and left their cage in the cart. It should be all right.'

I kissed Hal and winced as I bent to place him in the cradle Richard had acquired from the innkeeper. 'Does your father know they're with us yet?'

She shook her head, grinning triumphantly. 'He's off to meet with a Maidstone bailiff or some other goodman. I don't think he'll find out until we get to Halden.'

Fearful for their safety in the Tower without us, she and I had managed to lure the raven pair into one of the wicker cages that were used to carry live chickens from the market, intending to find them a safe roost somewhere in the Halden demesne.

'Well done, Maria,' I said, collapsing gratefully back onto the bed. 'You are a clever girl, who is going to make some lucky man a very organised wife one day.'

'Only if he likes ravens,' she commented over her shoulder as she left.

24

Our journey took us across the middle of Kent and by the time we had climbed into the High Weald my aches had eased considerably. I was actually able to look about me with interest and appreciate the beautiful vistas over land scattered with neat fruit and nut orchards, watered by steep river valleys and dominated by forests of magnificent oaks, now stripped of their leaves and showing their impressive skeletons of sturdy branches and gnarled trunks. I relished the flashes of colour as birds flitted through the high branches and the sharp tang of fallen fruit rotting beneath the bare orchard trees in their tidy hedged enclosures. Harvest was well and truly over and the earth was settling into quiet hibernation as it moved towards the winter solstice.

Sir Richard reined in his big bay stallion to bring it into line with my steady mare. He wore a cuirass over his boiled-wool gambeson and had a helm and mace slung from the pommel of his saddle, in case of any random attack by highway brigands, but we'd had no reports of troublemakers on our route. The children were all riding their ponies, with the exception of little Lizzie, who was nestled down in the well of the cart with Mistress Wood perched on the seat above her. A stack of baggage filled the space behind them.

'It's not far now, Joan. You have travelled well.' He glanced over my horse's head at the cart, beside which I had ridden most of the way. Hal was tucked in a box behind the driver, lulled to sleep by the plod of hooves and the sway of the wagon. 'Hal has too, it would seem.'

'Yes, but we must find him a breast nurse as soon as possible. Or else buy a milking nanny goat. This cow's milk does not agree with him. He has come out in spots.'

His face blanched. 'Not the measles?'

I shook my head. 'No, it's a milk rash – at least I hope it is. He's not feverish; in fact he doesn't seem to notice it at all. It just worries me.'

'I'll send out the harbinger to ask around the manor farms. He can gallop on now and get started if you like.'

I nodded. 'Yes, it's a good idea. The sooner the better.'

After our arrival at Halden Hall, it was some time before I had a chance to look around, because having slept through the last part of the journey following the dinner break, the baby was hungry and restless and Luce, who had ridden in the cart with him, brought him to me almost immediately to be fed and changed, apologising needlessly.

'I know you will want to look around, my lady, but Hal does not take well to my handling I'm afraid, and at least I can do the unpacking while you tend to him.'

Of course I took my son and attended to his needs without hesitation but it meant I had to leave Maria to take charge of the ravens and it was not long before Richard discovered them as she tried to smuggle them into the mews. Looking forward to getting in some hawking before he made the return journey to London, he had encountered his daughter in the bird-filled outbuilding, trying to find a suitable place for the ravens. Maria came to me in tears afterwards.

'It was horrible, Mother Joan,' she sniffed. 'He was terribly angry but he couldn't shout in the mews because it would disturb the hawks and so he grabbed the cage and took it outside, swinging it as if he wanted to hurl it away. Of course the ravens objected and started kronking loudly, so he strode off into the woods at the back of the house and just opened the door.' Her bright blue eyes were red from crying but she screwed up her face angrily and dashed the tears off her cheeks. 'You can imagine what happened. The birds scrambled out and flew off into the branches of a pine tree. They've gone, Mother Joan. We'll never get them back.'

I was trying to wind Hal, holding him over my shoulder and rubbing his back, and I had to contain my fury in order not to alarm him. He had taken some more of the fresh cow's milk we had obtained at the first of the Guildford farms we passed, as they'd had no other kind available, and I had to hope that the harbinger might have had more luck with his searches. Hal's face was spotted with little dots. I took comfort in the fact that they were white and not red, which would somehow have seemed more threatening.

I wandered to the window where the shutters still stood open. Outside the sky was a deep shade of purple – the sign of a storm coming? How would our ravens fare in a strange place in thunder and pouring rain? Surely they must have survived such conditions before. I tried to comfort Maria. 'You said they flew into the branches of a pine tree. There must be plenty of shelter among all those needles. Perhaps they'll roost there and we'll find them in the morning. We can't go hunting for them now, Maria. It will be dark soon.' I was angry with Richard but it would do no good to express that anger to his daughter.

'I simply do not understand you, Joan,' Richard began on a familiar note, when he strode through the door half an hour later and found me pacing the floor of the bedchamber, to and fro past the end of the velvet-hung tester bed, rocking my distressed, crying son, who showed no sign of going to sleep. His father suddenly abandoned indignation and peered anxiously over my shoulder. 'What is the matter with him?'

I took a steadying breath before answering. 'He has slept all day and seems to want to tell me that he has no intention of sleeping again before he has worn himself out. Either that or he is sick.' I turned to face my husband; a tracery of tears of worry and frustration must have been visible on my cheeks.

Richard reached out and took the baby from me. 'Here, let me try. He senses your distress.'

'Of course I am distressed,' I told him, grateful to relinquish my screeching burden for a while. 'Maria came and told me you opened the ravens' cage. She has been nurturing those birds for weeks and you just tossed them out.'

Hal had suddenly gone quiet, surprised by the change of bearer. Richard gave me a triumphant look. 'I have the gift,' he said smugly, then added, 'One cannot put ravens in with hawks and falcons, Joan. They are each other's enemies.' The baby lay peaceful and silent in his arms, gazing up at his father with apparent adoration. I was astonished and not a little jealous. I used my kerchief to remove the evidence of my weeping from my face and nose. The silence was blissful, even though it made me feel inadequate for not having 'the gift'.

'Could you not have told Maria that and let her find somewhere else to keep them? She loves those birds.'

Richard was doing some gentle rocking and Hal's eyes flickered shut. 'As far as ravens are concerned I do not understand either of you but I am sorry to have upset Maria. If she loves them so much perhaps they will stay nearby.' He looked around the room. There was evidence of baby care everywhere – discarded chemises, soiled wraps and a cradle in one corner. Someone had obviously prepared it for Hal. Richard walked across and placed the sleeping baby in it, tucking the coverlet around him. 'There. Let us send Luce in to watch him and tidy up the room. If you are up to it, I will take you on a tour of the house. You are mistress here now, Joan. You need to know your way about. Tomorrow we will find a breast nurse and someone to rock the cradle.'

To him it was apparently all so simple and I hoped it would be.

Richard explained that Halden Hall had started life a hundred years before as a simple farmhouse, when what was now the great hall had once been both barn and homestead. Later its upper floor had been removed revealing ancient oak roof timbers, and a chimney and hearth had been built on the eastern wall where a fire now burned brightly. A central trestle was already laid for a family supper, a sight that stirred my appetite. At the far end a carved wooden screen shielded draughts from the main entrance hall, which contained a fine wooden staircase leading to the new living quarters.

A couple of male servants had unloaded the baggage carts and were still carrying baskets and travelling chests up to the various bedchambers located in the upper floors of two wings, which formed a paved court. We squeezed past them to enter a covered gallery that linked these accommodation wings and from it there was a panoramic view down the lush green valley in which the house was set. Through diamond-glazed windows, in the deepening dusk I could just make out the wide moat at the far side of the front court and the stone bridge and gatehouse that spanned it.

'I cannot see clearly but I sense that from this spot in daylight you overlook most of your estate,' I said. 'It is a beautiful house, Richard. You must be very proud of it.'

'Well, the Halden estate is still my father's but he passed the house over to me when I started my family. My mother had died and my sisters married and left, so when he is not serving the king on a commission somewhere he lives with his second wife at one of our other manors nearby. They have no children. Its farm is where we stopped for milk on the way down but he is not there at present so we did not call at his hall.'

'Do the Guildfords hold a lot of property in this area then?'

He smiled. 'When you are more used to riding again I'll show you more of our landholdings. We'll make a tour.'

'It is a beautiful part of England,' I said. 'I'll look forward to that.'

The following day Richard took Maria, George and Pippa with him on their ponies, to follow up his harbinger's suggestions about possible nurses for Hal. Choosing to avoid the saddle for the time being, I decided to acquaint myself further with the house and its surroundings and, as it was a crisp and sunny day, I tied Hal into a shawl on my chest and ventured out through a back entrance to explore the rear court.

A high, crenellated stone wall defended the back of the hall, against which stood a range of timbered farm buildings and at one corner a small postern gate with a drawbridge that crossed the deep dry ditch beyond. This gave access to a sloping wooded area of mixed conifers, mostly dark-needled pines and graceful grass-green larches. Guessing that this might be where Richard had released the ravens, I found my way over the bridge and ventured in among the trees.

On the way out I had visited the large kitchen and had taken the precaution of procuring a bowl of raw offal from a puzzled scullion who was about to add it to the pottage cauldron perched on a seething-rack over barely glowing embers in the hearth. I hoped these bloody organs might be sufficiently tempting to bring our half-tame pair of ravens down from wherever they had taken roost the previous night. Emptying the bowl onto a stump, I slipped behind a nearby holly bush to wait, hoping Hal would oblige me by remaining quiet.

It was hard to keep an eye permanently on the stump but every minute or so I would peer around the bush to look for any arrival and after a while Hal became restless at all the bobbing up and down. When his eyes opened I knew my time in the woods was up. No bird or animal had shown the slightest interest in the bait but as I straightened up I caught a fleeting glimpse of movement among the undergrowth across the glade. It was not a raven because it had been pale in colour, even ghostlike, and it disappeared swiftly behind the trunk of a tree. Not an animal of any kind, I thought, but a human form – a child or a small man.

I called out. 'Who's there? Come out, I won't hurt you if you don't hurt me.' My heart was beating fast because I was carrying Hal and knew I could not afford to expose him to any harm.

There was no verbal response but a sudden crashing of movement through the undergrowth, a flash of what I took to be light-coloured clothing and the sound of twigs snapping. Whoever had been there, watching me or watching the bait, had beaten a hasty retreat. Reluctantly I abandoned my post and wended my way back to the postern, singing a soothing song to Hal to entertain him. But I was frustrated, wishing I had some good news to tell Maria when she returned.

Then, as I reached the bridge I heard the unmistakeable kronking call of a raven coming from within the wood. Typically, while I had been watching the stump, the raven – or ravens – had been watching me, cunningly waiting for me to go away, leaving it – or them – free to enjoy the bloody treat at their leisure. I could not run back because Hal was very obviously wide awake and hungry and his urgent cries would be enough to scare off any creature. But the call of the raven had been enough to convince me that at least one of them was there and presumably dining gleefully on the treat I had brought, so I had some good news to impart to Maria. The identity of the observer who had run away would have to be investigated later.

25

No one was more excited than Maria when she learned that her pair of ravens was roosting in the woods beyond the ditch. She took kitchen scraps out to them on a daily basis and brought me regular reports, while I was preoccupied with little Hal until the two local women Richard had managed to recruit began their work.

One was the breast nurse, Mistress Strood, a tenant farmer's wife who was willing to boost their income by sharing her plentiful milk supply now that her own year-old little girl was beginning to rely on more solid fare, and the other was Hetty, the sixteen-year-old daughter of a blacksmith from the local village of Rolvenden, who we employed to live in and officially act as the rocker of Hal's cradle. She also took a shine to Lizzie, who was soon following her around like a little dog, bringing her toys and treasures she found on their walks around the demesne. After Luce took Hetty under her wing, she became a favourite of the entire family and happily performed any task that was requested of her. In fact there came a time when I had to order all the older children not to overwork her.

Mistress Strood lived only a short walk away at the farmstead her husband rented from Richard, the closest to

Halden Hall. She came daily with her own toddler Sarah, who played with little Lizzie, and also brought fresh milk from her nanny goat to leave for Hal's night feeds. Within a week I had become confident to leave the little ones to them and pursue my usual household duties again.

Richard was far from happy about the ravens settling down in the home woods, pointing out as he prepared to mount up for a hawking session that George would not be able to practise flying his sparrowhawk there and would have to rely on the falconer taking him further afield when he himself was not there to do so. 'Every young man of gentle birth should know how to handle a hawk and George needs more practice than most because he seems to fear his bird,' he told me.

'He's suspicious of all birds and becomes too boisterous around them. He also believes you when you call the ravens carrion devils. Perhaps he should go with Maria and learn how to get close to them,' I suggested.

Richard took his horse's reins from the stable lad and pursued his theme. 'Well, he won't hear any praise for ravens from farmers around here, I can tell you that. They don't only feed on carrion. In the spring, boys of George's age are sent into the pastures to throw stones and scare them off because they attack the newborn lambs. Out hunting I've seen a flock of ravens gang up and feast on a live fawn if the hind is not close by to chase them off.'

I stood my ground. 'Well, she won't be, will she, if you're hunting her! I believe there is room in the world for all God's creatures, or else why would He have created them? And our ravens won't need to attack a living thing because we'll keep them well fed on the waste from our kitchen.'

My husband shrugged. 'Just don't be surprised if one day you find one of them doesn't return from a flight.' He sprang into the saddle.

'Maria will be heartbroken if that happens, so you'd better make sure it isn't you who is responsible.' My words followed him out of the stable yard.

Later that day that I went to the home wood with some pigeon wings and followed Maria's advice to sit in plain view rather than lurk in the undergrowth. She said that when they could see her, the ravens seemed happier to approach the bait, and it proved to be so. I had sat down on a fallen trunk not five yards from where I had placed the wings and within a few minutes both black birds were perched on the branch of a larch, each favouring me with a deep, unblinking stare. Having left Hal with Hetty, I felt free to simply sit and wait and take my cue from them. If they considered me their friend they would approach; if not they would retreat.

They did not retreat but nor did they rush to take the food. I thought perhaps they had already eaten and were not hungry but this was not the case. Instead they dropped to the ground one after the other in front of some bushes away to one side, prowling in the fallen pine needles, then gathering them up with their fierce beaks and throwing them consistently in one particular direction. I had the feeling that they were trying to tell me something and it was not long before I discovered what it was. We were not alone. Someone had been hiding in the undergrowth and was even now trying to slip away without revealing himself. But the ravens were not having that. When a stooping male figure in a filthy undyed hooded jacket made a break for the deeper shadows of the trees they took off together and began to round him up, circling just above his head, 'kraaking' and 'guerring' loudly in protest, forcing him to stop and turn around. It was a young man, or maybe he was still a boy, beardless, pale and skinny, with scraped knees showing through his ripped hose.

'Call 'em off, lady!' he yelled in alarm. 'I ain't doin' any harm.'

I rose from my fallen tree and moved towards him. The ravens withdrew and settled on another low branch to witness whatever might follow. 'Who are you?' I asked quietly. 'What is your name?'

He pulled off his hood to reveal a thick thatch of reddish-brown hair and a blue-black bruise across his left cheek. 'Simon, m'lady, but they call me Sim.'

'Who are "they", Sim; your family?'

He shook his head violently. 'Nah, just anyone.'

'Are you afraid of ravens, Sim?'

'Only when they flap their wings around my head.' He glared at the two birds on their branch.

I thought his language and attitude smacked more of the city than the country. 'You're not from around here, are you, Sim?'

He cast me a shifty look. 'Why d'you wanna know?' he asked.

'I'm just interested, but if you're hungry would you like to come with me to the Hall and I'll give you something to eat.'

He shook his head again. 'Nah, I don't like buildings. People shut you up in them. You bring food out here for the ravens; can you bring some here for me?'

It was logical. He definitely wasn't stupid. 'Very well; and if I say I'll bring some food that's what I'll bring – food and nothing else. You have to trust me. Can you do that?'

He gave it some thought. 'Mebbe. First let's see if the ravens do.'

Sitting himself cross-legged in the carpet of needles, his gaze swung from me to the ravens and then to the bowl of offal, as if he was asking them if they intended to eat it. I returned slowly to my fallen branch and sat down. For a few moments nothing happened then one of the ravens flew to the bowl and pecked at a large morsel, holding it up and letting congealing blood drip slowly from it before spreading its wings and flying off to a pine tree, where it disappeared into the bristling green branches. Sim gave me a sideways look and I put my finger to my lips. 'Wait,' I mouthed.

Almost immediately the second raven gave a loud grunt and swooped down onto the stump, clumsily knocking the bowl to the ground. Then it dived down and snatched up another, larger morsel of the offal and carried it after its mate, higher up into the branches of the same tree. Whether they ate it or cached it for a later feast there was no way of knowing but it was clear that they had accepted it.

I stood up. 'I'll fetch that food now,' I said. 'I hope you like venison pie, Sim.'

When I brought the piece of pie, wrapped in a napkin, there was no sign of the youth so I put it down on the stump where I'd left the offal and shouted loudly, 'I said I'd bring food, Sim, so come and get it or the ravens might take it.' Then I left the clearing, wondering if I would ever see him again and rather hoping that I might.

Richard and the older children came back from their

day's hawking flushed with success, the sumpter's panniers stuffed with birds for the game-larder.

'Luckily we didn't see any ravens, Mother Joan,' Maria said solemnly, 'because the falconer says they mob hawks and falcons. But my little merlin was brilliant. Father says we should watch out if our ravens encounter a bird of prey because apparently they can display quite amazing flying skills when they're seeing a falcon off their territory.'

Her father seemed to know a lot about ravens, I thought, for a man who professed to despise them. I wanted to tell her about my encounter with the strange youth but did not like to mention it in front of the rest of the family lest Richard might send out the huntsmen to arrest him for trespassing. So the next morning she took me by surprise when she returned from visiting the ravens' clearing carrying a rather ragged-looking napkin.

'I found this on the stump where we put the ravens' rations,' she said, holding it out somewhat gingerly, as if she thought it bewitched. 'It's a bit torn and dirty. I think the ravens must have been playing with it. How did they get hold of it, I wonder?'

I was surprised that Sim brought the napkin back because he could have sold it to some village goodwife for a ha'penny, which would have bought him some bread. 'I have a story to tell you about that, Maria,' I said, and did so.

She was interested but a little concerned. 'Were you not frightened, Mother Joan? The boy could have had a knife and stolen your rings or hurt you in some way.'

I frowned, touched that she seemed so worried for my safety and puzzled why this had never occurred to me. 'If you ever meet Sim I don't think you would suspect him of wishing you any harm, Maria. He is obviously not a bandit or a thief. To tell you the truth I was more anxious about his safety than my own. I'm hoping he'll come back again and then maybe I can help him a bit more than just taking him a slice of pie.'

Maria then surprised me further by suggesting that I should not tell her father. 'He's very protective of his property. He would probably arrest this boy if he spotted him or certainly set the dogs on him. I have seen him do so when poachers tried to take a deer from the park.'

I realised that she was right. 'Well, we don't need to tell him because Sim probably won't return and your father's going back to London tomorrow, so it's not necessary to worry him about it.'

'I won't tell anyone else either,' she said, 'because Bess would tell George and he would tell the park keeper and then Sim would be in the Cranbrook lock-up. What will you do if he does return, Mother Joan?'

Her question set me wondering. 'I don't really know. He's quite a character and I was surprised how much he appeared to respect the ravens.'

26

IN LONDON RICHARD DISCOVERED that there had been deaths in the royal household from the measles and the court and the Privy Council meeting had moved to the palace of Placentia at Greenwich. Realising he would not be using the Tower House for some time, he ordered it closed up and arranged for Martin the steward, Jake the cook and Hugh the scullion to travel down to Kent to bolster our country team of domestic servants. After attending the meeting at Greenwich he'd asked the king to excuse us from the court festivities owing to my very slow recovery from Hal's birth. We would all be together for Christmas at Halden Hall.

Richard's premature return jeopardised my plans for Sim. The presence of the ravens in the home wood had proved too much of a magnet for the lad. When I next took food out for them I caught sight of him once more, hovering around the clearing by their roost. A portion of our household meals was taken daily to the church of St Mary in Rolvenden to feed the poor and I began saving an extra ration to deliver to Sim. In return I gradually drew his life story from him.

He told me he was thirteen and, as I had suspected, he was not a local boy. He hailed from Maidstone, where his father was a porter at the busy docks on the River Medway. At age ten Sim had also been employed there as a runner, carrying whatever cargo he could lift or drag between the big river barges and the smaller wherries that bore bales and barrels and baskets up and down the higher reaches of the Medway and its tributaries.

'That's how I got here,' he admitted. 'My father took all the money I earned but then eventually, to pay off his debt to the dock tavern keeper, he sold me for a pound to a wherryman he knew. I didn't want to go with him 'cos I knew he was a bastard – but I had to. When we got up into the narrows, where he couldn't sail the wherry, he put me on an oar but I wasn't strong enough to row it upstream in the fast flows. That's when he started hitting me. It was him gave me this.' He touched his cheek. 'There are more bruises you can't see. I thought that sooner or later he would kill me, so one day when his back was turned after we stopped to make a delivery, I jumped ship. I didn't know where I was but I just kept running and somehow I ended up here. You won't send me back, will you?'

'No, Sim, I won't send you back and I won't hit you,' I said. 'But I will take you to the church and ask you to swear on the Bible that you won't steal from me or my family and you won't tell anyone else where you're from.'

He raised an eyebrow. 'Why? What do I get in return?'

'I'm hoping you will make friends with my ravens and I will pay you to feed them and guard them from harm. I can't always be here so I need someone to look after them for me. Will you do that?'

He sniffed. 'It doesn't sound like much of a job. Is that all you want?'

'At the moment, yes, but there might be other things when I find out what you can do. I'll pay you tuppence at the end of each month as long as you stay and we'll feed you and get you some new clothes. Does that sound fair?'

His eyes grew wide. 'That's two shillings a year.'

I was astonished that he was able to calculate that at all, never mind so quickly. 'Yes. As I said, there may be other jobs you can do as well as guard the ravens. After all they spend much time away from their roost.'

'When can we go to the church?' he asked eagerly.

'After I've told my husband about you. No, don't worry, I won't let him throw you off the estate but I'm sure he'll want to come and witness your oath. We'll go tomorrow. And I'll ask him if you can sleep in the stables. It must be freezing at night out here.'

Before I broached the subject with Richard I sent up a prayer to St Nicholas, hoping the patron saint of children would steer him to favour this unknown youth I'd taken under my wing. Remarkably Richard did not take much persuading, choosing to see the boy as a charitable case that would help redeem his own debt to the Almighty. He did however insist that Maria should not be alone in the clearing with the boy, a restriction she disputed bitterly.

'That's so unfair, Father! They are my ravens if they're anyone's and they answer to me best.'

He took a persuasive tone with his favourite daughter. 'Well, you'll have to let someone else get close to them as well, Maria,' he coaxed, 'because you go away to London and they'll need guarding then, won't they?'

His next suggestion mollified her somewhat. 'After we've

seen Sim take his vow tomorrow I'm planning to introduce Mother Joan to the shipbuilding business and I'm sure Mistress Wood will excuse you a day's schooling in order to come with us, Maria. You can see how they're getting on with your ship.'

Her face lit up. 'Oh yes! Do you think they'll have put my name on it yet?'

'Well, we'll find out, won't we,' he said, tweaking her cheek fondly. 'And you can copy my latest entries into the shipyard ledger for me. Your handwriting is so much better than mine.'

I was almost as excited as Maria at the prospect of visiting the Guildford shipyard, which she told me was less than an hour's ride from Rolvenden, where Sim took his vow in the church. We also introduced him to the village priest, who entered his name in the parish record and undertook to find him some fresh clothes from the village almshouse. 'It's just to tide you over, Sim,' I told him, 'until I can get some Guildford livery made for you. When you go back to the Hall the head groom will show you where you can sleep and eat with the huntsmen and stable lads. Then you can get food scraps from the kitchen and start making friends with the ravens. I'll hear how you got on tomorrow.'

Before mounting up outside the church I watched him follow the priest down the village street, head down and hood up, sensing his apprehension. I hoped he wouldn't run away again.

The High Weald of Kent consisted of a series of valleys and wooded ridges and Halden Hall was located near the end of one of these, before the land fell steeply down towards the sea. It was a glorious revelation when we suddenly emerged from a belt of trees onto the edge of the ridge's steep escarpment. Before us lay a sweeping vista over miles of flat marshland threaded with channels that reached out to the seashore like gnarled fingers. The waters of the River Rother had forced their way through the marsh leaving protruding islands and promontories that bordered a wide, winding estuary. On its shingle shores small timber-built villages clustered around sturdy stone churches, while flocks of hardy sheep grazed on the surrounding expanses of flat salty grassland under a pale autumn sky that seemed to go on forever, streaked with layered clouds of white and pearly grey.

'This is magnificent,' I cried.

'It's the Rother estuary, Mother Joan,' Maria explained. 'Most of this bank is Guildford land and you can just see the shipyard, tucked in below us under the hill.'

I followed her pointing finger and noticed the hulls of two ships, propped up on stout poles to either side, driven into the sand and shingle of the main shoreline. A number of men could be seen working from cradles slung off the ribs. One of the ships' hulls was considerably more advanced than the other.

'Is that the *Maria*, Father?' she asked. 'She's nearly ready for her superstructure isn't she?'

'Yes, it looks like it,' he replied, shading his eyes against the glare of the sky to get a better view. 'Last time I was here the shipmaster said they would put the nameplate on her very soon.'

Maria kicked her pony forward. 'Let's go then. I can't wait to see it.'

We took the steep zigzag path down towards the shore

at a careful walk. Richard glanced at his daughter who had ridden on ahead. 'Officially that ship is named for the Virgin but Maria prefers to believe it is named after her. The king wants to establish a Royal Navy to patrol the French coast for pirates and I will lease the *Maria* to his fleet and captain her myself.'

'Sailor, gunner, engineer and designer; your skills never cease to amaze me!' I was genuinely in awe.

He gave me a sly smile. 'It pays to make a king think you're indispensable.'

'Well, be careful you don't overdo it, Richard,' I warned him. 'Even the Almighty rested on the seventh day.'

'That is why I'm looking forward to a peaceful family Christmas. Only I forgot to tell you that it won't be just family, because when I was at the Tower I got talking to Sir Henry Wyatt and he let it be known that he would be alone at Christmas, so I invited him to join us.'

'Come on!' Maria's girlish treble sang out as she kicked her little grey mare into the final bend that led down to the Rother shore. 'I can't wait to see my name on the ship's stern.'

In contrast to her excitement, my spirits sank further with each of my horse's careful steps down the steep slippery slope, as I contemplated Christmas with Sir Henry Wyatt. Obviously I had not made my antipathy towards him clear enough to Richard and I could hardly refuse to entertain him now that the invitation had been made. Even so I could have wished that man anywhere but in my house on the anniversary of Christ's nativity.

27

PREDICTABLY IT WAS NOT the prospect of a lonely Christmas that had prompted Sir Henry Wyatt to wangle an invitation to Halden Hall. The real reason came towards the end of a private supper served on the evening of his arrival in Richard's solar. The children had been banished to their own quarters and, as it was still Advent, our meal had been restricted to fish and roasted onions. Even so it had been ample and, ignoring the fasting rule against alcohol, the two men were partaking freely of some local mead and spiced pears as a void.

'I have a proposition to put to you, Richard.' Wyatt's tone of voice was conspiratorial and immediately set my nerves jangling. I found it hard to imagine that any proposition from that particular knight was going to be legal and genuine and I shot a warning look at my husband but could not make him aware of it. 'I have my eye on a castle I wish to buy near Maidstone, which is in a sorry state of repair and is going to stretch my financial resources. However, as Comptroller of the Mint I am required to check their annual accounts and doing so has given me an unusual opportunity.'

'If you're thinking of cooking the Mint books I don't recommend it, Henry,' I was delighted to hear Richard say.

'I happen to know that the king keeps a sharp personal eye on those particular accounts.' He was careful to inject a strong note of humour in his voice when he said this.

'Ha, ha! No, I'm not foolish enough to do that!' Wyatt responded. 'The opportunity I am referring to is knowing the sources of the scrap precious metals, which are sent to the Mint for melting down. Much of it comes from former supporters of York, who are obliged to sell their plate in order to pay the fines that King Henry's first parliament has imposed on them, and I've made a note of those who reside in Kent and Sussex. Because many of them also need to mortgage their properties in order to complete the payments, my proposal is that we form a partnership to help them out.'

Richard frowned. 'What, lend them money to pay their fines? How's that going to help us? Most of them will probably fail to complete those payments, let alone pay off any further loans. We'll just end up out of pocket ourselves and we won't have impressed the king by appearing to support impoverished Yorkists.'

Wyatt touched his finger to his nose and shot a meaningful glance at me, clearly wishing I would disappear, and since I had a hundred and one things to do before the Twelve Days began I decided to take the hint. I could find out what this money-making scheme was from Richard later and I didn't anticipate it being either straightforward or legal. Nor did I think for a minute that Richard would even contemplate joining some hare-brained scheme to help Yorkists on the rocks. Apart from anything else, he already had too many calls on his time and received handsome rewards for his efforts both from the royal purse and his extensive businesses and landholdings. I made an excuse and left.

Later, having seen the babies into bed and comforted Maria, Pippa and Winnie, who were in tears after stirring each other's memories of their mother's sudden death almost exactly two years ago, I reflected how much had happened in my own life since marrying their father. It was less than twelve months since our wedding and although I believed his children tolerated my presence in their lives and the girls even called me Mother Joan, I still felt that I hardly knew their father. We'd had our differences, although we'd never had a blazing row, discovered a glorious passion or a violent dislike, but then we'd really spent little time together. Two weeks after our wedding I had returned to the queen's service and almost as soon as I took pregnancy leave, he had departed to captain his ship on Channel patrol for three months. Somehow we had achieved a healthy baby boy and I had survived his traumatic arrival, and now we were sharing Christmas together with a man who had threatened to exact revenge for my refusal to marry him. How different would my life have been if I had made the other choice of husband, I wondered? I found it impossible to imagine being Lady Wyatt rather than Lady Guildford. If Richard and I appeared to have very little in common, Henry Wyatt and I lacked anything at all, and yet ironically here we three were together, with one of us apparently unaware of the undoubted enmity that had grown between the other two.

Later in the marital bed, I pursued the subject indirectly. 'It seems strange that Sir Henry has no wife. I thought the king liked his courtiers to be married.'

Richard's reply came with a tipsy smirk. 'I expect that's

why he wants a castle. He needs it to tempt a bride. Because although he has the looks, he doesn't have the charm to attract the rich heiress he craves. I, on the other hand . . .' He groped for me unsuccessfully in the dark.

I didn't point out that breath smelling of alcohol and an ever-receding hairline hardly amounted to irresistible charm, or that I was scarcely a beautiful and richly dowered heiress. 'So are you going to help him finance this ambition of his by going into moneylending?' I asked, as he found me and I tried to fend him off.

I hardly ever refused him but somehow making love with Richard while Henry Wyatt was in the house produced a bad taste in my mouth. Even though he appeared to find me ugly and called me 'Blackbird', I couldn't help feeling that he might burst through the door at any minute, brandishing his sword and yelling, 'If I can't have her no one will!'

Richard's response to my question was not as definitely negative as I would have liked. 'What do you think, Joan? And why are you pushing me away?' At which he pushed himself away, rolled over and began to snore.

No matter how much I had to do, first thing next morning I could not waste an opportunity to make an excursion to the ravens' nest site. Nowadays I left their feeding to Sim because I thought it would bind the birds to him and in some way replace his family. We had learned no more about his background but he seemed to get on with the stable staff and be suitably respectful to the head huntsman and the falconer, so his appointment as raven keeper had not rocked the household regime.

He hadn't exactly got the ravens eating out of his hand but then I never wished them to be treated as pets. I wanted them to remain as wild as possible, having learned that if a raven pair settled on a nesting site, unless they were driven off it they would return to it every year during the breeding season, which occurred in the early spring when the most carrion was available to feed the young.

We didn't have to wait long for the pair to come and break their fast. Sim had sent a terrier out in the hayloft over the stables, where it had snapped up a rat, which Sim had then swapped for a juicy sheep's foot, to the dog's eager preference. But as the ravens caped their wings over the rodent corpse to begin enjoying their morning meal, I heard an unwelcome interruption from an all-too-familiar voice.

'Still consorting with the devil's spawn I see, Lady Guildford. I wonder that Sir Richard permits it.'

Chiming with my own intense aversion to this intruder, the neck feathers rose on both ravens as they backed away from their meal, 'kraaking' with alarm and flapping off into the shelter of their pine tree. Sim also backed off, his eyes flicking about with fear. Perhaps he recognised the under-lying threat in Sir Henry Wyatt's voice.

'God give you good morning, Sir Henry,' I said with an affability I did not feel. 'You are up early this Christmas Eve.'

'If you had opted differently a year ago you would have known that I am up early every morning.' He strolled across the clearing to where Sim was still attempting to dissolve into the undergrowth. 'Who have we here? A trainee for the devil's imp-school?'

I ignored his query and waved Sim away instead. 'You

have duties elsewhere, Sim. You may go.' The boy bolted out of the clearing like a hound on the scent.

Wyatt scowled and bent to pick up the rat's carcass by the tail, holding it at arm's length, dangling between us. 'Does Richard know you're breakfasting on vermin in the woods with a young man, Blackbird?'

I ignored his provocation in order to offer some of my own. 'Do you have a bride in mind for your fairy-tale castle, Sir Henry? Or will you have to get the king to find you a wife again? It didn't go so well the last time, did it?'

He looked as if he might explode with anger but instead he whirled the rat twice and spun it off in my direction. I felt the wind of its flight as it almost grazed my cheek.

Making myself walk slowly past him, I murmured as I went, 'If you had married me a year ago, you would know that I never eat breakfast. But it is served in the great hall. Rat is not on the menu.'

Fortunately Sir Henry did not stay until Epiphany; he left on Holy Innocents Day, when tradition dictated a regime of practical japes.

'Lest I be tempted to make you a colly pie,' was his own black joke as he bade us farewell. Luckily Maria just thought it a silly pleasantry but I understood his reference to the 'colly birds' or coal-black birds, from which Christmas cooks often made blackbird pie. Sir Henry Wyatt would never see ravens as anything but target practice for soldiers or ingredients for a pie.

The relief of bidding him farewell was followed by the delight of welcoming my mother who arrived two days later. Having been with Queen Elizabeth throughout her confinement and her churching, Mamma had at last managed to get permission to visit her first grandson. She came loaded with gifts, accompanied by Jess, her faithful servant, and a member of the royal yeoman guard, generously lent to her by the queen. 'For our protection,' she explained.

She had said all this before drawing me into a fierce embrace and plying my cheeks with warm kisses. 'Oh Gigi, it is so good to see you again but of course I am really here to see my grandson! I can't believe you've had a boy and Nicholas's Beth has not yet produced one. I gather you had a terrible time of it, which I was desperately worried to hear, but now I see you looking so well and beautiful I am happy.' I received another, even tighter hug. 'So – why are we waiting? Show me this miracle of yours immediately! I'm so excited to be Nonna to a little boy!'

I laughed happily. It was so wonderful to see her once more and sense her exuberant zest for life. 'Oh Mamma, surely you want to refresh yourself first. You have been on the road for hours. Hal won't be going anywhere in the next half hour!'

'No, no! Take me straight to him and ask your servants to bring the sumpter's panniers to my room so I can unpack his presents. They are all for him, of course – I have brought you nothing. Well – maybe just a tiny gift or two. Hal, you call him? I thought his name was Henry.'

By this time we had actually managed to enter the house and Martin the steward, who had heard her instructions about the panniers, immediately set about organising the house servants, leaving me free to usher her towards the nursery. 'Yes. Henry is after the king of course but we all call him Hal because there are just too many Henrys being born. Do you not like the name?'

My mother's brow creased into a frown. 'Yes, I like it well enough but Gigi, you might have told me in your letters. I have embroidered all his chemises with the name Henry!'

I had to smother my laugh then because Mistress Strood had emerged from the nursery with her finger on her lips. She had finished suckling Hal and both he and her little girl Sarah had been tucked up for their midday rest. My mother had to be content with a brief glimpse of her sleeping grandson before grilling the poor breast nurse about her routines and Hal's progress before I managed to tear her away, take her to her chamber and persuade her to prepare for dinner, which had been delayed for her arrival.

With the winter days so short and the meal being late, by the time we finished it was becoming dark and it wasn't possible to show my mother around the garden and grounds, but I did take her on a candle-lit tour of the house before we ended up at the nursery once more. But this time she was armed with her pannier full of gifts for her precious grandson and we spent an hour or more amusing Hal by showing him all the beautiful clothes his besotted grandmother had made for him during her embroidery sessions in the queen's company. I estimated that there were linen chemises in sizes that would take him up to at least three years old, little woollen jackets embellished with animals in bright coloured silks, sheets and coverlets for his cradle and cot, and a gorgeous stuffed linen dog to cuddle, with a bushy tail, embroidered eyes and nose and a bright pink tongue splitting his cheerful smile.

'And it is all washable, Gigi, because I know how easily these things get soiled by a small child,' she assured me.

'Oh, everything is beautiful, Mamma – you are an angel!

Up to now Hal has been mostly using Lizzie's outgrown things because, as you know, I have never been very good with a needle.'

She gave me a sage smile. 'Yes, Gigi, I've seen you fiddling with your embroidery; obviously wishing it was a book. Which reminds me to tell you that the queen misses you so much. She keeps asking me how long it will be before you come back. So I have to ask, are you coming back?'

The question perplexed me. When I had first left the queen's household I felt as if I had lost my sense of identity. Instead of being a member of the royal court, I was just another pregnant wife, lacking any purpose in life other than waiting to see if I would survive the dangerous process of giving birth. But now that I was the mother of a healthy boy, no matter how difficult the birth had been, I was proud of myself and of him. I suddenly realised that I had not read a book since Hal's birth, partly because I had taken weeks to recover my health and partly because I had lost the urge to use those qualities which I had previously considered so important: intellect, acumen, discernment. I was vegetating – but I was happy.

'I must admit, Mamma, that at the moment the only thing I miss about being a lady-in-waiting is the queen herself. Elizabeth and I are more than mistress and attendant, we are friends – have been ever since I looked after her when she arrived at Coldharbour as a confused, insecure girl. We have both changed but I believe we still have that early bond. So I would love to return to her company but, believe it or not – and I don't believe it myself sometimes – I would love to have another child, if God saw fit to allow it and to permit me to survive it.'

To my surprise my mother clapped her hands in the same delighted way she had done when Hal granted her a toothless smile. 'You can't imagine how happy it makes me to hear you say that, Gigi! It tells me that as well as being well read, super-intelligent and mistress of three languages, you are also a normal, loving woman, with a great deal more sense than I had at your age.'

No daughter could ever dismiss such a fond tribute from her mother, even if it wasn't entirely accurate. At the risk of squashing Hal, who was firmly ensconced on her lap, I flung my arms around her neck and kissed her. 'Why, thank you, Mamma! I don't think I've ever heard you speak so well of me. Just one thing though – I actually speak four languages – English, French, Latin and . . .'

She hugged me back and took my face between her two hands. 'Italian! How could I forget that!'

'And I should remind you,' I added, extracting myself and stroking an alarmed Hal's soft dark hair consolingly, 'that you also speak three languages and are a normal, loving woman. So it should come as no surprise to you to find that I am too – but it certainly surprises me!'

Sadly I waved my mother off on the day following Epiphany, after she had helped us all to take down the Twelfth Night candles, wilted greenery and tired wreaths from the walls and windows of the great hall. She said her week with us had been the happiest and most relaxed she had spent for years and I probably horrified Richard by saying it was time she retired from being at the beck and call of one queen after another and came to spend her golden years with us. He needn't have worried because there had been no chance that she would take me up on it.

'I will only retire when Lady Margaret decides to do so,' she said, having apologetically refused my invitation. 'We always said that if God granted us old age we would spend our declining years together.'

I had a mental picture of the two of them helping each other into their hair shirts and laughing together about how much they itched. They were two ladies who would never go weeping into their goodnight. For my part, after the hectic celebrations of the Twelve Days, I realised that I had overestimated the completeness of my recovery from Hal's birth and took to my bed with an ague and utter exhaustion. Then it snowed profusely and although Mistress Strood managed to wade through it from the farm with Sarah tied snugly against her chest, I did not venture out to test my strength until the thaw a fortnight later.

Sim brought me regular reports of the ravens' progress and soon after the thaw he told me that he had managed to climb the pine tree and look into their nest.

'There are four eggs, m' lady! So pretty – pale green and blotched brown.'

Maria was with me and gave a little cry of excitement, her blue eyes wide and shining. I was so thrilled that I asked one question after another without pause. 'Oh, Sim! Did they feel warm? Do you think they are sitting on them? What is the nest like? Is it secure and are the eggs safe or will they fall out? Oh, I wish I could see them!'

Sim tried to answer them all. 'They weren't warm but I waited some time after they flew off the nest before I climbed up. I can't tell the male from the female but I think the male does most of the hunting, only this time they both went together. The nest looks a mess on the outside, sticks pokin' out all over the place, but inside it's smooth and lined with fur and fevvers. The eggs look quite safe, 'cept I suppose a squirrel might carry them off, or a marten could but I haven't seen any about. The baby birds might be in more danger, always supposing they 'atch, o'course.'

'Oh, please God let them hatch.' I felt feeble, not being able to climb the tree myself. 'You'll have to be our eyes, Sim, but take good care when you climb. I'd hate you to fall.' A thought suddenly occurred to me and I put my arm around Maria's shoulders. 'And don't let Maria climb either. She can take foolish risks sometimes.'

Sim gave us a horrified look. 'She couldn't climb up there in a skirt, m'lady!'

I glanced at Maria before remarking, 'It might cross her mind to borrow her brother's hosen.'

She looked at me askance. 'I would not! They stink of manure.'

Maria and George were chalk and cheese, always at loggerheads, especially over the ravens. He had disappointed his father by showing little interest in the expected Guildford male occupations, such as weaponry, shipbuilding and sailing, preferring to disappear off to the Strood farm whenever he could, to help out in the fields and with the beasts. George was shaping up to be a farmer and of course, as a result, he shared their hatred of ravens.

At dinner, Richard asked if I would be ready to accompany him on a short journey the following day. 'I thought now that the snow has melted and you are feeling better we could visit some neighbours. It is not a long ride and we'll be back well before dark.'

Obviously I was intrigued. 'Certainly I will come. I feel guilty that I have not yet made acquaintance with our neighbours and tenants, other than Mistress Strood. Who are we to visit?'

Richard evaded answering my question directly but welcomed my enthusiasm, then went on to tell me that he would be returning to London for a special session of parliament at the end of January. 'Our ally Brittany faces another serious threat from the French king who is determined to annex the duchy to France by marrying the young Duchess Anne.'

'Really? The last I heard she was married already – to Emperor Maximilian, wasn't it?'

'Yes, but it was a proxy marriage which has not been confirmed or consummated. King Charles is also officially married but he seems to have acquired an annulment from the Pope. The whole affair is quite murky.'

'So what can King Henry do about it? Will he send an army?'

'I think not.'

I frowned deeply. 'So poor little Duchess Anne is going to be thrown to the French wolf?'

He shrugged. 'It looks like it.'

I pursed my lips, glancing down the trestle to where Maria was arguing with her brother Edward, home on leave from his page service in the king's household. 'I hope you won't be dealing so heartlessly when it comes to Maria's marriage, Richard.'

His response astonished me. 'At present I am not dealing with anyone regarding Maria's marriage. I think thirteen too young to be sent off into some strange household, especially now that she has a wise guide and counsellor in her stepmother.'

I could scarcely believe my ears. Had my laconic husband really just paid me the compliment of being a good influence on his favourite daughter? I had been seriously considering the queen's recall. Now I was being drawn the other way, not only by my own altered sense of motherhood but also by my husband's apparent approval. After one year of marriage might I have passed the good wife test?

28

THE MELTING SNOW HAD rendered the country tracks boggy and slippery and we had to keep our horses reined in to a careful walk, which gave Richard an opportunity to give me some background information about where we were going.

'During the last century, after the Black Death, one blacksmith's family from Rolvenden prospered more than most and when some land became available at the far edge of the village common they bought it and built a hall. Their name was Frensham so they called it Frensham Manor. That is where we're going today.'

'And do the Frensham family still live there? Is that who we're going to see?'

'No, because when the Duke of Buckingham led an uprising against the usurper, Squire Frensham and his son joined the troop my father and I raised in rebellion. Sadly they were both captured and imprisoned, as was my father but he managed to buy his freedom and a pardon from King Edward, whereas the Frenshams both died in gaol.'

'And you fled into exile with King Henry.'

'Yes, but recently I discovered that Squire Frensham's widow was living with her two daughters in dire poverty, so I bought Frensham Manor from them. They now live rent-free in one of our Rolvenden alms-houses.'

I was becoming impatient. 'So who lives at Frensham Manor now? Who are we going to visit, Richard?'

His pursed his lips and gave me a sideways look. 'I think I'll let you wait and see. We're nearly there anyway.'

We had ridden along a green lane, past a series of scattered cots; small farmsteads built in the Kentish style with vertical black timbers, interspersed with lath and lime-washed plaster and sheltered from the weather by steeply sloping roofs of sun-bleached thatch. But the house we reached after passing through a ragstone gateway was very different. Considerably larger than the one-roomed cots, it was roofed not with thatch but with striking red clay tiles, which lifted it from rustic charm to a stylish country residence. At one end of what was obviously the original hall was a new extension wing, with a third timbered floor raised under its own pitched and tiled roof. Tall ragstone chimneys on either end of the building indicated evidence of substantial fireplaces within.

'What an attractive place,' I commented to Richard, drawing rein to examine it in more detail. 'The tiles are beautiful and I see from the smoke that the occupants here keep their fires well stoked. Surely you can tell me now who they are, before I meet them?'

He shook his head stubbornly. 'No need,' he replied. 'I think we've already been spotted.'

The heavy studded oak door in the jutting porch was pushed open and a female figure emerged with her arms outstretched and a little girl hovering behind her skirts. I gasped and crossed myself in delighted shock.

'Rosie!' I scrambled from my horse as quickly as my skirt allowed, to receive her eager embrace. 'Whatever are you doing here?'

She gave me a rueful smile. 'It's a long sad story with a half-happy ending but you need to come in to hear it. And to see the house.' She turned to Richard, who had also dismounted. 'All is prepared as you requested, Sir Richard,' she said. 'Joseph will take your horses.'

A bearded man in a country smock had come round from the back of the house and led the horses away.

'Is this your little girl, Rosie?' The child who had followed her out of the house was studying me closely and solemnly. 'What is her name? Unless she would like to tell me herself.' I squatted down as I made this suggestion but the little girl was too shy to speak.

'We call her Betty. She was baptised Elizabeth – as are so many!'

'A young silkwoman in the making?' I suggested.

Rosie gave a little snort. 'Perhaps. I have so much to tell you. Come in and get warm first.'

Despite its lofty oak-beamed ceiling the great hall into which she led us was indeed warm, heated by a blazing fire. Two settles flanked the hearth and a sideboard displayed a selection of pewter cups and platters. Woollen hangings lined the walls and cushions eased the seats of the settles and window benches. A trestle table was laid for a meal in the centre. The house and the room puzzled me somewhat, because although I knew Rosie had married a London mercer, I had not thought him successful enough to afford such a comfortable and well-furnished country residence.

'When you have drunk some of this warm spiced wine I will take you on a tour of the house, Lady Joan.' Rosie filled two cups from the flagon warming at the hearth and carried them to Richard and me. I had not realised how much the ride had chilled me until the hot, aromatic liquid began to warm my blood.

With inner warmth came intense curiosity. 'How long have you been here, Rosie? Why have I not heard of your arrival so close to our home?'

At this point I detected a swift and silent communication pass from Rosie to Richard and my heart missed a beat. I looked closely at my friend with her English rose complexion and buxom figure and suddenly I felt my recent sense of marital success take a hefty knock. I had no reason to think it but could there possibly be something between these two that was about to turn my complacent world upside down? All at once the alcoholic drink had become a much-needed boost to my rocking equilibrium and I took several large gulps.

Rosie replaced the flagon beside the fire and watched me drain my cup. 'I promised Sir Richard to show you more of the house, Joan. So, if you're ready, we can make a tour,' she said.

Richard did not accompany us but took charge of Betty, whose willingness to go to him raised even more questions in my whirling mind, as we climbed the stair that led from the far end of the hall up to the first-floor chamber of the new extension. It was a large solar, with a sunny south-facing window overlooking a walled enclosure. Through it I caught a glimpse of dormant herb beds awaiting the kiss of spring and neat box hedges sheltering plots where flowers would bloom in summer. Beside these grew an orchard of fruit and nut trees, all neatly pruned, while a few pigs rooted about in a muddy pen set against the surrounding wall.

During the tour through bedchambers and attics, I could not rid my mind of that flash of communication between my friend and my husband and the fear that it posed some threat to my marriage. In the end, as we descended to the foot of the stair, I decided at least to settle the status of hers.

'Does your husband come often to the country, Rosie? I take it he is still in business in London.'

Her expression clouded instantly. 'No, my lady, he is dead. He died in the measles epidemic three months ago, along with our baby son. You had not been to the workshop for some time, so you would not know that I had a little boy, a few months before, I have now learned, you also had a son. I hope yours thrives.' On this final remark her voice cracked and her eyes filled with tears.

I rushed to wrap my arms around her; all suspicious thoughts banished from my mind. 'Oh, Rosie, that is terrible! I am so sorry. Why did you not tell me straight away? I have been wondering if you had left your husband or some-thing – but the measles – how unjust to steal both your men from you at once!'

She sniffed and dashed the tears from her cheeks. 'Yes, unjust is exactly what it was. God may have His reasons but only He knows what they were.'

'And so you have escaped to the country? Had he bought this place before he died?' I still could hardly believe that a man as young as he, however shrewd a mercer, had managed to amass sufficient money to purchase such a property.

'That is another story and one in which Sir Richard plays a part; let us join him again.'

I followed her back into the hall where, with his sailor's guise to the fore, Richard had been entertaining Rosie's little girl with a tale of the high seas.

'And so the mermaid dived into the sea and lived happily ever after,' he concluded hastily and rose from his settle as we entered. Little Betty immediately ran off to her mother. 'Have you had a good tour, Joan?'

'Not totally perfect,' I confessed, 'because Rosie says there is a story to it that concerns you.'

He sat down again, patting the seat beside him to indicate that I should take my place there. 'I hope you will think it has a happy ending,' he said.

I sat as directed and Rosie took Betty to the other side of the fire, which crackled as a log settled in the grate. She cuddled her daughter to her and kissed the top of her head.

Richard hesitated and cleared his throat. 'It all began when I went back to London before Christmas. The measles epidemic had been taking many lives, both in the city and around the Abbey and Palace of Westminster, but having survived the disease as a child, I did not fear catching it again. When I returned to the Tower the porter told me a woman had been asking for you, Joan, but he knew you were not there so he sent her away. I asked if he had taken her name and he gave me Rosie's and the address of the silk workshop.'

Rosie broke in here. 'It was so kind of him to come, Joan. I'd had to close the workshop because one of the girls caught the disease and I feared it would spread through the rest. In the event it was my husband and son who caught it and both died. We were in debt to the landlord and he repossessed our house, then my mother could not take us in because my stepfather had caught the disease. We were homeless and penniless and I thought of you, but you were not there. We were sheltering in the workshop when Sir Richard came. He was like an answer to my prayers.'

'As soon as I heard her story I knew that Rosie was the answer to my own problem,' Richard said. 'I had just sealed the deal on Frensham Manor and I needed someone to look after it temporarily, so I offered her the job.'

'I almost bit his hand off kissing it in gratitude,' Rosie said. 'By coming here we have escaped the measles and I have a home for Betty.'

Richard took my hand. 'Frensham Manor does not belong to Rosie, Joan. It belongs to you.'

I stared at him in horror, unable to grasp his meaning. 'But I have a home with you, Richard. Are you throwing me out?'

He laughed at that, saints forgive him! What was there to laugh about? One day he was telling me he approved of the way I guided his children, the next he was paying me off like an unsatisfactory servant and flaunting his doxy at the same time. I prided myself on being a strong-minded, capable woman but nothing in life had prepared me for the tumult of emotions I felt at that moment. When he took my hand I was too dazed to prevent it.

His voice reached me through a whirl of conflicting sensations. 'No, Joan, of course not! Halden Hall is our family home. I never thought it would be again after Anne died but you have made it so. Frensham will be your bolthole for when you need relief from us all. And you have not yet seen the pastures and the cots on the property that are rented to local people. The manor will provide you with an income. Rosie and Betty will go back to London when the epidemic ends and they have recovered from their loss. She will reopen the silk workshop. Then we can find a steward for the house and the manor and you can use it as you like. It is your security – a gift from husband to wife.'

My confusion dissolved into disbelief. I was speechless. Then out of my jumbled thoughts I selected one at random and clutched at it. He had made the purchase of Frensham Manor and installed Rosie here well before Christmastide. 'Oh, Rosie! You and Betty should have joined us for Christmas,' I groaned. 'Whatever did you do here on your own and then in all that snow as well? Richard, you should have invited them.'

My husband looked a little indignant. 'I did invite them but Rosie turned me down.'

Rosie nodded. 'It's true, I did. It was a very kind invitation but Betty and I were still in shock. She had lost her papa and her brother and I had lost my husband and my son. It was too soon for us to celebrate. We were just glad to be together and away from the sickness in the city. This is your house, Joan. We will not be here for long but we will be eternally grateful to Sir Richard for bringing us here when he did.' She stood up and lifted her daughter down from the settle, glancing out of the window at the bright sunlight. 'It is after noon. You must be hungry. I will serve dinner.'

Rosie left the room hand in hand with her little girl and I looked at Richard, my mind still unable completely to comprehend the situation. 'Is it really mine?' I asked him faintly. 'I don't deserve it.'

He gathered both my hands together and bent his head to kiss them. 'You nearly died giving birth to our son, Joan. I thought I was going to lose you and it was then that I realised how much you meant to me. You know I am not a romantic soul but this is my way of telling you that I am so glad you agreed to marry me. I know you did not really want to and you sacrificed your independence but you have nevertheless offered no resentment and shown my children patience and understanding. They do not call you Mother Joan for nothing and I have come to greatly appreciate your presence in my life. You should look on Frensham Manor as a gift of love from a humble knight to a beautiful lady of great and noble quality.'

As he spoke I could feel tears brim in my eyes and spill down my cheeks. Love had never been a word spoken between us, or one I had expected to hear, and yet my strong and silent husband had not only used it, but also added a compliment of a kind I had never thought to hear from anyone other than my mother. He had called me beautiful. My heart was beating so hard I was speechless. I could only press my lips to his in a passionate kiss, such as I had never offered him before. In response he released my hands and wrapped his arms around me. I could feel his heart beating as wildly as mine. In two people who had come together by arrangement something sudden and special had stirred.

Rosie fed us a tasty and simple winter meal of stewed bacon, onions and pease and with it some freshly made bread. Then, before the sun sank too low, Richard and I had time to ride the boundaries of the manor. We stopped on the crest of a hill at the edge of the common and from its height could view the entire demesne. Strip-ploughed fields ran down to the walled enclosure where the house lay nestled in its gardens, protected from the cold east winds by a conifer wood.

'I should have brought my ravens here to nest.' I patted my palfrey's neck and glanced round at Richard. 'Then they might not have disturbed your hawks and falcons. But it is too late now, they've laid eggs and are likely to return every year to the same place.'

Richard frowned. 'You didn't tell me there were eggs. Don't pin your hopes on them hatching, Joan. Those birds are very young to breed.'

'You'd prefer it if they didn't, I suppose?'

He shrugged. 'I'll never be fond of ravens like you are; I just don't want you to be sad if they aren't fertile. There will be other years.'

I gave him a rueful smile. 'I know you hate them but it has been kind of you to tolerate them.'

'I would do much more than tolerate a few ravens in order to make you happy,' he said, reaching out to lift my free hand. Then my taciturn, laconic husband made another unexpected gesture. He turned the edge of the glove back and kissed the skin of my inner wrist. 'I am only returning the favour you have done by marrying me.' Carefully he covered my wrist again and released my hand. 'I hope you will find happiness here.'

PART THREE

29

DESPITE RICHARD'S WARNING THAT the ravens were too young to produce healthy offspring, all but one of our eggs had hatched and so far the three chicks were thriving. I hadn't actually laid eyes on them until they were well feathered and venturing perilously close to the edge of the nest to stretch their wings, making me fear they might fall before they could fly. When they opened their beaks to call, I was startled by the bright red lining of their mouths, nature's way of attracting their parents to bring food, which they did, assiduously.

In June Maria launched the flag-decked ship her father said was named for her and we all stood on the shore and watched while a priest sang psalms as she poured holy water over the ambiguous bowsprit, which was carved in the blue robe and white veil of the Virgin but blessed with young Maria's beautiful face.

Richard and I moved up to London after the launch but the children remained by choice at Halden Hall and Sim and the ravens stayed with them. He was nervous of bringing three chicks to a place where other ravens might attack them. 'It's not that I don't want to come to London, m'lady. I'd like to see the big city and the Tower but maybe I could come next year, when the chicks are bigger.'

I missed them all, children and ravens, during my stay at the Tower House, but mostly I missed my little Hal, who had been left very contentedly with his nurses, but at least I managed to make a brief visit downriver to my mother, when the court was at Greenwich, and at last managed to refresh my friendship with Queen Elizabeth.

I kissed her hand as I knelt before her throne and was delighted that she seemed graciously excited. 'Oh, Joan, it is so good to see you again!' She signalled to a hovering page. 'Bring a seat for Lady Guildford. We have much to discuss. Tell me all about your little Henry. Does he thrive like Prince Arthur?'

I took my seat on the low cushioned stool the page produced. 'I'm happy to say he is very healthy, thank you, your grace. But your son will be four in September, won't he? Not a baby any more. I hear he was invested as Prince of Wales and sat the whole way through a ceremony and banquet with remarkable calm. Everyone is singing his praises.'

Her face clouded a little. 'Yes, he was beautifully behaved but I hardly had a moment to speak with him before he was carried off to his barge and taken back to Sheen Palace. Arthur has his household there now.'

'But the new princess has her nursery at Eltham Palace, I gather. How is she faring?'

'Oh, Margaret is well too, I'm pleased to say. One day we must try to get our babies together as playmates.'

'How lovely that would be,' I said. 'But they are both very young yet, your grace.'

I thought Elizabeth looked pale and strained and wondered if she was suffering some after-effects of Margaret's birth, but it was impossible to ask her in the formality of her Great Chamber. However, she invited me to join her for a private supper with my mother and Lady Mary Rivers, when more intimate conversation was possible, if restricted by the additional presence of the queen's younger sister Princess Anne, still chief lady-in-waiting and still possessed of a sharp tongue.

'When was your baby born, Lady Guildford?' she asked with an inquiring smile.

'Last year, my lady, at the end of September.' Her queries invariably had an ulterior motive and while she smothered a giggle I took a fortifying sip of the rather sweet Portuguese wine the queen's butler had selected.

'How exciting,' she said. 'As I remember you were married during Epiphany. How romantic to have a wedding-night child – but then you had no time to waste really, did you? Do you hope to have another soon, before it's too late?'

My mother gave a little gasp of indignation as I placed my cup carefully back on the cloth but I spoke up hastily, before she could intervene. 'If I do, princess, I shall keep my hopes as prayers, between the Almighty and me. We are all in His hands, are we not?'

The queen shot a frown at her sister and a smile in my direction. 'Well, I hope you know that if God does not grant those particular prayers, there will always be a place for you here, Joan. I sorely miss your friendship and your sage advice and hope one day you will return to my household. You have only to make your position known.'

I returned the smile. 'Thank you, your grace, I will be sure to do so. I wonder if you are still patronising the apothecary at Blackfriars? They always had supplies of a wonderful tonic, which fortifies the blood of women who have given birth. I remember that I bought some for you to take after Prince Arthur's birth.'

Princess Anne gave one of her sceptical snorts. 'It didn't do much good then, because it took a long time for the queen to conceive again, didn't it? There are three years between the two royal children.'

'It is not the time between that matters; it is the health of the mother and children. A mother with strong blood will have a strong child.' I leaned closer to Elizabeth and studied her face with its shadowed eyes and sallow skin. 'If you permit it, when I return to London I will have that apothecary despatch some of the tonic to you, my lady. How long does the court stay here at Greenwich?'

'That depends on the king,' she said. 'But at least another week, I think.'

'Good. And if I send it, will you take it, my lady?'

'I will see that she does.' This assurance came from dear Mary Rivers. No one could be more trustworthy than she, who still slept in the queen's chamber more often than not.

'Thank you, Mary; I will give the courier your name.'

The Lady Anne was not to be upstaged. 'It should come through the Lord Chamberlain's office, like all the queen's packages,' she persisted. 'And it should be cleared by the queen's physician. What is in this potion?'

'Dr Caerleon cleared it years ago,' I told her. 'He uses the same apothecary and will vouch for their skill and loyalty.'

'Nevertheless, I would like it double-checked. Do you not agree, sister?' Lady Anne clearly took the official part of her position very seriously but I wondered whether her attention to the practical tasks involved in serving the queen had improved at all.

Queen Elizabeth nodded somewhat wearily. 'You must do as you wish, Anne,' she said. 'But as you know I trust Joan implicitly and if she has confidence in the apothecary, as I know she does, then that is enough for me.'

My mother was swift to add her endorsement. 'I could not attend Joan's delivery but I was told it was touch and go, your grace. She hovered between life and death for days but as soon as she regained her senses she started taking the potion and has done so ever since. She looks very well on it now, do you not agree?'

Elizabeth nodded. 'Yes, Lady Vaux, she looks very well,' and at another snort from her sister added, 'which makes me wonder if she might not be *enceinte* again already. Selfishly though, I hope she is not, because I dearly want her back with me.'

'And I will willingly come,' I said with warmth, 'when Hal is on his feet.'

Elizabeth frowned. 'Hal?' she echoed. 'Ah, you call your little Henry Hal?'

'Yes, your grace. I hope the king would not be offended but so many children are given his name and we want our boy to stand out among them.'

The queen leaned over and squeezed my hand. 'As I am sure he will, Joan, considering the parents he has.'

On my return to the Tower House I learned that Lady Margaret was at Coldharbour and sent a message there to ask if she would accept a visit from me. It was some time since I had been to her London palace and the very smell of it as I entered brought back vivid memories of my childhood there and the later time I had spent within its walls with Elizabeth, before her marriage. The aroma was a mixture of spices and incense, reflecting the chatelaine's taste for fine food and strict adherence to church directives. She was celebrating the office of Sext when I arrived so I waited in the library, gladly picking my way along the shelves, mostly just touching the leather bindings with their gold-stamped titles and admiring their distinction.

Lady Margaret arrived as I was leafing through a pocket-sized copy of *The Dialogues of St Gregory*, enjoying the fine monkish script as a change from the thick black print I was now becoming used to.

I placed the book back on the shelf where I had found it and made a deep curtsy to the king's mother. 'I am honoured you could spare the time to see me, my lady. It is too long since we were last together.'

'Life has inevitably sent us along separate paths, Joan,' she said, expressing her favour as she usually did by tucking her hand into my elbow affectionately. 'How do you do, now that you are a wife and mother? And how is your little boy?'

'He is at home in Kent and I have not seen him for a week or two but I get regular reports from his half-sister Maria. She says he is growing more teeth, so I presume all is well.'

'And do you miss him when you're away?'

I thought it a strange question to ask a new mother but then Lady Margaret was no ordinary mother, having barely seen her own son between the ages of one and twenty-eight, only to be reunited with him as King of England. I found myself hoping Hal and I would have the same love and respect for each other as those two did now, despite our separations.

'I miss him terribly, your grace, and it surprises me to hear myself say that because I must admit that I never wanted to marry, let alone have children. But I now think very differently.'

'I am so glad to hear that. I never stopped missing my son for all the years we were apart and now I treasure every moment we spend together.' She squeezed my arm. 'Can you join me at dinner?'

'I would like that very much, thank you, my lady. I dined at Greenwich yesterday, when the queen almost begged me to return to her service.'

Lady Margaret paused in our walk towards the great hall to turn and look at me. 'She is very fond of you, Joan, but tell me, how did you find her? I have not seen her for several weeks and I thought she looked sickly then. She does not take easily to childbirth.'

'That's true. Before I came here this morning I visited the Blackfriars apothecary and arranged to send her some tonic. But I'm not sure that is all she needs. She seemed very tense, as if something was worrying her. It's a shame Lady Anne is not older and wiser.'

Lady Margaret surprised me then by making a disparaging noise. 'Phrrrh! Oh dear, yes, she is a disappointment. Elizabeth is very faithful to her sisters but she'll never confide in Anne the way she used to confide in the lovely Cecily.'

This made me smile inwardly because I knew that Lady Margaret had taken Princess Cecily under her wing when she was made chief lady-in-waiting, teaching her all the tricks of politics and diplomacy she'd learned herself at King Edward's court and from her powerful husband Lord Stanley.

He had played his cards so expertly throughout the tricky years of Yorkist rule that he had survived with his wealth and power intact. Nowadays however, although he and Lady Margaret were seen together at great court occasions, since the house had been restored to her possession I had never encountered him at Coldharbour, so I thought it safe to assume they were probably married in name only. In gratitude for his military support, the king had bestowed an earldom on his stepfather and made him a Privy Councillor but although he kept his own London residence, Lord Stanley spent much of his time on his estates in the northwest.

'Perhaps there is something affecting the realm that troubles the queen,' I suggested. 'Has anything untoward happened politically?'

The king's mother pondered this question seriously for some time before answering. 'There was recently a rumour that someone claiming to be Elizabeth's brother Richard had surfaced at the court of her Aunt Margaret in Flanders. But there are always rumours of York conspiracies emerging from that source. It's such a shame that no sign of those boys was found in the Tower at the start of Henry's reign. I'm sure their poor little bodies must be buried there somewhere and it would certainly put Elizabeth's mind at ease if they were found.'

'Edward of Warwick is still housed in the Tower, isn't he?' I remarked as we resumed our walk towards dinner. 'I wonder if his presence there troubles her? Perhaps she fears he, too, could disappear.'

'Oh, I don't think that could happen. He's living in the strict security of the Royal Palace. Perhaps you might pay him a visit when you're there, Joan?' Lady Margaret suggested. 'I would go myself but it would cause a fuss, whereas you are a familiar sight around the fortress and you might at least be able to reassure Elizabeth about the boy's health and wellbeing. I'm sure I could arrange it for you.'

Hesitant though I was to become too involved in Elizabeth's awkward family relationships, I felt I had no choice but to agree. I left Coldharbour with a handwritten letter from My Lady the King's Mother, affixed with her personal seal. 'Hand it to the Lieutenant Constable whenever you have time to make Edward a visit,' Lady Margaret said.

30

I CONFESS THAT I postponed visiting the young Earl of Warwick and returned to Halden Hall, where I enjoyed sunny summer days watching Hal crawl in the grassy clearing by the ravens' tree and then stand up and walk on his sturdy legs. Against my wishes that they should not be named, Sim had started calling the breeding pair Jack and June and at first, due to the toddler's initial stumbles and tumbles, they found Hal rather scary but then they seemed to realise that he was like their own chicks, gradually shedding his baby characteristics and exercising his limbs ready to fly, or in his case run. It might have puzzled them that his progress was somewhat slower than that of their own offspring, but quite quickly they took courage and began to tease him like they did Sim, running towards him with their lurching steps, which were amusingly similar to Hal's, and veering away just as he hoped to catch them. He found this endlessly entertaining, giggling with delight, and I took the birds' loud 'keeks' and 'kwaarks' in response to be ravenish laughter.

Richard came and went during this time, disappearing to supervise military business at the Tower, obeying several summonses to consult with the king wherever he was staying on his progresses around the kingdom and eventually taking his new ship, the *Maria*, on a month's sea trials in the Channel. Usually he sent word of when he was coming home but in October he arrived back to find me gone.

I had missed his messenger because I had decided to go to Frensham Manor, to make plans for some renovations. I left Hal with Hetty and Mistress Strood and spent a whole day making a thorough scrutiny of the house and outbuildings, climbing into nooks and crannies and taking measurements with a yardstick, making notes as I went. As dusk fell I washed off the dust and cobwebs and took some pottage I'd brought from Halden Hall and a jug of wine up to the solar, where I lit a fire against the gathering chill.

I set the pot on a trivet in the hearth and had taken only a few sips of wine when there was a sudden hammering on the main door of the house. We had not yet appointed a steward and I knew that Joshua, the groom and gardener, would not hear the knocking in his stable loft, so with slight trepidation I wrapped my stole around my shoulders and went to answer it. Not wishing to open to a stranger I peered through the porter's grille to see Richard standing in the front court holding his horse's reins, the steel cuirass he always wore when travelling gleaming in the moonlight.

'Have you shelter for a starving man?' he called.

I pulled the door open and slipped through. 'Only bread and pottage and a wife to warm you,' I said, receiving his kiss with a hug. 'I had no message you were coming.'

'And I had no message you were going,' he countered. 'Are we staying the night?'

'I'll have to ask the mistress of the house.' I closed my eyes as if consulting myself, opened them and nodded. 'She seems to be agreeable.'

'Excellent. Does she have a stable boy?' He raised the hand that held the reins.

I took them from him. 'She will play that role too. Close the door and follow me.'

I led them both around the house to the stable block and together we settled the horse with water, oats and hay and Richard carried his saddlebags past the silent kitchen to the rear door. 'If you have your dagger to hand we can cut some more vegetables for the pot,' I said. 'There is plenty of bread and wine.'

Before drawing his dagger Richard dropped his bags. 'But a man needs more than pottage, bread and wine,' he said, pulling me into his arms. 'Rosie has gone back to London so I take it we have the house to ourselves?'

I fitted myself against him, feeling the hard steel of the cuirass against my breasts. 'Except for Joshua, who is looking at us from the hayloft,' I murmured in his ear.

He released me and turned with an oath. There was no one there but I grabbed his dagger from its sheath and ran off with it to the vegetable patch. Of course he soon caught up with me but I was slicing away vigorously at some greens and he held back.

'It's a hunter's moon,' he pointed out, 'and you are my quarry.'

'So this is why you bought Frensham for me,' I said a little breathlessly. 'For indulging in some night-time hunting.'

'Why else?' he asked. With a soldier's sleight of hand he suddenly wrested the dagger from me and slid it back into its sheath. Then I felt his fingers on my bodice, feeling my breast, and his teeth gleamed in the moonlight. 'Where is our chamber, wife?'

I pushed his hand away and bent to gather up the greens in my skirt. 'Patience,' I said with a return smile. 'The back door is open and I can put these in the pot on the way,' I said, offering him my free hand. 'Come.'

In the solar I hurriedly pushed the greens into the bubbling pot on the trivet and when I turned around Richard had removed his cuirass, dumped it against the wall and was looking at me with a craving that was not for food. It was not an expression any wife could refuse, nor did I feel inclined to.

'In here then, husband, if your need is so great.' I took his hand again and led him into the main bedchamber. There was no fire lit and the room was cold but being alone with my husband in an empty house had sparked an ember somewhere deep in my being. It had been obvious to me for some minutes that a similar heat was burning in him and we were hardly through the door before we were clinging to each other, consumed by a furnace of wanton desire. He had lifted my skirt, hitched up my legs and backed me against the bedpost almost before I realised we were joined at lip and hip and I was experiencing sensations I had never felt before. We did not disturb the covers of the neatly made bed or remove more clothing than was necessary. What we did do was why the Church called marriage 'a remedy against fornication' and it satisfied a hunger I had not realised was in me.

Afterwards we both had a thirst though and as soon as we had caught our breath, laughed with slightly shamefaced amazement and adjusted our clothing, we returned to the solar and I poured him a cup of wine. 'I hope you have news to bring me, Richard,' I said, gesturing him to a settle close to the fire and sitting down beside him. 'We are starved of it here.'

This time his laugh was shameless and he clinked his cup to mine. 'That is not all we have been starved of it seems – but more of that anon, I hope! Firstly, I have been at court and I have a message for you from the queen. She almost begs you to come back to her service.'

'*Almost* begs?' I echoed.

'I went to her Great Chamber with the king and her first words to me were not of greeting but of disappointment. "I wish your wife were with you, Sir Richard!" Those were her exact words.'

'What excuses did you make for me?'

'None. I said you would be with her very soon.'

I reared up straight in surprise. 'Really? I thought you wanted me to play the mother and remain with your children.'

Richard gave a resigned nod. 'I do, but I detect that her need may be greater than theirs. Did you know she was pregnant again?'

'No. So soon? The king will be delighted.'

'He is and he too wishes you were there because the queen is not well.'

'Is it morning sickness again? She had it with her first.'

'No, the king says it is distress.'

'Why, what distresses her so greatly?' I asked, suddenly recalling my conversation with Lady Margaret earlier in the year.

Richard reached into the purse he wore on his belt and pulled out a coin. 'This,' he said.

I reached across and took it from him. It was bronze and about the size of one of the new silver groats that were pouring out of the Mint but it did not bear the head of King Henry wearing a closed crown. This one showed a much younger man – a youth, wearing a coronet. I tried to decipher the letters written around the rim but could not. 'It looks like a coin, but a foreign one.'

'No, it's not a coin,' he said. 'They call it a jetton in Europe and it's a gambling token. They're used instead of real coins at the card table.'

'Why should a jetton upset the queen?' I asked. 'She's quite used to losing at cards; not that she can afford to.'

He smiled. 'It's not the jetton itself that disturbs her, it's the head that's stamped on it. The words are in Flemish and it comes from the court of the queen's aunt, the Dowager Duchess of Burgundy, who as you know will do anything to rock King Henry's throne.'

'Ah. Whose head is on it and what are the words?'

'That of a youth, who calls himself Richard, Duke of York, and the words announce his claim to be the rightful King of England.'

'Prince Richard is alive?' I asked the question with shock and alarm.

Richard snorted derisively. 'No, of course not! This is some unfortunate lad, whom Duchess Margaret has dug out to impersonate the queen's younger brother. No one admits to knowing who he really is but you can be sure that the king's spies are actively working to find out. This fake coin has been minted in some numbers in Flanders to spread the word around the courts of Europe that a son of King Edward of York is still alive and the rightful heir to the English throne.'

'Another pretender,' I said flatly. 'No wonder Elizabeth is distressed. She loved those brothers of hers and she has always wondered what happened to them.'

Richard took a long gulp of his wine and nodded. 'She is utterly conflicted. Part of her longs to believe that this is her lost brother, while at the same time she realises if it is, he has a better claim to the throne than she does, or King Henry, with all the threat that contains for the growing Tudor dynasty. The king keeps telling her that there is no question of it being the real Prince Richard; that Duchess Margaret is fanatical about restoring the York throne and firmly believes that her brother – the usurper whom she calls King Richard – would never have ordered the death of his nephews, despite the indisputable fact that he stole their throne and they disappeared while under his care. But although the queen acknowledges these reassurances, deep down she still longs for one of her little brothers to be alive.'

'Only this lad in Flanders is not little,' I said, peering closely at the coin. 'By my calculations Prince Richard would be seventeen now and this handsome face looks about right: smooth cheeks, thick hair, jutting jawline. There are still many people in England who will want to believe it is a son of King Edward.'

Richard leaned forward and took the coin from me, carefully placing it back in his purse. 'Indeed. So the sooner he is unmasked the better, before Yorkist fever spreads like the sweat. Meanwhile our stock would climb high at court, Joan, if you were to return to the queen's service and restore her peace of mind in time for the next Tudor birth.'

'Yes, I can see that it would,' I agreed, half-heartedly.

We returned to the Tower House a week later and before I joined the queen at Sheen I decided to check on the other threat to the Tudor throne and took Lady Margaret's sealed letter to the Lieutenant Constable's office. Sir John Digby read it with a deepening frown.

'Access to the Earl of Warwick is very restricted, Lady Guildford,' he said. 'I have a list from the Constable of the Tower of those who are to be admitted to his chambers and your name is not on it.'

'Perhaps Lady Margaret was not aware that her authority ranked below that of Lord Oxford, Sir John. It is her personal request that I pay Lord Warwick a visit, which I would like to do before I return to the queen's service in a few days' time. If I cannot be admitted to his chambers perhaps I might encounter him elsewhere – in the privy garden perhaps? I understand he takes daily walks there for his health. When I next see her I would like to be able to reassure the queen that her cousin is being well treated.'

Sir John placed Lady Margaret's letter on top of the pile on his desk and drew a sheet of fresh paper towards him. 'I will keep the letter from the king's mother and give you a pass into the privy garden instead, Lady Guildford.' He selected a quill from the penholder before him, dipped it in ink and wrote for a minute or two before sanding it and adding his waxed seal. 'Show this to the duty guard at the privy garden gate. Lord Warwick walks there every day after Terce but be warned that he has company.'

I took the note from him with a smile. 'I'm so glad to hear that, Sir John. I had thought him a lonely prisoner.'

'Strictly speaking, Lord Warwick is not a prisoner but a guest of the king. Nor is he a sociable character. His constant companion is a dog. I hope you are as good with dogs as you are with ravens, my lady.'

Having no interest in hunting, I had never paid much

attention to the Halden kennels, so I sought advice from Richard about how to treat Warwick's unexpected canine companion. 'Get Jake to soak some bread crusts in gravy and toast them,' he advised. 'He does that for me when I need a supply for the Halden hounds.'

So it was with some trepidation and a pouch full of these doggy treats that I approached the entrance into the Royal Palace privy garden the following day. All I knew of Edward of Warwick was what I had heard in the queen's chamber after he had been brought to see his cousin Queen Elizabeth at Sheen Palace, four months before the decisive Battle of Stoke. His sister, Margaret Plantagenet, had also met with him, so that they could both confirm that he was the true Earl of Warwick and prove beyond all doubt that the boy who had been crowned King Edward the Sixth in Dublin was nothing but a pretender. At the time I had received the impression that the real Edward was a guileless, rather withdrawn twelve-year-old, who had been overwhelmed by the attention and had barely spoken a word.

The Edward of Warwick I met in the privy garden was nearly four years older, a rather gangly youth of fifteen, whose clothes looked a size too small and whose dirty blond hair badly needed trimming. I had asked that he should not be given any notice of my coming, fearing that he might take fright and keep to his quarters. So when I walked into the garden I acted surprised to see anyone else there.

He was certainly surprised to see me and immediately changed course in his walk, calling into the shrubbery to warn his dog. A small multi-coloured creature came bounding out from under the bushes, immediately saw me and rushed up yapping loudly. Edward turned about to run after him and they both appeared before me together, panting.

On the approach of the dog my first instinct had been to beat a retreat but stubborn pride made me stand my ground. It was only a little dog with its rather fragile-looking owner; they were hardly a threatening pair, and my skirts were good protection from an ankle-height attack. 'God give you good morning,' I said pleasantly. 'For November, it is quite warm I find.'

Both Elizabeth and Margaret had said Edward did not make eye contact but this boy stared at me accusingly and said rudely, 'Who are you?'

'My name is Joan Guildford. May I ask yours, and your sweet little dog's?'

'He is not sweet and he doesn't like strangers. His name is Castor.'

I dipped into my pocket purse and pulled out a few of Jake's dog toasts. 'Does Castor like treats?' I asked. 'I feed them to the ravens.'

Edward didn't answer so I tossed one a little distance to stop the dog nosing around my skirts and it ran away after it. 'You shouldn't be here,' said the boy, dropping his gaze. 'No one comes while I'm here.'

'Really? Why is that?' I was keen to keep him talking but he couldn't seem to find an answer and just frowned, staring at the ground. I waited.

Eventually he said, fidgeting, 'I don't know.'

'Does your dog bite? Perhaps that's why,' I suggested. Castor had consumed the treat and come bounding back for more. 'He's very lively, isn't he?'

'He's my friend. He lives with me.' After his first belligerent stare, Edward had kept his eyes averted, looking everywhere but at me.

'And what do you two do together?'

'Nothing much.' He'd begun to look restless. 'I must go now.'

'Why? Do you have lessons to attend?'

'No. I just have to go.' There was a pause but he showed no sign of leaving.

'Do you not have lessons then?' I wanted to have something to report to Lady Margaret and the queen.

'Castor wants another treat. Have you got one?' He cast a swift glance up at me and dropped his gaze again. He had spoken so quickly I'd had trouble hearing him but the dog was pawing at my skirt so I threw another treat to send it away. 'He likes them.' A sweet smile had transformed his features but it was directed at the dog, not at me.

Suddenly he opened up and his words came tumbling out so fast I had trouble keeping up. 'A man comes to teach me but I don't like him and never speak to him. But he leaves paper and pens and tells me to write something. I don't like writing so I draw instead.'

He stopped talking as suddenly as he'd started and began to look around, anywhere but at me. I wanted to grab his attention so I asked, 'What do you draw, Edward?'

His head snapped back and he fixed his eyes on me again. 'How d'you know my name?' he demanded.

He wasn't stupid, this boy, just different – awkward. I didn't want to tell him how I knew his name so I tested his memory. 'You told me before,' I said.

'Oh.' He dropped his gaze again. 'Did I?'

'If I come another time, will you show me your drawings? I'd like to see them.'

He called the dog. It bounded up to him and they set off down the path. Over his shoulder he shouted, 'I might. When will you come?'

'Tomorrow,' I called. 'I'll come tomorrow. Goodbye, Edward.' I watched him bend to pick up a stick from the ground and throw it for Castor. Just a boy and his dog, playing in a garden, but did he know how dangerous he was to the Tudor kingdom? I truly hoped not.

31

THE NEWBORN PRINCE WAS swathed in fresh linen and wrapped in a cloth-of-gold mantle when I carried him to the door of the queen's lying-in chamber to be shown to the king.

'I'm sorry, your grace,' I said with a curtsy. 'The queen apologises for not admitting you but as you will see the boy is a good weight and she has suffered sorely from the birth. She is presently being attended by the midwife and hopes to be able to receive you later, when she has had some rest. Sleep is the best healer in these circumstances.'

King Henry was visibly torn between concern for his wife and the desire to make first acquaintance with his precious second son. I understood that for him this male child must represent the confirmation of his dynasty, the spare heir that might guarantee Tudor rule into the next generation. He reached out and took the baby confidently in his arms, gently prising back the stole and linen to feast his eyes on the pink protrusions that confirmed his sex.

'He is a beautiful boy,' he said, the rising moisture in his eyes making him blink. 'Please give my dearest love and congratulations to Elizabeth and tell her that I will pray for her and for our new son. I pray God will bless her rest and heal her wounds. I'll go now and make arrangements for his christening. Tell her the Bishop of Exeter will perform the baptism and the godparents are already here at Greenwich. He will be named after me, as we agreed.'

He passed the baby back and I restored the folds of the mantle. Despite my disappointment in not conceiving again myself I was glad to have been at Elizabeth's side during the preceding months. However much she longed for one of her brothers to have survived, I believe she had truly needed the companionship of someone with my complete certainty that the youth on the jetton was an imposter, who had never set foot on English soil and was certainly not the boy Richard, who had been born to her mother in Shrewsbury seventeen years ago.

Now that he had checked the sex and health of his new offspring, the king's concern was all for his wife. 'If she is badly hurt should we not send for the queen's surgeon?'

'He has been consulted, sire, and was content to leave the treatment of the queen's injuries to the midwife. They do tend to have more experience and skill in matters of childbirth.'

King Henry studied my face at length before making a brief, decisive nod. 'Very well, I will rely on you to keep me informed of the queen's progress, Lady Guildford, particularly if there is the slightest sign of her condition worsening. I will tell the night guard to wake me immediately if you send word.'

I made another deep curtsy. 'I very much hope that will not be necessary, your grace.'

Like most men the king was not keen to hear the exact nature of Elizabeth's injuries as a result of the birth but they involved the midwife's skilful use of a fine needle and silk thread and were quickly treated, so that by the time I returned to her chamber she had been lifted from the delivery bed and was sleeping peacefully between clean linen sheets in her own curtained haven. At her request I attended the baptism that took place in the church of the Grey Friars, which was also the royal chapel at Greenwich Palace, re-named at the king's behest, who had taken against the name Placentia. Although not attended by so many members of the court as had been present at Prince Arthur's baptism, it was of similar splendour. The silver font had been brought from Canterbury and the infant was wrapped in an ermine-trimmed cloth-of-gold mantle to signify his royal status.

The following day the king created Prince Henry Duke of York. I assumed this was to done in order to nullify the bogus claim of the anonymous youth whose face appeared on the Flemish jettons. No public reference had been made in England to the emergence of this pretender but rumour was rife, especially in London, that the boy prince who had last held that title was still alive and living at the Burgundian court of the queen's Aunt Margaret. Richard had told me that King Henry's agents had in fact established that this youth, while claiming to have spent his childhood up to the age of twelve in England, spoke heavily accented English but was fluent in French and the Flemish patois; neverthe-less Duchess Margaret had declared him to be her nephew and kitted him out in purple silk and a gold collar to wear around his shoulders. However hard I tried to persuade Elizabeth that he was an imposter, it was not long before she admitted to me that she still held a faint, treasonous hope that he was her little brother.

'Until I set eyes on him and positively know him not to be Dickon, I will never be able to rid my mind of the possibility, Joan,' she had confided when we were alone. 'But I charge you, as you value our friendship, never to tell the king that I said this.'

Prince Henry was still a small baby when he was sent to join his sister Princess Margaret in the nursery household at Eltham Palace. I couldn't help thinking it a shame that, on King Henry's orders, their older brother Arthur was being brought up separately, far away on the Welsh March, being prepared firstly for his role as Prince of Wales and ultimately as the heir to the throne of England. As time went by Elizabeth felt this separation keenly. The journey to visit Arthur was an uncomfortable one of a hundred and fifty miles, mostly by horse or chariot, and took the best part of a week, whereas it was only a short trip by river barge from the main royal palaces around London to visit the younger children at Eltham, where they lived in the healthy atmosphere of their hilltop mansion with its piped water supply and improved drainage, surrounded by parks and gardens.

'Arthur will know his governor and tutors better than he knows his parents,' Elizabeth complained to the king.

'He will know his people,' King Henry insisted, 'particularly the people of Wales and the borderlands.'

Less than a year after the birth of Prince Henry, Queen Elizabeth learned that her mother, the Dowager Queen, was grievously ill and managed to pay an extended visit to her Bermondsey Abbey retreat, despite being in the advanced stages of her next pregnancy. When she left her at the end of May she knew that they were unlikely to meet again and ten days after entering her confinement she heard that her mother had died.

Elizabeth wept in my arms. 'She had such a chequered life, Joan, and at the end I was not even there to comfort her in death.'

'But your sisters were with her, your grace,' I said. 'The Princesses Anne and Katherine, and the Abbess of Barking even brought little Bridget from her convent to say farewell to her mother.'

'But my mother was Queen of England! A knell should have sounded in every town and city but there is silence. Why should she have asked to be buried at Windsor in the dead of night, with only her friend the Prior of Sheen and her chaplain to place her in my father's tomb in St George's Chapel? It's as if she felt God considered her unworthy of a queen's obsequies.'

'There is to be a grand Requiem Mass, is there not? Tomorrow, I believe. I'm sure there will be mourners and prayers and ceremonial then and those wonderful choristers will sing and your three sisters and your half-brother Lord Dorset and brother-in-law Viscount Welles will all take part.'

Elizabeth frowned through her tears. 'Why will Cecily not be there? She should be deputising for me and making offerings.'

'Lord Welles says she is ill. A miscarriage, I fear. Lady Anne will make the offerings.'

'Oh, poor Cecily!' Her countenance changed to one of genuine concern. 'She has had no joy from motherhood. And our mother lost her royal sons. No wonder she thought herself a failure!'

'I do not believe she did, your grace. Nothing that happened to her was her fault and the same applies to you. You must calm yourself and think of your unborn child. It will not be long before you are holding him or her in your arms.'

It was a girl, named after her mother and so recently deceased grandmother, the third royal Elizabeth in line. As soon as she was churched, the queen took the baby to Eltham, where she was to stay with her children for several weeks, and I was at last given leave.

It was months since I had seen Hal and he had changed from a waddling duck to a racing hare; his once-plump limbs transformed with growing muscle. Jack and June still teased him when we went to the home wood but the young ravens were no longer there. In the autumn they had been driven from the nest site by their parents and at Christmas Sim had taken the opportunity to transport the three juveniles up to London, where he hoped they would find a flock of other young birds, in which to complete their development.

I had been briefly to the Tower before coming down to Kent and was impressed at the work he had done there to encourage the raven flock to visit the alders on the green, building more roosting boxes for them to use later when pairs had formed. Sir John Digby had supported him and, perhaps due to the fondness that had developed between us as a couple, Richard had also favoured the idea, against the wishes of his friend Sir Henry Wyatt and the garrison commander. So although ravens were not permanently present in large numbers, at least three pairs had shown signs of settling and the archers were amused by the games and tricks Sim played with them and with the itinerant flock of young birds.

Politically, the Flemish pretender remained a persistent irritation to King Henry, who now referred to him as Perkin Warbeck, his spies having traced the young man's true family, living in the town of Tournai on the French border with Flanders. Duchess Margaret's protégé had left her court and travelled to Ireland, where he'd hoped to find a welcome and raise an army to take his claim to England, but he had not attracted enough followers and retreated to France. This had been the situation when the queen went into confinement and mourning for her mother and it wasn't until after I arrived in Kent that I learned of the subsequent dramatic developments.

My husband surprised me by calling his son Edward to Halden Hall from London to help him on an urgent recruiting campaign. 'The French king has publicly recognised Warbeck as Richard, Duke of York, and acknowledged his claim to the English throne,' he explained with bitter anger. 'It is only eight years since King Charles loaned money and men to King Henry to establish his own claim against the York usurper and now he is backing this Flemish imposter against him. He's playing a treacherous game and the king has sworn to stop him, so he's raising an invasion force to demonstrate his anger.'

I was flabbergasted. A few weeks ago Warbeck had been the subject of derisive laughter in the English court and now he was the cause of a declaration of war. 'And how many men are you obliged to muster here in Kent?' I asked. 'It will not be easy to get volunteers in midsummer, when men are needed on the land.'

'The king will not cross the Channel until October,' said Edward, now a strapping nineteen-year-old. 'And I will not be in the Guildford contingent. I will go with the king's henchmen, to guard his person.'

We had gathered in Richard's private office. 'That is a great honour, Edward,' I told him. 'You have done well.'

He grinned. 'Better than Farmer George anyway,' he jeered. 'Where is he, Mother Joan? Out digging in the fields? He certainly won't be in the tiltyard, I imagine.'

'George may not make a soldier, Edward, but he'll make an excellent estate manager.' I turned to my husband. 'Which reminds me, I need to talk to you about Maria. I think we may have a problem.'

His brow instantly furrowed but he put me off. 'Later, Joan. First I must go through the county muster rolls with Edward. Can you have supper sent here and a jug of wine? We may be some time.'

The midsummer moon had risen high above the casement frame before he came to our chamber but I was waiting, reading in the light of a fragrant oil-lamp. The smell of rosemary filled the room – an aroma I loved. Richard sniffed appreciatively. 'Mmm. That's very relaxing. What is it?'

'Rosemary,' I said, closing the book. 'It's supposed to keep you alert.'

He flopped down onto the cushioned window seat. 'I need the opposite – oblivion. I'm exhausted – and you were right. It's not going to be easy to recruit five hundred Kentish men for France. I worry that even on my father's lands there may be many closet Yorkists deterred by the prospect of fighting against someone they believe to be a living son of King Edward. Because my father was King Edward's Comptroller before he swore an oath to Tudor and became

King Henry's and retainers don't always stick by a leader who buys himself a pardon.'

'Is that what Sir John did?'

'Yes, and he wasn't alone. The royal coffers were empty when Richard died and Henry was susceptible to offers of gold coin and an oath of loyalty – still is.'

'You haven't bought Edward his place in the elite henchmen guard, have you?'

He shook his head with a smile. 'I didn't need to. He's impressed the king as a Squire of the Body. He's even on the court list of tournament jousters; not that there have been any tournaments lately.' He yawned and stretched his arms out with linked fingers, making his joints crack. 'Now, what's this about Maria?'

I took a deep breath. It was not a subject I'd been looking forward to broaching. 'She's sixteen and – how can I put it – restless. I think Mistress Wood had taken her eye off her and she's been allowed to go into the village and wander about the countryside with George, meeting all manner of folk. I'm not saying she's promiscuous or anything but I think she's become friendly with a young man of whom you would not approve.'

As I spoke Richard's face grew darker and darker. 'How has this happened? Is this because you have not been at the head of the household, Joan? Who is this young man?'

'As far as I can ascertain his name is Kempe, Christopher Kempe. He's the son of a farmer, one of your father's tenants. Do you know them?'

By now Richard had his head in his hands and his voice was muffled. 'Yes, I know the family. They come to the church in Rolvenden and the boys are often hauled before the village moot for various misdemeanours – mostly causing damage or trespassing with their dogs. There are three sons and they're all skirt chasers; that I do know. Do you think Maria has let this Christopher lout under hers? Please don't tell me she's breeding!'

I winced at his bitter, accusatory tone and coarse language, mainly because he was referring to his favourite daughter and I felt he should have more sympathy for a young girl who, without the necessary adult guidance, might have been led astray. 'It was Mistress Strood who told me about the gossip. I haven't actually confronted Maria yet. I thought you might want to do so yourself.'

He looked utterly horrified at the thought. 'Oh no, this is woman's work. I'm not going to ask her if she's been rolling in the hay with a local ruffian. I wouldn't trust myself not to take a belt to her. This would never have happened if Anne were still alive.'

I couldn't believe my ears. Was he really implying that this situation was my fault, when he had more or less ordered me to return to the queen's service, leaving his children in the care of their governess? My anger boiled over.

'That is grossly unfair! If anyone is responsible it is you. I re-joined the queen's service because you thought it would lift the Guildford standing at court. And it was you who decided to delay arranging a marriage for Maria because you wanted to keep her at home for longer. Then you left her to the timid supervision of Mistress Wood, who Maria can twist around her little finger. You have no idea whether your first wife would have handled this situation any differently, except that she never offered you the opportunity of raising your status so I suppose she would have been here for you to blame. You cannot parade a subtletie and eat it too, Richard.'

He was on his feet now, pacing the floor, clenching his hands together and shaking his head. 'All right, all right! I'm not blaming you, Joan, but neither am I going to confront Maria without you. We'll tackle it together.' He paused, turning to stare at me as I fixed his gaze with narrowed eyes. 'Now what?' he growled.

I put down my book to avoid the temptation to throw it at him and resolutely quashed my sense of injustice and indignation. Then I stood up in order to speak to him face to face, as calmly as I could. 'Well, Richard, if we're going to do this together we have to agree on how to handle it. If it turns out to be a harmless young girl's infatuation, which has gone no further than a few furtive kisses, that is easily dealt with, but if there might be a question of a pregnancy then that is another bowl of pottage. How do you propose to discover which is the case and what would be your reaction to the latter? Apart from thrashing her, which I refuse to even contemplate.'

I was pleased to note that he took a few moments to consider his response, although his disgruntled expression did not fade. 'Truly I can't think of any other way of finding out whether a girl might be pregnant other than just asking her. If that is too blunt a tool for you, then what do you suggest?'

'That we ask her gently and considerately if she has made friends with Christopher Kempe and then analyse her reaction. If she blushes and bridles and admits that she has, then we probe further but we can probably presume that it has gone no further than kisses. However, if she stoutly denies it and angrily asks how we got the idea that she was involved with anyone, we are probably in trouble. We may not call it love but that is what she believes it is and she will be trying to protect the boy from your wrath.'

He gave me a look of utter disbelief. 'How on earth do you come to those conclusions, Joan?'

I shrugged. 'I suppose because I'm female and it is not so long ago that I was her age myself. There's always a chance that she is already regretting the liaison and hopes to keep it from us entirely, in which case she is not pregnant, or at least does not know that she is. Of course then it will only be a matter of time before she and we discover it.'

Richard raised his eyes heavenward. 'Dear God – the mind of woman – how was it ever created?'

I ignored that jibe and said reasonably, 'The point is, do you have any suggestions as to how we treat those various possibilities?'

'I'm thinking that we should just arrange her a marriage as soon as possible; whether it has to be to this Kempe boy if it is necessary, or might be to someone of more worth, will become clear.'

'Do you know enough about the Kempe family to judge if they are worthy of Maria, Richard?' I asked gently. I understood how much this fall from grace of his favourite daughter had upset him.

The space between his brows creased into deep furrows of anguish. 'No, I don't, but I will make it my business to find out and if they are not I pray to God a marriage between us and them is not necessary.'

32

ALL RICHARD'S PRAYERS PROVED fruitless and the whole Guildford family attended the marriage of Maria to Christopher Kempe at the Church of St Mary the Virgin, a description that sadly no longer applied to our Maria. After being confronted with our suspicions, she confessed that she and the farmer's son had indeed become carried away by their teenage longings. The lax governess, Mistress Wood, had received her marching orders and Maria had been confined to the Hall until she appeared at the church porch to exchange vows with her chastened swain. I never discovered if he had been subject to any penance or punishment by his own family; I only knew that the dowry Richard had set aside for his favourite daughter's portion was drastically reduced.

In a tearful conversation with Maria before her wedding I asked her if she regretted the way things had turned out but she denied it and maintained that she was looking forward to being a mother. Her new husband was indisputably a handsome young man who was in charge of all the livestock on his father's farm and turned out to be a close friend of George's. It was not until after they were married that Maria discovered he had been putting out poisoned bait for the ravens. Their argument about this practice had caused the first of many bruises she received both before and after her baby was born. It was only much later that we discovered that she was paying dearly for her youthful misdemeanour.

Meanwhile Richard had mustered his troops aboard the ship *Maria* and joined the king's fleet at Sandwich, his contribution to the twelve-thousand-strong army intended to chastise the French king for harbouring the pretender, Perkin Warbeck. They began by laying siege to the fortified port of Boulogne but hardly a cannon shot was fired before a peace conference was called. Warbeck was eventually expelled from France as part of a peace treaty negotiated between the two kings; King Henry abandoned his siege and returned home and King Charles paid him handsomely to do so.

Christmas court celebrations were particularly lavish and held at Westminster Palace, which meant that Richard and I could stay at the Tower House and enjoy the company of our children as well. At three years old, Hal was enchanted by all the festive fun and entertainment he shared with the two royal children and on one occasion was ferried home to the Tower House fast asleep after midnight, having been found curled up on a window seat in the queen's Great Chamber.

It was during the Twelve Days, when we flitted between the Tower and the Palace that I became reacquainted with Meg Poyntz. She and her husband, Sir Robert, were among the guests invited to share the royal celebrations and had travelled to London from their Gloucestershire home, where I had spent time during the usurper's reign. When Richard invited Sir Robert to view the ordnance at the

Tower, it gave Meg and I an opportunity to catch up on our family news.

Although I felt slightly guilty about it, I did not tell her about Maria's misalliance and as George and Edward had chosen to accompany the two men, Pippa was the eldest of my stepchildren to join us around the fire in the hall.

'Pippa?' queried Meg, having been introduced. 'I take it that is short for Philippa, just as my name is short for Margaret. And how old are you, young lady?'

'I will be thirteen this year,' the girl replied proudly.

'Nearly grown up then,' Meg remarked with a smile, 'and only a little younger than my eldest son.' She turned to me, confidentially. 'Anthony is already thirteen and will be fourteen in the summer. Sir Robert is keen for him to go to the Inns of Court to study law but I would also like him to continue his military training.' She hesitated slightly before continuing. 'Would Sir Richard have any interest in taking him on as a squire, while also letting him attend the Middle Temple during the legal terms, Joan? Robert doesn't know I'm asking this but perhaps you would sound your husband out?'

'I'll do that willingly,' I replied. 'When you took me in at Acton Court, you asked me to teach Anthony to read and write and he was such a bright student. I'm sure he will excel at anything he sets his mind to.'

'Well, he certainly shows early promise in the tiltyard, so I don't think he will disappoint in that regard.'

I gave her a smile. 'I would be delighted to repay some of the hospitality you showed me. And Sir Richard could certainly use the services of a squire now that his eldest son has been appointed to the king's henchmen and George, whom you met earlier, shows more aptitude for farming than fighting.'

The matter was settled that evening and young Anthony Poyntz travelled to Kent the following summer, having completed his first term studying law in London. Richard had taken him to be measured for a harness, the elements of which could be altered as he grew, and he was proudly wearing his cuirass and leg armour over his doublet and hose when he rode to Halden Hall behind Richard, for the first time.

I greeted them outside the main entrance when they arrived and Anthony acknowledged my welcome with a remarkably stylish court bow. 'Greetings, Master Poyntz,' I said with surprise. 'I do not remember you performing such an elegant courtesy the last time I left you but then you were not quite six. Perhaps while you're here you might teach the Guildford men how it should be done?'

Smooth-cheeked and ash-blond, Anthony had matured into a youth who looked very like I remembered his mother at his age, when she had been celebrated among the court squires and young knights for her exceptional beauty. Had she been legitimate she might have married an earl but lovely Meg was the illegitimate daughter of the Dowager Queen's brother, Earl Rivers, and he had chosen to marry her to Robert Poyntz, an up-and-coming royal squire, who had also proved useful to him as an astute legal assistant on his diplomatic missions for the king. It was while serving on these that he had been of crucial help to the young Henry Tudor during his exile in Brittany and later received a knighthood as a result.

Only a few days after Anthony's arrival, news came that Richard's father, Sir John Guildford, had suffered a seizure at his home, a few miles from Halden Hall. Richard rode swiftly away with Anthony and a messenger at his back. Within hours Anthony had returned to tell us that Sir John had died soon after Richard's arrival and he was staying to discuss burial arrangements with his stepmother and the priest. The messenger had been sent to Canterbury Cathedral where Sir John would be interred, having established a chantry there, in anticipation of his death.

The young squire shuffled his feet, so I waited with an inquiring expression for he obviously had something else to say. 'Since George has gone off somewhere and Sir Richard is not here, I am free if you have any errands or tasks you would like me to do, my lady. I am not used to being idle.'

I smiled. 'That is good to hear, Anthony. In fact I have today received a delivery of books from London and I was about to round up Bess and Pippa and Winnie and ask them which they would like to study first. Every day one of us reads a passage and then we discuss it afterwards. It is educational but also interesting and can be fun. You're very welcome to join us if you would not find it tedious. First, however, we will go to the local church to offer prayers for their grandfather's soul, but I do not expect you to involve yourself in that.'

I noticed his eyes light up as I mentioned the reading class and was delighted but not surprised when he accepted the offer with alacrity. 'I love to read too, my lady,' he said eagerly. 'I would very much like to join your discussions.'

Anthony turned out to be rather an asset to our reading group because the girls were all quite struck by his good looks and vied with each other to impress him with their opinions. He found it hard to get a word in at first but when he did his comments were intelligent and often amusing, entertaining all of us. Subsequently we all looked forward to the occasions when he was able to join our discussions.

It was too soon after the birth of her baby boy for Maria to ride to Canterbury but otherwise, apart from little Hal and Lizzie, we all attended Sir John's funeral. It was nearly thirty miles to the famous cathedral and the older children were all able to ride their own ponies or horses. Since Sir John had been Sheriff of Kent several times, the funeral service the following day was well attended and so we were forced to spend another uncomfortable night at a hospice on the return journey. The younger girls were almost asleep in the saddle by the time we reached Halden Hall as dusk approached.

Hetty Smith, who had been taking care of the younger children, rushed out to greet us looking highly stressed. 'I thank God you are back, my lady! I thought you might have stayed another night away and I didn't know what to do. Hal is not well. He is hot and feverish and I think he may have an ague.'

I was off my horse and up the stairs to the nursery like a greyhound after a hare. Until that day Hal had been the healthiest child I knew; sniffles seemed to disappear in hours, coughs vanished overnight and he'd had none of the usual childish ailments – up to now. My heart was beating like a drum by the time I reached his cot and placed my hand on his brow. It was red hot.

'I've been sponging him down with cold water and for a while that helps but then the fever burns up again,' Hetty said. 'Do you think it's an ague?'

'I don't know, Hetty, but I do know that he mustn't get

305

so hot. I think we need a tub of cold water so that he can be immersed in it. Can you organise that with the steward and I'll bring him downstairs? He's been crying I expect, and that won't help. God and St Nicholas, why oh why did I have to be in Canterbury when this happened?'

But of course I was often away these days and illness could strike at any time. I picked Hal up and hugged him but he didn't really seem to know who I was. The house was stiflingly hot and I decided to take him outside. I fretted over what was making him ill, whether it was disease or something he had eaten or drunk. Our water was piped from a spring just up the valley but since no one else was afflicted I did not think there was any danger from that source. However, I had a great fear that it might be the scarlet fever, the cause of so many childhood deaths. There had been a case reported in Rolvenden and perhaps the heat had carried its miasma to Halden Hall. I prayed fervently that it was not the sweat, which had been claiming so many lives in a seemingly random way.

I asked Richard to get a swing-cot tied between two apple trees in the orchard and had the cold tub carried out to it, then I sat all night swinging Hal to let the breeze pass over him, singing to him and periodically cooling his fever in the tub, until at last I thought I detected a drop in the heat of his body. As dawn broke he opened his eyes and I held a cup of water to his lips. To my vast relief and delight he gulped at it as if he had just emerged from a desert. I fell to my knees beside his rocking cot and cried out my thanks to God and all the saints who protected children.

Unbeknown to me, Richard had been keeping guard at the orchard gate all night and heard my cries and prayers, but mistook them for anguish. He came running and calling, 'No, Joan! Do not tell me he is dead.'

I swept Hal out of the swing-cot and kissed his cooled cheeks. 'He is not dead, Richard; he is a hale and healthy Hal. Look!'

My little boy's bare legs were wrapped around my waist, his arms gripped my shoulders and he snuggled into my neck. 'Mamma, I'm cold!' he complained. They were the best words I had ever heard.

A little later that morning, when the sun had risen and I had fed Hal some bread and milk and tucked him back in his proper cot to sleep, I went out to the home wood to tell the ravens my good news. The original pair still nested in their chosen conifer every year but had not so far produced another clutch of eggs, although Sim and I lived in hope. He had brought out their breakfast of kitchen scraps and they were squabbling and play-fighting over them when I arrived.

Sim doffed the brimmed hat of homespun linen he wore all through the summer and gave me his familiar greeting. 'God give you good day, m'lady. All is well here.'

I nodded and smiled, more broadly than usual. 'All is better than you can imagine, Sim. I have wonderful news to tell the ravens.'

He had been unaware of the drama through the night and could not appreciate my elation. 'Best sit and wait until they finish their meal then or they'll not listen,' he said matter-of-factly, pointing to the log he had set against the trunk of a nearby larch tree.

Since he showed no personal interest in my wonderful news, I did as he suggested and waited, watching the flapping and 'kraaking' of Jack and June as they affirmed their bond over their food with a ritual caper that might have been thought a fight, if it didn't always end in mutual grooming and head-rubbing. I had seen it often and enjoyed it, only on this occasion the events of the last few days, culminating in the fear and worry of Hal's illness and the sleepless night, all caught up with me and I fell asleep.

I woke to a gentle pricking on my hand, which had dropped to my side as I slept. Still heavy-lidded, my eyes settled on the sight of a gleaming black bird gently lifting the skin of my upper hand in its mighty beak and dropping it without harm. Hardly aware of what was happening, I watched it do this several times before lifting my finger when it withdrew a little and stroking the smooth surface of its beak. A memory returned of my brief encounter with a raven on the Tower Wharf in the early days of my marriage, when I had been elated at coming so close to a wild creature, until it had ripped a hole in my thumb. This bird was kissing the same hand and yet the action was obviously done out of a wish to attract my attention, not to make me bleed. I could use the word kissing because it was perfectly obvious that was what it was but I could not tell whether the donor was Jack or June because they were so alike. Only instinct told me it was the female.

'I have good news to tell you,' I murmured as I stroked the shiny bill. 'Your youngsters are settling down at the Tower of London and last night my child Hal survived a terrible bout of fever and is recovering well. So God is good and we can celebrate, you and I, mother to mother.'

33

Sir John's death had considerably altered Richard's workload and I began to wonder if it had been such a good idea for him to take on the knightly training of Anthony Poyntz. Fortunately Edward Guildford was appointed joint Master with his father of the Royal Armouries, which meant that he was now mainly in London and could supervise Anthony's training while he was in the city attending his legal studies. Meanwhile Richard was largely in Kent, tied up with the affairs of the numerous Guildford estates that were now his, as well as overseeing work at the shipyard and on a new wall that was intended to keep the sea off the marshes at the mouth of the River Rother. He was made High Sheriff of Kent, responsible for justice in the county for a year and also inherited his father's crown post as Comptroller of the King's Chamber, which involved checking the king's annual accounts. Although we saw too little of each other, the Guildfords were heading for the top of the Tudor hierarchy.

I was frequently back with Queen Elizabeth, who now spent considerable time at Eltham Palace with her baby Elizabeth, four-year-old Margaret and two-year-old Henry and continued to fulminate over the identity of the young man we were calling Perkin Warbeck but who the elderly Dowager Duchess of Burgundy still persisted in promoting throughout Europe as Richard, Duke of York. Having been ejected from France as a result of King Henry's successful expedition he had taken refuge once more at her court.

'But despite exiling him, King Charles still stubbornly refers to him as the Duke of York and lately the young man even seems to have charmed the new Holy Roman Emperor, Maximilian,' Elizabeth confided in a whisper during her afternoon salon, drawing a fierce frown from her sister Lady Anne, who was unable to hear what passed between us but was probably convinced that it involved her. 'It seems that every monarch in Europe is in thrall to this imposter!'

In view of the consistent threat from across the Channel I had refrained from burdening the queen with a report of my visits to her cousin Edward of Warwick at the Tower, believing him to be of little significance now that the focus had turned to Warbeck. King Henry, furious that the imposter continued to represent a threat to his throne, decided the best response would be to plan a grand investiture of his younger son as the true-born and genuine Duke of York.

'I want it to be a truly spectacular event that will be the talk of Europe and so we'll wait until Henry is able to ride a warhorse,' he told the queen when he came to Eltham. 'When do you think that will be?'

Elizabeth laughed, thinking him to be joking. 'When he's thirteen or fourteen I should think, my lord. Do you want to wait that long?'

The king shook his head impatiently. 'Not to ride it in a

joust, Elizabeth, just to be able to stay in the saddle and look like a prince. He will be three very soon and he is quite tall. He should be able to straddle a horse by All Hallows.'

She was incredulous. 'At a mere three years and a quarter you would put Henry up alone on a warhorse? I cannot even begin to tolerate such a notion! He is still a baby, my lord.' She invariably addressed him as 'my lord' when she was at odds with him.

'I shall consult with the Master of Horse,' King Henry said, undeterred. 'I'm sure there must be an old warhorse in the royal stables that will carry him quietly and safely in a procession.'

'Even old warhorses can be unexpectedly frisky.' I was pleased to see a mischievous twinkle ignite in the queen's eye when she said this. Perhaps she was hoping to instigate a change of subject. 'Look at your Uncle Jasper. He's been quite frolicsome since he married my aunt Katherine. Can we look for more Tudor offspring from that source, I wonder?'

Jasper Tudor, Duke of Bedford, had visited Eltham quite recently, bringing with him a woman he thought would be a good governess for Prince Henry's household. Lady Darcy was finally retiring and when I showed Mistress Jane Howell around at the queen's behest I thought her very suitable for the job. Probably a few years younger than my mother, she was sprightly and cheerful and Welsh but, more importantly, she had looked after King Henry himself through his early youth. Now a recently widowed grandmother, I thought she seemed very capable of organising a staff of young nurses and perfectly able to sprint after a lively little boy, should it be necessary.

The king sent his wife a reproachful glance. 'All these years after their marriage I think we can forget any developments of that sort but they do seem quite well suited, despite the age difference. However, as far as Prince Henry is concerned I'm sure the Master of Horse will find a discreet way of tying him to the saddle so that he cannot fall off, even if his mount should prove skittish.'

A falsetto voice suddenly piped up from behind the queen's canopied chair.

'Skittish horsey starts to prance,
Leads the Prince a merry dance.
Little Princey waves his sword,
And falls arse-up upon the sward.'

Elizabeth felt in her pocket purse for a penny and tossed it to the source of the voice. 'Thank you, Patch,' she called, 'that's exactly what I fear.' She cocked her head to one side and raised an eyebrow at King Henry. The fool pocketed the coin with a smirk.

Henry pursed his lips but did not abandon his proposal. 'Sometimes I wish your aunt Margaret would tip off her horse that way. But at least even she might be silenced when all Europe is talking about the fabulous jousts held in England in honour of the real Duke of York.'

Elizabeth knew when she was beaten. 'As long as you don't have them put a lance in our little son's hand and send him into the lists,' she said and signalled to the musicians who sat silent in the corner. 'Let us have some music, minstrels – and some dancing, ladies! We need to be merry. Lady Guildford, can you teach the king the steps of the galliard? I don't want him showing England up when the Spanish embassy arrives.'

Anticipation of the Spanish embassy was somewhat premature, considering King Ferdinand and Queen Isabella had not yet confirmed the betrothal of their daughter Katherine to the seven-year-old Prince of Wales, but Queen Elizabeth had already ordered dance teachers to be hired to teach her attendants the steps of new continental dances. The galliard was the latest to take the courts of Europe by storm – an energetic and tricky processional dance, which I had still not perfected.

'Of course I would be honoured to do so, your grace,' I said, feeling my cheeks grow hot. 'But I really think instruction from one of the Lady Annes might be of more benefit to his grace.' Three ladies called Anne attended the queen and all of them were younger, nobler and nimbler than I was.

Elizabeth gave me her 'please don't argue with me' look and made an imperial wave in the direction of the clear space in front of the minstrels. It was aimed at the king as much as me and we both rose reluctantly to comply.

'You may not think yourself the best dancer, Lady Guildford, but the queen regards you as the best teacher among her flock,' King Henry said as he took my hand to lead me to the floor. The unusual rhythm of the music had us beaten for several minutes, inspiring childish titters among the maids of honour, but the king caught it quite quickly and started to enjoy the idea of the leaps that linked the steps.

We were both breathless and laughing by the time Elizabeth relented and ushered the youthful members of her troupe to replace us. 'But only until you have caught your breath, my lord; then your queen would like to take the floor with you so you can judge whether I have absorbed the steps of the dance.'

It goes without saying that Elizabeth danced it best of all.

Inevitably the king had his way in the matter of Prince Henry's triumphant ride through London. At the end of October the little boy was clad in a miniature knight's harness of polished and intricately engraved plate and strapped into a high-backed jousting saddle made especially to his measurements, upholstered in embroidered red velvet and girthed onto a venerable but gleaming black warhorse trapped in green and white Tudor livery. Flanked by his two great-uncles, Jasper Tudor, Duke of Bedford, and Thomas Grey, Marquess of Dorset, who rode smaller palfreys so as not to restrict the public's view of the main attraction, and escorted on foot by Yeomen of the Guard and the King's Archers, the young prince processed from the Guildhall, through Cheapside, around St Paul's churchyard, through the Ludgate, over the Fleet Bridge and all the way to Westminster.

Far from daunted by such a lengthy parade, Prince Henry had been in his element, waving cheerfully to the huge crowds, released from their daily toil by royal decree in order to express their affection for this charismatic little boy, who nodded and smiled and thoroughly enjoyed the noise they made and the flowers they threw. And the cheers multiplied when he managed to catch one red rose and use it to wave back at them with childish enthusiasm.

'It might have had a thorn on its stem, Mother Joan,' Bess Mortimer told me later as she described this incident, which she and the three younger Guildford girls had watched with their new governess from a bird's-eye viewpoint above the Temple Gate, courtesy of Anthony Poyntz. Richard and I had both been on duty at Westminster Palace, where there was a special banquet in the queen's Great Chamber, and only heard about the cavalcade when we got home to the Tower House that evening. 'He could have been hurt. I don't think he should have caught it, do you?'

Pippa was scornful. 'Of course he should. He had gauntlets on and anyway, who cares about a small scratch? Certainly not that little soldier. He took his hat off so many times that I'm sure he did it just to show us his bright red Tudor hair. He's a handsome little man, Mother Joan, even though he's only three. All the girls in the crowd thought so.'

'More handsome than his older brother, the Prince of Wales?' I inquired, amused.

She thought about it, then said, 'Well, we don't see so much of him, do we? Prince Arthur's handsome too but not so robust, I'd say. He looks as if he'd rather be holding a book than a lance, if you know what I mean.'

I smiled at her description, delivered with all the wisdom of an observant twelve-year-old. 'Like his father,' I agreed, 'although I'd like to point out that King Henry has won every battle he's ever fought. Fighting takes brain as much as brawn.'

There was plenty of each on show over the next week, as a series of tournaments were held to celebrate the little prince's elevation to his dukedom.

'King Henry certainly didn't spare the gold angels on that spectacular show,' Richard declared, after the banners and pavilions that he had designed had been taken down and the court had returned to its normal routine. 'We can only hope it achieved its purpose of taking Europe's eye off the pretend Duke of York and fixing it on the genuine article. Prince Henry was a star performer, wasn't he? He might have been born to it!' His little pleasantry disguised the weariness of a very tired man.

34

B Y MID-JANUARY IN THE following year there were signs
that King Henry's attempt to divert attention from the
Flemish pretender had failed and the repercussions caused
an upheaval in the royal court.

'Joan, you know your way around the Tower. Will you
accompany me to the chapel on the green? I have never
been to the people's church but I believe it is named for St
Peter.' The queen beckoned me from the front of her entourage, which had just disembarked from her barge at the
royal entrance by the Cradle Tower and was gathering in
the vaulted chamber at the foot of a spiral stair that led up
into the palace. This was an entirely unexpected visit, made
in the dawn light as the sun rose over the River Thames.

I stepped forward. 'Yes, your grace. It's on the other side
of the White Tower but not far to walk from here.'

She pulled her fur-lined cloak around her and went to
raise the hood. 'Can you arrange this so that I can see but
not be seen? I expect there'll be a lot of soldiers around and
I don't want to be recognised.'

I fixed the hood so that it hung over her face. 'That should
be fine as long as you keep your head down, my lady, and
just follow me.' I glanced around at the rest of the royal

attendants still standing at a discreet distance. Two of them were the queen's own yeomen guards who regularly stood sentinel at the entrance to her Privy Chamber. 'Would you not like your guards to accompany you?'

The hooded head shook in denial and she kept her voice low so that only I could hear. 'No, Joan; I want to go secretly and privately to pray. That is why I don't want to use the Chapel of St John or either of the oratories in the Royal Palace. Nor do I wish the king to know. He is very worried and distracted and I don't want to add to his distress. Let us just go quickly together. Perhaps you could tell your mother to instruct the rest to go to my apartments and carry on as if I were there already but not to be disturbed.'

On sudden and unexpected orders from the king we had left Westminster Palace very early, too early for the queen's chief lady-in-waiting to be up and dressed and so my mother was standing in for her. Moreover we discovered later that Princess Anne had been ordered not to follow the queen to the Tower but to remain in her quarters at Westminster. A deal of haste and mystery surrounded this dawn move to the royal fortress and when the two of us made our way out into Water Lane it was clear from the increased number of sentries on the battlements that the king's party was already installed. I could just make out his personal standard flying from the highest flagpole.

'King Henry must have arrived in the dark,' I remarked, as we were overtaken by squads of soldiers and scurrying clerks heading for the Wakefield Tower and the main entrance leading from the river to the Inner Court. 'Something crucial must be going on somewhere in the most secure part of the fortress.'

Her voice was somewhat muffled by the hood. 'Yes, Joan, something very crucial,' she said and I thought she might reveal more but she fell silent.

We took the gate that led directly onto the green and for once I did not look for ravens in the alder trees as we passed them, heading directly for the little church at the far end. The office of Prime was over and St Peter's was empty as we made our way up to the chancel, where a carved and painted image of the eponymous saint dominated a small side chapel. Its altar held a beautifully crafted and bejewelled gold reliquary, reputedly containing one of St Peter's finger bones, and Elizabeth went straight up to kiss it and leave a pouch of coins before it as an offering. I retired to the stone bench set along the outside wall and waited, wondering what urgent matter she was laying before the Apostle and what national emergency had caused the royal couple's sudden morning flit to the security of the Tower. My guess was that someone or something was posing a new threat to the Tudor throne and I found myself praying silently for the future of the reign on which my family and I so increasingly depended. I also wondered whether Richard had been called to join the king's deliberations, wherever they were taking place. As I had been serving the queen at Westminster since the Twelfth Night celebrations ended, we had not been in each other's company for the past week.

When we left the church I managed to get a glimpse of a pair of ravens perched on the battlemented wall that divided the green from the street on which the Mint was located, its chimneys presently smoke-free during the winter lay-off. The birds were clearly a pair because they were busy preening each other. We soon hurried away, however, when our presence attracted attention from a passing troop of archers who began offering us coarse soldierly comments. Had they known they were addressing the Queen of England they might have adjusted their language but Elizabeth simply followed me, head down, as we ducked behind them into the tunnel under the Coldharbour Gatehouse, which led to the Tower's Inner Court. When she pushed back her hood, the guards on duty in the archway were dumbfounded to recognise her and immediately drew back their pole-arms in salute to let us pass.

The yeoman guard at the entrance to Elizabeth's Privy Chamber revealed that a messenger had delivered a note for the queen from the king. Freed of the hood's shadow, I noticed the blood drain from her face when she heard this and she sped off towards her quarters leaving me trailing in her wake. 'Thank you, Lady Vaux,' she said as my mother pressed the sealed note into her hands.

'Have you learned anything about why we're here, Joan?' my mother asked in a whisper, keeping her eye on Elizabeth as she read the contents.

'No, nothing. She just made an offering to St Peter and prayed for a few minutes, but she is obviously extremely worried. We may find out more now.'

But the queen folded the note, saying simply, 'The king requests my presence in his Privy Chamber. There is news from Flanders.'

She refused the bread and milk my mother offered to break her fast and insisted on leaving at once for the King's Lodging, a short walk away through a connecting gallery. It was only when I entered the council chamber with her that I realised that my husband was among those seated around the table with the king. Richard rose as soon as he saw that it was me accompanying the queen and fielded a dismissal signal from the king's own hand as he bowed to greet the queen.

'I'm afraid you must leave us, Joan,' he muttered, taking my elbow to escort me to the door. 'Word will be sent when the queen is ready to leave and I hope I may see you this evening at the Tower House.'

'What is going on?' I whispered back. 'The queen is as tense as a bow-string.'

'Top secret, Joan, but I'll probably be able to tell you tonight.'

The queen dined with the king and his councillors and in her lodging her attendants ate a mess of meat and vegetables sent from the officers' kitchen, but I had little appetite. After the meal I would have liked to have gone to the Tower House but the yeomen guards told me that the wharf area was closed off and required a special pass for access. I hoped Richard would obtain such a pass so that we could go home in the evening and made the excuse of seeking some fresh air in order to return briefly to the alders on Tower Green, hoping to sight more ravens, but none came. Sim was back in Kent and it was obvious that no one was tending the roost boxes he had built or putting out any tempting treats. I feared that my dreams were becoming reality; the ravens were abandoning the Tower and in the king's council chamber the legend was being fulfilled.

At sunset the queen returned but she was tight-lipped and agitated, picking fault with the arrangements for supper and becoming angry when there were no musicians available to play soothingly for her. I felt relieved when Richard came to request my release for the night and she agreed to it, stressing that she would need me first thing in the morning.

With George, Hal and Lizzie at Halden Hall and Edward occupied at the royal armouries in Southwark, when we reached our house on the wharf we were bombarded with complaints from Pippa, Bess and Winnie about not being able to take their ponies out to the fields behind Tower Hill. 'The grooms said no one could leave the fortress,' grumbled Pippa. 'So we've been cooped up in the house all day.'

'Mistress Brook sent us to make a list of everything in the kitchen store cupboards instead,' added Bess. 'It was so boring and then she wouldn't let me read your copy of *The Canterbury Tales*, Mother Joan.'

'Your governess is quite right, Bess,' I told her sternly. '*The Canterbury Tales* is not for maids of fifteen.' Bess sorely missed Maria, who had always been her reading companion. I did not imagine that Maria had much time for reading now that she was a mother and a farmer's wife.

'If the fortress was not in lockdown I would have banned you from the fields anyway,' Richard told her. 'Tower Hill is crawling with troops at present and no place for girls of any age.'

Pippa's ears pricked at that. 'Why is that?' she asked. 'Are there going to be executions? Can we go and watch?'

Her father's brow knitted. 'Not as far as I know – and no, you certainly cannot!' he growled. 'Take some cooking lessons from Jake if you're bored. That at least might be of some help when you have a household to run.'

'I shall have a cook in my household, unless you marry me to a pauper, Father, like Maria.' Pippa was becoming quite a little madam.

'Maria chose that path herself,' Richard snapped. 'So behave yourself if you wish to be well dowered.'

At this point I decided to shoo the girls up to bed, being impatient to get Richard to myself and find out what was occurring in the kingdom to cause royal tears. He was pouring himself a second cup of strong wine as we headed for the stairs and I promised myself a cup when I had settled his daughters and ward.

He must have read my mind for he brought the flagon of wine and another cup to our bedchamber in due course and poured my portion immediately. 'At last!' he sighed as he handed it to me. 'This has been a dreadful day.' He gulped the contents of his cup before putting it down and shrugging off his doublet. 'I cannot wait to go to bed.'

'Well, do not give yourself a sore head for tomorrow if there's another awful day in store,' I said, taking a large sip.

He bolted the door and came to unbuckle my belt. 'Let me take your gown, then turn around and I will unlace your kirtle. It will be safer if we muffle our voices behind the bed curtains before I tell you about it. Nothing of what I say from now on must leave this room because I shall be clapped in irons if it does.'

Within minutes we had drawn the curtains around the bed and when I heard what he had to say I was not surprised that he still spoke in a whisper. 'It seems unbelievable but Perkin Warbeck, the pretender who professes to be Richard, Duke of York, has not only managed to persuade the two most powerful rulers in Europe to endorse him but has also corrupted one of the king's closest courtiers. Henry refuses to believe it but it seems undeniable that his Lord Chamberlain is guilty of treason.'

I was astounded. 'Sir William Stanley – a traitor? But he was responsible for turning the tide of battle against the usurper. He practically put King Henry on the throne! Why would he of all people turn coat to York?'

Richard sighed and scratched his head. 'It would seem impossible. After all he also fought at the battle of Stoke and has sworn loyalty to the king several times since, most recently when he was made a Knight of the Garter. But there is damning evidence. Henry is in a state of shock because Sir William has travelled secretly to Flanders and there is a reliable witness who heard him say that if, when he met him, he was sure Warbeck was King Edward's son, he would not take up arms against him; which is surely treason.'

'No wonder the queen is so distressed. She must be torn. Who is this witness?'

'A man called Sir Robert Clifford. He managed to join Stanley's covert trip by feigning Yorkist sympathies but is actually a double agent, under the king's orders. He has just returned and is being held in the Tower for his own protection, hence the tight security. The king has cross-examined him today in the presence of the queen, because of course if this young man really is her brother – well, she loses her status as King Edward's heir.'

I gasped in disbelief. 'Dear heaven! What would happen to the Tudor claim – to her husband and children? England will be torn apart again. Is it really possible, Richard?' I sank the rest of my cup of wine in one gulp.

Richard took a deep breath and expelled it noisily. 'Who knows? King Henry is convinced Prince Richard died with his brother in the Tower but obviously the lack of their bodies remains a huge stumbling block. Stanley has not yet returned from the Duchess's court and this whole situation has to be kept under wraps until he does, because he will be arrested as soon as he steps off the ship. Then there will have to be a trial and if he is found guilty of treason there is the question of the sentence. Most of our meeting was spent trying to persuade Henry that the death sentence is essential, if only to discourage other high-ranking men from committing treason.'

'But the Stanleys command the loyalty of a huge part of England. Surely they will expect the king to commute the sentence.'

'Not if the Privy Council has its way. By the way, you'll be interested to know, Joan, that Sir William's first wife, now deceased, was also the mother of Francis Lovell, the man who organised the failed attempt on the king's life in York seven years ago and brother-in-law to your brother.'

I narrowed my eyes at him. 'My goodness, King Henry really married Nicholas into a nest of York vipers, didn't he!'

He reached out to put a consoling hand on mine. 'Lucky you married such a staunch Tudor supporter, isn't it?'

I snatched my hand away. 'I haven't forgotten that you practically accused me of being a closet Yorkist for speaking to my brother's wife at their wedding, Richard. I'm surprised you wanted to marry me at all!'

His smile in return was gleeful. 'I only did it to please the king,' he said and rolled over to fling his other arm across me, more or less pinning me down. 'There was no question of pleasing myself, of course.'

He seemed to have forgotten his exhaustion. I struggled against his obvious intention but only half-heartedly. I used the excuse to myself that I was still hoping to conceive another child but I knew it was wishful thinking. The days of hiding that traitorous piece of jet beneath my tongue were long gone and there was no brother or sister for Hal. However, opportunities for paying our marital debt did not come very often nowadays and when they did I had to admit that I enjoyed them.

Sir William Stanley and the rest of his party were arrested when they stepped off the ship a few days later and he was brought straight to the Tower as a prisoner. I thought it dreadful that his trial was held before his brother, Lady Margaret's husband, Lord Stanley, Earl of Derby and to everyone's surprise Sir William admitted his treason, probably expecting his sentence to be commuted to imprisonment. But there was no change of sentence and in a cold February dawn, before the city awoke, he was taken out to Tower Hill and beheaded.

But that did not put paid to Perkin Warbeck – or bring the ravens back to the Tower. The roost boxes sat empty in the trees, neglected in a kingdom in distress. The guardians of the Tower of London had gone. Who knew what would happen to England now?

35

KING HENRY'S REACTION TO the latest Warbeck episode was to insist that the two unmarried York princesses should now be safely wedded to Tudor loyalists, before any rebel with an eye on the throne took them willingly or unwillingly before a priest. Fifteen-year-old Princess Katherine was quickly betrothed to William Courtenay, the son and heir of the king's companion in exile, Edward Courtenay, Earl of Devon; a union which, when finalised at the altar after the necessary papal dispensation, might well have suited a young couple who were already quite attached to each other.

The other match, however, was not so much to the lady's liking. Princess Anne had now been the queen's chief lady-in-waiting for four years – an uncomfortable four years for those of us who had been obliged to work with her. When a very young girl during the usurper's reign she had been contracted to marry Thomas Howard, the grandson and heir apparent of the Duke of Norfolk, but when King Henry had won the throne, Anne had assumed that the betrothal would be annulled, because the old duke had been killed fighting for the usurper, his heir had been imprisoned and the Howard family had lost their lands and titles. So when he reached his majority Thomas had nothing to recommend him, not even a knighthood, and status-conscious Lady Anne could not stomach the ignominy of marrying a commoner. Thomas, on the other hand, insisted that the betrothal should stand, doubtless expecting to retrieve at least some of the family wealth and status as a result.

In view of Anne's scathing remarks about my own marriage, I had felt a certain venial pleasure when King Henry ordered the marriage to go ahead. Despite the groom's lack of rank, their wedding was lavish, paid for from the royal purse, and attended by the king and queen, who settled generous gifts and annuities on the couple. And of course it wasn't long before the Howard family were restored to some of their titles and lands. I had to be content with my reward, which was Anne's replacement as chief lady-in-waiting by the queen's cousin, the beautiful, charming and intelligent Lady Elizabeth Stafford, sixteen-year-old daughter of the Duke of Buckingham.

However, I did not enjoy serving under this pleasant new regime for long, because in the early summer Hal was taken ill again with the whooping cough and I hastened down to Halden Hall to nurse him, leaving the king and queen to make their annual progress without me. Thankfully Hal made a swift recovery from the worst part of this dangerous childish illness but it took him several weeks to get back to the lively, healthy five-year-old he had been before the whoops set in.

My protégé Sim was now training under Richard's head huntsman, working with the horses and the hawks, as well as still spending time with the ravens, bringing them treats and playing games with them. When I could leave my vigil over Hal, I went to reacquaint myself with Jack and June and watch the three raven chicks they had hatched in the early spring fledge from the nest.

Later, after Hal was well enough to venture out with me, I told Sim about the neglect of his roost boxes at the Tower but he just shrugged. 'To be honest, m'lady, I don't believe that story about ravens bein' guardians of the Tower. I think they just live their lives the best way they can and if that means roostin' in the alders, well an' good. If not – too bad. They're prob'ly cleverer than most of them soldiers anyway.'

Although I couldn't agree with him about the legend, I had to admit he had a point about the soldiers. I was lazing against a tree trunk on my favourite log when a familiar voice broke into our conversation.

'I knew I'd find you here.'

I looked up in surprise. 'Anthony! What are you doing here? We weren't expecting you for another week. Has the legal term ended early?'

Anthony Poyntz crossed the clearing with lithe, youthful steps, making his familiar flourishing bow when he reached my side. 'You obviously haven't heard from your husband lately, my lady. He sent me a letter by special messenger ordering me here as soon as possible.' Sinking down beside me on the log, he was immediately leapt on by an ecstatic Hal.

'Tony! Tony! You're back! Can we have a sword fight?'

Anthony pushed him off gently and gave him a friendly punch on the arm. 'Cheeky young whelp! You're the only one who calls me Tony but I suppose I'll let you. Are you capable of fencing with a fully trained squire though, I wonder?'

'Course I am.' Hal waved an imaginary sword and lunged at him. 'See, I've been practising. At least until I got the whooping cough.'

Anthony glanced at me in alarm. 'Oh, that must have been a bit of a scare. He seems pretty well now though. Back to his disrespectful self.'

I smiled and gave a sigh of relief at the same time. 'Yes, he's fine again but it wasn't nice. What has Sir Richard summoned you for?' I felt slightly nervous of this development. Anthony was nearly seventeen now, well trained in arms and old enough to be recruited for active service.

'He's mustering a force to guard the Kent coast – orders from the king. Apparently there's a report that the pretender has hired mercenaries in Flanders and they're embarking on ships at Sluys. Agents report that they're heading for Deal. I've never been there but I'm told it's on the coast between Dover and Sandwich and it has a shelved beach; a good place to land troops. It seems the pretender has big ideas of staging an invasion.'

I looked at him, wide-eyed with horror. 'How big?'

Anthony shrugged. 'I've no idea. I can't imagine he's managed to gather a vast army. It'll probably be just a token gesture.'

Hal wriggled off his hero's lap and picked up a fallen twig to use as a sword. 'Will you be fighting them, Tony, for real?' He made wild thrusts.

Anthony grabbed the other end of the stick as it flashed close to his face and stood up. 'If any Flemish fool dares to step onto English soil he'll be a dead man, Hal, believe me.' He poked the stick lightly into Hal's chest. 'Dead – as – a – doornail.'

Richard rode in a few hours later with Edward Guildford at his side and a column of men at arms behind them. 'I've been on a recce at Deal,' he revealed. 'Edward brought men from London and has picked up more on his way down here. They can all camp in our home pasture tonight and we'll head out to recruit at Smallhythe and along the Rother shore tomorrow. We need to be back in Deal at full force by tomorrow night.'

I cast my eyes over the troop of men at arms and archers dismounting all around the stable yard and my heart sank. 'We don't have enough meat to feed all these men. Shall I send Sim to the Strood farm to tell George to kill a couple of sheep and bring them here?'

Richard frowned and handed his courser's reins to a groom. 'Is George playing farmers again? He should be here protecting you and the children. But yes, that's a good idea. There'll be men among this lot who can butcher the meat and they can cook it over campfires. That way you won't need to worry the kitchen. Except for the family, of course.' He rubbed his stomach. 'George had better make it three sheep. I think I could eat a whole ram myself. I've ridden fifty miles on short rations today.'

I went to the strongbox to fetch a gold angel for Farmer Strood. He wouldn't be providing any sheep without recompense and I had no doubt he'd be keeping the fleeces. It had been a huge relief when I heard Richard suggest the home pasture for the camp because it had occurred to me that the soldiers might pitch their tents under the ravens' nest, which would have troubled me greatly.

As we were making arrangements a courier rode in with a letter from my mother. The royal progress had reached

Lancashire and was staying with Lady Margaret at Lathom House, the palatial seat of the Stanleys and home of her husband Thomas, Earl of Derby. My mother wrote that the queen was missing me and especially my apothecary potions, because she was riding on without revealing that she was once again pregnant. For my part I was pleased that the king and queen were far away from Kent and this alarming threat to the Tudor reign. I thought of how many times my mother when young must have waved her husband off to fight during the worst of the civil wars thirty years ago, only to lose him to the second York incursion ten years later. Was this new threat the work of yet another York prince making an attempt on the English throne? Or was it just a Flemish burgher's son with a handsome face and the gift of the gab, as the king's spies maintained? Either way, I realised it was all too possible that my husband and his young recruits might fall foul of an invading army. That evening, as the smell of roasting mutton filled the air, my thoughts were gloomy and my appetite non-existent.

Only four days later they were back, fewer in number but not because they'd had casualties. The Flemish mercenaries had been routed on the beach at Deal, hundreds killed, and hundreds more captured. Few of Richard's troops were killed or injured, but a number of them were marching the captives to await ransom in Dover Castle. The rest of the futile invasion force had fled back to their ships. No one claiming to be Richard, Duke of York, had set foot on English soil.

'That Perkin Warbeck fellow is no battle commander!' cried Edward at the celebration feast we held in the great hall. 'He might have convinced the courts of Europe that he's a lost English prince but he never showed us any sign of leadership. His ship was hove-to well offshore and there didn't seem to be anyone issuing orders to his men. We were all hidden in the dunes and the poor saps just walked up the beach into our range. When the arrows started to fly they turned tail and ran back to their boats. It was laughable. King Henry has nothing to worry about from that source!'

In September the adult ravens stopped feeding their offspring and I decided it was a good opportunity to take Sim and the chicks up to London, hoping that quieter times at the Tower would have allowed the usual autumn gathering of the juveniles and our three might join the 'conspiracy'. It would give Sim a chance to spruce up the roosting boxes and me an opportunity to check up on Edward of Warwick, who I'd been unable to visit when the Tower was in lockdown during the Stanley crisis. I wanted to be able to report on his progress to Elizabeth and Lady Margaret when I took up my place once more in the queen's service on her return from the royal progress.

By now the guards on the Privy Garden were used to my occasional visits to Edward of Warwick and I had asked Jake to make me the usual gravy crusts to treat his dog. Though when I entered the garden there was no sign of either of them. 'He's in there somewhere,' the guard had said, 'but he's not at all happy.'

After a brief search I found Edward hunched on a turf seat in a corner of the shrubbery, out of sight of the windows of the royal palace. There was no sign of the dog. 'Where's Castor?' I asked as I approached. 'Is he hiding from me?'

'He's dead.' Edward said this in such a flat, matter-of-fact way that I might have been fooled into thinking that he was unmoved by the demise of his beloved pet but I knew better.

'Dead?' I echoed, shocked for the terrier had been a lively young creature. 'How did he die?'

'I don't know. Somebody killed him. It could have been you with your gravy biscuits.' Still the same indifferent tone.

'It certainly wasn't!' I exclaimed, appalled at the thought. 'When did it happen?'

'A week or so ago. He found something tasty under a bush then not much later he started shaking and before anyone could help he was dead.' He looked up at me then, but only briefly then turned his gaze away. 'It wasn't your biscuits was it? You haven't been to see us for a while.'

'No, I'm sorry. It hasn't been possible. You must miss Castor badly. Might it help if I found you another dog? A puppy you could train?'

He shook his head violently. 'No. They won't let me keep it.'

'Who are "they"?' I asked with a frown. 'Why shouldn't you have another dog?'

'Because they say it smells and fouls my chamber. But that isn't true. Castor never did that.'

Edward hauled himself off the turf bench and I suddenly realised that he was not a boy any more. This was a young man of twenty, more or less the same age as his namesake Edward Guildford, yet so very different. For whereas my stepson was broad-shouldered and muscular, capable of firing an arrow up to three hundred yards and manhandling a

334

heavy cannon into position, this Edward was a puny lad, tallish but thin and pale, with the air of someone who couldn't summon the energy to wield a quill, let alone a sword. Yet he was not backward, as his tutors had labelled him, just a poor conversationalist though a talented artist – I had seen his sketches on previous visits and they were good. He certainly lacked confidence and motivation but who could blame him, having been shut up in the Tower for ten years without any prospect of leaving? And now his boon companion was gone, apparently killed by some unknown poisoner. I couldn't imagine who might have performed such a callous act and to what purpose?

After shuffling his feet indecisively for a minute, as if he had something more to say to me, Edward of Warwick suddenly turned and walked away without another word. I called after him but he did not heed me and quickly disappeared through the surrounding shrubs. I was left contemplating what, if anything, I could tell the queen about him. The constant flood of rumour concerning the pretender Perkin Warbeck had left Elizabeth still unable to completely accept that he was not her younger brother Richard grown to manhood, yet also troubled by the threat he posed to the Tudor throne and her young family. With all this on her mind, how could she cope with hearing the present plight of her young cousin, another living threat to the Tudor future now also grown to manhood?

Wearily I took Edward's place on the turf bench, aiming to use his quiet corner to mull the situation over, but the silence was broken by the snap of a twig under a heavy foot and the sudden emergence of a hooded figure through the bushes.

'You obviously have a habit of making trysts with young men in shady places, Blackbird,' the intruder said.

A voice I knew and abhorred; one that drew me to my feet in fear and loathing. 'Sir Henry Wyatt! Have you been following me?'

He moved nearer and I backed away but he still bore down on me. Under the shadow of his hood I caught a glint of evil intent in his eyes and experienced a lightning jolt of alarm. But before I could obey it and run he had grabbed my arm. 'Yes Blackbird, I have been following you.' He thrust back the hood of his cloak and pushed his face right up to mine, his sharply trimmed beard scratching my chin as he spoke again. 'And I'm sure the king would be very interested to hear that the wife of his trusted Master of Ordnance has been holding clandestine meetings with a highly suspect Yorkist conspirator, right under the noses of his Tower guards.'

'Ugh!' Disgusted by the putrid smell of his breath, I twisted my head away and tried to wrench my arm free, without success. At the same time the feel of his nails digging into my flesh through the cloth of my gown inspired my anger. 'And I'm sure the king would be horrified to hear that the Master of his Jewel House was molesting the wife of his Master of Ordnance,' I snarled through gritted teeth. 'Let – me – go!'

Unexpectedly he did, but not without a violent push, which flung me backwards onto the turf bench, where he immediately followed, throwing himself on top of me and pinning me down with his body. His heavy weight knocked the breath from me and his cloak enveloped us both, so that although I tried to struggle and bring my knee into what I hoped would be painful contact with his crotch, I found my arms and legs entangled, unable to move freely enough to use any force. My mouth was not covered however and when I'd managed to gulp adequate air into my lungs I used my tongue to lambast him with all the ire and spittle I could summon.

'You are a hideous monster, Henry Wyatt! With an evil mind, a poisonous tongue and an unnatural hatred of women and ravens.' I reared my head up to stare fiercely into his baleful gaze. 'I will not be bullied by a man who struts like a cockerel and is all bluster and no charm. Why the king cannot see you for what you are I do not know, but if you believe he will trust your word over mine or my husband's you are more stupid than your looks might indicate. Now get off me!'

Perhaps my words and my animal glare had weakened his resolve, or else he realised that he'd let his craving for revenge get the better of him, because all of a sudden I sensed his moment of doubt and knew that I could throw him off, which I did with a grunt of effort, watching him scramble away from me in a flurry of cloak and the terrifying sight of his hand on his sheathed dagger. Nevertheless I took my time regaining my own feet, watching him watching me and determined not to reveal the chilling fear that gripped my guts. Whether he still intended to rape me I couldn't tell but my every instinct told me that only moments before, he had. Now all I wanted to do was get away from him. So, in a sudden whirl of skirts I turned and ran. I didn't look back to see if he'd tried to follow me but once I was out of the shrubbery and in full view of the royal palace windows, I knew I would be safe.

36

I DID NOT TELL Richard of my meetings with Edward of Warwick or my frightening encounter with Sir Henry Wyatt. Being thoroughly convinced of male supremacy in all matters, he hated me pursuing my own agenda and I had only recently received his grudging permission to pursue my mission to bring the ravens back to the Tower. I realised now that the higher Richard and I climbed in the favour of the king and queen, the fiercer and more irrational Wyatt's craving for revenge might grow, but I could devise no way of halting it other than by avoiding him, which as the new chief lady-in-waiting had taken over the task of handling the queen's jewels, might now prove relatively easy. Besides, the queen grew more and more reliant on my friendship and service and I couldn't risk any hint of dishonour jeopardising that. A fact that was amply demonstrated by a troubling letter penned by one of the queen's clerks, which found me a few days later.

To Joan, Lady Guildford from Her Grace, Elizabeth the Queen,
The queen deeply regrets to inform you of the sudden death of their grace's youngest daughter, Elizabeth, on

the fourteenth day of September at Eltham Palace. As
you will understand her grace is profoundly shocked and
in deep mourning but asks me to request that, out of the
love and loyalty you have always shown her, you present
yourself to Eltham Palace as soon as possible in order to
assist in the arrangements for the princess's exequies,
prior to the conveyance of her body to Westminster for
funeral rites and burial in due course. Her grace is also
concerned for the welfare of her other children, at a time
when they will be much troubled by the loss of their
sister and in need of comfort and counselling, which she
is certain you are admirably equipped to provide.

The queen sends her earnest hope and belief that you
will find it convenient to render this service in all
possible haste.

Written at the dictation of Her Grace Queen
Elizabeth at Sheen Palace on this sixteenth day of
September, in the Xth year of King Henry VII.

I was at the Tower House with the intention of returning
to the queen's service as soon as I received word that she
and the king had returned from their summer progress. Its
contents brought tears to my eyes.

Hetty Smith was with me as I intended installing her as
my chamber servant at court in place of Luce, who had
become betrothed to a London tailor and loth to leave the
city. She was wielding a broom in my bedchamber and
looked startled when I walked in, as if she'd been caught
out in a naughty act.

'I noticed some dust in the corners, my lady,' she said a
little sheepishly. 'I hope Luce won't mind.'

'Don't worry about Luce. She has more than enough to do and would welcome the assistance. But I have more important tasks for you right now, Hetty. Get ready to pack very quickly; we're not going to Sheen Palace, we're going downriver to Eltham instead.'

'Is there something wrong, my lady?' She was eyeing me curiously, no doubt detecting the remnants of my tears for the baby princess.

'Yes, Hetty; Princess Elizabeth has died suddenly at Eltham and the queen has asked me to go and comfort her sister and brother. So could you give my black mourning gown a brush and I'll change into it quickly before we go? This one I'm wearing can be left here because I don't think I'll need it before Christmas. I am charged with comforting the living children and bringing the little girl's body to Westminster for burial.'

She looked perturbed. 'That is a sad thing to do, my lady.'

I nodded. 'Yes, Hetty, it is. The queen must be devastated. I only hope her deep sorrow does not affect the next babe she is carrying, because it is at an early stage and not due until spring.'

A harbinger was sent on ahead of us and when we docked, as far up the River Lee as our barge would go, there was a cart waiting to transport the baggage up the hill to Eltham Palace and horses for us to ride. It was only a mile or so but by the time we reached the drawbridge over the moat it was dusk and the torches were being lit. I wondered if the children might be in bed but Princess Margaret and Prince Henry were waiting for us by the fire in the great hall, two red-eyed youngsters dressed in royal mourning blue. Although the prince was a year and a half younger than his sister, it was he who stepped forward first to greet me.

'Welcome, Lady Guildford. The queen informed us of your coming and said we are to consider you her loving ambassador.'

He was four years old and my heart ached at his polite bow and correct form of address, obviously quoting straight from his mother's letter, formal words that seemed completely at odds with his hoarse voice and brimming eyes. I sank onto my knees, so that my face was level with his. 'Thank you, your grace,' I said softly, wrenched by his shaky breathing and the sight of his well-bitten lip. 'I feel sure that were your lady mother here, she would take you in her arms and give you a hug. Would you perhaps permit me to do that for her? I may be no substitute, but if you close your eyes you might imagine for a moment that I was her.'

I opened my arms to him and waited. For a brief moment I thought he was going to turn away but then he all but threw himself at me and wrapped his arms around my neck, almost dislodging my tight-fitting brimmed coif. Gently I reciprocated, hugging him to me, closing my eyes and imagining him to be a smaller version of Hal, trying to match my breathing to his jerky sobs. When I opened my eyes, my gaze met Margaret's, only a yard away and full of yearning. I extended one arm in her direction and she shyly moved to fit herself into the embrace. I could feel both their hearts beating, faster than mine and very distressed. For a moment I regretted making the offer. How could I possibly be a substitute for their mother?

When they withdrew I rose and stepped back. They

expressed their own misgivings by exchanging glances with rather sheepish expressions.

'Thank you for coming, Lady Guildford,' Princess Margaret said with stilted formality. 'It is kind of you.'

'I assure you I would do anything for your royal mother and equally for you.' I risked a little smile. 'Anyway I was about to go upriver to her at Sheen Palace, so all I had to do was turn around and take the boat down the river to you.'

When I explained that I had been asked to make the mourning arrangements for her sister, Princess Margaret offered to take me to the palace chapel. 'Lizbeth is there,' she explained. 'People are taking turns at guarding her.'

When we entered the chapel, two nurses were kneeling beside the tiny bier and their murmured Ave Marias, mingling with the intense aroma of incense and candle wax, filled me with desolation. The three-year-old's body had been dressed in a pale blue satin gown, trimmed with white ermine, and her gold hair was lying loose about her shoulders. Regrettably, under the overriding church smells, I detected a faint whiff of decay and realised that it was time the embalmers were summoned. I felt a fierce sense of anger and regret that a child with everything to live for should have been snatched from life at such a tender age.

'Why did she die?' the princess asked in an undertone. 'I'd rather it was me that died.'

I turned to her with concern. She was not quite six. It was a sad sentiment from a little girl who had every reason to look forward to a golden future. 'We cannot know when or why we die, princess. God chooses our coming in and our going out. At least she did not suffer long.'

Her response made my eyes brim with tears, instantly

conjuring memories of my own Hal. 'Maybe not long but she did suffer. She had whooping cough and they said that a blood vessel burst in her throat and she choked. They wouldn't let me go to her until they'd cleaned up the blood.' She looked indignant, angry to have been prevented from comforting her little sister in her final moments.

Mistress Howell, Prince Henry's governess, arrived at this moment, clearly alerted a little late to my arrival. Having greeted me she went to whisper something to the kneeling nurse, who rose and took Margaret's hand to lead her out of the chapel.

'It is really time she was in bed, Lady Guildford,' the governess said when the little girl was out of earshot. 'Princess Margaret is a melancholy child at the best of times and this has made her worse.'

I nodded. 'She said she wished it had been her that died.'

'I greatly fear that life might always be a disappointment to that little girl. Her confident younger brother can laugh and cry with equal ease but Margaret always walks under a dark cloud.'

After I had bidden the royal children goodnight, I saw the castle chaplain and asked what arrangements had been made for preserving the body, relieved to hear that embalmers had been summoned from London and would be arriving the next day. By the same barge came letters from the royal household giving details of arrangements for the princess's funeral. The embalmed body was to be sealed in a lead coffin and kept at Eltham until the end of October, when it would be taken to lie at rest in Westminster Abbey while a full state funeral was arranged, to be led by the Archbishop of Canterbury and the Lord Chamberlain.

A full state funeral for a little girl of three! As his reign progressed it became clear that King Henry was employing every possible opportunity to promote his Tudor dynasty, even using his young daughter's obsequies as a demonstration of Tudor eminence. I wondered what his queen thought of these arrangements. Compared with the secretive midnight interment three years before of her mother, the former queen, it occurred to me that Elizabeth might find this grand funeral of the Dowager's three-year-old granddaughter glaringly inappropriate.

37

AFTER THE LITTLE PRINCESS'S funeral, I accompanied the queen on another pilgrimage to the Shrine of Our Lady at Walsingham in Norfolk, once more to pray for a son. Three months later, back at Sheen, she gave birth to another girl but even so she desired her to be called Mary.

Towards the end of May she took the new baby to the nursery at Eltham Palace, prior to setting off with King Henry on a summer progress along the south coast. I went with them, travelling via castles, abbeys and priories to Southampton where we took a ferry across to the Isle of Wight, a wild and beautiful place, which sadly suffered frequent and devastating raids by French and Spanish pirates. On returning to Southampton I had to excuse myself from the remainder of the progress, so that I could attend Edward Guildford's wedding to Eleanor West, a daughter of Sir Thomas West, Baron De La Warr, one of the king's military commanders and a childhood friend of Richard's.

The wedding was held at the bride's home of Broadwater on the Sussex coast and the newlyweds were to set up their household nearby at Offington Hall, Richard's birthplace and one of the Guildford manors I had not previously visited. We travelled back in glorious sunshine along the

Sussex Downs into the Kent Weald. Richard took eight-year-old Lizzie on a pillion saddle but I was absurdly proud of my little Hal, who at age six had ridden his own sturdy pony to Offington and now rode him all the way back. The rest of the summer was spent between Halden Hall and Frensham before I returned to the queen's service in September.

After the fiasco on Deal beach the young man who still called himself Richard, Duke of York, had made his way to Scotland. 'King James is treating that cowardly son of a Flemish burgher like royalty and even promising to help him invade England!' Henry fumed, storming into Elizabeth's solar after receiving news that the Scottish king was providing the pretender with silks and furs and armour. 'What's more, he's married him to some woman called Katherine Gordon, who is apparently the daughter of an earl. Not that a Scottish earl can be ranked anywhere near equal to an English one.'

'And will he invade England?' Elizabeth asked. I could hear the tremor in her voice as she once again faced the thought of Henry heading off to battle in his own kingdom.

'I doubt it.' The king's reply was scathing. 'King James has got enough problems keeping his own nobles under control without taking England's northern cohorts on. No, the Earl of Surrey is my lieutenant on the Scottish border and he and his son have orders to frighten the daylights out of Warbeck.'

'Oh, poor Anne!' Surrey's son, Thomas Howard, was Elizabeth's sister Anne's relatively new and recently promoted husband. 'She is only just pregnant. I would be with her if I were not that way again myself.'

'Let Cecily or Katherine go to her then,' said Henry callously and quickly amended his tone on fielding the queen's angry frown. 'But I'm sure this will all be over long before Anne's child is born and without a gun being fired. The King of France has sent Warbeck packing, Emperor Maximilian has banned him from his court and I'm certainly not going to give the upstart the satisfaction of thinking the King of England rates him as an opponent worthy of his personal attention.'

'But supposing . . .' Elizabeth's voice trailed away and everyone knew what she dared not say.

Curbing his anger, King Henry leaned forward to take her hand. 'Can you really believe that your royal brother Richard, who were he alive might now be a trained knight of twenty-two, would have sent his men to land on the beach at Deal without leading them himself? Any genuine prince would be the first to set foot in a kingdom he believed to be his, ready to rouse his supporters to his standard. We know who this nonentity is who cowered aboard his ship and he is no son of your warlike father – decidedly *not* Richard of Shrewsbury!'

She gave a sigh. 'I am sure you're right but I would dearly like to see that for myself.'

'In that case I will send an order to Lord Surrey to instruct his commanders that however cowardly he is, Warbeck is to be taken alive and brought captive to the Tower of London. Then you can confront him and put him in no doubt that his insolent impersonation is over.'

'And what will you do with him then, my lord?' she asked.

It was his turn to sigh. 'In truth I don't know. It entirely depends whether there is any merit to be found in him.'

King Henry's analysis had not been far wrong. When they disembarked at Berwick on Tweed, Perkin Warbeck's promised Flemish 'force' proved to be merely sixty strong and few Yorkist supporters flocked to the official Duke of York red, gold and silver battle standard King James had scurrilously presented to him. So after the Scottish king learned of the considerable numbers Lord Surrey had mustered to confront him, he swiftly withdrew his own army back into Scotland, where a letter awaited him from King Henry demanding that he surrender the pretender or prepare for war with England. Within days King James had hired a ship and cast Warbeck, his Flemings and his unfortunate young wife from his kingdom.

'Which means King Henry will have to deal with him eventually,' my mother remarked tartly as we walked together from our chambers at Sheen Palace to our duties at the queen's disrobing. The news had arrived at court that day, sent from Scotland by fast courier.

'How do you know he'll come to England?' I asked. 'He's tried once and he's a bit of a coward by all accounts.'

'Have you not heard, Gigi? The queen's Lord Chamberlain holds half of southern Ireland and he says his tenants will refuse to allow Warbeck into Cork or Waterford again and there's no support for him anywhere else in Ireland, so it's either invade England or sail into the sunset for that poor fool now.' My mother could be quite cruel sometimes. 'Unfortunately the king might have made things easier for him by sending his tax collectors into Cornwall to finance the reinforcements on the Scottish border. Because it's so far away the Cornish have always been excused from paying tax for that purpose – until now, and apparently they're on the march to protest. If the pretender gets to hear that, he'll be landing there and making common cause. That's if he's got any sense.'

I stared at her, amazed. 'How do you know all this, Mamma?'

Sometimes my mother could be more Italian than English. She put her finger on her nose and gave me an enigmatic smile. 'I keep my ear to the ground.'

My grin in return was cheeky. 'Aren't you getting a bit old and stiff to manage that?' In truth I had been trying to persuade her to retire from royal service for some time. She was in her mid-fifties and I thought she deserved to enjoy a quieter life.

'I've told you, I'll retire when Lady Margaret does.'

'That's all very well but she gets waited on hand and foot, whereas you're doing the waiting and the queen is demanding. For instance when did she last give you time off?'

My mother cast an anxious look behind us to make sure no one was listening. 'She doesn't give time off, as you well know, Gigi. You have to demand it and I don't have the excuse of a husband and children like you do.'

'Surely you can give your family as an excuse? Your little grandson would love to see more of you and you know you can stay with us any time – or if I'm not at Halden and you want peace and quiet, there's always Frensham. The renovations are finished and I'm going to hire a steward for the manor soon, so it'll be at your disposal.'

I felt her take my hand as we walked along. 'I do know that and I love being with Hal – growing so big and strong but still a charmer. What a shame you never managed to have the little girl you wanted – and there's your brother's wife giving him nothing but girls!'

I suddenly realised something. 'You don't like Beth, do you, Mamma? Is that why you'd rather not go to Harrowden?'

She lifted her chin defiantly. 'I'm allowed to prefer my own daughter's company over my in-law's, surely – but that's enough of that.' We had reached the entrance to the queen's Privy Chamber. 'I bet you tuppence they're all talking about Warbeck and Cornwall in the queen's dressing room tonight.'

I didn't accept her bet because I knew she'd be right. The Cornish rising was the only subject occupying the court for the rest of the week. An emergency meeting of the Privy Council was called to discuss what action should be taken.

'The Cornish rebels are moving fast,' Richard told me afterwards. 'It's quite a horde of roughnecks – mostly miners and fishermen. Fifteen thousand have left Cornwall apparently – but a blacksmith with the unlikely name of Michael An Gof seems to be the ringleader. I expect he can wield a hammer but I fear most of them will be cannon fodder. King Henry is leaving tomorrow to muster his forces south of the capital, in order to keep them off London Bridge, and the queen is going to Eltham to collect the royal children and bring them to the Tower, in case the rebels should try to take them hostage.'

'That sounds a bit desperate,' I exclaimed. 'Is it really as bad as that?'

He made a dubious gesture. 'The king seems to think so. Anyway he's not taking any chances. At least that trouble-maker Warbeck hasn't put in an appearance – so far. Let's hope he's lost at sea.'

'What are your orders?'

'Edward and I are to bring out the guns and hold them ready to deploy. I don't imagine the rebels have too much ordnance so we should be able to inflict a lot of damage without suffering too much ourselves.'

I shuddered. 'Will you take Anthony Poyntz to the muster? Is he still in London?'

'Yes, he'll already be with Edward at the Tower. I'm going there first thing tomorrow to get my harness oiled and my sword sharpened. I presume you'll be going to Eltham with the queen by barge, then coming back up to the Tower. You should be there before the rebels get anywhere near London.'

'I very much hope so! You will look out for Edward and Anthony, won't you, Richard? Neither of them has seen battle action before. I'd hate to have to tell Meg Poyntz that her son has been injured in your service, or worse.'

He gave me one of his ironic smiles. 'And what about your husband, Joan? Are you at all worried for his safety?'

'Of course I am, Richard, but you're a battle-hardened soldier. You know how to look after yourself. It's your turn to show the young ones how to do it.'

'So you'll blame me if one of them gets hurt?'

I felt my blush rising. 'Yes, no – you know what I mean. I'd rather the Cornishmen turned around and went home but I suppose that's not going to happen. I'll pray for all three of you.'

He took my hand and kissed it. 'Well, that is reassuring, my lady.'

38

BEING UNABLE TO SLEEP, I was sitting under the alders at dawn on the following Saturday waiting for the ravens to wake up, when I heard the guns speak. They had rolled only the smaller cannons out of the Tower, pulled over London Bridge by the same teams of oxen that hauled the scrap silver and gold into the Mint. At the same time a number of larger guns had been deployed on the bastions to defend the royal family, in case the unthinkable happened and the rebels managed to get through the king's substantial forces and storm the Tower's walls. At the brief but deafening fusillade the few ravens that had recently returned to the boxes rose into the sky, 'kraaking' in alarm, and headed out over the city to look for shelter elsewhere. I sent up a quick prayer to St Francis that they would be back. The kingdom and the Tower could not afford to lose any guardians if the legend was to prevail.

Scrambling to my feet, I made a beeline for the Queen's Lodging. I had not been scheduled on duty for her robing that morning but I knew the royal children might be alarmed by the sound of the guns. My own family were at Halden Hall and as the Cornish rebellion escalated I had suffered only one moment of concern, when someone had suggested that the rebels might attempt to rouse the volatile Kentish Men to join them in their rebellion, but nothing had come of it. I was glad to find that Prince Henry and the baby Mary had both slept through the distant thunder of the guns and only Princess Margaret was awake and trembling in the arms of Jane Howell. Both were still in their chamber robes.

The curtains were open on the big tester bed. 'It's only practice shots,' I told Margaret, jumping up to sit beside them. 'When they're in the field, the gunners always have a practice at first light, just to check that the cannons are firing properly. The sound carries a long way. They're probably in position on a hill somewhere across the river.'

'Are they our guns or theirs?' asked the princess, putting her hands over her ears as another salvo sounded.

'Those are cannons,' I repeated. 'They're kept here at the Tower. I haven't heard that the rebels have hauled anything of that size as far as this. In fact I'd be surprised if they have any artillery to speak of.'

'That's not very fair,' she protested. 'If we have big guns and they have none.'

I quashed the temptation to smile. 'There is nothing fair about war, I'm afraid. If you have guns you use them – if not, and the other side has, you're in trouble.'

'I'm glad I'm not a boy,' she said earnestly. 'I wouldn't like to face such weapons and have to pretend not to be terrified.'

Mistress Howell released her charge and slid off the bed. 'I think you'll feel much better after some breakfast,' she said. 'Let's get you dressed, shall we? Then you can go and see your lady mother. I expect she'd like you to go with her to the chapel, to pray for your father.'

353

I nodded. 'You go and wake Prince Henry. The queen would like them both to accompany her, I'm sure. I'll help the princess to dress.'

'We don't call him Henry any more, Mother Guildford,' Margaret revealed. 'He likes to be called Prince Harry.'

As I wrung out a soft linen cloth to give her to wash her face, I reflected that it was lucky I had decided on Hal for my own son's diminutive.

Through the morning we heard no news from the field of action, although after they had broken their fast I took the prince and princess up to the roof of the White Tower to see if we could discern any evidence of military activity on the other side of the river. There was a series of bangs, and clouds of smoke rose from the direction of Deptford, where a bridge spanned the River Ravensbourne tributary and the Thames made a big meander around extensive marshland before passing Greenwich Palace. After that the guns fell silent and I told the children this must be because they wouldn't want to fire on their own men once the two armies met. There could be no doubting that there had been a major clash of arms at the Deptford Bridge.

We were all picking without appetite at the dishes put before us in the Great Chamber at dinnertime, when a herald arrived and bent his knee before the queen. I took instant comfort from the fact that he looked pristine in his splendid tabard, lavishly embroidered with heraldic symbols, thinking that if there had been fierce fighting he might have collected some mud or even blood spatters.

'Your grace, I come with glorious news from the mighty Henry Tudor, King of England and Wales and Lord of Ireland. His army has routed those who tried to rebel against his reign and taken captive the ringleaders, who will soon be brought here to the Tower to face justice. His grace is presently at the entrance to London Bridge, raising to the honour of knighthood the heroes from London, who came out to defend their city against invasion. Subsequently the king and his retinue will progress to St Paul's Cathedral to hear Mass and the king will lay his battle standard on the altar in gratitude to the Almighty. He begs me to inform you that immediately afterwards he will come here to greet your grace and his children who, God be thanked, remained safe within these stout walls.'

Queen Elizabeth rose from her seat. 'I thank you, most honourable Richmond Herald, for bringing us this extremely welcome news. We greatly rejoice that Almighty God has guided the king to vanquish those of our subjects who have misguidedly taken up arms against us.' She picked up her jewelled cup and raised it high. 'I drink to a victory which will, I am sure, restore our appetites for a meal that hitherto we have been unable to consume with any relish. If it is your wish, the server will find you a place so that you may enjoy a well-deserved dinner before you leave us.'

Later, when the cloths and trestles had been removed, we all rose and applauded as King Henry entered the Great Chamber and ceremoniously knelt before the queen's canopied chair to kiss her hand and place a somewhat battered sword at her feet. 'This is the sword given to the leader of the rebels by Lord Audley, who alone among my nobles chose to support the rising. I and my loyal commanders dedicate our victory to you, my queen, and to our children.'

Behind him knelt his battle chiefs, still in their armour and their action-scarred surcôtes, bearing their coats of arms.

355

Beside the king's Lord Chamberlain, Lord Daubeney, were Lord Oxford and Lord Suffolk and Richard was the fourth among them. I felt a stab of pride. It was the first time I had witnessed him in his guise as a military leader and the king's next words filled my cup even fuller.

'And as I see you have Lady Guildford among your attendants, it would be a suitable time to announce that I have this day on the field of battle elevated Sir Richard Guildford to the rank of Knight Banneret, in recognition of his skilful command of a brave and quick-thinking company of gunners and militia. His fellow commanders all recognised the effort and dedication that had gone into their training and the zeal with which they executed their duties.'

Her page bent to lift the sword into the queen's hands and she stood up, holding it out like a cleric carrying a cross. 'I accept this trophy with pride, my lord, and congratulate you and your commanders on your success in preserving our throne and our safety. If it please your lordships to rise, we will provide meat and drink for such noble victors.'

They all rose as one but the king declined her offer of food, declaring, 'We will drink a toast, if you will be so kind, but we are all too battle-stained to remain welcome for long in the company of ladies.' He took the sword from her and gave it to one of his retinue before lending his hand to lead her into the centre of the room. It seemed strange to think that such a crucial battle had been fought only a few miles from the city walls.

As pages ran to supply cups and flagons of wine, the queen's ladies mingled with the heroes of the day. Naturally I made my way directly to Richard, noting tell-tale signs of soot on his armour and a few small blisters on his right hand. 'Congratulations on your promotion,' I murmured, reaching up to kiss his cheek. 'But you will have to enlighten me about the significance of Knight Banneret over Knight Bachelor.'

I had expected this to evince a smile but received only a worried frown. 'It has to do with the permitted shape of the battle standard and the size of one's retinue,' he said, wincing as he took my hand and led me into a quiet corner. 'But there is something more important to tell you, Joan; there was an accident during the firing of one of our cannons and Anthony received a bad burn on his left arm. Edward has taken him to our house on the wharf and I think you should go there as soon as possible. It may be wise to send for a physician.'

I felt my stomach clench. Fire was one of my worst fears, because we depended on using it day in and day out, for light, for cooking and for warming our homes; yet it was one of our greatest enemies. Burns were notorious for developing into killer wounds within days. 'How bad is it, Richard?' I asked, my voice trembling with alarm.

He shook his head. 'I don't know. It's under his vambrace – you'll see when it's taken off. Go, Joan – go now. I'll make your excuses to the queen.'

39

ANTHONY WAS SITTING ON a bench in Richard's ground-floor office, still in his armour minus the helm, his face chalk-white. He did not appear to notice my arrival; did not seem to be aware of anything. Luce was sitting with him, trying to get him to talk, but he remained mute, his pupils pin-pricks.

The maid rushed to meet me, desperate for reassurance. 'I have not treated him or removed his armour because I was not sure if that was the right thing to do. Master Edward was not very helpful when he brought him here. He just told me Master Anthony had been injured and that he had to leave.'

I took a quick look at the vambrace on the squire's left arm and I could see that it was blackened and buckled, the effect of having been subjected to heat and a violent thump. There was also a sinister smell of roasted flesh. I wished I could have heard more details of how it had happened because clearly Anthony was traumatised. 'I'll have a look at the wound, Luce, but I think it would be wise to take him to a bedchamber first. I'll need your help to get him up the stair.'

We managed to get Anthony to his feet and I took his

injured side, wondering if I could get his arm over my shoulder so that I wouldn't have to hold it near the injury. However, when I lifted the upper part of his arm he gave a blood-curdling scream of pain and I nearly fainted myself. But the jolt had brought him back from the brink of unconsciousness and he looked at me with sudden recognition. 'Lady Joan!' he croaked. 'Thank God!'

'I know you're hurting, Anthony, but we need to get you up the stairs. Do you think you can lean on me and Luce and we'll help you to a nice comfortable bed and some treatment for your arm?' As I spoke I edged myself as gently as I could under his armpit so that his damaged arm hung around my neck. He gasped but he did not cry out. 'Well done!' I said. 'Now just a few strides to the stair and we can take it slowly up.'

Gradually we edged him up and into the first chamber on the landing. It contained a large four-poster bed but I made him sit on a bench until we had removed his armour and I had taken a good look at the state of his arm. Fortunately a knight's harness was chiefly designed to protect the front of its wearer and between us we managed to remove the separate pieces without causing him too much discomfort. I left the damaged vambrace until the last and sent Luce off to find clean linen and cold water, while I gritted my teeth and gently undid the buckles.

Before I lifted the scorched and dented steel plate away I asked Anthony if he could tell me how the injury came about. His voice was weak and I had to lean close to hear what he said. 'I was standing behind the gun, near the pile of cannonballs, because I was responsible for loading them. There was one in the tube ready to fire and the gunner had fed the gunpowder and the wad in behind it. But when the cannon fired one of the bands holding the barrel together snapped with a bang. I ducked away but a shard of red-hot iron flew off and hit me on the arm. It stuck to the steel of my vambrace. I couldn't shake it off. By the time I did the steel was boiling hot and I felt a searing pain . . .'

Reliving the event made him weak and he slumped down. I thought he might slip to the floor but fortunately Luce came back and helped me to heave him up again. In truth he wasn't very heavy and it came home to me vividly that he was only eighteen and probably had a good deal more growing to do. I prayed this fearful wound on his arm would not fester and rob him of the chance to do it.

With a linen napkin soaked in water I started to remove the damaged item of armour. I assumed that the skin would have blistered and stuck to the sleeve of his chemise and I hoped to be able to soak it off, to preserve the protection it would afford the deeper layers beneath.

But it was not to be. Anthony's eyes were wide with pain and shock when he saw the raw flesh slowly emerge below the vambrace as the metal and the roasted skin both clung to the linen and peeled away. A long agonised keening sound seethed through his gritted teeth, then silence fell as the poor boy fainted.

Luckily we managed to stop him falling and took the opportunity to untie the laces of his points and separate his chemise from his hose without causing him any more pain, which the action certainly would have done had he still been conscious. Any thought I'd had of preserving the skin vanished, for the once-white linen and the blistered skin were now fused together and the garment had to be lifted over his head with the vambrace still attached. The open wound with its blackened edges and bright red veins oozing his lifeblood now lay in plain view. It was a dreadful sight and all I could do was cover it with fresh wet linen and send Luce to fetch one of Richard's clean chemises. I cut its left sleeve off at the elbow before we gently dressed him in it and lifted him together into the bed.

Richard had suggested calling a physician, but I had more faith in the queen's favoured apothecary and, leaving Luce to keep an eye on the patient, I changed out of my court gown into a simple kirtle and cloak and set off to take a ferry to Blackfriars. Luckily it was June and the day would be long enough for me to get there, have a consultation and be back before dusk. All the same the torches were ablaze on the Tower gates and walls when I finally returned, my basket laden with suggested salves and potions and my head full of advice on the treatment of burns.

Richard and Edward were both waiting anxiously for my arrival. They had been to see Anthony and were alarmed by the fact that he seemed to be in a state of extreme distress. 'He is shivering violently, Mother Joan,' Edward reported. 'Even though Luce has lit a fire in his chamber and he has plenty of bedcovers.'

'It is delayed shock,' I explained, repeating what the apothecary had warned me about. 'It is one of the early effects of a bad burn. And it is a bad burn. Have you seen it?' I had asked Luce to keep lifting and moistening the bandage because I did not want the linen to stick to the open wound. Another suggestion of the apothecary's had been to leave the wound open to the air. 'But not until you have him out of London, my lady,' he had added. 'The air here is too noxious but clean air will help the wound to close, which is the best way to stop it festering.'

The two men looked horrified at the thought of actually seeing the result of the cannon's explosion and had clearly avoided looking. 'It was fortunate there were not worse injuries,' Richard said. 'It could have backfired on the whole crew, but luckily the ball had already passed through the barrel and the gun only shed one joint. Unfortunately it caught poor Anthony. He will recover though, won't he, Joan?'

I sighed. 'I can't be sure. With any injury there are many things that can go wrong and the apothecary said that burns are the trickiest. Most importantly he advised that Anthony be taken out of London into fresh country air, so tomorrow I would like arrangements to be made to take him to Kent. He is young and strong and we must pray that all goes well.'

Richard undertook to inform the queen's vice-chamberlain of my departure but delegated to Edward the task of arranging the journey and escorting us to Halden Hall. 'The king has called another meeting of the Privy Council at Sheen in two days' time,' he said apologetically. 'And I must attend, because although we are celebrating a victory today, Henry is worried that King James and the pretender might have planned a pincer movement, intending to invade the kingdom from both north and south at the same time. Our forces must be redeployed accordingly.'

It was not until we retired to bed that I could inspect the blisters on Richard's hand where it had caught the remnants of the charge, which had caused the gun barrel to explode. I applied some of the salve I had acquired from the apothecary and we agreed that Richard should write to

Meg and Robert Poyntz to tell them of their son's injury. 'But do not make it sound too terrible,' I warned him. 'I believe Meg is pregnant and we mustn't cause her any shock.'

Edward did his best, hiring a more comfortable chariot than our own rattling baggage cart in which to convey Anthony to Halden and silencing the squire's weak protests that he could easily ride there with a curt, 'No, you can't, Poyntz, you'll make the injury worse and anyway you couldn't control your horse if it was spooked. You'll just have to lie back and take it like a girl.'

Although I couldn't approve of his way of expressing it, his coarse order had the desired effect. Worryingly however, by the time we reached Halden it was obvious that Anthony had a raging fever and my heart sank when we had to summon two of the strongest grooms from the stables to carry him up the stairs to bed. I made him eat some bread and milk, drink a goblet of ale and a good gulp of poppy juice, then I prepared to spend a long night doing for him what I had done for Hal when he had his unidentified fever, sponging him down and fanning his hot body, as well as periodically washing his wound with another of the apothecary's recommendations – diluted vinegar. He fell quickly into a state of restless unconsciousness, so at least he didn't feel the agonising sting of it.

The night was warm so neither chemise nor covers were necessary, or even desirable in the circumstances. At first I wrung out napkins in cold spring water and placed them on the bare skin of his torso until they dried out from the heat of his feverish body, while I wiped his face and neck with wet, soft linen waste. As I fought against sleep myself, a terrible guilt assailed me and I berated myself, as if the potentially fatal injury was my fault, having encouraged Meg and Robert Poyntz to send their precious son to serve Richard as a squire. In the flickering light of the lantern I had placed beside the bed I imagined how I would feel if this were Hal lying senseless beside me. My eyes closed in horror at the thought and perhaps for a few brief moments I fell asleep and then suddenly awoke, to find that what I had thought I was dreaming, I was actually doing. Had it been my own son I would have been hugging him in maternal consolation, kissing his cheeks and running my hands through his hair, and to my consternation this is what I was doing to Anthony. My hand had abandoned the wet cloth and was wandering freely through his thick blond hair and my lips were on his cheek.

The sudden sound of his voice made me snatch my hands away. 'Lady Joan,' he murmured, stirring. 'Honoured lady.'

I felt a surge of shame, as if I had been caught in carnal sin. I made the sign of the cross and pressed my fingers to my mouth – the mouth that had been so close to his only moments ago. My utterly unconscious actions felt terribly wrong and the guilt redoubled in my mind. Then Anthony tried to roll over, crying out in pain when he caught his wounded arm in the sheet. I bent swiftly to pull him back and turn him onto his other side. Then I loosened the bandage and lifted it to see if the burn was oozing pus again. If my patient's voice had not completely turned my thoughts back to the stark reality of the situation, the smell of his decaying flesh certainly did. This time my hand wandered to his forehead in a cool nursing capacity and my heart fluttered with relief in the rising hope that his fever was retreating.

The following day he seemed a little better and when Hetty came to relieve me we discussed whether there was anything else that could be done to encourage the skin to regrow over the suppurating wound. I told her about the apothecary's suggestion that the best thing was to leave it uncovered in the fresh air, but the wound affected most of his arm between the wrist and the elbow and I didn't see how that could be achieved without risking knocks and further pain and damage.

Hetty lapsed into silence for a minute or two and then said, 'There's a craftsman in the village who makes baskets out of osier stems. Perhaps he might make one that could be tied over the arm to protect the wound but with a mesh open enough to let in the air. If I made some measurements I could take them to him and see what he thinks.'

'That is a brilliant idea!' I cried. 'Impress on the weaver how essential it is that the basket can be easily buckled on and off with one hand and isn't too heavy. It could be some weeks before the wound heals and Anthony will need to be able to do it himself. Oh yes – I have great hopes for this basket-vambrace, Hetty!'

And it worked. The basket was made in a day and it kept Anthony's bedclothes off the wound at night and let the good clean air of the Kentish Weald do its healing work in the daytime. At first he fretted over the smell of his wound and waited impatiently for a scab to slowly grow over what had started as an alarming ten inches of blood and pus; a sight he could barely bring himself to look at, let alone leave open to the elements. Then, as he slowly became accustomed to wearing the basket, he grew irritable because the scab itched and he could not scratch it, but I put all this fretting down to delayed shock and a lingering fear that he would never recover enough strength in the muscles of his arm to perform as a knight in the field of battle. However, when his fever had completely gone and he regained his appetite and some of his strength, he became more optimistic. He realised that here was an opportunity to turn his attention to something other than the law or knightly pursuits and he took to wandering out to the shade of the home wood and sitting on my log seat with a book.

Often when I had completed my domestic chores in the morning I would join him and we would discuss whichever book he was reading and watch the ravens feeding their chicks. Frequently Jack and June came down to the ground to amuse us and several times Sim climbed up to the nest to give us a report on the chicks' progress. I had thrust the memory of the guilty and sinful feelings that briefly assailed me during the initial crisis of Anthony's injury into the depths of my mind, promising myself that was where they would stay.

As the summer gave way to autumn Richard and Edward were still involved in crushing the Cornish rebellion, which had been revived by the inevitable arrival of Perkin Warbeck, who as Lord Ormond predicted, had been given short shrift in Ireland and forced to beat a hasty retreat. He sailed his rag-tag army and poor pregnant wife to a beach near Land's End, took her to the protection of the nuns of Syon on St Michael's Mount, where he left a totally inadequate garrison, and then proceeded to sweet-talk the gullible Cornish dissenters into supporting his march north. They even took him to Bodmin and proclaimed him King Richard the

Fourth. But true to his usual form, when his ill-armed force moved into Somerset and his scouts reported that a substantial royal army was approaching he panicked, abandoned them and fled into sanctuary at Beaulieu Abbey, hoping to escape retribution in the depths of the New Forest. Meanwhile in lonely confinement in her island refuge, his wife miscarried their baby and was taken by King Henry's agents to throw herself on the king's mercy.

'Which was readily given,' Richard related when he returned from what he called a tedious expedition in which hardly a shot had been fired. 'But there was no sanctuary for Warbeck at Beaulieu. When a troop of the king's men hammered on the gate, the abbot was easily persuaded that protecting such an undeserving asylum-seeker was not worth incurring the wrath of God or the king. Warbeck is to be paraded through London in chains and confined in the Tower. Though frankly I think they should sling him into a distant dungeon and throw away the key.'

While I wouldn't have couched it in such drastic terms I found myself agreeing with Richard's instincts but I was also well aware of the queen's continuing ambivalence about the true identity of the pretender. She still had not completely satisfied herself as to whether or not the face she had seen on the Flemish jetton was that of her younger brother and now she had the pretender's Scottish wife confined in her household. Therefore I was not surprised when the following day I received a note in her own hand and under her personal seal, asking me if I was ready to return to her service. Its final passage convinced me that I had to be.

*They are bringing the prisoner to the Tower in a few
day's time and I would greatly appreciate your help in
finding a place from which I might obtain a clear view
of his face, without revealing myself to him or to anyone
else. The king has said he will have the pretender
brought before me but I prefer to choose my own moment
and to avoid him seeing me. You know the layout of the
Tower Joan, and you are the only one I can ask to help
me in this endeavour.*

I sent an immediate reply by her own messenger to say I
would be at the Tower in three days' time and entirely at
her service.

When I saw her barge dock at the royal river entrance I
donned my fur-lined cloak and packed a spare one of Pippa's
into a leather satchel, thinking that any cloak of the queen's
would look far too luxurious for our purpose. I did not wait
for a summons but set out to make my way unbidden to
the queen's lodging, knowing I would be expected. I had
asked Martin to find out where the prisoner would be
confined so that we could take up a position somewhere on
the route.

The queen took me and my mother to her solar and
dismissed her other attendants. 'You know that you are all
sworn to keep silent on this matter,' she told us. 'I want a
chance to discover once and for all if this man is or is not
my brother Richard and one good look at his face will tell
me.'

'Do we know roughly when Warbeck should arrive at the
Tower tomorrow, your grace?' I asked. 'We don't want to be
standing around anywhere too long or we'll attract attention.'

'I think we'll all be able to hear the noise of the crowds as he passes down Tower Street,' said my mother. 'And I don't imagine they'll be singing his praises.'

'Some of them may still believe he is the true Duke of York,' Elizabeth pointed out. 'They might be cheering him.' Her expression was glum and her fingers fidgeted nervously with the fabric of her gown. It was obvious how much she was pinning her hopes on this encounter and how torn she was about the outcome. 'And part of me wants to join them but then what would that mean for the king and our children? Oh why can't this nightmare be over and done with?'

I summoned my most soothing voice. 'Tomorrow it will be and I'm certain you will know him for an imposter once and for all.'

At noon the following day we heard the loud jeers and cat-calls carry over the castle defences as we stood on the roof of the Wakefield Tower and watched the mounted procession of guards and their prisoner turn out of Tower Street towards the Barbican and disappear within its high walls. This was our cue to hurry down the spiral stair and walk briskly along Water Lane to tuck ourselves under the gateway arch that led onto Tower Green, just as the caval-cade appeared through the Moat Gate and people scattered to avoid it, some of them joining us in our shelter. A phalanx of men at arms closely surrounded the prisoner, who was laden with chains and riding with his hands fastened behind his back. He was bareheaded and jerked his gaze from side to side as if constantly on the lookout for any sign of help or danger.

Stains left by a hail of vegetable missiles spattered his clothes but he did not look cowed by his hostile reception.

Even stripped of his silks and furs and clad only in a dull brown tunic and hose, he looked proud and defiant as he lifted his chin to check the guards on the walls, their bows drawn ready to react to trouble. I felt Elizabeth stiffen beside me, as if in that moment she saw something that shocked her. She shifted the hood of her cloak back a little to get a clearer view and I saw her brow crease into a fierce frown.

My heart skipped a few beats as I noticed that she had failed to remove her coronation ring. 'Your ring!' I hissed. 'Hide your ring.' She hastily tucked her hand back under her cloak but her expression was suddenly transfigured so that she looked almost euphoric.

'It isn't Richard,' she whispered as the prisoner's horse carried him beyond our view. 'It can't be him! Oh thank God!'

PART FOUR

40

'For the love of God, Hal, come down!' My heart was thumping in my chest like a troubadour's drum. 'If you fall you're dead!'

I had entered the home wood to find that my precious nine-year-old son was two-thirds of the way up the pine tree where the raven pair had produced another clutch of eggs. We knew this because Jack was away searching for food and June was sitting tight on the nest, otherwise I suspected they would both have been mobbing Hal as he hauled himself from branch to branch.

'I just want to see how many eggs there are,' Hal called back. 'It won't take me a minute.'

I was helpless. In less than that minute he could be lying lifeless at my feet. Hal was a strong and agile boy and he had great faith in his own physical ability – too much faith in my maternal opinion – but I knew there was nothing I could do to get him down safely and so I had to summon the same faith and reinforce it by praying to every saint I could think of to preserve him. I closed my eyes and concentrated on that, remembering the number of times I had watched Sim climb the same tree without a qualm. But Sim wasn't my own flesh and blood and he'd been older than Hal when he'd first started guarding the ravens.

Even with my eyes closed I knew when Hal had reached the nest because I heard June give a keek-keek of indignation, indicating that he had dislodged her in order to count the eggs. 'Four!' he yelled triumphantly. 'Well done, June – ouch!'

My eyes flew open. 'What's happened?' I shouted. 'Has she pecked you?'

'It's nothing,' he called back. 'I'm coming down now.'

Down was always more dangerous than up, so I didn't cease praying until I heard the thump as he jumped from the lowest branch onto the carpet of needles at the foot of the tree. I gave a sigh of relief. 'Thank you, Lord,' I said, crossing myself and turning my fury on Hal. 'You are never to do that again, do you hear me? Even if you survived a fall from that height you'd probably break a leg or crack your head open. And then how would you ever become a knight?'

'Yes, Mother,' he said with feigned remorse and sucking his bleeding finger before exclaiming jubilantly, 'But four eggs! That's a record, isn't it? I hope they all hatch.'

I grabbed his hand and inspected the damage. It was only a small scratch and licking it was probably as good as any other salve. He was so young and enthusiastic; I couldn't stay angry with him for long. 'Yes, so do I. But you may not be here to see it, Hal, because the queen wants me to take a post as governess to the two princesses and she's suggested that you come with me to Eltham Palace to join Prince Harry's household. What do you think?'

I had expected him to be excited at the idea but he looked

rather doubtful, kicking away at the pine needles while he gave it some thought. 'Prince Harry's nearly two years younger than me, isn't he? Won't I have to let him win at sports? And will I have to bow to him and call him my lord all the time?'

I smiled and ruffled his hair. 'Well, he is a prince, Hal. I think you'd have to sort that out with him but I suspect he won't want anyone to *let* him win. On the other hand I hear he's very good at sport and French and Latin. He's a bright boy, they tell me.'

'Who are "they"?' he asked pertinently, then screwed up his nose and made a funny movement from side to side with his mouth to express diffidence. 'Oh well – I suppose I could give it a go. When do we start?'

'I thought we might go to Eltham tomorrow, so you can have a look and meet the prince. You can make up your mind afterwards.'

But Hal was too astute for that. 'No. If I go there and meet the prince and then say I don't want to join his household he may never forgive me. People don't like being rejected, especially princes I should think. Whenever you're ready to go, lady mother, I'll be with you. I'll get on fine with Prince Harry. I'd be a fool not to.'

I gave him a big hug. Sometimes my son took foolish risks, like climbing trees, and sometimes he showed the wisdom of a person twice his age.

It was late March and I'd only arrived back at Halden the previous day, having attended the birth of the latest addition to the royal family and the churching of the queen afterwards. She'd had another problematic pregnancy but the birth had been unexpectedly easy and the boy had been baptised Edmund, after his grandfather, Edmund Tudor. Before she set out to take the baby prince to the nursery at Eltham Palace, Elizabeth had given me leave to come down to Halden in order to make arrangements before I started in my new post.

'I know you will not want to be separated from your own son on a permanent basis, Joan,' she had said. 'So I suggest you bring him with you and let him join Prince Harry in his household. It will do Harry good to have an older boy to compete with, and meanwhile you can keep a motherly eye on them both and keep me informed of their progress. I have recently appointed a protégé of the king's lady mother as Harry's tutor. He's a young Cambridge scholar, who she says is also a musician and a poet, so perhaps he will encourage the boys in some of the gentler arts.'

At the same time as the queen was offering me a post, the king had asked Richard to take on a tricky mission to Flanders. Perkin Warbeck had made another feeble attempt at invasion somewhere near Land's End, attracted a couple of thousand more Cornish malcontents and led them through Devon into Dorset. But when confronted with a formidable and well-equipped English army, the Flemish merchant's son had abandoned his men once again and fled to sanctuary with the monks at Beaulieu Abbey. However, King Henry had persuaded the abbot that such cowardice did not deserve God's protection and had taken Warbeck captive, hoping at last to bring the nerve-wracking saga of that troubling pretender to an end.

Meanwhile Queen Elizabeth's fiery cousin Edmund de la Pole had inherited the Suffolk estates but, due to his drastically reduced income, been demoted to Earl rather than Duke.

Angered by a tenant's jibe about being a pauper he had lashed out, was accused of murder and had fled to the continent to avoid justice. Fearful of any genuine nephew of Edward IV roaming loose among the treacherous courts of Europe, at the latest meeting of the Privy Council King Henry had tasked Sir Richard Guildford with fetching him back.

So in the face of our extensive royal duties it looked as if we would see little of each other during the coming year. Many noble marriages faltered in the face of royal demands on their time but on a personal level ours had progressed on a fairly even keel, perhaps because we had married with low expectations, which had shifted from time to time but never out of control. We no longer felt the sudden bursts of passion we had enjoyed in the early days of Frensham but neither had we abandoned all need for occasional conjugal confirmation of our marriage.

Most of Richard's older children were now well settled. Following Edward's wedding, George Guildford reached his majority and he and Bess Mortimer had married as planned and taken possession of her various manors in Essex, where they now lived. Of his girls, Maria remained stuck as a farmer's wife with only the one little boy and regrettably I saw little of her. Pippa was betrothed to John Gage, the elder son of a Sussex knight whom she would marry next year and meanwhile she practised her housekeeping skills at Halden Hall. Richard was in negotiation with a Kent family for a good marriage for fifteen-year-old Winnie and she and eleven-year-old Lizzie were still taking lessons along with Hal from the governess Mistress Brook, who had proved a great asset. I knew Lizzie would particularly miss Hal when he joined Prince Harry's household.

A couple of weeks later our cavalcade to Eltham made quite a column. Two of our stable grooms, armed against highway robbers, also led extra horses, so that Hal and I would have spare mounts at the palace. Our large farm wagon, pulled by a pair of Halden ploughing oxen, was stacked with chests full of our belongings. Hetty and Sim sat up beside the carter, she to serve as my personal maid and he to supervise the instalment of our four chosen hawks in the royal mews before returning with the cart.

'I suppose when it comes to falconry, I get to fly a kestrel, while Prince Harry gets a peregrine,' I heard Hal grumble to Sim, riding his pony up beside the wagon.

'Sim's going to the Tower after he's done his work at Eltham Palace, Hal,' I said, urging my palfrey a little closer to my son's. 'I've asked him to repair the roost boxes on the alder trees to see if we can attract more ravens to return. If there's a busy roost there again we could take Jack and June's chicks to join the juvenile group in the autumn. That's if you can tear yourself away from your prince and your kestrel.'

'I'm more likely to be tied to a desk and a Latin grammar,' he said glumly. 'Or learning how low to bow to lords and ladies.'

The nearer we got to Eltham, the more nervous Hal became. I couldn't blame him. I was used to being in the company of the royals, with all the protocol and etiquette that demanded, and he had only been at court during one Christmas, when the rules were more relaxed. I kept silent on the subject but I knew there was a steep learning curve ahead for my beloved son. 'Well, if you don't like it, Hal, you can always come home to Halden you know,' I said sympathetically.

I received a scathing look. 'And give up all hope of a knighthood? I'm not that stupid!' he said.

As we crossed the Eltham drawbridge, the sight of her personal standard flying above the royal apartments told us that the queen was still in residence, clearly taking her time to see baby Edmund settled, not that he would be aware of anything much yet, apart from his crib and his nurse's breast.

However, as I had already known, I had two very different princesses to mentor and the difference between them was made immediately obvious. We had arrived at Eltham the day before Princess Mary's birthday and when the two girls were brought to the queen's solar to greet me she could scarcely keep still for excitement. She just managed to make me a beautifully executed curtsy before announcing, 'Good day, Mother Guildford. Today I'm two but tomorrow I'll be three.'

I looked into her intense grey eyes and experienced an entirely unexpected surge of emotion. There before me was the realisation of the beautiful golden-haired girl I had dreamed of bringing into the world myself after Hal's baby smiles had erased my fear of giving birth. Not that my colouring was likely to have produced such a fairy-tale creature but God had not granted my wish anyway. Instead, He had now given me this manifestation of the daughter of my dreams, to care for and nurture.

I squatted down to her level. 'And what plans do you have for celebrating that amazing day, princess?' I asked.

Mary's smile plucked further at my heartstrings. 'I will have a special dinner and then my lady mother will read me a story. She is best at reading stories.'

I looked up at Elizabeth and I could see that praise from

her little daughter was worth all the jewels in her crown. But she was careful to share the joy. 'Then Margaret will play the lute to accompany your pipe. Won't you, Meg? We're going to have a concert.'

'And a dance,' Mary added, doing another little jig on the spot.

'And what will you have for your special dinner on your birthday?' I thought of the feasts I had conjured up for Hal's celebrations.

Nine year-old Margaret intervened when Mary obviously didn't know how to reply. 'It's Lent so we won't have meat but the cook says he has a lobster with her name on it.'

The queen looked surprised at this. 'Does he? How clever of him. That will be a treat.'

'Yes, but this one is *mine*,' Mary said determinedly.

'Don't you think you might share it with your mother and sister?' I asked gently. 'I'm sure you can't eat a whole lobster.'

Mary's bottom lip protruded in a pretty pout. 'Maybe not but Harry gets some first.'

Elizabeth and I exchanged glances and I stood up. 'Mary is very fond of her big brother,' she admitted and slipped her hand into Margaret's. 'And Meg doesn't much like lobster, do you, dearest?'

The older girl shook her head and bent to whisper in her sister's ear. Mary giggled and Margaret spoke for both of them. 'We thought you were going to bring your son with you, Lady Guildford. Is he here?'

She had blushed quite pink when she said this but the queen intervened. 'I think Meg took a shine to your Hal when he came for Christmas at Westminster,' her mother confided. 'They're much the same age after all but I expect

Harry's showing him around, isn't he? It will be so good for him to have a companion nearer his own age. His other pages are wards of the king and at least six years older than him. We'll get them all together at supper.'

I learned later that Prince Harry's younger pages had come and gone quite frequently, unable to keep their tempers when he lost his or else not bright enough to stomach the prince's keen desire to win at all times. I crossed my fingers and hoped Hal would weather the storms to come. Nine was young to start as a page but not unusual.

He was lucky that the first sign of conflict did not involve him but made him aware of where danger might lie. It came at dinner the next day when the coveted lobster was paraded around the great hall at the birthday celebration; rivalling a goose for size, it was gilded and decorated with rows of pearls; aquamarines represented the sea and two large red rubies replaced its eyes.

'The jewels are a present from the king, Mary,' her mother explained. 'He will have an item of jewellery made for you from them, when you decide what you might like.'

Mary clapped her hands with pleasure and I was surprised that she knew exactly what she wanted. 'I like the pearls best,' she said. 'I would like a crown of pearls.'

Prince Harry was sitting on her other side and leaned close. 'But pearls are my birthstone, Mary, so I should have those. I could have them sewn onto a pair of sleeves for my birthday in June.'

Mary was quite firm in her response. 'If you take my pearls I won't give you any lobster.'

'If you don't give them to me, I won't dance with you ever again,' the prince declared, his temper rising.

Mary shrugged and turned away from him. 'I'll dance with your new page then. I expect he dances better than you anyway.'

Angrily Prince Harry beckoned Hal over from the pages' corner. He approached eagerly and bent his knee as he'd been taught.

'Can you dance, Hal?' Harry's face was like thunder, screwed up into a fierce frown. 'My sister Mary says you dance better than me.'

Margaret spoke up in Hal's defence. 'No she did not. She said she expects he does.' Her cheeks were pink but she obviously couldn't let someone she considered her friend be bullied by her little brother. 'Do you, Hal?'

Hal's eyes widened and he raised his shoulders doubtfully. 'I don't know. I've never seen you dance, sir, but you'd need two left feet to dance as badly as I do.'

That made the prince laugh. 'Ha! We'll have a contest after dinner then.'

At this point the queen intervened. 'By all means do that,' she said, 'but neither of you gets the pearls because they are mine. Your presents are the aquamarines and the two rubies, Mary. And so is the lobster. When the carver has portioned it Hal can bring the dish and you can tell him who you'd like to offer it to.'

As Hal rose and backed away I gave him a sly nod of approval. When he offered the lobster around, Princess Mary left her brother to last and after the prince protested that she had broken protocol she smiled her best three-year-old innocent smile and asked, 'What's pro-to-col, Harry?'

41

IN JULY RICHARD APPEARED at Eltham Palace, having succeeded in extracting the Earl of Suffolk from Guînes Castle in the Calais Pale, where he had been enjoying the hospitality of the Constable, who was apparently oblivious of the 'wanted' status of his guest.

'So with Warbeck safely locked up in the Tower and Suffolk back under his eye, the king is now reasonably satisfied that his throne is safe,' Richard told me, lying back wearily on the comfortable curtained bed in the spacious chamber allocated to the princesses' governess. 'By the way I brought Sim and Anthony with me and will take them on to Halden. Sim's had a difficult time at the Tower because your roost boxes had all been removed.'

'What? Completely taken away? By whom? Did he find out?' I was incensed and suspicious at the same time, because I could guess immediately who was the malicious perpetrator of this vile deed. But what had stirred Sir Henry Wyatt's ire from dormant to active once more?

'He said it was done by some of the moneyers from the Mint. I suppose they must have been under instructions though.'

'By a Comptroller for instance?' I suggested.

He sat up, surprised. 'You think Sir Henry Wyatt did it? But why would he?'

'Don't you remember? He once shot a raven with a handgonne when I was feeding it on a Sunday. He hates them and he hates me. Are those good enough reasons?'

He sank back again, tired from his long, hard ride from London. Richard was in his mid-forties now, a veteran of much work, assiduous training and many battles. He wouldn't admit it but his body was beginning to feel the effects. 'No, not really; he's never indicated any vindictive streak as far as I'm concerned.'

'Lucky you,' I remarked dryly. 'Have you eaten anything today or shall I send Hetty for some food?'

He lifted his head again. 'Yes please. Can she get hold of some at this hour?'

The children were in bed and it was long after supper had been cleared from the great hall but there would still be scullions cleaning pots in the kitchen court. 'I'm sure she can. It will only be bread and cheese though – and maybe some fruit.'

'Sounds like a feast. Could she get some for Sim and Anthony too?'

'Yes, but pull your boots on again. We'll have to go and eat it somewhere else. I don't like crumbs in my chamber, they bring vermin.'

'But I noticed you have some wine on the buffet. Let's have a cup before we go.'

I poured two cups and laid two more with the flagon on the tray for Sim and Anthony.

July had been hot and instead of sitting in the stuffy servants' hall we took our meal out into the herb garden behind the kitchen, which was fragrant with its scented planting and had benches where cooks and gardeners could sit and take a break from their daily toil. Not being familiar with the layout of the palace Sim and Anthony followed Hetty to the kitchen door and then, when she knew she had led them to us, I saw her slip away to her own evening rendezvous with one of the royal grooms that she was sweet on.

I had seen little of Anthony since his horrible burn had healed and he'd regained his fighting fitness. He'd returned to his law studies in London and spent the legal holidays serving in the small entourage of young knights and esquires that Richard had acquired in accordance with his Knight Banneret status. Anthony was now approaching his majority and in a few weeks would be returning home to be married to the Somerset heiress to whom he had been betrothed some years before. I would sadly miss the gallant way he always greeted me, as he did now, like an awestruck squire addressing his honoured lady, going down on one knee and bowing over my hand. He attributed his survival from his injury entirely to my care and said, often and with simple and endearing devotion, that he owed his life to me. I prayed that his intended wife, whom I had never met, would love and appreciate the handsome, literate, charming young man she was about to marry.

Richard always teased his squire when he saw him make his chivalrous address. 'One day you'll find you've worn a hole in the knee of your hose, my lad!' he remarked this time. 'I thought you'd stopped reading those mawkish Arthurian tales now you're back in military mode.' Romance was still not a word that featured large in my husband's vocabulary, even though I'd been shown that he understood its power when he gave me Frensham Manor.

Anthony took it all in good part. He rose to his feet and made a flourishing bow to his knight. 'They have a great deal to tell us about life out of armour as well, sir. I'm still learning about both.'

My husband used his belt knife to cut a piece off the loaf Hetty had brought and another off the wedge of cheese. 'Well, come and eat something now and feed your belly. And you too, Sim; there's wine too.'

'Do you want to hear how your son's getting on with Prince Harry?' I asked, cutting bread and cheese for the two young men. Sim thanked me and took his food and drink to sit apart on the next bench, always aware of the social gulf between a knight and his servant.

Richard swallowed his mouthful. 'Yes, I'm sorry I arrived after his bedtime. Your last letter implied that he was struggling a bit. Are things any better now?'

'There was an incident when the prince climbed a tree in the park and called Hal to come up with him but he refused, remembering what I had told him about never getting to be a knight if you broke a limb falling from a tree and warned the prince accordingly. Luckily the tree wasn't very tall because Harry did fall but was only winded. Unfortunately the prince then informed his governess that Hal had told him he would never be a knight. He is rather prone to not quite telling the whole story and I had to go and establish the truth, otherwise Hal was on the way home.'

'Poor little Hal,' his father sympathised. 'Serving royalty is like being constantly on a cliff edge in a blindfold. You never quite know which way to step, do you?'

'True, but Hal is learning and he has an agile mind, so

he usually steps in the right direction, which either means telling a joke or suggesting a game. The prince loves that about him. I don't think he'd want him to be sent home like the others.'

Richard cut himself some more cheese and picked up an apple. 'Here, Sim, catch. Do you want to come and tell my lady about the raven boxes?' He selected another apple for himself and watched Sim approach and sit down on the grass in front of our bench.

'I wanted to write, m'lady, but my letters aren't good, despite your efforts to teach me. The ink spatters everywhere.' He threw his apple from one hand to the other nervously. 'I'm not sure it's worth replacing the roost boxes. There are very few ravens around the Tower now, since the fire.'

'Fire?' I echoed, horrified. 'What fire?'

'The men who pulled down the boxes stacked them against the wall under the trees at the back of the copse. Then someone else must have noticed them there and put a torch to them. All the wood is burned. Even worse, several of the trees caught fire too but luckily alder don't burn very well. Of course the few ravens that were still roosting in the branches all flew and they haven't been back since. I don't think they'll come now.'

I felt tears spring to my eyes and brushed them impatiently away. 'Oh Sim, this is terrible news. So there are no ravens at the Tower at all now?'

He shook his head and bit into his apple. There was a guilty look on his face, as if he felt the ravens' departure must be his fault.

'This is disastrous,' I said indignantly. 'Did you inform the Lieutenant Constable?'

Sim hastily swallowed his mouthful. 'No, my lady, because I was told he knew. He'd been asking questions around the garrison 'bout who might have lit the fire.'

'And did any of the soldiers know who he suspected?' My anger was building again because again I was certain what the answer would be.

Sim frowned. 'It's only rumour but the arrow is pointin' at the man who runs the Jewel House. But he's a knight and no one is going to point the finger d'rectly.'

I met Richard's glance and fielded his fierce shake of the head. His message was clear. He didn't believe it was Sir Henry Wyatt and didn't want his name mentioned. I shrugged and sighed. 'I don't suppose they are,' I said regretfully. 'And it sounds like you don't think it's worth replacing the boxes. But would you, Sim, if I asked you?'

He took another bite of his apple and chewed it, ruminating. 'Of course I would, m'lady, if you asked me.'

'It would just be nice to take Jack and June's new chicks up there when they're ready. The others have done well finding mates during the autumn roost.'

'I'll build the boxes when I get back to Halden and then you can decide what you want done with 'em. How's that?'

I smiled at him. Since I rescued him, cold and hungry from the forest, he would do anything for me. 'Good, Sim. That's good.'

42

AT THE BEGINNING OF November I left instructions for Jane Howell to supervise the two princesses' lessons for a few weeks and took leave to travel to Halden to collect Sim and his roosting boxes and take them to the Tower of London. I was pleased to discover that Sim had been having riding lessons from Richard's Master of Horse and was now sufficiently skilled to be allowed to use one of the Guildford palfreys instead of bouncing painfully alongside the carter on the baggage wagon, which contained eight new roosting boxes as well as my clothes chest. It meant that we could talk together en route, rather than having to shout over the sound of the ironbound cartwheels rattling over the ruts on the ill-kept Kentish roads.

'You know Sir John Digby is a supporter of the ravens, Sim. What was the real reason you didn't consult him about the identity of the arsonist who burned the trees?'

He gave me an astonished look, as if I had uttered an expletive. 'He's the king's Lieutenant Constable, m'lady! He wouldn't give someone like me the time of day, let alone take notice of any complaint I made.'

I frowned. 'Is that really so? He may be an officer of the king but Sir Richard outranks him as Master of Ordnance and you wear his livery.' I gestured at his green jacket, which bore at the shoulder a black saltire cross on a silver ground between four sable martlets: the Guildford coat of arms. 'I'd say he was duty bound to at least hear what you have to say.'

The young man flushed and hung his head, making no response, and I spoke again, less harshly. 'Remember that next time, won't you? Your livery gives you status, Sim, especially in the Tower. When the new roosts are in place I shall go and see Sir John and I believe he will agree to my request that protection be given to the ravens. They are the guardians of the Tower and an important symbol of King Henry's reign.'

'Are they, m'lady? I would have thought a king would want an eagle or a gyrfalcon rather than a raven.'

I shook my head. 'Eagles and falcons are solitary top predators who live off the flesh of their prey. King Henry desires to rule an orderly and prosperous kingdom where his subjects can live in harmony with their neighbours and the rich share their wealth through charity with the poor and needy, just as ravens roost together and share the carrion they find with other members of their community. They are symbols of stability and order and their presence demonstrates the role the Tower plays in keeping the king and the kingdom safe.'

I was not sure if he followed my reasoning but he rode on with a thoughtful expression on his face. The next day it was still daylight when we reached the Tower and after stabling the horses we went straight to the roost site to see how the trees were faring. Luckily alders are a hardy species and most were looking well set for the winter, showing only a few scorch marks along their bare branches, some late-dropping catkins and a glut of brown seed cones. Having become used to seeing at least one roost box in each tree I made a prayer to St Francis to enable Sim to erect enough of them before winter set in to attract a fair 'conspiracy' of ravens.

As I mentioned this to him, I gradually became aware of sounds coming from up in the tree above us. Normally ravens did not make many soft noises, preferring to honk and 'kaark' loudly and make their presence felt; only sometimes the younger birds made a noise like small pebbles rattling musically under shallow, fast-flowing water. It was usually made to greet a friend or a family member and gradually I became aware that this might be what we were to the two birds sitting side by side on a branch above us.

'They might be Jack and June's chicks, Sim,' I whispered, suddenly frightened of alarming them by speaking too loudly. 'Or at least one of them is. Perhaps it remembers our voices better than we remember theirs.'

'If one is our chick, it must be a nestling from two years ago,' he responded eagerly, while the soft 'kerrring' sound drew significantly closer. I chanced a swift glance up into the tree and saw the birds moving further down, one after the other. At any time, even when they'd bonded and paired up, it was difficult to identify individual ravens, because they were so alike; black, luminous wing feathers, those deep, unblinking brown eyes and short ruff feathers at the neck, which fluffed up at times of pleasure or alarm. Only their 'moustaches' were variable, the pinfeathers that rooted where the beak erupted from between the eyes and lay at varying length and thickness along the top half of the hooked upper mandible.

'I think I recognise that one.' Sim pointed up at the bird making the sound. 'He always appeared to have a cheeky grin. See how his mouth turns up at the edges?'

'I just can't believe we are remembered at all, after so long,' I responded, my voice breaking with emotion. 'Have you got any treats?'

Sim usually had wafer crumbs or nuts in his pockets but on this occasion, at the end of a long ride, he had only a handful of oats – not the ravens' favourite food. However he cast it on the grass below the tree and the vocalising raven dropped down to investigate. Then Sim made a little run at him, just as he had always done with the young ravens that had hatched at Halden Hall. It was an invitation to play and the bird responded with a little run of its own, first of all in the opposite direction, then darting back to make a teasing peck at Sim's ankle before veering off again. Sim gave me a triumphant look. 'It's definitely the cheeky one!' he cried. 'This is how we always used to play.'

I watched him set off under the trees, weaving in and out of the trunks, closely pursued by the bird on its long leathery legs and sharp-clawed feet, flapping its wings with excitement but not actually rising off the ground. I laughed with delight and above me on its branch the other bird issued a series of rasping honks, which I took to be from amusement. Then, out of the corner of my eye I caught sight of a figure standing in the gateway, silhouetted against the pink clouds of the evening sky and framed by the arch. His arms were folded across his body and his feet were spread in a tyrannical pose that vividly expressed disapproval, but when he noticed I had seen him he turned abruptly on his heel and strode away out of sight. I knew who he was though – Richard's friend Sir Henry Wyatt, Comptroller of the Mint, Master of the Jewel House and my bête noire.

Two days later, having chosen the trees for the new roost

boxes with Sim, I decided to confront Sir Henry over the wrecking of the old ones and the fire. I had to wait for Richard to leave before I could do so however, because I knew he would not approve. After he had broken his fast I found him in his office, poring over some new design, which he hastily covered up when I entered.

'I'm glad you came, Joan,' he said immediately. 'I've just heard from Sir John Digby that the king has ordered the garrison strengthened, so you'd better take care around the precinct because there will be soldiers who don't know who you are. They can be troublesome around women when they aren't aware of the consequences.'

I gave him a rueful smile. 'Thanks for the warning; you're right, obnoxious remarks can be passed. Did Sir John give you any idea why the garrison is being strengthened?'

'Some prisoners are being questioned, I gather. It must be a matter of state importance.'

'I'll warn Sim. He's installing the new roost boxes this week so he'd better keep a low profile on the green. Sometimes he gets involved in an exchange of banter with the archers. I don't want him marched off to a dark cell. He has work to do.' A second thought occurred to me. 'Might it have something to do with the Spanish wedding?'

In May there had been a proxy ceremony at the Prince of Wales's palace in the Welsh March, when Prince Arthur and Princess Katherine of Aragon had been provisionally united, with the Spanish ambassador deputising for the bride. This began the process of marriage according to the treaty drawn up between King Henry and the king and queen of Spain. Princess Katherine was due to come to England after Christmas, when she would be fourteen. This marriage was the basis of an alliance of extreme importance to Tudor standing in Europe. Anything that might jeopardise it would be severely dealt with.

Richard gave me a quizzical look. 'What makes you say that?'

'The fact that the pretender Warbeck and the Earl of Warwick are both held in the Tower at present and either one of them could be the focus of a plot against the throne, which would undoubtedly threaten the Spanish alliance.'

Richard's shrug did not convince me that he knew nothing of the reason for the high level of security. 'There's been no mention of anything like that in the Council,' he said.

I scoffed at that. 'As if the Privy Council is your only source of information!'

He rolled up the design he had been studying and tied it up. 'I must go. I have a ferry waiting to take me to the Woolwich armoury. Edward has a problem there. I'll see you later.'

I set the matter of a plot against the state to one side to consider later, because Richard's departure left me free to tackle Sir Henry Wyatt. When I ventured out I immediately noticed there were more archers on the walls than usual and extra sentries on the towers where state prisoners were held. I was well known to the men who regularly guarded the Lieutenant Constable's house, located on the green, and so I was admitted without fuss and my business with Sir John Digby took little of his time. I asked him about the increase of the guard but he just said it was an exercise. However, I was so closely quizzed by the guards on duty in the big Coldharbour Gatehouse leading to the Inner Court, which protected the entrances to the White Tower and the Royal Palace, that I knew there was more to it than that. The general atmosphere within the whole fortress was distinctly tense. I had to show my permit from the king before I could gain entrance to the Jewel House.

It would be the first time I had confronted Sir Henry Wyatt since he had made his frightening attack following my last encounter with Edward of Warwick in the Tower's privy garden. I had to summon all my courage to climb the stairs to his office but he appeared either to have no recollection of it or else no sense of chagrin or remorse.

'I'm surprised they let you in here, Lady Guildford.' It was with obvious reluctance that he offered me a seat.

'I do have a letter of trust signed and sealed by the king, Sir Henry, which I presume, as a member of the Privy Council, you have also,' I said.

His already grim expression became a scowl. 'Whatever possessed him to grant one to a woman?' he muttered, as if I were not in the room.

'Perhaps the fact that I am entrusted with the education of his children,' I suggested. 'But I am not here to argue my merit or my loyalty to the crown. I wish to know on what authority you ordered the removal of the roost boxes in the alder trees on Tower Green and, more hazardously, had them burned?'

The knight's scowl became a look of angry disbelief. 'What on God's earth led you to believe I had anything to do with those incidents? I am Master of the Jewel House, Lady Guildford, not Keeper of the Green.'

I stared down his attempt at intimidation, although my heart felt as if it was swooping and swerving, like a flock of starlings on the wing. 'You are also Comptroller of the Mint, Sir Henry, and it was a gang of your moneyers who were seen pulling down the roost boxes. And you must admit that you have frequently and publicly expressed your hatred of the ravens.'

'I very much doubt if there is a soldier in the garrison who does not hate ravens. And I may be Comptroller of the Mint but that does not mean that I control the men who strike the coins. The moneyers work to the Master of the Mint, so perhaps you should be taking your hysterical accusations to him, my lady.' He finished this tirade with such a fiercely sarcastic grin that I could see the blackened signs of rot on his gums. It stirred an awful memory of his fetid breath on my face as I fought him off.

'Clearly you have not kept in touch with the Lieutenant Constable, sir; because if you had he would have told you that he has banned the archers from using the ravens as target practice and given permission to any soldier who wishes, during his spare time, to help erect the new roost boxes that will go up from today.'

The withering smile altered only slightly. 'I don't believe you will find a line of soldiers queuing up for that dubious privilege, madam.' He stood up. 'You have climbed the stairs in vain and now, unless you wish me to call my squire to assist you from the building, I would like you to take your leave. You may have little to occupy your time but mine is in high demand.' He moved around the desk in such a predatory way that I truly thought he might try to eject me bodily.

I rose with slow decorum, taking time to adjust my skirt, brush imaginary dust from my sleeves and pull on my gloves. Adopting a tone as icy as his, I made him a minuscule bow. 'I fear there could be more call on your precious time than you may have envisaged, Sir Henry, for the Lieutenant Constable intends to serve you personally with a further demand — requesting compensation for the damage done to the Tower walls and trees by the moneyers, who were apparently not aware that you wished to keep your name out of their acts of vandalism.'

I did not wait to witness his reaction to this pronouncement but made my exit. The door had not closed, however, before I heard his exclamation of fury and allowed myself a little smile of satisfaction before heading for the stair.

Something about this episode and my earlier conversation with Richard made me take a detour to the privy garden before leaving the Tower's Inner Court. It was about the time of day when I had been accustomed to find Edward of Warwick taking exercise there but when I showed my now rather well-thumbed permit from the Lieutenant Constable the duty guard shook his head.

'No admissions allowed to the garden at present,' he said, handing it back and eyeing me closely. 'Aren't you the lady that visited Lord Warwick sometimes? The lad with the dog?' When I said I was he added, 'He don't come here any more anyway. I think they must have moved him.'

43

'Your guess about the Spanish wedding being involved was right, Joan,' Richard revealed, having invited me once more into his office for privacy. 'King Ferdinand wrote to King Henry, making it clear that Princess Katherine would not be travelling to England while the Earl of Warwick lives. So a scheme was hatched to incriminate him in an escape attempt.'

'But how, Richard?' I asked, shocked. 'Warwick has never shown any inclination to escape, not even after Warbeck tried to last year. Anyway so few people even know what he looks like that he could probably walk out of here without being recognised, but then where would he go? And the queen would tell you that he hasn't the mental aptitude to hatch a plot.'

'That may be so but it doesn't stop York supporters from wanting to use him as a figurehead for rebellion, which is what concerns the Spanish monarchs. Edward could be said to have a better claim to the English throne than Henry, and Ferdinand and Isabella want him out of the picture permanently, by fair means or foul.' Richard drew up a chair for me and we sat across from each other at his big drawing trestle. 'Having no wish to resort to murder, King Henry consulted a soothsayer to advise him. Perhaps he hoped he would predict Warwick's imminent death but he did not. And now his astrologer has been called in, who told the king that during this year just one man's death will prevent many hundreds more. It seems to have aged Henry overnight.'

'In other words he feels his throne shaking under him again,' I said dismally. 'Where is all this leading?'

Richard gave a hoarse laugh. 'Ha! That's just it – nothing is clear except that somehow, Warwick and Warbeck were able to meet right here in the Tower with what they believed to be a couple of Yorkist conspirators, who had apparently been able to get themselves hired as gaolers. The plot was theirs – or at least planned by whoever planted them. The idea was to start a fire near the gunpowder store, which would cause the garrison to panic and the guards to unlock Warwick's chamber, who would then open the gates to the Yorkist outsiders. Then Warwick would declare himself king and order Warbeck's release. But here is the truly relevant part of it. Apparently there are witnesses who heard Warwick say that if he was convinced that Perkin Warbeck really is Richard of York, he would concede the throne to him. Like Sir William Stanley, that is what puts him in line for the scaffold.'

I made a rather unladylike noise. 'What, just like that? It's preposterous! Warwick wouldn't have the nerve or the guts for such a scheme.'

'You keep implying that,' Richard said, 'but have you seen Warwick since he came to the Tower?'

This question came like a bolt from the blue because I had not told Richard about my visits to Edward, and now I was obliged to come clean. 'Well yes, I have, because Lady Margaret asked me to check on him. I reported back to her and the queen the same thing Elizabeth has always believed, that although he may be a prince of the blood, Edward of Warwick is mentally incapable of being even a puppet king.'

I could see my husband's intense hurt and anger that I had not revealed these visits to him. I could also see fear in his expression as he locked eyes with me. 'Why did you not tell me this, Joan? You have put yourself into an extremely dangerous position. Does the king know?'

I shook my head, alarmed at his evident distress. I was beginning to wish I hadn't told him. 'I don't think so, unless Elizabeth mentioned it. But I'm sure she wouldn't. She and Lady Margaret just wanted to be sure that Edward was being well treated. Anyway I haven't seen him for at least two years. Not since Perkin Warbeck was brought here. As you must realise, I had absolutely nothing to do with this conspiracy.'

'I believe you, of course I do, but it could still get you in trouble if someone in the Tower knew.' He took my hands in his across the table. 'Was anyone else there with you when you visited Edward? I can't believe no one has mentioned your visits in the Privy Council. Its members have ears and eyes everywhere. How many times did you see him?'

'Only three times in the privy garden, and there was no one with him, except his dog. Honestly, Richard, I just met a lonely youth, who had only a small dog for company. He loved that dog, but it died. He believed it was poisoned.'

'What did he say to you? Did he ever ask you to help him escape?'

'No. I don't think the idea ever occurred to him. He had no interest in life outside the Tower. He was allowed to take his dog for a walk in the privy garden every day and this was his great pleasure. Otherwise he had a few books and a supply of pens, ink and paper but he only used them to draw – mostly pictures of his dog as far as I know. He showed me some and actually they were very good. He told me that a priest visited him every week but it was hard to get him to say anything very much apart from that.' I withdrew my hand from Richard's and clasped mine together, blinking back tears. 'Are they thinking of doing what the Spanish want? Will he go to the scaffold? I honestly don't believe he's any harm to anyone, Richard.'

He leaned his elbows on the table, shaking his head dolefully. 'I'm sure you're right, Joan, but that's not the point, is it? The point is that King Henry won't get the marriage he desperately wants for Prince Arthur unless Edward dies. And as a result of this abortive attempt to seize power it's now possible to make sure that happens, legally and with the full force of the law. There will be trials and I just hope and pray that you don't get swept up in the scheme in the process.'

'I don't see how that could happen,' I said, although I was far from confident, once again recalling my frightening encounter with Wyatt following my last meeting with Warwick. 'It's the queen I will worry about. Not in Warbeck's case because she only saw him once and she instantly discarded the possibility of him being her brother, which was a great comfort to her. There should have been a scar on his neck from some boyhood sword fight with young Edward of York but it wasn't there. How is she going to feel though when her undisputed cousin Edward, whom she sees as a poor, guileless innocent, is sent to the scaffold, as the result of a plot entirely contrived in the King's Chamber?'

'Terrible,' Richard admitted. 'But she's as keen on the

Spanish marriage as Henry is. I'm sure they will have discussed it.'

'Perhaps they have, but simple soul that Edward may be, he is her close kin. The thought of him laying his head on the block will be torture for her. Will he be executed on Tower Hill?'

'It hasn't been decided yet. Warbeck will go to Tyburn first and is scheduled for the traitor's sentence of hanging, drawing and quartering. But the king intends to commute it to a simple hanging if he agrees to make a full public confession that he is an imposter and definitely not a son of Edward the Fourth.'

I shivered. 'I thought he'd done that already, but I suppose if it's made in the face of death and divine judgement that would be a powerful admission.'

'But Warbeck's death will not satisfy the Spanish king and queen. It's Warwick they want dead and he has pleaded guilty to treason. I cannot see how the king can possibly commute his sentence.'

'I do not want to be here when that poor young man goes to Tower Hill, Richard,' I said, rubbing my temples in distress. 'I cannot bear to hear the roar of the crowd as the axe falls. I will go to Eltham Palace as soon as I see the ravens begin to come back in numbers.'

For once Richard was quite positive about the ravens' return. 'Well, I hope they do, Joan, because the kingdom has been rocking uncomfortably in their absence.'

After Sim and I had seen at least ten ravens fly in to roost together in the new box shelters set among the alders, I told Hetty to pack my travelling chest. On Tower Green the following day Sim watched the pretender tied face down in the traitor's position on the hurdle and then followed the grim procession along Cheapside, through the Newgate and down the long road to Tyburn. Afterwards he came to tell me that a pair of our ravens had followed the hurdle all the way and watched the hanging from a tree. Even though I cherished their presence, I shivered at the thought that they might have taken the pretender's eyes before coming back to roost that night.

'Did the condemned man speak, Sim?' I asked.

He gave a noncommittal shrug. 'I think he might 'ave but there was so much jeerin' and shoutin', m'lady, I doubt if anyone actually heard what he said.'

Nevertheless Warbeck's scaffold confession that he was not a son of King Edward the Fourth, and therefore not the rightful king of England, was printed and posted all over the city the next day and no doubt in due course on every market cross in the country.

No announcement had yet been made about Warwick's execution when I was intrigued to receive a formal invitation from My Lady the King's Mother to attend 'a solemn ceremony' at Coldharbour Palace the following day, a place which I had not visited for several years. Walking up from the private wharf through the long sloping garden, I remembered when a certain knight had sought me out there and more or less accused me of being party to a Yorkist conspiracy against the king. His attitude that day had been very different from the belief he had shown in me lately, when I told him of my meetings with Edward of Warwick.

At the Coldharbour dock my mother pounced on me,

having clearly waited there for that very purpose. Her words came out in a great rush, even as she kissed me in greeting.

'I have not had an opportunity before this to tell you that I am leaving the queen's service and joining Lady Margaret in her retirement, as I always said I would. I should have written to you but anyway I have told you now before anyone else does and I know you will be pleased.'

This news came as a total surprise but before I could discover more she whisked me off to the palace chapel to join a small congregation of women, led by the queen, to witness Lady Margaret take a solemn vow of chastity and declare her intent to retire into the country.

I was surprised but not amazed and later having invited me to share her barge back to Eltham Palace, the queen explained further.

'Lady Margaret is not becoming a nun but she will dress in sober apparel and live a chaste and quiet life in her own homes with your mother as a constant friend and companion. I must say that I will miss Mother Vaux immensely but I believe Lady Margaret intends to keep permanent and separate accommodation for her husband and for any of her friends and family who choose to visit her, so you should not feel excluded from your mother's company. However, from now on My Lady the King's Mother will only attend royal occasions of great significance, if the king specifically requests it.'

I studied Elizabeth's face, pondering what significance this arrangement might hold for her. For much of her life as King Henry's wife she had been obliged to share his company with his mother who, although a kind and generous person, was also a forceful and determined woman. If Lady Margaret was now taking a significant step back from public life, might her daughter-in-law at last find her rightful prominence and power in the land? I thought I could detect a certain relish in the way Elizabeth described the very private life the king's mother intended to lead – perhaps even a hint of triumph.

But she had not asked me to take a seat beside her on the barge merely to discuss her mother-in-law's new status and it was not long before she changed the subject.

'I'm so happy that Prince Harry and your Hal have struck up such a close bond of friendship, Joan. It pleases the king and I enormously because we have been vexed that several young boys have previously been obliged to leave his household. But I am personally a little worried about Arthur. When he joined us in the summer I thought he looked rather too thin.'

I did some quick mental arithmetic. 'He is just thirteen now, is he not? I think young boys often grow upward fast at that age. I feel sure he will flesh out in due course. Certainly my stepsons did.'

'You always know how to reassure me, Joan. I trust you are right.'

She fell silent at this point and I wondered if she might make any reference to the two current executions, which had such relevance to the Spanish wedding. Although she had satisfied herself that Warbeck was definitely not her brother Richard she had nevertheless, at the king's request, taken his pretty Scottish wife into her household. I pondered what future she now saw ahead for his unfortunate widow. As for the matter of Edward of Warwick's impending execution,

I dared not even mention it unless she did. The queen I knew now was a very different woman from the girl I had first served at Coldharbour all those years ago.

I took a sideways step towards the subject. 'The Prince of Wales is as good as married now, isn't he, your grace? How does he feel about that?'

Her face lit up. 'Arthur and Katherine have been exchanging letters and they are so enchanting. I must show you some of hers while I'm at Eltham. They write in Latin because that's the only language they have in common but Queen Isabella tells me her daughter is taking lessons in French. I would much rather she learned English but I don't feel I can say so, not while Arthur refuses to learn Spanish. He says the princess is going to be Queen of England and should learn our language. He does not need to learn Spanish because he will not be going to Spain. I take his point, don't you?'

I couldn't help smiling. 'Yes, your grace, I rather think I do. However, while they both have Latin I suppose at least they can converse together, even if it is a rather formal, diplomatic language. Do you know yet when she will arrive in England?'

'It should be early next year but we might delay the wedding until after Arthur's fourteenth birthday. I think we must be careful of his health while he is growing so fast.'

'They are both young, after all,' I agreed. 'There is plenty of time.'

She frowned and dropped her voice, so that those seated nearby might not hear. 'The king does not agree, Joan. I tell him that but he wants the marriage confirmed by consummation because he desires the security of England's firm alliance with Spain.'

I lowered my voice to match hers. 'Even though his own birth, when his mother was only thirteen, cost her dear? I mean she never conceived again.'

'No, and they both nearly died. I believe it has influenced her whole outlook, that and losing control of her son at an early age; that is why she and the king contrived to have Arthur reared in a separate household from the rest of his family. Separation from his mother forged Henry into a strong and independent character and she believed it would work for Arthur. I will not forgive Henry for agreeing to that. And now that she has retired from an active court life I hope I will be able to stop competing with her for influence over his decisions.'

At this point Elizabeth gave me one of her dazzling smiles, the kind I had not seen her use for years. 'And that is another thing I trust you not to repeat to anyone, Joan.'

Two days later at Eltham Palace the queen received news that Edward of Warwick had been taken to the scaffold on Tower Hill and beheaded. Elizabeth showed me the official notice bearing the king's seal and we both wept. 'He was the last in the male line of the House of York,' she said through her tears. 'What a cursed family we were.'

44

'No, no, not the blue gown! I will not wear that one. The green one is prettier.'

Princess Mary was having one of her outbursts over what she would wear to greet her parents, who were riding via Eltham on their way to Dover to take ship for Calais. Her nurse had called me to deal with the problem because I was the only one the little girl would listen to when she got into a fret. Although the queen came frequently to visit her children it was a great event when the king came with her, for Mary worshipped her father.

I knelt down beside her, taking her hand and engaging her eye to eye. 'Do you not remember, Mary? You spilled gravy down the green gown and it has taken some time to clean it. So you cannot wear that one but if you wish you could put on the red one with your cream kirtle underneath, or the black velvet with the red bodice. His grace loves to see you in black, it is his favourite colour.'

I knew what colour she would choose when she had recovered her composure. The black velvet was her most fashionable gown and even at four years old, Mary was obsessed with the latest fashions.

Her grey eyes always darkened to slate when she became

angry and they glared back at me intensely for a few seconds as she considered her options. Then the rosebud lips widened into a smile and she nodded. 'I had forgot the gravy, Mother Guildford. I will wear the black gown. But not the red bodice; the one with fur on the skirt.'

The fur she mentioned was white winter ermine. This was her most expensive gown. And why not? I thought, the king is coming. 'Yes, that one is beautiful and your pearl pendant will look lovely with it. I'm sure your lord father will be pleased.'

'What is Margaret wearing?' Mary always wanted to outshine her elder sister and invariably succeeded, because she had inherited her mother's thick red-gold hair, alabaster skin and dimpled chin, whereas Margaret resembled her father, fine mouse brown hair, rather sallow skin and a pointed chin. On her, black looked funereal.

'The pink satin kirtle under her cream wool gown; she looks her best in light colours, doesn't she?'

Mary smiled at that. 'We will look good together. But the king likes black velvet best.'

I made no comment. Peace had been achieved. I tried not to let it be known how much I adored this little fairy princess, despite her occasional tantrums and her irrational phobia about having wrinkles in her hose. She was a feminine echo of her brother Henry, an intelligent perfectionist, fond of music and dancing and impatient with anyone who couldn't keep up with her quick grasp of new subjects. She had started to study French with her brother's tutor and could already make rudimentary conversation. Had she been a boy, she, too, would have ridden through the crowds in London at three years old and if she did not wear skirts she could have climbed a tree like Hal. Unfortunately she was not as sturdy as the boys and her health sometimes gave cause for concern. I prayed that she would survive the dangerous early years of childhood when, as we had learned from the death of her elder sister Elizabeth, a random illness could claim a young life almost without warning.

There had been a serious outbreak of plague in London and the court was making sure to avoid the disease by keeping well away from the capital. After Christmas Richard had based himself in Kent until he came to Eltham to visit me and Hal and to join the royal entourage on their journey to Calais, where he would be one of a team of councillors and advisers to the king. The royal trip abroad was intended partly to avoid the epidemic and partly to further seal a family alliance with Archduke Philip of Austria, who would soon be Prince Arthur's brother-in-law, because his wife Joanna of Castile was Katherine of Aragon's elder sister. The plan was to reinforce the dynastic ties further by arranging a contract between Mary and their baby son Charles, only three months old as yet but who might, should he survive to adulthood, become heir to nearly half of Europe. So much power hovered around these young scions of the great European monarchies; it was no wonder King Henry was eager to establish his Tudor dynasty among them.

Soon after the royal cavalcade left Eltham, rumours began to circulate that the plague had started to claim victims south of the River Thames, and the decision was taken to move the royal children north for safety. Arrangements were hastily made for them to stay at the Bishop of Ely's palace at Hatfield. We moved there in easy stages and the journey there gave them a chance to visit parts of their father's kingdom beyond the royal palaces along the Thames. The older children loved Hatfield. Its winding passages, extensive parkland and ancient oaks and yews made a new and exciting playground.

Sadly, while their parents were forging new and magnificent family links in Calais, as if to demonstrate the fragility of the young lives on which they were based Prince Edmund was suddenly found dead in his cot. Once more the whole household was plunged into grief and I arranged for the older children to hold vigils and obsequies in the palace chapel. I had thought that the queen at least might hurry back to England, but King Henry must have persuaded her that there were important treaties to conclude because it was decided they would defer the baby prince's funeral until their planned return to London in June. Edmund's little body was encased in lead and he was eventually buried in Westminster Abbey beside his sister Elizabeth, in the chapel devoted to St Edward the Confessor.

The two princesses particularly missed their baby brother. I would sometimes find Mary sitting in his empty nursery, as she mourned her little playmate, with whom she had built castles out of wooden bricks and at whom she had giggled as he staggered on wobbly legs after the soft ball she liked to throw for him. Margaret, older and more soulful, recalled her sister Elizabeth lying on her bier at Eltham and another family death only served to exacerbate her already gloomy view of life, so I was relieved when Lady Margaret made the journey from her home in Lincolnshire to bring comfort to her grandchildren. Not only relieved for them, but relieved in my own sore heart as well, because with her came my own dearest Mamma for a fortnight's visit.

When the king and queen travelled back from Calais they went straight to Canterbury where Archbishop Morton, King Henry's eminent friend and adviser, was gravely ill, before attending Prince Edmund's funeral at Westminster Abbey, which the plague had fortunately failed to reach. Released by the king to attend to his own affairs, Richard came straight to Hatfield. I arranged a private dinner in a separate chamber so that we could converse together and Hal asked if he could invite Prince Henry to join us.

'Gather round, I have some news,' Richard announced as servants laid out dishes along the cloth-covered table before we took our places. 'I am honoured that the king has nominated me to the late Viscount Welles' seat as a Knight of the Garter, which, as you boys should know, is the highest rank of knighthood in the realm and the greatest chivalric honour a man can receive.'

Princess Cecily's husband and Lady Margaret's half-brother, John Welles, had been another sad death in the royal family. It had occurred the previous year, not long after the double blow of the death of his two young daughters. Cecily's marriage, begun rather amusingly and romantically during Epiphany at Greenwich Palace, had lasted only twelve years and she was still in deep mourning for the husband and children she had loved and lost. Not only was Richard being honoured with the Garter, he would be taking the Garter seat in St George's Chapel previously occupied by the king's half-uncle and one of his closest allies.

I had thought myself emotionally drained by the death of Prince Edmund but it appeared that I was wrong, because my eyes suddenly filled with tears and I gasped, 'Oh Richard, that is utterly marvellous! Congratulations.' Impulsively I took his hand and kissed it, at the same time sinking into a deep curtsy. Elevation to the company of the Garter Knights was like being handed a key to the kingdom. It was an honour only exceptionally achieved by a commoner, being more usually granted to royalty or the nobility, whether English or foreign.

Although typically a man of restraint, on this occasion Richard raised me up, pulled me into his arms and kissed me passionately on the lips. Being thus engaged, I could not see what Hal and Prince Henry thought of this but I could hear their barely concealed sniggers. When Richard finally released me he turned us both around to face the boys and addressed them with a wide smile of his own. 'I wish it to go on record before witnesses – by which I mean you, Hal, and you, my lord Henry, when you have both finished smirking! – that a great deal of the credit for this distinction is due to my beloved wife. Without her devoted service to Queen Elizabeth and to the children of the king, I do not believe I would be receiving this honour. So when the time comes for me to be installed, I very much wish you, Joan, to be there.'

'And when might that be?' I asked. 'Is it not generally around St George's day at Windsor Castle?'

'Yes, and being the turn of the century that would have been a particularly memorable date, but I'm afraid the plague and court mourning for Prince Edmund's death have prevented the annual ceremony of the Garter this year and so it will not be until next spring. However, that also looks like being a year of great note because it will almost definitely include the wedding of Prince Arthur to Princess Katherine of Spain and I have already agreed to organise the secular celebrations, which the king intends should be the most spectacular Europe has ever seen.'

After the king made his garter of appointment known, there were celebrations in most of the places Richard worked and at many of the country homes of courtiers he had worked with and of course we held a banquet and entertainments at Halden Hall for the family and local dignitaries. Due to the plague epidemic the exception had been the Tower of London, which had been carefully locked down for the duration.

By the time the service at St George's Chapel came to be held on the saint's feast day in April, the king had also nominated Sir Thomas Grey, the son of the Marquess of Dorset, and his trusty chief minister and Lord Treasurer, Sir Reginald Bray, as Companions of the Garter and so the three new knights were installed together, among such other assembled members of the Order as had been able to attend. Afterwards, the king and queen staged a sumptuous banquet in St George's Hall for their families and friends.

In order to attend all these events I had been frequently absent from Eltham Palace and so it was really no surprise when, at the Windsor banquet, the queen suggested that I should return to her service at court.

'I intend to bring Margaret into my household this year, Joan,' Elizabeth said. 'She will be twelve in November and it will be good for her to make friends among the maids of honour and learn more about the workings of a royal court. You have done such a wonderful job calming Mary's volatile temper that I think now she will gain most from sharing Harry's tutors and music and dance instructors. Those two seem to get on so well together, I think it wise to take Margaret out of their orbit and give her a chance to shine elsewhere. I hope you will take her under your wing here at court. It may not be long before she has to go to Scotland and she will need all your encouragement and sound advice. But I do hope you will allow Hal to remain at Harry's side at Eltham. It would be a pity to separate two such good companions.'

I was relieved to hear her last remark because there was no doubt she was right. After nearly two years together, Harry and Hal were like brothers; inseparable, sharing tutors, confessors and instructors, ponies, jokes, pranks and even Harry's princely tester bed. Other young men served in his household but none could claim quite the level of friendship that existed between these two young Henrys. And Princess Mary also held an important place in their lives; she was regularly invited to share their games, making them laugh at her antics on the tennis court, showing them up on the dance floor and even wildly wielding a wooden sword against their superior fencing skills. It was not difficult to read between the lines of the queen's request and conclude that Elizabeth was worried that Princess Margaret felt excluded by the close friendship that had developed between these younger children, and I had to agree that she greatly needed the boost to her confidence that a closer relationship with her mother might provide. And if she could also be guided into good friendships with one or two of Elizabeth's young maids of honour, she would be a happier little girl.

'I am content to be of whatever service I can to Princess Margaret, your grace,' I was obliged to agree. 'And when she comes to court it might also be a good idea to encourage her to talk to Lady Gordon, who must have good knowledge of the Scottish court and way of life. I believe that would be of great help to her.'

Now officially a widow since Perkin Warbeck's execution, Katherine Gordon still graced the queen's court and the other ladies had mostly taken to her.

It seemed that Elizabeth had as well. 'Yes, King Henry suggested that too. It is a good idea but it must be under supervision. Margaret knows nothing yet of Warbeck and I would rather she did not.'

In the hotbed of female gossip that was the queen's household, I didn't believe it would be possible to keep such information from the princess but refrained from saying so. Among the more scandalous stories circulating at present was a suggestion that the beautiful Lady Gordon was a frequent visitor to the king's chamber but either Elizabeth had not yet heard it or else she deliberately turned a deaf ear. For my own part I believed that any long gaps between Elizabeth's pregnancies were due more to her own fragile health, rather than King Henry's roving eye. Despite the stresses of monarchy and the strains exerted on their reign by successive Yorkist claims to the throne, they gave every impression of being as faithful a couple as Richard and I were, at least as far as I was aware.

Curiously Richard's elevation to the Order of the Garter and his appointment as chief co-ordinator of jousting and processions for the impending royal wedding seemed to have encouraged his attendance in my bedchamber. Whereas while I was spending much time with the royal children at Eltham Palace, his marital visits to my apartment had become relatively few, my return to the queen's household introduced something of a change. Nights spent sharing my bed increased from rarely to more often than not, to the extent that I was obliged to arrange for Hetty to take accommodation in the servants' dorters of the various palaces to which the court moved. Not only did this increase our lovemaking but it also meant we shared considerably more details of our daily activities.

Similarly, because of the plague epidemic, I had not been to the Tower of London or checked on Sim and the ravens for some time. Happily the dreaded disease now seemed to have abated and the court had moved down the Thames to Westminster for the first time since Prince Edmund's funeral. In the lassitude following one of our newly enlivened bedtime frolics, Richard revealed that he'd received an invitation from the Lieutenant Constable of the Tower to attend a banquet in celebration of his Garter installation. 'You've probably had quite enough of toasting my success, when most of it is down to you, Joan,' he said, 'but nevertheless I hope you will come. The king and queen are attending so you'll probably be there with her anyway.'

I raised my hand to give him a gently admonishing pat on the cheek. 'Please stop claiming I am responsible for your KG, when you know it is a well-deserved reward for your own tireless service to the crown. Of course I'll be there. And if you've received a communication from Sir John Digby, has he made any mention of the ravens by any chance?'

'Oh yes, I almost forgot. The ravens are there but apparently Sim has been carted off to the Fleet gaol for some unnamed felony. I thought to look into it when I get to the Tower tomorrow.'

I sat up abruptly in the bed. 'What! You tell me that as an afterthought! What is this felony? When did it happen? Did the letter say?'

Richard shook his head. 'No. It could have been any time in the last few weeks, I suppose.'

'The Fleet is a sink of filth and disease, Richard! It may even still have cases of the plague!' I made the sign of the cross. 'I'm coming with you. St Jude protect Sim!'

45

IT COST RICHARD A gold angel to bribe his way into Sim's cell. He would not let me go with him and when he returned from the Fleet his expression was grim and his clothes stank like a latrine.

'Sim is not ill but he is very thin and listless. He's been in there for a month and didn't really seem to know why. Two sergeants came to arrest him and just took him away. There's been no charge and no contact with the outside world since. There are about twenty men in his cell and the place is damp and infested. I think he thought we'd abandoned him.'

I was distraught. 'We have to get him out, Richard! How do we do that? Must we bribe the gaolers or can we use the law? Maybe Anthony can help.'

Richard shook his head. 'Anthony is in Gloucestershire. He's newly married and I can't ask him to come to London just now. I think we'll have to throw money at the gaolers if we want him out quickly. I'd like to know who's responsible for this gross injustice though.'

'Oh, I think I know who that is but the first thing to do is to speak to Sir John Digby. I'd like us to do that together, if you can spare more time today.' I believed this was Sir Henry Wyatt taking revenge for my accusing him of arranging the sabotage of the roost boxes and the subsequent fire.

We passed the alder trees on Tower Green on the way to the Lieutenant Constable's house and found plenty of evidence that ravens were still using the roost boxes but no sign of any birds. I hoped they were all out hunting carrion but I worried that the garrison soldiers might have turned against them during the plague epidemic. Certainly there were plenty of feathers about, which might have been indication of hostility but equally might have been due to the start of the moulting season. We couldn't see into the roost boxes because that involved climbing the trees but I thought there was every likelihood that they hadn't been cleaned out since poor Sim was marched away.

Sir John was unrepentant about the arrest. 'Yes, I agreed to call in the sergeants because I was told that scrap metal was being regularly stolen from the carts while they were waiting to offload at the Mint stronghouse. The raven boy had been seen hanging around there at unloading time.'

'Did it occur to no one that Sim might be scaring the ravens off the gold and silver, rather than stealing it?' I asked, trying to contain my anger. 'All corvids love a bit of glitter. Why were the carts not kept covered?'

'I don't know, my lady.' The Lieutenant shrugged and turned away from me to seek support from his fellow official. 'I am not responsible for the management of the Mint, as you know, Sir Richard.'

'So it would appear it is from Sir Henry Wyatt we must seek an explanation,' responded my husband. 'But my servant was working in the Tower precinct when he was arrested and I think we might at least have relied on some questions being asked, Sir John. After all he wears the Guildford livery and he is a trusted servant of some years' service, not just a vagrant newly off the streets. How do you suggest that we extract him from the Fleet? Or at least obtain some legal notice of the charge he faces.'

'Perhaps Sir John would respond to a letter from the king,' I suggested slyly, growing more angry by the minute at the casual attitude of a man I had thought one of my supporters. 'King Henry is due here this week and will be disappointed when I cannot show him the raven sanctuary I promised, with the man I appointed in charge.'

This at last wiped the ineffective smile off Digby's face as he stood up to indicate that the conversation was over, but it didn't diminish his patronising tone of voice. 'I wouldn't bother the king if I were you, my lady. He is coming to celebrate Sir Richard joining the august ranks of the Garter Knights as you know, and also to discuss arrangements for the jousts and archery competitions due to follow the royal wedding later this year. I hardly think the ravens will be very high on his agenda.'

'You may be surprised, sir,' I informed him, pointedly neglecting to say farewell and sweeping through the door, which Richard held open for me. I decided that Sir John Digby had been seeing too much of Sir Henry Wyatt.

Back at the Tower House we went straight to the strongbox in which the household funds were secreted and filled a small purse with silver coins. 'I really object to greasing the palms of those grasping, dim-witted gaolers,' Richard fumed as he hid the purse deep in his belted doublet.

'They'll only drink themselves even more stupid in the Tabard Inn.'

'But it will save Sim's life, Richard, which will be your good deed for May Day,' I said, giving him a grateful kiss.

When Sim arrived at the Tower House I hardly recognised him. He was filthy and his clothes were in rags, dangling off his emaciated frame like seedpods on an ash tree in winter. Tears stung my eyes at the sight and I wanted to hug him, except that I thought he might break; then all at once he flung himself at my feet and grabbed my hand to kiss it.

'Thank you, my lady! Thank you for rescuing me. I thought I was going to die in that stinking cell and no one would know.'

I glanced over his head at Richard, who nodded vigorously. 'He needs food and rest, Joan; lots of both.'

I bent to pull him to his feet. 'I am so sorry this happened, Sim, and that we were not informed. Your arrest was a criminal mistake and it is Sir Richard you should thank for getting you out of the Fleet. We intend to find out who put you there; meanwhile what he says is right. First you must eat, then you must strip off those horrible rags and I will get Hugh to fill a bathtub. And then, finally, you can sleep.'

I wanted him to use the curtained bed in what had once been Edward and George's chamber but he said he would rather sleep on the floor, like he always did. We compromised with a fresh pallet and he slept the rest of the day and a night. When he finally woke and rose, he insisted on going back to the raven roost but he went in fresh clothes, with a full stomach and a pouch full of bread and cheese. The only concession he would make to his weakened condition was to agree to use a ladder to get up to the roost boxes. In two days they were all fresh and clean and the ravens were playing with him on the grass again.

Meanwhile Richard at last managed to attend to his latest royal assignment, planning the processions, jousts and tournaments, which the king wished to take place around the time of Prince Arthur's wedding. The Spanish ambassador reported that Princess Katherine had at last bidden a final farewell to her parents at the Alhambra Palace in the south of Spain and she and her fifty-strong entourage had begun to make their way north to the port of La Coruña, there to take ship for England. They had more than six hundred miles to travel overland which, with scheduled rests and visits to shrines en route, was expected to take the best part of three months. Remembering my family's long journeys across France when I was a child, I didn't envy her the trip.

At the banquet held in the Tower to celebrate Richard's Garter knighthood, he and I sat in places of honour beside the king and the queen and Elizabeth confided her worries about the dangers involved in making such a long and hazardous journey.

'Princess Katherine is only fifteen and has just bidden farewell to her mother and father, probably for ever. I worry that she will be lonely and miserable, even though she writes to Arthur that she cannot wait to meet him. Also I am told that central Spain is very hot in the summer months and I fear she may become ill.'

'I understand completely, your grace,' I responded dutifully. 'As a mother you put your own daughter in the same situation but a princess is educated to the idea of leaving home at a young age, is she not? That is certainly what I have aimed to do in supervising your daughters' education.'

'Perhaps I am being too sensitive,' the queen admitted. 'After all when I was a girl I was quite ready to go to France and marry the dauphin and was even angry when the French king reneged on the contract my father had made. Perhaps we grow less adventurous as we get older. The journey Princess Katherine has ahead of her would daunt me but . . .' She dropped her voice to finish this remark, 'the king is more concerned about what she looks like when she gets here than whether she is happy to make it.'

I bit my lip in order not to smile, thinking that in order to find his son's Spanish bride stunningly beautiful, King Henry needed only to gaze upon the heaped gold of the enormous dowry her father was contracted to pay. Moreover, when successfully concluded, this marriage promised to fulfil the king's long-held ambition to place the Tudor dynasty high among the great royal houses of Europe, putting his throne on a more secure footing than he had ever felt it to be. It was typical of a man of King Henry's perfectionist ways also to require wondrous beauty in the lady who brought this security to his reign.

When Princess Katherine finally reached her port of embarkation there were further delays, because persistently adverse winds prevented her ship sailing. By the end of August the king was becoming exasperated, especially after the Earl of Suffolk bolted once more across the Channel and this time straight to the court of his Aunt Margaret, taking his younger brother Richard with him. Once more the Dowager Duchess had scions of York to succour and promote and use to threaten the Tudor throne.

King Henry's great consolation was to move into his newly built palace of Richmond, named for his father's earldom in Yorkshire and based on the old palace of Sheen, which had been badly damaged by a fire three years before. He had lavished enormous amounts of money creating a residence to rival any of those he had experienced during his long exile in Brittany and France.

The gardens there were spectacular, dotted with flower-filled knot-beds and ornamented with decorative poles supporting painted heraldic beasts – lions, greyhounds, yales and dragons but sadly no ravens. A hedged avenue led down to a sporting enclosure, providing bowling alleys, archery butts and tennis courts. As the warm weather persisted into September, King Henry was frequently to be found on an open tennis court, working off his frustration on his tennis coach and a bucketful of small leather-coated wooden balls. During their summer break, the royal children had also come to sample the new palace and he put their sporting prowess to the test, impressed by the standard of tennis displayed by Prince Henry and my Hal. I felt a surge of pride when Hal, spurning the notion that royalty should always win, had no compunction in defeating his princely friend in front of his father, albeit only by a very narrow margin. Prince Harry gave him a peeved punch on the shoulder before they wandered off together, arm in arm and laughing.

'I'm older than you so I should win!' claimed Hal.

'Age before beauty!' cried Prince Harry, preening.

'Those Spanish sailors are a bunch of cowards!' King Henry exploded while walking to Mass one mid-September morning. While the sun still shone down on England, he had received yet another letter from the ambassador reporting delay due to adverse weather conditions. 'Wind is what fills the sails, for the love of God! I'm going to send my best English sea captain over to Spain to show them how to sail the princess to England!'

'Might they not take offence at that?' the queen suggested mildly.

'Let them!' the king declared. 'It's time they learned who rules the waves.'

Queen Elizabeth offered him a patient smile. 'I think you'll find the Almighty does, my lord.'

But Henry was not deterred and despatched a certain Captain Butt with some success, for in the first week of October word reached the court that Princess Katherine had at last arrived at Plymouth. I had been grateful not to be among the ladies Queen Elizabeth selected to travel to the southwest to greet the bride-to-be and her entourage. A cavalcade of chariots and spare palfreys was also sent from the royal stables to transport them to London. No expense was spared.

The king and queen moved up to London and King Henry ordered celebrations to begin. The Tower became the focus of pre-wedding activity. A temporary tiltyard was built in the Inner Ward, transforming it with a blaze of colour as the flags and banners of the participating knights were raised around the walls and viewing pavilions were erected for the royal family and senior officials. A more extensive tournament was planned for after the wedding but this joust was to be an opening salvo, to whet Londoners' appetites and encourage enthusiasm for the Spanish alliance.

I was among the queen's ladies in the silk-hung royal

426

pavilion, when two royal scouts arrived during an interval between jousts. The first handed a sealed note to the king and announced that Princess Katherine's procession had crossed into Hampshire and the second reported that Prince Arthur's column was halfway to London from the Welsh March. The king perused the note and immediately sprang another of his impulsive decisions, the like of which had characterised this long and tense build-up to his heir's wedding, and which brought a temporary halt to Richard's carefully orchestrated entertainment programme.

'I can bear the anticipation no longer, Elizabeth,' Henry declared, handing her the note. 'Your Lord Chamberlain says the princess intends to rest a few days at the Bishop of Bath and Wells' lodge at Dogmersfield. I'm going to divert the Prince of Wales to a meeting in Windsor and then we can ride on together into Hampshire to make a surprise visit of welcome to the princess. I'm sure young Arthur is as keen to see his future wife as I am. We have all waited too long.'

Elizabeth said little in response at the time but later, to those of us helping her to change before attending a private supper in the King's Chamber, she gave her true reaction, after I had remarked that she seemed a little agitated.

'Well, yes I am, Joan. Firstly because it was I who sent Lord Ormond to escort the princess to London and it should have been to me that he addressed his note. Had I read it before the king did, I could have counselled him against his wild notion. It is never a good idea to take a high-born lady by surprise. She likes to present herself at her best advantage or she may not choose to present herself at all, thereby causing offence to the unexpected visitor, when really the fault is theirs for imposing themselves without warning.'

We had removed her heavy gabled headdress and I moved forward with a lighter, close-fitted jewelled silk hood. As I adjusted it over her frontlet she gave me a sympathetic look. 'I'm sorry to tell you, Joan,' she continued, in a tone that sent a shiver down my back, 'but the king has also asked me if I will release you to accompany him to visit the princess. Although she has been learning French, Henry fears that despite their expertise in written Latin they may need an interpreter in order to make themselves clearly understood and believes the princess will surely appreciate any help of that kind coming from another woman, rather than a man. I'm afraid I felt obliged to agree your assistance in the matter.'

I completed my efforts with the headdress and stepped back to view my handiwork. 'I'm flattered that his grace should consider me capable of serving him in that way, my lady. And may I add that this new headdress looks beautiful on you.'

Elizabeth smiled. 'Thank you, Joan, and since you remark on the headdress I think I will risk a glance in the mirror before I venture out.'

I adjusted the looking glass for her. 'If you were to send a courier with me I could keep you informed of how the meeting goes, your grace.'

This suggestion inspired another royal smile. 'What a good idea! Please arrange one. I believe the king wishes to leave early tomorrow but I will see you at disrobing, won't I? I will confirm everything then.'

As dusk fell over the Tower, I took the opportunity to

go and watch the ravens coming in to roost. Autumn was a good time to gauge their numbers, because it was when the juveniles flocked and relationships were formed. Sim was on the green as usual, laying some meaty treats, gleaned cheap from the city shambles as the butchers closed their shops. The older and more confident ravens were already gathering on the lower branches, preparing to pounce on the best morsels.

'Any trouble today, Sim?' I asked as he threw down the last of the gory contents of his bucket. 'I worried that the cheers at the jousting might frighten the young birds off.'

Sim shook his head. 'Looks like the same number as usual, m'lady.'

'That's good.' I settled down on the grass, careful to avoid any of the places he had cast the bloody meat. Sim had recovered physically from his imprisonment but he was a much quieter man, as if his cheeky humour of the past had all been erased by his gaol ordeal. I felt pangs of guilt that he had felt so abandoned and because I still had not managed to confront Wyatt about the arrest. 'Anyone been about?'

'Only the Lieutenant's guards and they don't bother me.'

'I've got to leave tomorrow so I won't see you for a few days, maybe a week. Make a note for me if you see any birds pairing up. It's going to be very busy around the White Tower in November because of the celebrations for the Prince of Wales' wedding. There'll be music and fireworks. I hope that doesn't frighten the ravens. Will you warn them, Sim?'

He nodded. 'I'd better do that.' Sim set great store by telling his charges what was happening around them, perfectly convinced they understood. 'Thanks for the tip, m'lady. I hope you have a good week, wherever you're going.'

'I'm going with the king to meet the Spanish princess; the one all the fuss is about.'

He looked impressed. 'You're moving in grand company these days, m'lady. You and the master.'

I nodded solemnly. 'Luckily yes, so we were able to get you out of the Fleet. But do you know, Sim, I'd rather be sitting here talking to you and watching the ravens than eating sturgeon at the king's table.'

46

WHEN WE REACHED THE bishop's palace in Hampshire, we were greeted by the queen's Lord Chamberlain, the Earl of Ormond, but not with much enthusiasm. 'I fear this may not be a convenient time to see the princess, my lord king,' he said regretfully. 'She stopped here for a rest and has not been rising before midday. She always attends Mass immediately after dressing and then breaks her fast. She does not receive anyone but her duenna and ladies until mid-afternoon.'

The king's brow darkened. 'Just inform her that we are here, Ormond, eager to greet her and introduce her to her bridegroom.'

Lord Ormond ushered the royal party into a reception chamber and departed to do the king's bidding but within a few minutes he had returned, looking crestfallen. 'The duenna says, regretfully the princess is unable to meet your graces at this time.'

Prince Arthur wasn't satisfied. 'Are you sure she has asked her, Lord Ormond? I really thought Princess Katherine would be eager to see me,' he said and began studying the rings on his fingers, as if seeking solace from them. The ride to Dogmersfield had brought colour to his cheeks and in his deep red sable-trimmed Italian brocade doublet and polished riding boots, he looked every inch the royal prince. 'After all, we are as good as married.'

King Henry drummed his fingers on the arm of his chair. 'I knew they had something to hide!' he muttered.

'Give me pen, ink and paper,' demanded the prince. 'I will write a personal note to Katherine.'

Disappearing again briefly, Lord Ormond fulfilled his request and took the resulting note.

'Make sure it is given to the princess herself, Ormond,' ordered the king.

Some time later, when the drumming of the king's fingers on the arm of his chair had reached fever pitch, the door of the reception chamber was suddenly thrown open and a dark-skinned guard in a gilt-edged black helmet, gold-tasselled black jacket and carrying a fierce-looking pole-arm, stamped into the room and shouted something in Spanish.

The attendant yeomen guards standing behind the two royals sprang to attention and the king and Prince Arthur stood up. Through the door came a bejewelled figure dressed almost entirely in gold satin, lavishly embroidered in red silk, but the most striking feature of her apparel was a black lace veil arranged to completely obscure her face. It was impossible to know if this was the Princess Katherine but at least the curtsy she made was graceful and fluid, certainly worthy of a princess.

The middle-aged lady beside her spoke in French. 'I am the princess's duenna, Doña Elvira, appointed by Queen Isabella. Because of the respect she owes the prince, she has consented to meet with your graces.'

I looked at Prince Arthur and sympathised with the frustration that was written all over his face. Perhaps he did not fully understand the duenna's heavily accented French and it was hard for a putative bridegroom, so keen to see his bride, to have ridden all the way from the Welsh March, only to be confronted by a black lace veil.

His father spoke up for him, using his perfect French. 'Does the princess have a condition that prevents her showing us her face, Madame?'

The duenna gave a nervous tinkling laugh. 'He! He! No, your highness; Spanish protocol says that she must remain veiled until she is married.'

I translated for the prince who gave a smothered exclamation of disbelief. 'Then how does a man know exactly who, or even what, he is marrying? She is not very tall. She could be an ape, for all I know.' He said this to his father in English.

Doña Elvira looked puzzled, not understanding. She shook her head stubbornly. 'This is the rule, it is protocol, messires.'

'It is not English protocol, Madame,' King Henry said, again in French. 'I expect the princess does not wear a veil in bed. If she prefers we will wait until she retires and come to her bedchamber to see her.' When the duenna gave another nervous laugh he added sternly, 'I am not joking, Madame.'

Prince Arthur frowned. He sensed his father's anger and perhaps feared that it would frighten the princess. To my surprise, and probably to that of everyone in the room, he moved purposefully forward to stand before his betrothed.

'Thank you for coming to England, Katherine,' he said gently and earnestly in Latin. 'It must have been a weary journey for you and I have waited so long to see the face of my bride.' He stretched out his hands and touched the edge of the lace veil, saying softly, 'May I?'

We all held our breath and Doña Elvira made an exclamation, 'She will not understand you!' and stepped protectively towards her charge but the princess raised her hand to halt her. Then she inclined her head forward and said very quietly, '*Sí*.'

Arthur slowly lifted the veil, moving closer in order to fold it over the high-backed comb that held it in place. There was an audible sigh as everyone released the breath they had been holding and Princess Katherine's sweet, still childishly round face was revealed, framed by two smooth wings of bright gold hair. Softly curved lips held the hint of a smile and her cheeks and brow were smooth and fair, like pale pink marble, clearly well protected from the burning Spanish sun. Her eyes were cast demurely down until she lifted them to gaze upon her bridegroom's face, when they were disclosed as intriguing pools of deep blue-green, like the seas she had crossed to reach him.

'You are beautiful, Katherine,' Arthur said, in a voice filled with awe. 'I am so happy you are to be my wife.'

I wrote of this touching scene to the queen as promised, including the general difficulty over communication, and this led to her agreeing to temporarily assign me to the bride's household for the days leading up to and following the wedding. Days in which my grasp of Spanish improved considerably and I tried to encourage Katherine to increase her regrettably neglected understanding of English.

The princess's party was housed in the Archbishop of Canterbury's Lambeth Palace and I found myself translating between the palace staff, the princess's entourage, the Spanish ambassador and the king's Lord Chamberlain about the extensive arrangements already in place for the wedding celebrations. It was a task I found extremely taxing, given the differing attitudes and expectations of the two courts and countries, not to mention the need to translate everything into written Latin, so that the princess could approve the plans. Each night I went to bed with my head spinning, my mind a blur of languages, personalities and protocols and my cheeks aching from smiling.

Later, the incident I remembered most vividly of that exhausting few days was a comical dispute over Princess Katherine's mode of travel for her formal entry procession into London. Queen Elizabeth had ordered a chariot uphol-stered in cloth of gold and bedecked with red and white silk roses but the Spanish officials flatly refused this arrangement, maintaining that until she was married the princess remained a Spanish noblewoman and therefore would make her first public appearance in the mode and livery of her country of birth. For this very purpose special robes and accessories had been brought from Spain and her royal highness's favourite mount had been transported all the way to England at vast cost and at the particular insistence of Queen Isabella. She had insisted that the princess should not be introduced to the people of London sitting low in a chariot but riding high on a velvet-covered saddle, brilliant with sparkling jewels and girthed on a mount trapped flamboyantly in the Spanish fashion. When the queen's Master of Horse heard this he was delighted by the novelty and spectacle of it, until he was shown the mount involved, which was not as he had imagined, a high-stepping and spirited Spanish stallion, but a great thick-headed, long-eared Spanish mule.

'She will be a laughing stock,' he confided to me, after his cautious protests had been dismissed by his Spanish counterpart with much hand-flapping and finger-snapping. 'The English regard mules as beasts of burden, not noble processional steeds.'

I, too, had seen the animal in question. 'But it is a beautiful beast, is it not? It is certainly tall and I thought that pale gold coat and the way it carried its head were distinctive. The princess is happy to ride it and the crowds will certainly see her up there above all the horses in the procession. But most importantly the mule is calm and steady. It will not tip her off at the first rousing cheer.'

After he heard the outcome of this difference of opinion the king made a suggestion to his Master of Horse. So when the procession made its slow way across London Bridge, up the length of Gracechurch Street and down Cornhill to Cheapside, the princess was cheered ecstatically by the crowds, which thrilled to the music of her lively minstrel band and her spectacular Spanish apparel, capped by a wide-brimmed, pink cardinal-style hat, worn over a pearl-trimmed white coif with her bright hair caught in gold netting hanging loose down her back. Many also applauded the way she rode astride on the distinctive long-eared mule with its red and gold trappings, ignoring the spare chestnut palfrey, caparisoned in Tudor green and white and equipped with a modest side-saddle, which was led some way behind her in case of need.

The procession ended at St Paul's Cathedral where Princess Katherine made an offering and heard Mass. The alternative palfrey was led, unused, back to the king's stables in the Tower of London.

47

L ATER I PRAYED THERE was nothing prophetic about Princess Katherine choosing to ride astride an infertile mule, while ignoring the fertile palfrey following behind. This notion struck me a few days before the wedding, as I was conversing with the princess during one of our regular English classes and trying to respond tactfully to her apparently innocent inquiry regarding the difference between kissing a man and consummating a marriage. As I did so I felt sad that such a vital and intimate matter had not been tackled before she left Spain, either with her nurse or, preferably, her mother. At this early stage of our relationship, I did not feel qualified to provide a detailed answer to her question.

Meanwhile the pace of wedding preparations had increased to a gallop. During the sixteen years of his reign King Henry had acquired a reputation as a charming but somewhat detached monarch, who had adopted his mother's tendency towards controlled consumption and strict adherence to religious fasts, with the result that he was of slim build with a lifestyle verging on Spartan. He rarely over-indulged in food or drink himself but, when fasts permitted, provided generously of both for his friends and guests. For this all-important wedding however, expenditure on every form of indulgence went through the palace roof. Money appeared to be no object and he spent lavishly on banquets, entertainments, gifts and apparel, financing distinctive new liveries for all his household servants and officials.

Nor did he stint on his own raiment. Whereas he usually wore elegant but muted colours, frequently black, albeit often trimmed with expensive furs and jewels, for the wedding of his precious son and heir he splashed out on glorious fabrics, providing copious cloth of gold in assorted colours for his queen and her chosen ladies in waiting and indulging in an ermine-trimmed robe and mantle for himself, fashioned from an elaborately patterned crimson silk-velvet from Milan, worn with a jewel-encrusted silver breast-plate and ruby-studded belt, all of which must have cost him a king's ransom. Ambassadors and representatives of the royal houses of Europe had been invited to attend the wedding, on the understanding that they would report back to their own monarchs on the wealth and splendour of the English court and the strength of its alliance with the burgeoning imperial empire into which Prince Arthur was marrying.

For her part Princess Katherine's parents had provided her with a gold and white wedding gown of fabulous fabrics and tailoring. The secret of the unusual bell-shaped design of the skirt was revealed to the few of us who watched her try it on as a fine linen underskirt sewn with a framework of hoops, so that the material of the kirtle's skirt and the gown were draped over it like a tournament tent over its supporting poles, lending the wearer an illusion of gliding rather than stepping jerkily across the floor. Inevitably it was a fashion swiftly copied by English tailors and grew more and more popular among the ladies of the court who, failing to pronounce the Spanish word for it, called it a 'farthingale'. It amused me to see that those who chose the widest form of it found entering a room rather difficult, due to the need to tip the farthingale in order to get through the door sideways, thus risking exposure of an unladylike expanse of leg and ankle. Fortunately the princess's version had been fashioned discreetly enough to allow her to avoid this costume blunder.

I didn't have the privilege of witnessing the wedding itself, which was solemnised on a high platform covered in red velvet, built where the transept crossed the nave of St Paul's Cathedral and witnessed by the nobles of the court, the Lord Mayor and aldermen of London and all the capital's most influential citizens and merchants. The latter in particular would be celebrating because the treaty established by this marriage perpetuated England's freedom to trade with Flanders and the Low Countries, restoring the greatest source of London's wealth.

My task of the wedding day was not with the bride or groom but with Prince Harry and my son Hal, preparing them both for their allotted roles. Prince Harry would be escorting the bride down the long church aisle and up the steps of the platform to meet his brother and, while the princess was assisted by six maids of honour who carefully adjusted the jewelled coronet that held her long golden hair in place and carried the remarkable embroidered train of her voluminous bridal veil, Prince Harry had help only from me and Hal to smooth his royal purple mantle and sparkling doublet of silvered cloth, embellished with gold roses. He went into church bareheaded and it was remarkable how similar was the colour of his Tudor red-gold hair to that of his brother's Spanish bride. They might already have been the brother and sister they were about to become. Hal carried the train of his royal friend's mantle as they left me at the church door, where I had made last-minute efforts to smooth the wrinkles in their respective hosen and whispered good luck messages in their well-scrubbed ears.

I had a seat beside Richard at the wedding banquet, which was held in the Bishop of London's palace within the walled precinct of St Paul's. It was a feast eaten off a fortune's worth of gold plate and drunk from a precious regiment of jewelled cups and flagons. Afterwards the young newlyweds were separately escorted to their nuptial chamber and laid together, blessed in the bishop's vast episcopal bed. I was privileged to witness this event, in what seemed to me a weirdly canonical setting for what should have been a joyful family affair. But this dynastic union was so much more than that, endowed with the hopes and prayers of two nations and fraught with such great expectations.

Later, ensconced with Richard in our own well-used marital bed in the house on Tower Wharf, I could feel little joy for those two young people, who were hardly more than children, lying alone together for the first time. Would Arthur ever fulfil the great hopes his father had for his kingdom's future? Did Katherine really know what miracle of royal progeniture was expected of her slight, childish body? Did either of them even know how to go about begetting it? I felt that their happiness, if they were to have any, depended on them somehow understanding that whatever their dynastically greedy fathers wanted from them, time was on their side; and I prayed that they were intelligent enough to know this and wait.

Following the wedding there was a rest day, when participants and guests had time to recover from all the celebration and ceremonial and the bride and groom were given some private time together, for there was to be little of that in the days to come. I was on standby in case there was a need for interpretation but I was hoping for a day of rest myself.

Richard could not relax because tournaments were planned in the Great Court at Westminster, due to begin in two days' time. His team of workers had been busy erecting stands and tents for the competitors all through the wedding day and would work on until the last minute, laying gravel and sand on which to build the lists. Each of the main contestants had been asked to provide a dramatic spectacle on making his entrance into the arena and much ingenuity and construction was being employed in workshops all over the city to provide thrills and entertainment for the thousands of spectators and to compete for the substantial prize in gold offered for the best entry. After the jousts there was to be a banquet in Westminster Great Hall, with pageants paying tribute to the new Spanish alliance, when Prince Arthur was to perform a dance with his Aunt Cecily and Princess Katherine with one of her ladies. Finally Princess Margaret and Prince Harry were to display the fruits of all their sessions with their dancing instructor.

'Harry is enormously excited about performing his high leaps in the galliard,' Hal had told me in confidence. 'I just hope he doesn't fall over or, even worse, trip Princess Margaret up. It would cause great mirth no doubt, but Harry would be mortified.' Hal conveyed these thoughts with such a huge smile and a wicked glint in his eye that I had to warn him sternly not to be the cause of any such mishap or be seen to laugh if there was one. 'Would I do any such thing, Mamma?' he asked with all sincerity and innocence. 'Which is not to say that I wouldn't secretly enjoy it if it happened!'

But all that was for the future; my main aim for this day of freedom was to go to the raven roost shortly before sunset to find out whether the birds were massing during this great carnival of the Tudor reign or if they had shown their disapproval of all the commotion by making themselves scarce. Meanwhile, apart from the servants I had the Tower House to myself and ate a solitary dinner, which was surprisingly interrupted by a visit from Sim, who entered with a look of nervous awe on his face.

'I have had a visit from one of the king's yeomen, m'lady,' he said and I could see that his hands were shaking as he twisted his doffed cap round and round in agitation. 'He came to ask me when would be the right time for the king to pay a visit to the ravens.'

I smiled at his evident panic. 'But that is excellent news, Sim. It means that we may have his grace on our side. What did you tell the yeoman?'

'I just said that the birds came to roost at sunset and the king should come a short time beforehand. Will you come too then, m'lady? I wouldn't know what to say.'

My reply was instantaneous. 'Of course I will come. I am thrilled that the king is taking an interest in the ravens and I will remind him that their very presence ensures the safety of the Tower and the kingdom. What will you do, Sim?'

His eyes grew wide and his shoulders hunched with indecision. 'What I usually do I suppose – feed them some treats and have a bit of a play, if any of them are brave enough to approach me with the king there.'

'That will do nicely,' I told him. 'And because the king is a calm and composed person, it is my guess that they will be plenty brave enough.'

48

Towards the end of that bright November day the sunset was impressive. Dying rays caught horizontal layers of low puffball clouds, turning them several shades of red from pink to crimson and the reflecting waters of the Thames to a burning ribbon of fire. Crossing the moat by way of St Thomas's Tower, I peered through the window from which I had spied the first raven I had ever dared to touch, all those years ago during the early days of my marriage. With my forefinger I felt the scar on my thumb, left by that raven's sharp bill as a reminder of my temerity in thinking it was a creature to be tamed. Then I shaded my eyes against the fiery glare of the river and caught sight of a gilded barge approaching the wharf, glittering drops falling from the blades of its busy oars. Only one golden vessel plied the waters of the Thames and it belonged to the king. I whirled away from the window and ran on down the spiral stair. Sim had been right; King Henry was coming to see the ravens.

Moments later I walked through the gate archway that led onto Tower Green and stopped in my tracks. Sim was standing beneath the alder trees with his bucket of meat treats in one hand and his trusty brown cap in the other, his expression one of abject terror. I did not need to see the face of the man who was towering over him with his back to me and I strode up behind him with my finger to my lips to stop Sim reacting to my arrival.

'God give you good evening, Sir Henry,' I said very loudly, so that Wyatt would hear me over the sound of his own harsh voice, which was threatening poor Sim with fire and brimstone. 'You must have heard the news that the king is coming to see the ravens. No doubt you are eager to associate yourself with his enthusiasm for the guardians of the Tower.'

Sir Henry's tirade ceased abruptly and he swung round, his mouth twisted in an ugly sneer. 'Lady Guildford! As usual you are sadly deluded if you think King Henry would be coming to the Tower to visit the ravens. He is far more likely to pay a visit to the Mint, where commemorative gold coins are being struck to mark the marriage of his son and heir to the Spanish princess.'

'In that case why are you not there to wait on him, Sir Henry? Instead of here, frightening my servant with your ugly threats.' I had barely finished speaking when the sound of a trumpet pierced the quiet of this public day of rest and a chorus of alarmed raven calls answered it, as a score or more rose up above the alder trees to swirl in the brazen sky.

Sir Henry's jaw dropped in shock as he saw six yeoman guards, in their distinctive tawny livery and shouldering their raven-beaked halberds, step smartly through the gate arch, while safe among them walked the slim, straight-backed figure of King Henry the Seventh. Sim promptly dropped to the ground on his knees, bizarrely hugging his bucket of treats as if his life depended on them, and Wyatt bent low in a practised courtly bow. I, too, made a royal curtsy as the king strolled free of his guards and approached, signalling me to rise.

'Lady Guildford, how kind of you to meet me here when you must be fatigued after all your efforts yesterday. You and your son were a great support to Prince Harry performing his role as groomsman to his brother and I thought the whole day rolled along like a well-oiled cart-wheel.' He turned to Wyatt with a raised eyebrow. 'I did not expect to see you here, Sir Henry, having heard you were no friend to the Tower ravens. Have you perhaps had a change of heart?'

Wyatt's reply was almost drowned by the ravens dropping back into the branches of the alders on a rumble of wings and a crackle of protests. 'Er, no, your grace – that is, yes. I have a certain interest.'

Having only caught the words 'certain interest', the king nodded appreciatively. 'Good, good. They are indeed interesting and I hope we are about to see more of their famed intelligence. Would that be the task of your assistant, Lady Guildford?'

Sim was still on his knees, clutching his malodorous bucket and apparently unable to interpret the monarch's signal that he should get to his feet. So I approached him and bent to put my hand under his elbow. 'You can stand now, Sim,' I murmured and added more firmly, 'the king would like to see the ravens play.'

The young man rose to his feet and sheepishly backed off to start throwing his teasers under the trees. Careless of the presence of royalty in their midst, within less than a minute the ravens began to drop down to snap up their portion. They did so in some form of pecking order, picking up their treats one after another and returning to a branch to consume them, taking a perch as if according to rank. The two earliest contenders were also the largest birds and probably the oldest. Perhaps they were two of the chicks that had hatched in the home wood at Halden Hall and were the most familiar with Sim. They commandeered the lowest branches while the younger and more nervous birds flew further up to consume their evening treat.

'I think I counted twenty-four birds, would that be right, Lady Guildford?' the king asked. 'They are very impressive-looking creatures, aren't they? Imposing, in fact; I don't think I have paid them enough attention in the past.'

'Many Londoners call them the guardians of the Tower, your grace,' I responded. 'And believe that while the Tower stands the kingdom will prosper and thrive. That is why these ravens choose to roost here and why we give them food and water and a safe place to sleep. Safe, that is, until disbelievers chose to pull down the roost boxes and set fire to the trees that sheltered them.'

I cast a surreptitious glance at Sir Henry Wyatt when I said this and saw him glower back but the king was distracted by Sim, who was waving a succulent piece of red meat at the two leader birds, urging them back down from their perches with a series of low, keening calls. Dropping to the ground both ravens swayed up to him on their gnarled-twig legs, eyeing the juicy meat with lidless brown eyes and nodding their heads enthusiastically.

'You can have them but you have to catch me first!' Sim shouted and began to run in and out between the tree trunks, abandoning his gory bucket. One of the two immediately chased after him, flapping its wings to get up speed and making short, low-level flights from one trunk to the next, landing for several long, loping strides in between. Meanwhile the other raven, the larger and more cunning of the two, sidled up to the abandoned bucket and poked its head over the rim. With a triumphant 'kwaark!' it tipped the bucket over and quickly dived into its murky depths, only to emerge with an unmistakeable smile on its face and a large portion of liver clamped in its bill.

King Henry began to laugh heartily. 'Ah, the clever creature knew it was there. Just look at its air of triumph! Those eyes are so expressive, are they not? They are indeed noble birds, Joan. You must bring the queen here one day. She would love to see them, I'm sure. Do you ever feed them yourself, or do you leave it to Sim – was that what I heard you call him?'

I confessed that Sim handled the bloody tit-bit but I fed them wafers and cakes. 'And I come here whenever I'm at the Tower, your grace. I find it hard to keep away. But it's not all games and laughter. They are emotional birds.' I showed him my blemished thumb. 'I have the scars to prove it.'

Sim seemed to have forgotten his fear of the king in his rapport with the ravens and came back to chase the larger one off the bucket and attempt to take back the slice of liver, but the bird was having none of it. Of course in order to hold on to his treat he could not use his beak to peck Sim and so the lad was able to tease the raven, threatening to catch it by clamping the bucket over its head. It was a game they must have played frequently because the bird teased him back, waiting until Sim was only a yard away before ducking off and darting up behind him to splatter his hose with liver blood. It was the smile on the bird's face after this achievement that completely convinced me it was one of the ravens Sim had played with as a chick in the Halden wood and I was delighted to make the link between my two lives.

At this point Sir Henry excused himself to the king, pointedly ignoring Sim and me, and took himself off to the Mint. But the king did not leave until the last glimmer of daylight had surrendered to the stars and the ravens and the darkness became one. I hoped he was a convert. He had certainly enjoyed the interaction between Sim and the birds and, having watched Sim stroke their breast feathers, even made a tentative approach to do so himself. However, the big raven recognised his wish to be friends by giving him a little nip on the ankle.

'A great compliment, my lord,' I assured his grace, having checked that no royal blood flowed. 'This bird does not kiss just anyone's feet.'

'I've had much worse attacks from my pet monkey,' King Henry admitted.

The following day after attending Mass and making offerings at the altar of St Paul's, the king and queen and the newly wedded prince and princess dined together again at the Bishop of London's palace. I was in attendance on the queen and therefore ushered to her ladies' table, entertaining my fellows with anecdotes about the king's visit to the Tower. As My Lady the King's Mother had come out of retirement to attend the wedding celebrations, my mother was also

449

seated with us and happily next to me, so I managed to tell her quietly about the encounter with Sir Henry Wyatt.

'I know for a fact that he was responsible for both the destruction of the ravens' roost boxes and the false accusations that got poor Sim thrown into the Fleet prison, so when I saw him haranguing Sim again I had to intervene. But fortunately the king chose to come and visit the ravens at that very time and made it clear to Sir Henry that he thought the ravens should be encouraged and protected. You should have seen Wyatt's face when King Henry called them "noble birds"! It was a picture!'

But the ravens had done far more than enliven my days and haunt my dreams, for the king chose this banquet, in the company of the bishop, the Lord Mayor and aldermen of London, to call for attention and announce that their city had received a blessing from God.

'We sing the praises of noble birds like eagles and falcons but yesterday I had the privilege of spending time in the company of a gathering of ravens at the Tower of London,' he began. 'I believe some people call such a gathering an "unkindness" or a "conspiracy", but these black birds, so often harried and hated, showed me no evidence of wickedness or scheming; they displayed characteristics and traits of the sort God only grants to the highest of His creations.

'In the eyes of these ravens I saw empathy, sympathy, co-operation, intelligence and humour, and the fact that twenty-four of them are choosing to spend their nights in the shelter of the Tower while it guards and defends London suggests to me that they are sent by God to ensure the safety and prosperity of this city and its people.

'We men envy birds their capacity to fly, not only because

it enables them to look down on the earth and see our faults and weaknesses but also because it takes them nearer to heaven than we can ever hope to get in life, placing them high in God's favour. We should admire and promote the raven – not deride and destroy it. I have been told there is a legend that if the ravens leave the Tower the walls will crumble and the kingdom will fall, and recently there has been a concerted effort to drive them away. The person who told me this legend and who has done the most to encourage the ravens back is their champion and friend, Lady Joan Guildford.

'Now that I have seen her efforts with my own eyes, I wish to acknowledge that after the dreadful epidemics of measles and the plague and the risible attempts by imposters to threaten the Tudor throne, by luring the ravens back to the Tower she has effectively preserved peace and prosperity in the city and ensured the kingdom's orderly progress back to health and wealth.' He raised his heavy jewelled cup. 'I would like to raise a toast to Lady Joan Guildford, The Lady of the Ravens!'

'This is not right,' I murmured. 'I only do the organising. Sim does all the hard work.'

'Hush, Gigi,' my mother whispered. 'Enjoy your moment in the torchlight. They don't happen very often.'

'To the Lady of the Ravens and the Guardians of the Tower of London!' bellowed the City Cryer from behind the Lord Mayor's chair. 'Long may they preserve our walls!'

All eyes were on me as the toast was drunk. I had never learned to control my blushes and now the blood rose inexorably up my neck and into my cheeks. Nevertheless I felt a sense of jubilation. King Henry was right; whether it was down to the ravens or his own determination, there was no longer any reason for him to feel his throne shaking under him and every reason to celebrate a secure future for the Tudor dynasty and a prosperous outlook for his kingdom. I stood up. Bravely I raised my cup and cleared my throat. 'To the ravens!' I cried.

We were only in the second year of a new century. Prince Arthur and his Spanish wife were seated beside the king and queen. This was not an ending; it was a beginning.

GLOSSARY

aiglets: metal tips on laces to aid threading and stop fraying

attainder: loss of all civil rights on conviction for high treason

attire: a knight's complete set of arms and armour for going to war

chaperon: style of head-hugging hat, often with scarf attached

chrism: a holy oil or unguent used in baptisms and coronations

clerestory: upper story in a church, with clear windows to light the nave

comptroller: auditor of accounts

cord-laces: like modern shoelaces, threaded through eyelets on garments

gallowglass: a professional soldier-retainer of an Irish chief

gongfermer: refuse collector and sewage-tank emptier. A life short-lived!

harbinger: scout who travels ahead to bring notice of an arrival

Moot Court: a parish or manor meeting where petty crimes were judged

passementerie: the craft of fashioning silk into decorative items

Placentia: 'Pleasance' – original name for the royal palace at Greenwich

poniard: short, dagger-like weapon worn in a belt-sheath

portcullis: a wrought iron gate defence – image used as a Beaufort badge

subtletie: an artistic confection of marzipan paraded at a feast

sumpter: a packhorse

usher: a senior yeoman* of the guard in the king's household

vervain: a form of verbena used in apothecary to treat pain

villein: a serf, member of a Norman lord's estate, bound to his service

ward: child in custody of the crown – orphan or father killed or captive

*yeoman: a smallholder of land – not rich enough to be 'gentry'

AUTHOR'S NOTES

It's not often that inspiration for a novel comes out of the blue in the middle of lunch – but that's just what happened with this one. My publisher and editor had invited me and my agent to discuss my next book in a very pleasant restaurant, which just happens to be located on the Thames, opposite the Tower of London. When they asked what I intended for my next novel, my mind went blank. That is until I looked across at the famous Tower and said, more or less out of the blue, 'It might be set in the Tower of London.'

This idea seemed to go down well and all sorts of helpful suggestions were made about my approach but little in the way of plot – mainly because there wasn't one. But weirdly, the nub of it came to me in a dream that very night when one of the historical characters I had used briefly in a previous novel suddenly re-presented herself – Joan Vaux, a commoner in a royal household. Joan was a highly intelligent, second generation immigrant, whose mother had arrived in England from Provence in the train of Marguerite of Anjou, Henry VI's queen. Looking back I realise that she could easily have written her own biography and perhaps had it published by the Caxton Press. But it would probably have been in Latin and since she didn't write it, 500 years later I decided to do it for her and, through her eyes, bring to life the early and perilous years of the Tudor regime.

This element of the book was greatly helped by the historical fact that Joan had served Henry VII's queen, Elizabeth of York, as a woman of the bedchamber and, after her marriage to Sir Richard Guildford, as a lady-in-waiting. Before that she had by chance been raised in London, in the household of Lady Margaret Beaufort, Henry Tudor's mother. So Joan knew the city well and, after marrying Sir Richard Guildford, the king's Master of Ordnance, she had a home in the Tower. Eureka! All I needed then was a plot – and there were plenty of those during the first tenuous years of the Tudor regime.

Where contemporary sources mention appearances or foibles I take great pleasure in using them, as with King Henry's small blue eyes and bad teeth, which caused him to smile without showing them. I've never seen a Tudor portrait where the subject is smiling and showing teeth; except maybe a child whose milk teeth are all present and correct, as in the terracotta bust believed to be of Henry VIII as a child, which is in the royal collection and attributed to an Italian artist called Guido Mazzoni. He does look cheerful though.

If you have enjoyed Joan's story so far, don't wave her goodbye. There is more of her long and fascinating life to recount, including a mystery, a remarkable second marriage and a close relationship with Katherine of Aragon – plus of course, the early (and relatively happy!) years of the reign of Henry VIII. I suppose it was inevitable, having started the 15th century with the birth of his great-grandmother Catherine de Valois in *The Agincourt Bride*, that I'd get to him eventually. Stay with me!

Joanna

ACKNOWLEDGEMENTS

When it comes to thanking people who have helped to bring a novel to the reader's attention it is hard to know where to begin.

But, I'll start by thanking my very good friend Jenny Brown, who has been my agent for ten years now and read and advised on every version of every book I have written since; who sat with me in the restaurant overlooking the Tower of London as we discussed this one and negotiated the resulting contract – a tower of strength and a great companion through my writing career.

Next on the list must come my editor Kate Bradley, by now unquestionably another good friend as well as an excellent and ruthless critic and adviser. Every writer needs one and sometimes they're lucky enough to get two, as I was for this book when the multi-talented Susan Opie joined the team, providing a much-appreciated extra voice on the early manuscript.

Then we come to the all-important people who handle the way the book reaches the readers; grateful thanks to Holly Macdonald for the gorgeous jacket design and to Terence Caven for making the maps and family trees not only decipherable but also elegant. Jaime Witcomb was once again the publicist, and a new face and name on the team is Rachel Quin, who handles the marketing; grateful thanks to them both. So you can see what a many and talented group is behind me, all led by the one and only Kimberley Young, who as publisher has always been a great supporter of my books. Huge thanks to them all and to you, the reader, who has either bought or borrowed *The Lady of the Ravens*. I do hope you have enjoyed it and might consider reviewing it on a platform of your choice so that other people can consider its allure.

Aside from the publishers, I also had much help from Charlie Oven in the press office at Historic Royal Palaces, who facilitated my research at the Tower of London and steered my path to Christopher Skaife, the Warden Ravenmaster and the source of much ravenish legend and behaviour. Two books also aided my research on these remarkable birds: Chris's own recently published memoir *The Ravenmaster* and *Mind of the Raven* by Bernd Heinrich, who I believe is generally recognised as the chief guru on the subject! Through their insights, I have grown to greatly appreciate the raven character and I hope this is conveyed in the pages of my novel, although any mistakes I have made regarding their raven habits and characteristics are entirely mine and none of theirs.

As far as the history of the early years of the Tudor reign is concerned, my chief guide was Alison Weir's seminal work *Elizabeth of York, The First Tudor Queen*, which I thoroughly recommend to anyone looking to delve further into this fascinating period of English history. Of course there were contemporary sources as well, such as Polydore Vergil's biography of Henry Tudor and I have to thank Kevin Clancy, Director of the Royal Mint Museum, for the inside story on the Royal Mint and a beautiful copy of his *History of the Sovereign*, which was first minted in the reign of Henry VII.

For the country episodes in the novel, I had excellent help from the staff at the library in the beautiful medieval town of Rye and from Edward Barham, present owner of much of the land around 'Halden Hall' and 'Frensham' who supplied me with historic maps of the area. Last but not least, a nod to the ladies of the Church of Saint Mary the Virgin in Rolvenden, who interrupted their flower-arranging to tell me stories of the Guildford family and the beautiful area in which they lived.

Thank you all so much!

ENJOY MORE RICH AND COMPELLING NOVELS FROM JOANNA HICKSON

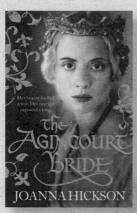

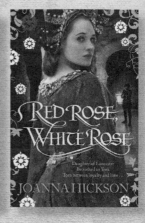

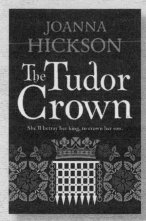

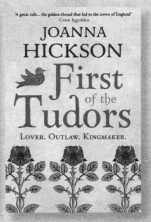

'A great tale... the golden thread that led to the crown of England'
Conn Iggulden

JOANNA
HICKSON

The Tudor
Crown

She'll betray her king, to crown her son.

JOANNA
HICKSON

First
of the
Tudors

LOVER. OUTLAW. KINGMAKER.

ALL AVAILABLE NOW